WISHBONE

Also by Marcia Golub

Secret Correspondence (novel)

WISH-BONE

A NOVEL BY

MARCIA GOLUB

BASKERVILLE
PUBLISHERS, INC.
DALLAS • NEW YORK • DUBLIN

This book is a work of fiction. Names, characters, places and incidents are either the product of the author's imagination or are used fictitiously. Any resemblance to actual events or locales or persons, living or dead, is entirely coincidental.

BASKERVILLE Publishers, Inc.
7616 LBJ Freeway, Suite 220, Dallas TX 75251-1008

Library of Congress Cataloging-in-Publication Data

Golub, Marcia.
    Wish-bone : a novel / by Marcia Golub.
        p. cm.
    ISBN 1-880909-26-X , $20.00
    I. Title. II. Title: Wishbone.
PS3557.0453W5   1995
813'.54--dc20   94-40986
                                                                CIP

All rights reserved
Manufactured in the United States of America
First Printing, 1995

*For Bob, who stands by me,
and for Zachary, who's too young to read this*

In memory of Stuie Bleckner

It is desirable that the inmate should not have at all, or, if he does, should immediately himself suppress nocturnal dreams whose content might be incompatible with the condition and status of the prisoner, such as: resplendent landscapes, outings with friends, family dinners, as well as sexual intercourse with persons who in real life and in the waking state would not suffer said individual to come near, which individual will therefore be considered by the law to be guilty of rape.

Vladimir Nabokov
Invitation to a Beheading

If wishes were horses beggars would ride.
—Anonymous

ONE

It was apple weather and Mabel Fleish's nose was cold. She held a tissue to it as she slipped off her shoes. "Nubi," she called, holding the door. A large white dog bounded in. "You're a mess," she said, wiping his paws with a rag before letting him into the kitchen. He ran the length of the house while she hung her jacket on a hook, then returned to nuzzle his snout in her crotch. "Sit," she said, pushing him away. She put cider in the refrigerator, took out an apple. Washed it, kissed it, bit its cold skin.

It was autumn again. Burning leaves, crispening air. Sweaters that seemed like old friends. The college town of Winegarden, New York, was filled once more with students, and even they seemed fresh in the red and gold light. It was the season of beginning—if only there was something to begin. Mabel hadn't begun work on a new novel yet. She didn't feel finished with the old one. Images, scenes, phrases kept occurring to her for a book that was already written. The publication she had once hoped for now seemed the granting of a fairy wish: There were hidden consequences. Before, she had taken chances because she had nothing to lose. Now she had everything.

The mail was on the kitchen table. She flipped through bills and pleas till she came to a small envelope. It had no return address, just the letters *BB* in the corner. Her chest constricted with crazy hope. It had been twenty years. "Exactly twenty years," she realized with a start. Beau was dead but she opened the envelope, ready to believe in miracles.

Words floated in an alphabet soup. The letters were cut out, not typed, but because the typeface and size used for each letter were identical they seemed to have come from the same book. She read the message several times, trying to understand.

"Mthr," it said, "dghtr, sistr, wfe: Ill git you bck if it tkes yr life. You had no rt to rt such lies. Ill cut the trth betwxt yr thighs— Bone."

"It can't be," she said, the page trembling in her hand. She'd gotten correspondence from a ghost once before, so she knew the dead had their tricks. But Bone wasn't dead. He was never alive. How could she be haunted by a figment of her imagination? "You're a character in a novel," she said aloud, then knew she wasn't alone.

Ana stood in the doorway. Mabel looked up with a quick smile, folding the note as if absentmindedly.

"Hello, sweetie," she said. "You're so quiet, I didn't hear you come in." She slipped the paper into her jacket while taking out her cigarettes. "Would you like an apple? I was at the orchard."

The eleven-year-old gave her mother a contemptuous look. "You didn't hear me say Pammy's on the phone, can I sleep over?"

"Didn't you just sleep there last night? Or were supposed to. Pammy canceled, didn't she? No, maybe it's not such a good idea."

Ana glared. "Why? It's important. We're having a bridal shower for Barbie, then a wedding. You can't make me miss it."

"Oh, I see. I didn't know it was an occasion." Mabel smiled. "I was going to make roast chicken, you love roast chicken. I'll tell you what. How about if I drive you over after dinner?"

Ana rolled her eyes. "I just told you. Don't you listen? Pammy's mother said she'd pick me up on her way from the market. We're having pizza. And I happen to despise roast chicken."

Mabel was looking for matches and gestured her annoyance. "Oh, I don't care—you're sure Mrs. Stein doesn't mind? Next time—"

Ana ran upstairs before Mabel finished talking. A few minutes later she came down, opened the refrigerator. "Don't just stand there," Mabel said. "Take what you want and shut the door." Ana took an apple, was about to bite it when Mabel said, "Wash it first." The girl grunted but did as she was told. She leaned on the sink and stared at her mother.

"Where'd the mail come from?" Mabel asked nonchalantly.

"A man in a skeleton suit dropped it off." Mabel stared till Ana laughed. "I'm kidding, Ma. You know joke, like ha ha? Frank's too fat to wear a skeleton suit."

"Yes, of course. I was uh...thinking of something."

Ana closed her face. "You're always thinking of something. I guess I'm too boring for you. I'll go up to pack, so you can be alone with your thoughts. I hope you'll be very happy together."

"Wait a minute," Mabel called. "I didn't, I'm, you know. Have some cider. I got it at the orchard. It's fresh and—"

"I'd rather drink blood." The girl stomped up the stairs.

"Then do," Mabel yelled, starting after her, then stopping herself. She lit a cigarette instead. Her hands were shaking. *Damn,* she thought. *Why do I let her get to me?* She knew she should talk to her, calmly, but she was anything but calm. She inhaled deeply from her cigarette, put it in the ashtray. Went upstairs, knocked on the door. Ana was only a child. It was up to Mabel to set things right.

"Honey," she said. "I want to talk to you a minute." She turned the knob. The door was locked.

"Go away," Ana said.

Mabel stood outside the door, listening to sniffles. If only there were a way to take back words, events, things that happened that should never have happened. "Ana, sweetie, I didn't mean—"

The door opened partway. "Ma, I want to be alone. I know you didn't—oh Ma, don't *you* cry."

She couldn't help it. "I'm sorry," she blubbered. "I just...I offered you cider and—"

Ana came into the hall. "Don't cry, Mommy," she said, letting herself be embraced.

Mabel brushed the bangs from the child's eyes. "You can sleep over Pammy's, sweetie. I wish we didn't have to fight like this so much. Over nothing."

Ana pulled away and walked to the bathroom to rinse her face. "I'll be down in a minute," she said, but Mabel didn't move. "Ma," Ana said. Mabel nodded, then returned to the kitchen. Her cigarette was one long ash in the tray. She lit another, put it on the counter, and began to prepare dinner.

She washed the chicken, placing it on a paper towel. Rubbed its belly with oil. Shook out salt as if it were talc, tried to wipe some off. She lifted it by the legs so she could slip another towel underneath. It lay on the counter like a baby. "Chicken," she said. "A nice roast chicken. A delicious roast chicken." Without preheating the oven she shoved it in, not wanting to give it a chance to grow a penis and head. She knew too well who the baby was, the danger of letting him in. She peeled carrots, thinking "shame shame." Took out a tomato, rinsed it. Took out the lettuce. Washed each leaf like a plate. Still thinking about him.

Had Ana caught her? Mabel knew she scrutinized her daughter for evidence of the evil seed, but she didn't know if Ana knew. Seth would have been eight years old. He would have been upstairs playing with his trucks or annoying his sister. They might at this very moment have run to her, asking her to arbitrate some childhood dispute. Instead she was trying to find excuses for herself that didn't lay the blame on Ana. The girl was only three at the time. Mabel had let her guard down, for one moment. For one terrible moment she said, "I am a writer," instead of, "I am a mother." And she was going to pay for the rest of her life.

She put the salad in the refrigerator, wishing it were as easy to put away thoughts. She spilled dog food in a bowl, called Nubi. Opened a bottle of red wine, poured a glass. She remembered there was something she wanted to forget. Then remembered what it was. Death chuckling in a tub. Seth had fallen asleep in the car. She had brought him in, put the groceries away. She was preoccupied with an idea for *Bone*. Her writing back then was stopped up by baby bottles, diapers. When a space opened in her day she didn't question it. Ana was playing with her dolls. Seth was napping. Was there anything wrong in stealing away to jot a few notes? Ideas flowed till five pages later she became aware of a sound.

She went over the event, as she did too often when she was alone. As if she could find some detail, some implausible fact or hidden watcher or unrealized event that would enable her to point and say, "There. That's the proof it didn't happen." A babysitter pulled the plug. Ana was too little to lift the baby. The pipes were frozen. "Seth is alive," she would cry. "I know he's alive."

Instead the story continued as it always did. She approached the bathroom. Opened the door. "Ana?" The little girl held her brother by the foot. Scrubbing his foot with a bar of soap. The rest of the infant undulated beneath the laughing water. "I gave Sethy his bath," she told her. "Dirty baby. Dirty dirty dirty baby."

"Okay? Ma, yo, anyone home?" Ana turned the faucet off in the sink. "Remember me? Your only daughter?"

Mabel looked up. "Oh hi, dear. I didn't realize I left the water running. I'm so absentminded lately."

"Lately? Listen, Mrs. Stein is waiting. I'm going."

Mabel reached for a kiss, but Ana scurried past, clothed once again in preadolescent coolness. Mabel followed her and waved at her back, gesturing hello-goodbye to the woman in the car. She was about to close the door when Ana pushed back in. "I forgot my Barbie case." Mabel went to keep Mrs. Stein company.

"It's funny, isn't it?" she said. "One minute they're like teenagers, next minute they're playing with dolls." Olga Stein laughed. "Yeah, I know. Pammy asked for a training bra for her birthday and a bridal gown for Barbie."

"And they're so touchy. At least Ana is. I mean, I know it's hormones, but sometimes I think that's just an excuse for acting like a, oh hi, dear. Have you got your Barbie now?" The girl held up her case. There was a plastic man in her other hand. "Is Ken sleeping over too?"

Ana rolled her eyes. "Of course. After the shower it's Barbie's wedding night." Mabel and Olga gave the girl surprised looks, then burst out laughing. "The mouths of babes," said Olga, driving away.

Mabel returned to the kitchen. She looked through the oven window at the small naked carcass. "What a good little chicken you are," she said, then bit her lip. It hadn't browned yet. It would be easier when it browned. She busied herself with the broccoli. The air was cool. The day darkening. The only thing Mabel didn't like about the fall was how quickly the light faded.

She was opening the oven door to baste the chicken when Percy came in. He took her around the back as she bent over. "Write any great novels today? Where's *l'enfant terrible?*"

"Sleeping over Pammy's, where else?"

"Well then," he said, raising his eyebrows up and down like a malevolent Groucho, "how's about some minky soup later?"

"After dinner." Mabel laughed. "You clean the tub. It's dirty." She forced a picture from her mind, wondering whether such dangerous words as *tub* and *dirty* conjured visions for her husband. Checking her jacket pocket for her cigarettes she felt an envelope. She was about to take it out when she remembered and decided to keep it secret for a bit longer. "How's the new class?"

Percy shrugged. "I feel like they're the same people dressed in different bodies. The eternal class. Same wise aleck in the back, same ass kisser in the front. There's always one person who makes intense eye contact, smiling at everything you say."

Yeah, Mabel thought. *The one with hot pants for you.* "What about Wutzl? Is he back?"

"Is he ever! 'Furnival, my lad.' How can anyone say 'Furnival, my lad' with a straight face? Oh, that reminds me—faculty Halloween party on the 31st, as usual. Mandatory costumes. Come on, Mabel, don't look at me like that. It's not so bad, is it?"

"No. Just a reflex, I guess. Things are better since *Bone* came out—I was working on it for so long I used to think people doubted its existence."

"You acted like that too."

"Well, no one ever talked to me, Percy. Now they line up to ask if I wrote *Bone* with a pen or a computer." Percy laughed. "What you drinking? Vino, my little minky?"

Mabel finally found her cigarettes next to the ashtray on the counter. "Can you do me a favor," she asked, "and take the chicken out of the oven?"

After washing the dishes Percy filled the tub and lured his wife upstairs. She didn't take much luring, looking forward to the luxury of bathing with him as much as he did with her—one of the things they used to take for granted before they had a child. Naked and chilled she put one foot in and was standing on it before she realized the water was too hot. "We're not lobsters," she yelled. "What are you trying to do, boil us alive?"

"Oh, come on," Percy said. "I need a hot bath, Minx. My back's killing me." He stepped in and was sitting down before Mabel could convince her first leg it was okay.

"Let some water out," she said. "It's too full."

"It's not even to the top."

"Yeah, Percy, but I'm getting in. A body displaces its weight in water, or however that goes. And this body doesn't want to mop the floor."

Percy pulled the plug, stopping the drain a moment later. He lay back. Mabel wrapped her legs outside his. He soaked the loofah and told her the latest faculty follies. She leaned against the porcelain, admiring her husband's strong body and dark curls. She wondered why, as much as she loved him, she couldn't be faithful. Every time one affair ended she questioned why she sought recognition from strangers. She knew of course. Beau. Her sixteen-year-old lover. Always perfect, always dead. *I won't anymore*, she resolved. *Now that Idi Masambe and I—*

"Did you hear me?"

Mabel blinked. "No, I'm sorry. What did you say?"

"Oh, never mind. Forget it."

"No, Percy. I was just daydreaming. What is it?"

"If you can't listen when I talk, then skip it. Your dreams are more important than anything I have to say."

"Will you stop? You sound like Ana. Dr. Xavier told you not to take it personally. Just because your mother did it—I'm not Hannah. It's different with me. Dreaming's my business. Dr. Xavier—"

"I don't think you should talk about Dr. Xavier when you're not seeing him anymore." Mabel made a face. "What were you so busy thinking about when I was talking?" he asked.

"If you must know I was thinking about Ana. We had another fight. About the stupidest thing. Apple cider. But what really bothers me is I can't help thinking we made a mistake when we named her. No really, don't look at me like that, it's going to make problems for her later. We should have called her Hannah, if you wanted to name her after your mother. But this way she's bound to see herself as the Anna in my book."

"Minky, the kid's only eleven. She's not going to read your book for a long time. We'll deal with it then."

"Yeah, well she's older than you realize. Hand me the soap, Pook. Thanks. Look, Pooky, I think it's dangerous to read a book written by a parent, even if the book were *Heidi*, and *Bone* is most assuredly not *Heidi*. But to read about a woman with the same name as you, a woman who gets into a sadomasochistic relationship with a demonic character—you really think Ana can handle it? I mean, could you? You can't even handle your mother ignoring you when you were growing up. What if she had written a novel about a man named Percy who gets raped by a tribe of Amazons? Careful, the water's going over."

"I'd thank her." He splashed Mabel's chest. "No, seriously, all *I'm* saying is I don't think we have to worry about it now. When the time comes you'll explain stuff, that the orgies refer to Canaanite fertility rites, that your Anna is named for Anathe and Inanna, Bone for Baal. That's all. Ana's smart. She'll get it."

"You think so," said Mabel. "I'm telling you I've gone over this in my head a hundred times. It's not so simple. We made a mistake. She was an infant, we forgot she'd be a woman."

"Anyway, Ana's not the same name as Annabelle."

"You know I changed it to Annabelle at the last minute, for exactly this reason. Mostly she's Anna in the book, there were too many rhymes and puns by that point. Maybe I should have given the book up when I got pregnant, sacrificed it for her—is that what you think? I mean, I love Ana, but *Bone*'s my child too."

"Nobody thinks—"

"I just want to ask you something. I named my Anna first, right? before our Ana was ever conceived—but just tell me, did you expect me to change my character's name? Forget the year I'd already been working on *Bone*? Be honest."

"Of course not. I told you nobody thinks that."

Mabel shook her head. "We should have named her Hannah."

"Ugh. Would you do that to your own child? Listen, this is ridiculous. I don't want to discuss it. There's nothing we can do anyway. You want to change our Ana's name? Your Anna? So forget it. We'll talk to her when the time comes."

"Talk about it how, Percy? When?"

"I'll discuss it with Dr. Xavier, okay? Or you can. He thinks you should come back. Give me your foot."

He soaped Mabel's toes, rubbing the length of her sole.

"Maybe you're right," she said. "Making a mountain...mmm, that feels great." She relaxed. Percy dipped her foot in the water, then put her toes in his mouth. She closed her eyes. Beau stared back. He was always there, inside her eyelids. Faded now, his darkness gone gray. Just a pale afterimage when she tried to recall his face. Except for his eyes, shining blue through the shadows.

Beauregard Barbon was sixteen. He would always be sixteen, while Mabel was twenty, thirty, soon fat and forty. She tried to imagine him her age. That's how *Bone* began. Bo Bone was based on the dead boy, grown up in fiction. She had imagined Beau a man, like the many in whose arms she sought him, and was surprised when Bo turned out to be a malevolent being. Wanting to exorcise his charm through her art she hadn't known fiction cast its own spell. Then she saw what she couldn't when she was sixteen. That Beau had had in him a sweet wickedness all along.

He was strange, Beau Barbon, caught up in witchcraft, voodoo, gris-gris, stuff he said an obeah woman taught him before his family moved to Brooklyn. He could persuade her to do anything. She would never have gone to Rosemary's house with anyone else, walked the snaky path alone to enter the old woman's shack. She certainly would never have taken off her clothes in that dark, dirty place with anyone else. Making love there the first time, Beau's shirt and pants spread on the floor beneath her, the blood on his shirt. "I'll keep it always," he said, "a memento. Maybelline, why can't you be true?" She laughed. He put the shirt to his face, inhaling as if it were a red and white bouquet. "Friday, Maybelle? Midnight."

Percy put Mabel's foot in the water. She opened her eyes. "Other foot," he said, doing a more rudimentary job, swishing his fingers between her toes. "You were off in space."

"It puts me in a trance when you do that," she said. "Like I haven't any bones. Here, give me your foot, let me do you." She rubbed her thumb along his arch, working his metatarsals gently. She soaped his calf, kneading the long muscle. Percy sank low in the tub. He groaned softly to let her know he was alive. She put his leg in the water, resting his other foot on her thigh. She soaped and massaged the calf, thinking about the strange letter in her jacket. Her first thought had been that it was from Beau. Before she even knew it was the anniversary—twenty years today she hadn't kept her word, and Beau was dead. A death never confirmed, but she knew.

She should talk to Percy about the threatening letter. She didn't know why she didn't—except it was her secret. Maybe she still thought it was from Beau? She shook her head. No, there were really only two possibilities: Either it was written by a real person who wanted to scare her, or else she was going mad. Having gone there before she knew you couldn't always tell when you were traveling. Maybe that's why she didn't say anything.

For a moment she looked at Percy's long naked body in the water, remembering a time of babies behind doors, in ovens and refrigerators and tubs. It was a terrible thing to hear water running and never be able to shut it off; to hear a baby crying and not be able to stop his tears. Whichever way she went the sound didn't get louder or softer. She could never find the little boy lonely in death. The time she opened the door and saw the giant body in the bath— as big as the tub itself and oddly glowing—she had no sense of something strange. She mentioned it to Percy as if it were an ordinary occurrence, except "you never saw such a clean baby," she told him. "Such a clean clean clean baby."

"Do my back?" Percy asked. "It really hurts today."

"Sure," Mabel said. "Turn around." She ran the soap along his spine, working up a lather. The suds acted as a lubricant so she could slide her fingers into his tight muscles, probing under the wings of his shoulder blades. She massaged his neck, squeezing the tendons, then leaned forward to rub her breasts and belly against him as if she were a sponge.

Her husband's body was lean. He was tall and fit. He swam regularly at the college, his skin always gave off the faint scent of chlorine. Beau's body had been young, hard. She longed to feel him fill her again, and again. The first time she'd entered Rosemary's house he hid from her. She was angry and scared. He was not at the gate as he had promised. "Beau?" she whispered in the yard. No reply. She walked along the path to the old woman's house, calling his name every few steps till she got to the door, still calling. She went into the parlor. There were rags on the windows. She realized with a start they had once been curtains. "Beau," she said, "if you don't come this minute I'm leaving." She turned around to head for the door. The moon was staring like a hollow eye. He grabbed her. She screamed. "Shhh, honey," he whispered. "It's only me." She pounded him, furious at how he'd scared her until he took her wrists and held them away, kissing her. "Take off your clothes," he said. "I want to see you naked in the moonlight."

"That feels great," Percy said. "Let me do you now."

Mabel twisted in the tub. When he dripped warm water on her back her nipples hardened. She rinsed the suds off her breasts, dipped the washcloth and let it mold to her chest. "Let's add more hot," she said. Percy opened the drain to let water out. He and Mabel held themselves away from the faucet while the scalding water ran. Percy closed the drain, Mabel shut the faucet. He rubbed her back with the loofah. "Don't worry about Ana," he said. "I'm not," she said.

When Beau entered her he was slow and careful. It didn't hurt much, not right away. Then it hurt forever.

He was in love with death. His suicide had more to do with that than with her. For almost a year he and Mabel had kissed and held each other in the way of sixteen-year-olds, in parks, in basements, in cars, going so far and no more, always someone else around. Then he discovered the old woman's house and said it was haunted.

Rosemary had been murdered. He told her of the rituals he did there at midnight, violent acts performed on small animals. He and another kid were studying to be warlocks. They wanted her to join them. She was appalled but fascinated, shivering with a feeling not unlike delight. "Obeah lady used to watch me taught me stuff. I'll teach you. If you love me you'll come." For a year there had been clothes bunched up or opened, a window of warmth, a glimpse of skin. "It's time, Maybelline," he said. "We're not children anymore."

If only she had gone to Rosemary's house the second time, as she had promised. Instead she felt too sick with guilt, and desire. At midnight she took off her clothes and went to bed, imagining him, the salty taste of his neck, the strange light in his eyes. At three she was still up. Dread overcame her. She dressed, climbed out her window, down the trellis. Ran through empty streets. The gate creaked. She was afraid of the bushes. She stood at the door calling. No answer. She thought she knew his tricks. He was laughing in the next room. She went, it was empty. The laugh came from the room beyond. She followed the sound, found no one. The laughter was beyond and beyond, always at the next place, till she'd walked through the house, staying to the edges of the floor, as he had showed her, so she wouldn't fall through the holes. She couldn't find him anywhere, and finally she left.

She was still angry the next day when he didn't meet her at the fountain in the park. And Saturday night he didn't call. On Sunday she dialed his number. No one answered. She rode her bicycle past his house. It was closed up. Monday she stopped by Saint Francis High School, looking for him before going to her own school. She saw a group of his friends, asked if they knew where he was. "Haven't you heard?" the redhaired boy said. "Beau killed hisself. Jon Smelcks told me. His old lady's already left town. There's an article in the paper." She walked by his house after school. She saw the FOR SALE sign on the lawn. She called his number when she got home. An operator's voice said the phone had been disconnected. By then she knew the rumor was true; she had gotten his letter.

"Lean back," Percy said, holding his wife's soapy back to his chest, pulling her down into the water.

"I don't want to crush you."

"You won't. Rest against me."

Mabel leaned back. "That was a great massage," she said. She splashed water on her chest. "But you know what? I'm not comfortable. I'm turning around." Facing Percy, she saw him semi-erect. "Here, let me do that," she said, taking the soap, rubbing it gently into his pubic hair. She encircled him, working up a lather, squeezing and pulling, taking pleasure in his hardening. She opened her legs and let his buttocks slip from her thighs, submerging him. Then she raised him up on her legs again, bending over to take him in her mouth. She remembered the envelope with the Bs in the corner, just like today's, only it was Beau's letter then. Coming home Monday after school, finding it. The postmark showed it had been mailed Saturday. She took some comfort in that till she realized he'd have mailed it after midnight Friday, when she didn't show up. She knew then he wrote the letter in Rosemary's house, waiting for her. She saw him in the dirt and gloom, the gray curtains pointing their filmy fingers. Why had he brought a stamped envelope and paper to that haunted, abandoned place of love? Unless he planned it all along.

The suicide was neither confirmed nor denied. Mabel was afraid to go to the police. She couldn't ask her parents for help. They didn't like "that Christian boy" she was dating any more than Mrs. Barbon did her son's little "Jewess." The Barbons, mother and son, just disappeared. Maybe Mrs. Barbon took Beau's body back home for burial. Mabel didn't know. She didn't know why Jon Smelcks said Beau killed himself. The article in *The Brooklyn Wing* only mentioned the discovery of a boy's nude body. His name was not given because he was a minor. She didn't tell anyone about the letter.

"Maybelline," Beau wrote, "why can't you be true guess I'll never know why you couldn't love me a little but I love you always even when I'm dead and gone. I know you never loved me like I love you or you'd be here in my arms. I can't live without you can't bear I mean so little to you can't forget your body in the dark. I know what I have to do. On my grave see they write I died of love. I Love You Always—Beau."

He was dead, and she was thirty-six, still expecting to run into him, receive another letter. He would be sixteen, strong and hard, she a virgin opening in the moonlight. He was more in love with death than with her, and now she knew firsthand death's seductive ways. Seeking the company of dangerous men—the first time, when you didn't know what might happen, who the naked stranger was, what he wanted, what he would do—anything could happen. Even love after death.

She swallowed, keeping her head down and her husband inside her mouth for a few moments before gently letting him fall into the now tepid tub. She leaned back. "We should get out."

Percy's eyes were dreamy. "Not yet."

"We're turning into prunes."

"Let's add more hot. I want to soak my neck." He let water out while she let it in.

"Look at my hands," she said, showing her waterlogged fingers. "What was it you were saying to me before anyway? You know, when I was daydreaming and you got so offended?"

"When? You mean when we first got in? I don't, oh, I know, not such a big deal. Just, I think you should read *The Counterlife*. I'm finished with it. I'll leave it on your nighttable. But, you know, it's like what you were saying about Ana and Anna. I mean, it seems to me Roth creates fiction out of his life, while you create a life out of your fiction. What I'm trying to say is, he takes life material, deconstructs it, then deconstructs that. It's brilliant. Funny too. Nobody does the Jewish family better. The way he plays with the metafiction, well, read it, that's all."

Mabel was accustomed to Percy's reading recommendations. He had once been her professor, after all. But something about this irked her. "I was planning to," she said. What had he meant, that she created a life out of fiction? Looking at the wet tiles, their double bunch of laundry on the floor, her image in the mirror—a woman with her hair in a trash bag because she'd forgotten to buy a shower cap—she was struck, as if looking at a movie.

"It's funny," she said. "About Philip Roth, I mean. Could he ever imagine two strangers talking about him like this in the tub?"

"If anyone could," Percy said, "he could. That's the nature of celebrity, don't you think? People in Chinese restaurants, on toilets, in bathtubs are reading your book, and you don't even know they exist."

Mabel shivered. *Someone could be thinking about me at this very moment*, she thought, *up to his neck in hot water*.

"Hello? Come in, Mabel." Percy shook her foot. "Did we?"

"I'm sorry. What did you say?"

"I said, Did we get any mail?"

Mabel's eyes narrowed. "Why do you ask?"

"Why? Because I want to know if we got any mail. You know, bills from the oil company, invitations to bar mitzvahs."

"Just junk. Advertisements. Solicitations. I threw them out." Now would be the time to tell Percy about the letter. Instead, she observed him. Did he know about her affairs? Who would have a better reason for wanting revenge, who would better know how to terrify her? He might...but that was ridiculous. All Percy had to do was be unfaithful himself. He had opportunities. She knew about the hot English majors who came to his office, to "discuss my paper with you, Professor Furnival." After all, she had been one.

"Hey," she called out. "You're pushing me."

"Sorry," he said. "I just want to get my neck in the hot water."

TWO

Rufus Wutzl, professor emeritus, gazed out the window of his office, thinking about a book he had just finished reading—for the third time. Thinking in fact about a particular chapter he had read many more times than that. His hands were clasped on his stomach. He had the hard, round belly of a thin man gone fat. The bottom buttons of his vest were undone to accommodate it.

Someone tapped at his door. He turned to face a young lady asking if she might disturb him to discuss her thesis. "No trouble at all, my dear. Sit down. What is your name again?"

"Iris Specter, sir," she said. "You know...I took your course in English Romantics last year? I'm doing my thesis on Byron and—"

"Ah yes, Lord Byron, quite a chap. A gadabout, you know. You're familiar with the particulars of his ah imbroglios with his hm-hm"—he cleared his throat to indicate quotation marks—"'sister,' aren't you, my dear?"

"Well, yes, I am, but I don't think that enters into it. You see, I want to discuss his poetry in the context of..."

Dr. Wutzl turned his attention to the girl, to her full cherry lips in fact. He smiled wisely, nodding his head to convey concerned engrossment. He wondered if she were in the habit of sucking red cough drops. Or lollypops. Such pouting red lips could not be natural, and yet just as surely she was not wearing lipstick. She looked so sweet and did not appear to be wearing any makeup. In fact, she did not appear to be wearing a bra.

Ah, youth, thought Dr. Wutzl. What need had youth for the stays of the establishment? The young threw caution to the wind, dancing unfettered by the restraints of responsibility that came with age such as his. It was ironic really that the girl wore such a virginal look. The things one heard of happening in the dormitories. Coeducational sleeping arrangements. Brazen female students, lascivious and shameless. All they thought about was sex. Scandalous. They couldn't keep their minds on their work. Just sex and more sex. It was a wonder they took the time to come to class. But what could the administration expect when they put healthy young boys in dormitories with healthy young girls, no chaperones? The girls were said to walk the halls in their flimsy nighties, not even aware that they were arousing heat in the young males. Their gossamer gowns...they never wore underclothes. Who could blame red-blooded American boys for staring down passageways at them as they brushed their long silky hair, giggling together in groups of two and three, graceful arms beckoning the boys to come, come and put skin lotion on me. My skin is so soft, my lips cherry red. My breasts are full and—

"Dr. Wutzl?"

"Yes, well I agree with you in principle, but I don't think you're quite ready for that discussion. You need more preliminary research. Study the material that has already been written. Have you read my book on the Romantics? Ah, good. Come back to talk to me again. My door is always open. I hope I will see you soon. You're an enchanting young lady. You have some thought-provoking ideas about the English Romantics."

The girl uncrossed her legs and stood up. "Thank you, Dr. Wutzl. Just talking to you has helped."

"Glad to be of use, my girl. We all need our sounding boards, and what could be a more pleasurable use for a semi-retired professor like me than to be knocked upon by your young, uplifted mind swelling with ideas?" The noon bell rang, but Dr. Wutzl's stomach had gurgled the time ten minutes earlier. He took his stick and began walking home. The inestimable Mrs. Wutzl would no doubt have a delicious hot meal waiting. He strolled slowly along the paths of youth. Hungry students on their way to the cafeteria cut across lawns to get around him. He set on his face the preoccupied look of an elderly professor contemplating a magnum opus and his own mortality, yet when he saw someone he knew he made sure to signal with a wave of his cane. He wished to be remembered as a kindly old gentleman never too busy to help a young scholar in his pursuit of knowledge, so it was a surprise that none of the faculty did more than wave back. Except Percy Furnival, who signaled he was late for something by pointing to his watch.

Fool. Furnival was nothing but a prissy pedant who could not control his own wife. Nonetheless Dr. Wutzl would have liked to speak with him. It was not so much interest in what Furnival had to say as the hope of catching a scent of the elusive Mabel Fleish. Her affairs were the scandal of the campus.

"Young man," Dr. Wutzl said, stopping a student by hooking him with the handle of his cane. "I say, don't I know you?"

"Yes, Dr. Wutzl. I'm Horace Byrrd. I studied the English Romantics with you. How are you?"

"I'm fine, fine, but why haven't I seen you? I hope you haven't given up pursuing your academic career, by any chance."

"No. I graduated last year. I'm a teaching assistant now, in your department, as a matter of fact. I majored in bio but cha—"

"Yes, yes, well that's very interesting. I must be going. Mrs. Wutzl is waiting. A pleasure to see you, my lad."

Dr. Wutzl ambled off, all but oblivious to Horace Byrrd shaking his head. *Of course*, Wutzl thought. *Horace Byrrd. That scandal last year. Him and Mabel Fleish.*

He savored the gossip he could recall like someone finding bits of an enjoyable meal still stuck between his teeth. It had something to do with the pair going up the mountain, being found naked in a swimming hole. *In flagrante delicto*, no doubt—that was how he remembered it. Mabel Fleish taking the long hard strokes of a strong woman, darting from one end of the rocky pool to the other, Horace Byrrd in hot pursuit. Glimmering like a mermaid, the temptress, laughing, her breasts floating on the silvery water, wet and full, their buoyancy a seeming miracle. Dipping her red hair into the water, exposing her long neck to the young man who took her then, in the water, holding her easily, moving her easily in the water, and just at that moment of unabashed bliss, their animal howls breaking the serenity of the mountain woods, Professor Hazel and his wife, decently clad in bathing suits, their peanut-butter sandwiches in their knapsack, came upon the couple coupling. Disgusting. After all, the swimming hole was used by other people. In fact, Dr. Wutzl used to go there himself when he was younger. Of course, even then there was a certain amount of amorous play in the woods, frolicking. Not that that was why he went. He enjoyed the peaceful quiet of the mountains in which to read the poetry of the English Romantics.

Really, Mabel Fleish was not to blame if that prissy Furnival could not control her. "Spare the rod, spoil the child," he imagined advising his colleague, stroking his cane. "Women are children, my lad, regardless of what those so-called feminists say. They are our responsibility. A husband must tame his wife, whip her into shape. Look at your wife's book. Can't you see what she's crying out for? Rule her with an iron hand, my boy, *and* a velvet glove."

Mabel Fleish, her dark red hair and black eyes. He'd always had a weakness for women with freckles, but he hadn't understood the potential of such a woman till he'd read *Bone*. Now, after reading it again, and again, particularly the chapter in which—

"Hello, dear," Mrs. Wutzl said, greeting him at the door, which she opened before he rang the bell (an act of precognition that greatly annoyed Dr. Wutzl). She took his cane and presented her dry lips for a kiss. He allowed her to brush his cheek. "Lunch is almost ready. Why don't you relax in your study a bit?"

"Thank you, dear. I believe I'll do that." He went into his room and closed the door before pulling out his copy of *Bone*. He opened to his favorite chapter and began reading with a sigh.

It was the scene in which Bone uses Annabelle to build his "pulsation machine." Dr. Wutzl read it, imagining the red-haired Mabel Fleish as the hub. When he was done he read on to the penultimate chapter. Anna's lover Matt had just found her imprisoned in the "bonehouse." Unaware that Bone was waiting inside, he tried to squeeze through the tiny window and got stuck. Bone, gloating, brandished his ax—"So, Death, you have come stealing into my palace"—then chopped Matt to bits.

"No doubt about it," Dr. Wutzl said to himself. "Canaanite source material." He'd been reading a lot of mythology lately as he worked on an exegesis of Fleish's book. He hoped to show the world that the old professor still had some juice. Just the night before he had read the tale in which Mot, the death god, entered Baal's palace through its one tiny window. "Only," he said aloud to an imaginary audience, "in the myth it was Baal who was chopped up. Poetic license? Or had the author some intention that..." *Hmmm*, he thought. *Intentional fallacy. Rephrase.* He sighed and picked up a heavy tome on ancient middle eastern fertility rites. "But Puissa[*nt*] Bl said, 'Make not a w[*ind*]ow in the house,'" he read; "'A casement with[*in the pa*]lace.'"

Since his infatuation's beginning, months before, he had spent much time imagining the lectures he would give on *Bone* as well as the erudite conversations he might have with its authoress. How impressed the world would be with what he now knew about the gods. How impressed she would be. If only she could see him as he really was, the vital, throbbing man inside this dry shell.

He picked *Bone* up again, turned it over. "Heartstopping," he read, "...thrilling...woman kidnapped by crazed lunatic, forced to be his slave." "...explosively honest." "Compelling exploration of a woman's psyche as she deals with the anger, the terror...the desire." "Retelling of an ancient myth. A lost child...descent into madness. In the Hades of sexual humiliation and grief Anna must fight to win back her son."

The novel had gotten some good reviews, some mixed, but mostly it was ignored—till now, when suddenly there was this glowing piece in *The New York Review of Books*. Did it signal the beginning of *Bone* getting the recognition it deserved? He hoped not. *He* wanted to be the agent of its success. How grateful the authoress would be. How humbly he would insist he'd had nothing to do with it, *Bone* was merely getting its due. The review in his briefcase had ruined all that, for indeed he'd had nothing to do with it. He took it out with a sigh, intending to read it before lunch; instead he turned to *Bone*'s flap copy.

"Mabel Fleish's astounding first novel about a woman's descent into the underworld of drugs and prostitution. She would stop at nothing to bring back the dead. Meet

"ANNABELLE DUMUZEL—young, beautiful, provocative. The mother of a sixteen-year-old boy was a woman of thirty-five. Was it a crime for a mother to be a woman? Would she have to pay and pay for her sins?

"TED DUMUZEL—a boy who desperately craved a father...and was willing to do anything for the one he found.

"The BONERIDERS—sex- and drug-addicted cultists willing to prostitute themselves for the love of

"BONE—religious leader? Drug pusher? Sexual monster? What was the source of the demonic power that made women—and men—willing to do anything for him?"

The crass commercialism of this appeal annoyed Dr. Wutzl, but he savored the images it conjured. Just seeing the characters' names in print titillated him with jolts of recognition, as if someone referred to incidents in one of his own dreams.

He put the open book facedown in his lap, contemplating the author photo on the back. Funny how you misjudge people at first, he thought. He had not highly regarded Mabel Fleish until her book came out. Oh, he recognized she was pretty enough, Percy Furnival's pretty red-haired wife. But she seemed rather stupid, if the truth be known. Her grin too wide and goofy, her stutter annoying. She *umm*ed and *like*d and *whatchamacallit*ed like a sophomore. Vapid, never anything to say. Because she saved it for her pages. Yes, there was such depth of soul in *Bone*, such wisdom about the nature of man...and woman. One would never have expected it from the giggly, shy shadow who accompanied Percy to faculty affairs, standing at his side, half a step behind.

Rufus Wutzl tried to remember her as she had been then. Was she already having all those affairs? He couldn't remember, he hadn't been interested enough to notice. She was like maple syrup to him then, a sticky red sweetness he found cloying, with her face like the Vermont Maid. In looking back, he recalled a young man. Army jacket. Funny name. Something like Walker or Skip. Not a student, if he remembered correctly. A vagrant. Before Horace Byrrd. Did he and Mabel? No, he thought with a pang. Not Ryder.

Ryder. That was the chap's name, Wutzl thought, smiling as the piece of memory floated back. He recalled him now. A strange name for a strange man. Fancied himself a poet. Wutzl often came upon him sitting on a rock, scribbling in a notebook, acting the part. Nothing Dr. Wutzl despised so much as pretention. What in the world could Mabel have seen in Ryder?

Mabel, ah. He had always thought she had an intelligent face— till she opened her mouth. If only he had seen then what he now knew was inside. He could have offered fatherly advice about her writing, she might have opened to him, as she had opened to so many other men, including that scruffy Ryder Somebody no doubt. Now that he thought of it, he was sure. There had been rumors. He hadn't paid attention, but the sordid information nested in his memory, tormenting him now, as he was tormented by visions of her with Horace and Furnival and all the young men in the English department, many of the students, one after another, sometimes at the same time. The harlot. Yet it was true—there were many more orifices in the body than people realized, and they could all be stimulated to... Furnival probably didn't know that. *Mabel*, he sighed. *Someday I'll make you see in me the inner bone of a man.*

He took out a notepad and began a letter. "Mabel," he wrote, then blacked out the holes in the vowels. He drew rectangles around the consonants and filled them in. It was probably better to leave the woman unnamed, like the Dark Lady in Shakespeare's sonnets. Let posterity wonder. "Beloved," he wrote, then "Blvd," then blackness. After all, he had a wife to consider. If Death took him unawares—

"Luncheon," said Mrs. Wutzl, barging into his study without knocking, a habit Dr. Wutzl had tried unsuccessfully to break her of for years. She glanced down at his book and he squirmed, as if its open pages were the wet, spread lips of the woman whose picture gazed up from his lap. "Are you coming, Woofy?"

Dr. Wutzl cringed. "Ethel, I've asked you not to call me—"

She sniffed. "You used to like it," she said. "You used to say it made you feel like a wolf. You'd kiss me—"

"My dear, it's no longer fitting for a man my age to be called Woofy. Nor is it fitting for a woman yours—"

"Well! I'm sorry then, hmph. You needn't go on, Rufus. I know what it is. It's that girl. Ever since that girl published—"

"What girl? Whatever girl are you alluding to? I don't know of—"

Mrs. Wutzl huffed. "Well, never mind then, hmph. If you can't even admit it, this silly infatuation that indicates you're entering your second childhood, then I don't wish to discuss it. Come eat your luncheon, Rufus." Ethel walked briskly from the dining-room table where her husband had taken his seat. She soon returned, putting dishes down with a clatter. "That Mabel Fleish just better watch herself," she said, and marched off.

What did she mean by that? Dr. Wutzl wondered, his eyes narrowing as he thought about his wife's face. Could she be up to something? A moment later he laughed. There was nothing diabolical about Mrs. Wutzl. She was a simple woman, incapable of duplicity. He let the thought of her become background noise, like a radio playing in another room. Forgetting his momentary suspicion he spooned clotted cream on his strawberries, then buttered a piece of bread. He was about to begin the article in *The New York Review of Books*—a periodical he considered his easy reading, as he mentioned to most of the faculty and many of the students, joking how he reserved the tabloid for reading during meals, on the train, and "whilst performing other necessities of life"—when Ethel returned. She pushed the swinging door so hard it knocked into his mahogany secretary. He showed remarkable restraint in saying nothing.

"There's chocolate cake, too," she said, putting the dish before his nose. "Tell me when you're ready and I'll bring in the whipped cream and coffee."

"Thank you, dear," Rufus said. "You shouldn't have bothered baking today. It's still so warm. But you are a most splendid *pâtissière*. Have we any maple syrup, by the way? I have a hankering for maple syrup with my berries."

THREE

Ethel Wutzl walked into the kitchen, still hmphing through her nose. The old fool. No fool like an old fool—how often her mother told her that. But there was another saying her mother repeated even more: The way to a man's heart is through his stomach.

She went to her shelf of cookbooks, pulled down the black one Rufus jokingly called her gramarye. Why, just last week her mother had reminded her of a special recipe in it. She'd been hoping to hear from Felix, but he must have been too busy to call, you know children. Mother came instead. She had plenty of time on her hands, what with being dead and all, and a mother was still a mother, no matter. As soon as the seance began, Madame Tchernofsky started looking Ethel over in that special, maternal way, so she knew Mother would be dropping in. The urge to let go and fix her hair had been terrible, but she resisted. Mother glared through Madame's eyes, then spit out, "*Soufflé au Chocolat*. The way to a man's heart." Mother was right. Mother was always right. Ethel made it that night, and Rufus kept smacking his lips. Of course, if he had known it was her mother's suggestion.... Rufus liked Madame Tchernofsky even less than he had her mother. The whole concept of spiritualism annoyed him.

That was because he was a young spirit (according to Madame). He did not have as highly developed a soul as his wife.

Mrs. Wutzl turned quickly to the recipe for double-dip chocolate-chip pudding cake. She knew the spell by heart and only wished to confirm her memory of it. She had decided to make Rufus something especially good tomorrow, his favorite dessert. Why shouldn't he have it, despite what the doctor said? *A bit of wifely magic*, she thought. *That'll fix him good.*

Ethel held *The Gourmand's Companion* to her chest and started thinking of that skinny Mabel Fleish, her whole skinny family. God only knew what gave poor Percy Furnival the strength to stand before his classes day after day. And that little girl—it was a crime a child should be allowed to become skin and bones because her mother was running around. Everyone knew Mabel Fleish was too busy writing down her dirty dreams, researching them in the flesh, hmph—the women in the beauty parlor all said so—to cook a decent meal for her family. Why, Ethel Wutzl had seen her on more than one occasion buying a barbecue chicken in the supermarket. As if there were anything to roasting a fresh chicken! You just patted the breast with a mixture of olive oil and chopped garlic, sprinkled paprika, salt, and pepper on its skin, stuffed it with its own broasted innards and toasted bread pieces. What could be simpler to cook? Then your family could sit down to a wholesome homecooked meal instead of a cold, unwashed, barbecue chicken. They wouldn't all look like they were fainting from one moment to the next.

Women like Mabel Fleish, these young (though she was not so young as she acted) career gals, well it was a shame, a shame that women like that had families and women like Ethel Wutzl were childless. Not that she would have wished on her what had happened, but wasn't it just desserts? If the truth came out she was probably running around even then, while her baby drowned in the tub.

Poor little boy. If that sweet child had been hers he'd be alive today. She would have watched him carefully, never letting him out of her sight, she'd have watched his every move. At lunchtime she'd have met him outside the playground with a glass of milk. When he came home there'd have been fresh cookies waiting. He would have grown up plump, healthy, fattened like a Christmas goose. The gloss of good health would have made his hair shine.

Ethel blinked hard, longing with all her soul for such a child, wondering why God hadn't seen fit to give her one—or, rather, why He had changed His mind. Instead He went and gave him to that horrible Mabel Fleish. Hussies like that had babies pop out of them like toast while good women like herself remained fruitless. She had begun studying the ways of the Lord in an effort to understand the answers to such questions. Though she still didn't, she'd come to feel on almost personal terms with the Divine. She now tsked her tongue at God, as if He were someone she thought had committed a peccadillo.

Pouring half-and-half into the Wedgewood creamer that, together with sugar bowl, had been a wedding present from her favorite cousin, she sighed. Who was Ethel Wutzl after all, she philosophized, to question the mysterious workings of God? And, really, she had no complaints. It wasn't as if Felix didn't keep in touch. And she had Rufus. He was child enough for her. There was nothing she liked better than pleasing him. She had gotten to his heart through his stomach many times before, and would again. When Mabel Fleish's book was on the trash heap where it belonged Rufus Wutzl would still be sitting at the table, licking his lips and gazing with love on the face of his esteemed wife.

Ethel poured heavy cream into a bowl. She took out her whisk and began whipping it. *That Mabel Fleish,* she thought, *probably never whips for her husband.* She added sugar and beat the cream faster till the froth formed a hard, pointy peak when she touched it with her finger.

She put a wooden spoon into the bowl and took it out to her husband. He liked to lick the sides. She couldn't see any reason to deny him that pleasure. As she came into the dining room, she was pleasantly annoyed to see he had already helped himself to a piece of cake.

"Rufus," she said. "I told you I was whipping cream."

Dr. Wutzl looked up from his periodical, a guilty look on his face. "I'm sorry, dear. I couldn't wait."

"You are so naughty." Mrs. Wutzl laughed. "Such a naughty-naughty boy." She put the bowl before him, smiling until she saw the wide-mouthed caricature of Mabel Fleish in *The New York Review of Books.* "What's *she* doing there?" she complained.

"She who, dear?" said Dr. Wutzl.

"She who indeed! That 'woman,' although another adjective would be more appropriate."

"You mean noun, dear. 'Woman' is a noun, not an adjective."

"Oh, for God's sake!" Ethel said as she stormed off. *The letter,* she thought, then pushed it from her mind. She returned with a pot of coffee and a cup and saucer, which trembled alarmingly as she laid it before her husband. He didn't notice. He had returned to reading about that, that *witch,* although she could think of another adjective, she thought, mentally sticking her tongue out at him, to describe a woman who had all the men sniffing around her like a pack of hounds. Look at him, the old fool, that dazed, enchanted smile on his face. Why, he didn't even realize she could see it. He never believed she had ESP, though she could read his mind now when she wished she could just throw it in the garbage along with that trashy novel he was so all-fired hot about too.

"That girl just better watch out," she said ominously.

"Hmmm," said Dr. Wutzl, not looking up. "Why's that?"

"Can't you listen to me when I talk? You'd think I was a wall, for all the attention I get. Because *someone* might read her novel and think that's what she wants. Or deserves. Someone..."

"Mmmm," said Dr. Wutzl. "Mmm-hmmm."

She crossed her arms over her chest. "Will that be all, Dr. Wutzl?" she asked.

"Maple syrup," he said. "Would you be so kind as to—"

"Oh here. Here's the damn syrup right in front of you. And here's the cream for your coffee. Just you wait. I'll fix you. Just see what I make tomorrow."

Rufus Wutzl smiled, revealing chocolate on a front tooth. He rubbed his belly. "You are a most excellent wife, my dear."

Mrs. Wutzl stomped into the kitchen and took down *The Gourmand's Companion* again. Was double-dip chocolate-chip pudding cake the answer? Perhaps Charlotte Malakoff au Chocolat would be better? It took a lot of work to make the ladyfingers, light and airy, then the chocolate-almond cream filling, but Rufus would just die when he tasted it. Particularly if she used dark Lindt chocolate and added a layer of crushed nuts. Butternuts would be delicious. And she could make a goose *cassoulet*, if the butcher had any fresh-killed goose. Or she could use lamb. Or pork. Maybe she would make an asparagus cream soup too. Yes, after eating a meal like that he wouldn't soon hunger for Mabel Fleish.

FOUR

Percy was working late in the library. Ana was upstairs with her dolls. Nubi was asleep in his corner. Mabel, alone in the living room, took an envelope out of her pocketbook, then went to her desk for her journal. Someone had left the scissors and tape out. She put them back in the drawer, her eye falling on the *Bone* galleys inside. Why was she saving all those pages of type, she wondered. Superstition—or was it because words, once committed to print, had a life of their own? She paused, opened another drawer, took out a folder buried beneath stationery, and sat on the couch.

Upstate New York was having a spell of Indian summer. The windows were open, the blinds were raised. The panes, black with night, were like eyes, but she did not pull the shades. She stretched her arms overhead, curling her legs beneath her. Under the gaze of invisible strangers she felt oddly seductive and moved as though juggling balls. Reaching her hands under her blouse she unhooked her bra and pulled it out her sleeve like a magician. She put it on the couch and picked up the envelope. In it was a Xerox of an article. She held it but didn't read it. Instead she thought about a man. A young man with long white hair. A disdainful smile and funny name too. What was it again? Herm? Yes, Herm Kwestral.

Earlier that week she had driven to the city to meet her agent, who wanted to discuss her new book. Only she didn't have one.

"You know what your problem is?" Max asked, his bowtie bobbing like a rooster's wattle. "You have great ambition...to fail."

After lunch she had gone to the library, to look up the one small article she remembered about Beau's death. *The Brooklyn Wing* had run a story about the discovery of a body in a ruined building on Flatlands Avenue. The adolescent boy, it said, had apparently overdosed on sleeping pills, but his nude body showed signs of mutilation. It was not clear if these were self-inflicted. There were no indications of other intruders. Still, the police were looking into the possibility of a cult ritual. The symbols cut into the boy's body and smeared in blood on the floor matched those found on the corpses of a variety of small animals, including several dogs and cats belonging to residents in the area. The victim was a minor, age sixteen, his name was not given.

Sitting in the too-bright living room now, Mabel felt as if she were on stage. She held the article in her hand and looked at it as if she didn't know what it was. She remembered how, after finding it in the library she had had to put her head down on the microfilm viewer, sitting that way till someone tapped her shoulder to ask if she were done with the machine.

She now put the article on the couch beside her and picked up the folder. In it were two letters. One was Beau's suicide note. The other was the letter from "Bone." She looked closely at the yellowed paper, observing how Beau had made his *a*'s like stars. She kissed the page, then impulsively, shamefacedly, put it in her blouse, holding it against her breast. She peeked inside the neck of her sweater to see her nipple pressed against his pen. When her hunger for a lover changed to an infant's for a mother she pulled it away and returned it to the folder. She placed the article between this note from Beau and the one from "Bone," and closed the file. She wondered why she still hadn't said anything to Percy about the crazy letter. Even when he came upon her reading it and asked what it was she had said it was her shopping list. After slipping it back into her jacket she snuck glances at him to see if he would explore her pocket. He didn't. That was the thing about Percy. He was so trusting. So easy to cuckold. It was like tricking a baby, hardly fair game. Percy deserved a better wife, she thought, one who plotted hearty, wholesome meals instead of steamy novels and amorous escapades.

I won't do it anymore. She made a fist, as if her determination were something she could grasp. Why was it, she wondered, that sexuality and creativity were tied in this perverse bondage anyway? The side of her that loved life loved Percy; the other side wanted to die. Percy was familiar, safe. She didn't thrill to any danger in his touch. They had a good sex life, but she didn't moisten at the thought of him, as she did when contemplating a stranger like

Kwestral.

She smiled at the memory. His whiteness, as of someone dead...but for his intensity. He had a long neck with a protruding Adam's apple. When he swallowed, it bounced deep down, then high, before resuming its place in the middle. His thin hook nose had dilated, aristocratic nostrils. But it was especially his weird, albino, looks that grabbed her.

After leaving the library she'd gotten into her car, planning to escape the city before being trapped in its rush hour. Instead she found herself driving to Brooklyn. She went to the station house in the neighborhood she'd grown up in. The desk sergeant was bored but not very helpful. "Why do you need to know about a death that happened twenty years ago?" he asked, looking at her suspiciously through the smoke of his cigarette. She started to answer when the phone rang. He held up his hand to her, mumbled a few phrases to someone named Itchy. Two cops walked by with a pizza. Another cop, an older one, had a container of coffee in a white bag with an onion bagel. He took out the bagel and started to munch. Mabel read a sign that said, "Old Complaints To Be Filed R.I.P."

The desk sergeant hung up the phone. "That boy was my friend," she told him. "My first lover, if you must know." He shrugged. "I'm a writer," she said. She held his glance, touching the corner of her lip with her tongue. Promising something. Nothing. "I need this material for my next book." He sat up taller, gave her a half smile, which she returned. She watched herself. She watched and swelled with hate. The red hairs on his arms saluted, then something closed behind his eyes. A female cop walked by, another one took a pad off his desk. She heard someone ask a drunk, "What were you arrested for then?" The phone rang again. A presence stood between them, and Mabel knew she had lost. She turned around.

He was sitting on a bench when she first saw him. She gasped at his whiteness in the dim, windowless room, then caught herself, covering her reaction by pretending she'd just thought of something. He was so pale he looked unformed, featherless somehow. He stood up when she turned, opened his mouth like a young bird asking for worms. There was mutual recognition. She knew she could never have forgotten looks such as his; still, she felt she knew him and couldn't think how. Then she knew. The sullen mouth, the insolent eyes, so disconcerting in a baby face. Except Beau was dark. And dead.

"I overheard your conversation," he said. "Hope you don't mind. Maybe I can help you. I'm a reporter. I work on *The Brooklyn Wing*. If you tell me what you're looking for I'll check the morgue."

"Morgue? It was twenty years ago. I hardly think—"

He laughed. "That's what we call the room where old clips are kept. It's extensive. Not just *Wing* stories."

"Well, I don't know how newsworthy this is, although *The Wing* did run a story. He was just a kid when he died." She started to tell him about Beau.

"Wait," he said. "Let's go someplace else." He invited her to a coffee shop. There she told him the facts about her dead friend, and he told her a bit about himself. She was impressed. It had taken her many years to get published, and he, by his own estimation, was doing quite well as a journalist. He was young to be as successful as he was. She said as much. "Not as young as I look," he said, which made him seem even younger.

She smiled into her coffee cup, stirring, stirring. "So, you're a journalist. What exactly do you do on *The Wing*?"

"I'm a crime reporter." She didn't say anything, just looked. He continued, as if compelled to correct any misconceptions he may have fostered. "Actually I'm a stringer. But I get a byline and my stuff's published regularly."

"That's great," she said. "But hey. I don't want to put you out. Aren't you supposed to hang around the precinct, stuff like that? Won't it be inconvenient for you to go to the office, to the 'morgue'"—she giggled saying the word, indicating quotes around it by flexing her fingers—"to help me?"

He looked down, his blush deepening the hitherto mild contrast between hair and skin. "I write obits too," he admitted. "Three times a week, freelance. On their computer."

"How fascinating," Mabel said. He seemed suspicious of her enthusiasm, as if he thought she was funning him. He continued speaking only after she reassured him of her interest.

"Actually, it is kind of interesting. People call in with deaths all day. You know—Grannie. Sis. I don't do the big names. They're done in advance anyway, updated when need be, especially if Mr. Rich N. Famous is sick. But these others, well someone has to take grief and whip it into shape. We're mostly a local paper, after all.

So I sit at their computer three days a week, waiting for Death to ring. Here, let me present his calling card." He took out his wallet, pulled an embossed rectangle from it. In addition to his name and number it said, "Deathly Prose, Reasonable Rates."

She laughed. "You have a way with words." She liked him. He was only a boy, it was as wrong to think about him the way she was beginning to as it would be if their sexes were reversed. Robbing the cradle. But it felt like robbing the grave. She'd always had a weakness for death. She was drawn to his lack of color. At first it was repellent, but, as they talked, she contemplated making love to a body so hairless and fair. It might seem pure. Like making love to an infant—what's so pure about that? she asked herself—or a veal sausage. She laughed aloud.

"What's the joke?"

"Nothing." She waved her hands helplessly, trying to regain her composure. Everything about him just then made her laugh. He had quirky ways. That hat he was wearing—right out of a forties movie. Bogey in *To Have Or Somethingorother*? He held his cigarette like a disaffected Russian. She liked him. She imagined their bodies entwined, then shook her head.

"No, what?" he asked. She didn't respond. "So, what about you?" he said. "You're a writer. What have you written?" He sat back, looked at her, taking her in as if drinking her. She felt her nipples harden, wondered if it showed.

She told him about *Bone* and was pleased that he'd heard of it.

"That makes you one of fifteen," she said.

"Metafictional mystery—I read that somewhere recently. In a review. Hey, I'm into mystery—detective, gothic, spy stuff too—but I've never read a metafictional one. What the hell does that mean?"

She shrugged. "I didn't write the line. Send a letter to *The New York Review*."

Kwestral signaled to the waitress with a movement of his hand that looked like studied rudeness. "More coffee," he said, staring at Mabel as he ordered. She thought, not for the first time, how absurd her life was, the conversations she had with people once they found out she was a writer. Idi Masambe wanted her to admit that her writing oppressed the masses in South Africa, which was why finally she broke off with him. He was a madman, and madmen were exciting in the beginning. Then they got on your nerves. And Ryder, a guy she'd seen for a while, kept reading her stuff, accusing her of stealing his ideas. She shivered, thinking how he'd tell her to stop reading his mind. Did hairdressers have such conversations? Waitresses?

"I have to get going," she said.

"You do?" His voice squeaked. He deepened it, tried to make it gruff. "Give me your number. I'll call you, if I find something one day when I don't have too much death on my hands."

She fought the urge to tweak his nose, wrote her name and number instead. "See you around sometime, Death," she said, handing him back his card. She walked out the door slowly, knowing full well that his eyes were on her. She could feel them stroking her thighs.

Smiling, remembering this, she sat back on the couch like someone digesting a sumptuous feast. Suddenly the living-room phone rang, startling her from her reverie. She jumped to answer it. No one was there. Shrugging, she hung up. She tried to recapture her mood, but the sound had cut through it. She felt herself watched by unseen eyes. Staring at the phone she willed it, dared it, to ring again.

FIVE

Kwestral was alone in a room of mirrors. Out the window he could see the crescent moon. Other than that, the windows were black, shiny with night. They reflected him like more mirrors all around. He saw himself, thin, bent, like a crescent moon himself, sitting at the rowing machine closest to the window wall.

"Ready?" the screen asked. He checked his posture in the glass, pulled his abdomen up, breathed into his back. He took up the oars, the screen fired. Two cartoon figures in boats began rowing. Kwestral's man easily maintained speed against the pacer as the long-haired albino leaned forward, pulled back.

Row, row, row your boat, sang an inane voice to the squeaking of his seat. He tried to drown it with fiction. *Plot*, he commanded himself. There was a detective novel he wanted to write but never seemed to have the time. Working two jobs—stringer and obit freelance—left him little energy for another kind of writing. Now he was alone, with no demands on his mind but those self-ordained. He could plot a novel or sing nursery rhymes. *Plot*, he told himself. *Row*, ordered a different master.

He didn't have a plot, that was the problem. He did have a character though, and liked nothing better than to think about her. Just, she had this disconcerting way of turning back into a woman, a woman he didn't want to want. There was something too...too carnal about her. Her lips, bloody with life. Her hair, wild. She was dirty sex, a woman tusseled from between sheets.

And yet something drew him. The way she laughed, her body shaking like a belly-dancer's. Her tongue lingering in the corner of her mouth. Vitality, that's what she had, and he didn't. Part of him wanted to suck the life from her, the blood that colored her. *Row*.

Just thinking about her made him feel faded. *Rowrowrow.* Why? What had she done? She'd written a novel, big deal, he'd read it. Trash. Good trash, well-written and all, exciting, provocative, and the prose was, well...she was the poet of pornography. Still, there had to be something more. Soul, her book lacked soul. No, that wasn't it. Too much soul. Yes. Revealed too much. More than a man wanted to know. *Gently down...* He grimaced. *Gently down the gently down...* He forced his face to relax, leaned back. *Gently down the stream.*

All right, it was an okay novel, it had good bits, some nice writing, suspense, but there was something about it he didn't respect. She seemed too much like her main character, that was it— dirty in her desires, uncontrollable till controlled. Fiction should be controlled. It should be...fictional. Autobiography disguised as fiction, oh, anyone could do that. He could do that. The Confessions of an Albino Obituary Writer. Not to say that that wouldn't be interesting. One was almost inclined to call her Annabelle instead of Mabel; even the names were close. Admit it, though, her writing was good. And she was, well, sexy. Getting on in years but still it was flattering to have a woman like that attracted to him, though that only proved her lack of worth. *Row row row row.*

There were two types of women in his experience—one, repelled by his lack of pigment; the other, attracted to it. That the second type existed at all was a surprise he knew he should feel grateful for. Certain women had a way of seeing past his freakishness—but to what, he couldn't help wonder. Pity? he thought, and his stomach churned acid. He didn't know what they saw, but he could see them see it. Maybe it was just the perverted pleasure of fucking a freak. He'd read a porno comic book once about Snow White and the Seven Dwarves—all at the same time. That was Fleish. He knew this from having read her book. He knew her secret desires as well as if she'd whispered them in his ear, handing him a cord.

Even if he hadn't read her book he'd have known. He had this "gift," this way of reading people, and she was like one of those detective novels he'd read through in a night.

Row your boat, row your boat. He should call her though, as a courtesy. Let her know what he'd found out about her old boy-friend. He pulled at the oars thoughtfully. How would she respond to what he'd learned? Lean back, pull, stretch.

He'd spent much of the past week in *The Wing*'s morgue on

Fleish's account, researching death instead of writing about it. He couldn't help fantasizing her reaction to his information. He thought of her face, raised up like someone staring at the moon. *Row*, he told himself. *Row, row, row.*

Beau Barbon never came up in the news. Would she be pleased to learn he was still alive (as far as the news went)? The dead kid was named Larry Lazar. Kwestral had had to call his contact in Crime Analysis to find that out. *The Wing* hadn't followed up much on the story. Did she know Lazar? He felt a pang of jealousy and imagined it was contempt. Carnivorous female, he thought, eating young males like potato chips even then. His pulse raced with fear for a moment, as if he watched himself sleepwalking toward a vampire.

She isn't real, he told himself, and to prove it he tried to picture her face. He could only come up with the head shot on her book. He sighed, fingers of sweat tickled his neck. "I want to sleep with you," a voice said. "To *sleep*. With you." A song began to sing in his soul.

He reached, as if for his reflection. "I want to sleep with you. To *sleep*/ With you." Pulled back. Reached again. *Life is but a life is but a life is but a.* "To fall/ Unconscious/ To breathe your breath." *Life is but a.* Dream woman, he called her, not real at all.

But we are always dreams of each other, he thought. Especially in sex. We touch but do not enter. Skin repells skin. We lie together, dream separately. Take turns speaking, hear our own fantasies echo back. ("Your spirit disturbs mine as our bodies/ jerk and rest/ like puppets/ pulled by dreams.")

That girl in college, they hadn't even gone to bed, but she kept calling, dropping him notes, going places she thought he'd be. Flattering, to be the object of someone's obsession. Annoying too, and frightening. What did she know of him? Nothing, except that he was whiter than moonlight. Was that the source of her attraction? Didn't that prove something wrong? She wanted to believe in what she saw, and when someone sees so clearly what isn't there, that person might be mad. "As sin," his mother always said. Was sin madness then, did evil not exist? Finally he'd stopped being polite, stopped returning her calls. Would run into her now and then, would wave and walk on. That time he was having coffee with Lou, she sat at a table nearby, crying. "There's a beautiful girl behind you," Lou said, "crying." There she sat, shameless, tear-streaked. As if they had ever had anything going. As if it hadn't all been in her head.

Life is but a... He yearned forward, toward an attainable disdainable woman he didn't want to want. He imagined her arms. He leaned back, pulled her on top of him, and they began to dance. He pushed faster, she rowed in counterpoint, facing him, pulling as he pushed, pushing as he...oh, *life is but a life is but a.* "I want to sleep with you," sang his soul. "To die the little death nightly in your arms." *Life is but a dream.*

The gun shot off, the screen grew blank. The race was over, he'd won. The screen demanded he cool down, congratulated him as the pacer rowed off in defeat. It told him the particulars of his heart rate, the number of calories he'd consumed. Kwestral put the oars down, pulled off his shirt, wiped his face and underarms with it, sniffed it for the secret pleasure of his smell.

He got into the shower, let the hot water beat on his head. Life is but a dream, he thought, sounded kind of Hindu. He whistled a few bars before he realized what he was doing and stopped.

Got out, wrapped a towel around his waist. The workout had given him a high. He felt capable of anything. Saw himself from all angles in the mirror-paneled locker room, thought he looked good. Lanky, but muscles were starting to pop. Of course he was still as white as the locker room attendant's coat. He waited for Charlie to use his skeleton key to unlock his door. Yeah, he thought, he felt good. It was a shame to get dressed. Wearing nothing but a towel cinched about his waist he felt rugged, not skinny. There was no one in the locker room. Just him and Charlie. He looked at his watch. Almost nine. Not too late. He could call.

He took out change, found his card with her number on it. "If you learn anything," he remembered her saying. "Please. You must help me. You're the only one who can."

Kwestral's chest filled with manly gas as he walked in flipflops to the telephone opposite the hair blowers. His scapulas shone like dinosaur plates, he thought, seeing them in the mirror while he dialed.

The phone rang a few times, then she picked up. "Hello?" She sounded distracted. Busy. Like someone interrupted, kept from doing something important to do something mundane...like answer the phone. "Hello, hello?" He hated the phone, especially if it rang when he was writing. "Who is it?" She'd despise him if she heard his voice.

He hung up fast, afraid she'd recognize his breathing. Stepped back from the phone, as if it were coiled to strike. Saw himself in the mirror, a gawky ghost. Looked about twelve. Skinny, no meat, all bone. Adolescent leper, people running from his bell. *Hey, I'm twenty-six years old*, he thought. He pulled the towel tighter around his waist, walked back to the locker. The attendant made a face when Herm asked him to open it. He apologized for bothering him again so soon. Semi-naked, cold, shriveled and bent, he stood waiting as the middle-aged man in medical whites sighed and took out the key.

The hospital room in which his father died was flat white. Herm had felt as if he and his father, draped sheets all around, were part of an alabaster relief, something on a temple wall. "Cop Shot," the headline ran, "Aiding Lady of Night." His father was dead. Like all heros, dead as a god. Kwestral was fifteen. "If anything ever happens to me," he used to tell him, "you're the man of the family." Over and over. "Remember, son." As if he could forget. His father's face, dead already though still in a coma. The beard growing, the horror of shaving that undead face as it turned itself to hair. The beard grew so fast. You wouldn't think the body would waste energy when there were more important things to do. Like heal. Like live. He'd spend all day in that room. Wouldn't go to school, no matter what his mother said. Read to him. The newspaper (his father liked to keep up, especially with sports). A detective novel. The whole family loved mysteries.

So he read to him, and read and read. He didn't know what else to say. What do you tell a dead man? What do you talk about when you're fifteen and your father's turning gray on a slab? On day five he put the book down and looked at the old man. He wasn't old, but he looked old, dying. "Don't worry," he said. "I'll take care of Mom. You can count on me." That's when his father's face began to twitch. His eyelids fluttered, his mouth grinned. For a moment Herm thought he was waking up, that he'd open his eyes, open his mouth and say, "Just wanted to hear you say that, son." Then that horrible deathgrin contorted his lips, his face became a mask, and it was clear this was no joke but what they'd been waiting for.

Kwestral knew he had given his word, whether his father heard him or not. It was something he had to live by. So he was twenty-six years old, still sleeping in the room he'd grown up in, eating meals made by Mom. He and Mom sitting alone in the big house, reading side by side. "How was your day, dear?" Like being married to an old wife. Stuck in a role assigned by his father—man of the family. Never a man.

SIX

Mabel looked at the clock. It was getting late. Percy would be home from the library soon. She had told him she was going to work on a new story. So far all she'd done was reread old letters and an article about a dead boy while mooning about a kid named Kwestral. She caressed the purple file, caught herself doing it, put it on the couch beside her. Definitely not, she told herself. If he called she wouldn't meet him. Dr. Xavier said she was acting under a compulsion. She'd show him she wasn't.

Beau, she thought suddenly. If he hadn't been jealous he'd have been amused. Jezebel, he called her. She hadn't even known what a Jezebel was. Beauregard No Regard, she taunted back, more right than she could have known. Twitching animals. "You have to see these things, Maybelle." He told her he had powers, he would share them. "Beauregard No Regard," she whispered now in the empty room. "I was just one more little animal you made twitch, wasn't I?" She opened her journal and wrote, "I still haven't told Percy about the letter. Because of Beau? Do I really believe it's the message I've been waiting for? That's nuts. Still, I don't want to scare him off."

The porch wind chimes began to make music. She knew it was nothing but the announcement of a breeze, still the ghostly gaiety hinted of a different intrusion. She shivered, but fear was not unpleasant. *Beau*, she thought, then heard voices upstairs. Her fear grew cold as she listened to the male and female voices. When she recognized Ana assuming Ken's low pitch and Barbie's high she laughed. "Infernal midgets," she said. "Can't wait till she's old enough to throw them out."

Whenever she went into her daughter's room her dolls stared in their malevolent, plastic way. Who was to blame for Seth's death if not them? On that horrible day, when she heard Ana chattering to them, she had been lulled into thinking it safe to leave the little girl with her sleeping brother.

The bells rang again. Mabel didn't look up. She flipped the pages of her journal, thinking how many times she had looked for someone to blame. There were over twenty notebooks full of accusations. The dolls were at fault, the stars were at fault, the three-year-old was at fault. The reality was, and Mabel knew it, she had not wanted another baby. She had willed Seth's death. And she would never forgive Percy for implying as much. "Why weren't you watching him?" he said. Why indeed! No subsequent kindness on his part could ever counter the accusation that still rang in her ears.

A long, terrible cry cut through her thoughts. She looked up, startled, as though the wail too accused her. Shorter cries followed, right outside her window. Mabel willed them away. They wouldn't leave. "Go to sleep, Sethy," she whispered. Anubis, in his corner by the radiator, looked up. His ears twitched. He heard it too? Then it couldn't be a ghost.

"A cat," Mabel said, laughing in relief.

Nubi got up, looked out of the window, searching for the yowler. He walked over to her, put his head in her lap, wanting to be petted. He had a wicked grin, his mouth slightly open. He smiled in the wolfish way of white shepherds, panting. Drool made his teeth shine. "Go away," she said, but he would not leave off burying his face in her crotch. The dog had such insistence about his demands she sometimes fantasized he'd rape her. She imagined herself naked, getting out of the bath, bending over to pick up a towel, Anubis knocking her over, her head hitting the floor. When she came to she would wonder at the wetness from her center, dripping like a wound.

She shook her head. How did she come up with so many disgusting ideas? And why? She pointed to the corner. "Lie down," she commanded, as if summarily dismissing a courtier who'd made untoward advances. The dog slunk away, glancing back lasciviously. He sat in his corner, worrying a piece of paper. "What's that?" Mabel asked. She took the white sheet from him, wondering how it had gotten in. On it were individual letters taped together to form words.

It gos accdng 2 the bk.
2 see me act you got 2 look.

I see a ghst. The ghst is me.
You clsd the bk so I cnt see.

Lfes a bk. Yr bks my lfe.
I cut yr pctre w my knfe.

All humn lfes a play, Wil sd.
At ths bks end wil bth be dd.

Mabel got up, went to the window. She looked out. The night seemed calm. Deceptively. None of her neighbors were sitting on their porches. No one was walking by. She put her head back in and was disconcerted to find Anubis behind her. It was not the first time she felt as if he were a man in a dog mask. She couldn't shake the uneasy feeling that at the very next moment he'd have pushed her into invisible arms.

"Where did this come from?" she asked, terrified he'd answer. Instead he went to his bowl and lapped water noisily.

She took out the first letter from Bone, read it again. "I better tell someone about this," she said. But she was stirred by the scent of secret. She opened her journal. "Are other authors," she wrote, "haunted by characters in their novels? Am I mad?" Bone was based on Beau, she knew, but even as she wrote him into existence he had rebelled, becoming the character *he* wanted to be. And here he was, back from the dead (or soon-to-be-remaindered), to continue his story beyond fiction.

She shook her head to ward off dream. "I can't think about this now," she said aloud, as if for someone else's benefit. She lit a cigarette, opened her journal at random. Her eye fell on an entry in the middle of the page. "How can I lie to you?" she read. "You know I went into labor as though marching to my execution. When I heard the baby was a boy my heart hardened. But I swear I didn't want him to die."

She shut the book. Of all the pages to open to! As if the alphabet, which she'd served for so long, had turned against her. "What I need," she told herself, "is another novel to work on. Then I wouldn't keep going over this stuff." She stood up, stretched,

making a show of comfort. "What I need," she said, "is a drink."
She poured herself a scotch. Drank two large gulps. Steam shot out
her ears. Her stomach lurched in rebellion, then said okay. She tried
to forget what she had been working on while Seth drowned.

It was a coincidence that her own son was dying at the same
moment she had been jotting notes on Ted's death. Ted was the son
of a fictional character. Annabelle was not real, Ted was not real.
Writing about Ted had not caused her baby's death.

Seth was an infant. Ted was sixteen. Seth drowned in a bathtub.
Ted died of an overdose. What had drugs to do with an infant's
body jerking beneath water? Ted ran away to become the coke cunt
of a stranger called Bone, supplying the charismatic cult leader with
money earned from his prostitution. Annabelle went to confront
Bone, and fell under his sway. What had any of that (which Mabel
had been scribbling while the water ran) to do with the death of a
baby? Bone twisted things around. Like a snake, he was danger-
ously hypnotic. Charming. The skin fell back, revealing the bone.
"Whose fault is it," asked Bone, "if he looked for in me what he
never got from you?" No, couldn't you see, couldn't Percy and
everyone see—writing about the death of a fictional son had not
caused a real son to drown.

Mabel was accustomed to sifting her soul for fragments of
character. Almost nothing shameful got past her without being
imprisoned in a book. Long before she conceived of *Bone* or Seth
she recognized the strange bond between mothers and sons. She
had based Annabelle partly on her memories of Mrs. Barbon, an
attractive blonde too young to be a mother. At sixteen it struck
Mabel that Beau had an odd relationship with her. When she was
around she stroked Beau's face, he kissed her hand. She was no
more than thirty-five, single, walking around in a skimpy robe. She
left Beau alone many nights, while she went off, carousing with
lovers. He carried her picture in his wallet. "Isn't she beautiful?"
he'd ask his friends. Mabel pouted. "Why don't you carry my
picture?"

She condemned Mrs. Barbon with an adolescent's morality,
believing she would never be provocative with her own son. But
once she gave birth to Seth she understood. Diapering him she
listened to her own fantasies, as if eavesdropping on a stranger. "He
wouldn't know what I was doing if I took his tiny penis in my
mouth, but wouldn't it tie him to me forever?" She hadn't done it

of course, just as Mrs. Barbon probably hadn't done anything more to Beau than flaunt her body. It was just the realization of what one could do. In the mundane world Mabel had been businesslike to a fault, washing Seth. It was enough that she had thought of it, made note of it. Someday, if ever she had the need, it was there for her fiction.

Wasn't that the problem? she thought now. Her allegiance had always been first to her writing, then to her children. Still, it was better than some of the things you heard. Ryder's mother used to put him down a well. He hadn't told her much about his childhood, but one night he had trembled in her arms, crying as he told how she had done it first for an hour. She kept lengthening the time he had to spend in the well. "To teach me," he said, "a lesson." The last time days must have gone by. The hole above him darkened, grew light. He began screaming again. If that man hadn't heard him what might have happened? "Don't ever shut me up in the dark," he'd cried to Mabel, telling her. She'd comforted him as if he were her child.

Now she opened her book, about to write down some memories of Ryder, laughing when she thought that such life-story plagiarism was just what he had accused her of. That was when she noticed an eerie light in the next room, reflected in a mirror. When she moved it moved. She danced with it, thinking it had to vanish into an oddly magnified speck of dust. It didn't. She rose to investigate. "Nubi," she called, slapping her thigh. "Here, boy." The dog jumped up to accompany her down the hall. She didn't believe it was a ghost. And if it were, what could a dog do? Still, she felt better in the company of a living thing. She got to the back room and saw it was the moon peeking through the window, its image caught in the mirror on the closet across from it. She shut the blind. "Good boy," she said, petting Anubis's long, pointy head. His eyes gleamed in the dark. He smiled and sniffed.

She returned to the couch. The wind chimes rang. She pulled her blouse tight around her, sorry she had taken off her bra. She looked down the dark passageway to the room she had just left. The mystery she now saw was even more disturbing—nothing, yet she knew she was seeing the reflection of darkness. As if whatever spook was there was watching her still, but better hidden.

A dead beau, a dead baby. Whose spirit was pulling at her breasts tonight? "Beauregard No Regard," she called softly, "is it you?" If Beau had had any regard for her, he would not have killed himself. He would not have written that horrible letter, laying the blame at her feet like a bloody John the Baptist's head. Playing with matches, guns, drugs, voodoo. If he killed himself it was because death was his mistress, not her. She wished he would return from the dead so they could argue it out. She wanted to explain why she hadn't come that night. She wanted it so much that, twenty years later, she still awoke to find her face wet, knowing she'd cried in her sleep. She wanted him to take her down to his underworld of crazy ideas, make her stay with him forever. Memory had faded him into a gray boy, but his eyes still burned in the dark. They saw through her dreams till she became the ghost.

She remembered how, just a few days before his death, they were in his house. His mother was away, *with one of her lovers, no doubt,* she had thought. Beau offered her a cigarette.

"Know what this is?"

"A home-rolled smoke," she said.

He laughed. "Boo," he said.

"I'm shaking."

"Honey, don't you know what boo is?"

"What ghosts say?"

Again he laughed. "It's marijuana."

"Beau, are you crazy? Put it away. Throw it away. You'll get arrested. Addicted. You'll go nuts."

He wrapped her hair around his hand so that the tendrils looked like streams of blood. He pulled her close. "Stop it, Beau. You're hurting me." He kissed her so hard she felt his teeth through her lips. Then he pushed her away.

"If you love me you'll try it." His eyes looked through her, as if she had no clothes. She remembered dancing naked in the moonlight, how he had held her, made love to her, so sweet so gentle. "Ah, Beau," she said, as he lit the joint. He inhaled deeply, then handed it to her. "Don't exhale," he said. "Don't cough." She couldn't help it. She choked. "Here," he said. "Suck it from me." He took a long, hard pull, then put his lips to hers, gently opening them with his tongue. Slowly he fed her the smoke from his lungs. She tried to pull away, but he held her, forcing more smoke into her lungs. She thought she was suffocating and pushed away as if he were trying to kill her.

"Well?" he said.

"Well?" she said.

"Feel anything?"

"I don't think so," Mabel answered. "Except hungry. Did your mom leave you anything to eat?"

He laughed in jerking motions so strange that she thought of a snake shedding its skin. "Let's go in the kitchen," he said. There they found a coconut. Mabel held the hairy head while Beau hammered nails into it. She enlarged one of its eyes, milked the nut into a glass, offered it to him. "I don't much care for it," he said. "You drink it." She did, secretly pleased to have the whole glass for herself. He cracked the head, peeled back the skull, putting pieces of the white meat into a bowl. "Let's wait till it chills," he said, putting it in the fridge.

He led her first to his mother's room. Mabel would not lie on the bed. He took her then to his own room.

They lay down and kissed. Only a few nights earlier they had made love for the first time, but Mabel was afraid. "What if your mother comes in?"

"She won't care. What do you think *she's* doing?"

She let him open her clothes but would not take them off. They struggled. He was stronger and could have overpowered her but didn't. Instead he lay back, putting her head on his chest. He held her breast, fondling it as he spoke. "You know about that old woman, don't you? Rosemary whose house we were in? Well, the way I heard it was she was alone one night. And this crazy man come. He had an ax, and he—"

"Beau, stop. What are you telling me this for?"

"You know you like it. Don't you?" He stared into her eyes. His eyes were dark blue then, almost all pupil. She felt goosebumps, her nipples elongating. He pushed her bra up, took her breast in his mouth, then he lay back down. "They didn't find her body for a week. By then it stank. There were rats."

She held him. He slipped her open blouse off her shoulders, unzipped her shorts. She didn't struggle.

"That's where you like it," he said. "In the dead woman's house. Aren't you my Jezebel? You don't even know. Oh, you are my honey, aren't you?" He pulled down her shorts, her underpants. He put his pillow between her legs so he could "dream of you later." Terror was a form of foreplay.

Afterward she felt the hot of him pool in her seat at the kitchen table. He took out the coconut. The cool white meat was waiting. They shivered with pleasure as the water dripped on their thighs. Outside, humid vegetation breathed at the window as if watching children at play.

Mabel went into the kitchen for an apple. She could still hear the murmur of Ana acting out her childish games with Ken and Barbie. She smiled. Her daughter was young. What *would* she do when, in a few years, Ana asked to read *Bone*? Maybe Percy was right. She wanted to believe it. After all, she was a writer, she made her living by blowing things out of proportion. Ana was nothing if not a matter-of-fact child. It was entirely possible that she'd say, "Aw, Ma, I know Anna's not me. You didn't even know me then. She's just a character in a novel."

She heard the telephone ring. It caught her unawares for the second time that night. Startled, she took a deep breath. "Hello?"

"Hello, Anna," said an oddly familiar voice.

"This isn't Ana," Mabel said. "Who's this?"

"It wasn't nice of you to write such nasty things about me, Annabelle." The voice was muffled.

"This is not Annabelle. You have the wrong number."

"No," said the voice. "I have your number. I know what you want. I'm going to get you back. See you soon, Annabelle, honey."

The phone went dead in Mabel's hand. She stared at it, unsure now if she'd heard the voice or dreamed it. She looked around, terrified by all the open black windows. Backing into a corner she sat on the floor with the blank wall behind her, watching the windows to see if anyone tried to enter. She heard steps outside. Saw a face at the window. Before she could focus on it, it was gone. There was the sound of footsteps on the gravelly path, footsteps going up the stairs to the porch. Someone kicked the door. Mabel pushed herself further back, staring with horror as the person on the other side kicked harder. What should she do to protect Ana? *Whatever happens*, she thought, *make it happen only to me. Make it happen to me.*

The door opened, revealing an angry Percy Furnival, his arms full of books. "Why didn't you open the door? Didn't you hear me?"

"I-I-I was napping," Mabel said.

"On the floor? What's the matter? What happened?" He put

down his books, put his arms around her.

"You're trembling, Minky. Tell me what's wrong. I know you weren't napping. I saw you when I looked in the window."

"Oh, was that you? You scared me. The most terrible thing is happening. Here, look at this. I just found this letter." Mabel showed Percy the latest note from Bone, then told him about the earlier one and the phone call, watching as disbelief spread across his face. "I knew it," she said. "You don't believe me. That's why I didn't tell you. You won't believe it till my naked corpse is found in the woods."

"Minx, I think you should see Dr. Xavier. He's been ask—"

Mabel pushed him away. "Dr. Xavier, my ass. I'm never going back to that quack. Maybe he's the one doing this, did you ever think of that? Trying to get me to come back." She was sorry she said it. It sounded paranoid even in her ears. "You think I'm crazy. You don't believe me, do you?"

"I believe you believe it."

"Goddammit, Pooky! And what about the phone call? Do you think I called myself? How would I—"

"Did anyone else hear the phone ring?"

"Ana's upstairs. Maybe she heard it. And besides, if anyone could have cut out the letters and pasted them on a page, that anyone could as easily be you. I don't mean you did it, I just mean I could accuse you as—Pooks, don't look at me that way. Pooky!"

"Minky, it's better if—"

"Listen to you two," Ana said, coolly eyeing her parents from the stairs. "I feel like the child of cartoon mice."

"Ana, you heard the phone ring just now, didn't you?"

"No, Mumsy." She smirked. "I didn't. I was in *my* room. The phone in my room didn't ring."

Mabel looked at Percy. "That's because it was this phone, the one down here in the living room. It's a different number."

Percy nodded his head, glancing at Ana, telling Mabel with his eyes that they'd discuss it later, after the child went to bed. "How about some ice cream?" he asked, clapping his hands. "What do you say we cartoon mice have us some cheese?"

SEVEN

When Ana finished her ice cream she went upstairs. She could tell by the furious murmuring that began when she left that her parents were having a discussion. "Mommy and I are not fighting," her father had said often enough. "We are having a discussion." Last year when the teacher separated her and Pammy for hair-pulling she told Mrs. Lee they were having a discussion.

She went into her room. "Mommy has a lot of nerve," she told Barbie and Ken, "asking me if I heard the phone."

"What phone?" said Barbie, hanging up her pink princess.

"Who were you calling?" Ana asked. The dolls stared. "You heard me. What are you looking at?" she asked Barbie in her Ken voice.

"Nothing," squeaked Barbie. "I wasn't calling for help."

"I'm going to punish you," said Ken. "I'm going to-to-to radish you." *That isn't right,* Ana thought. She pulled a copy of *Bone* out from behind her headboard, turning to the first of several pages marked with turned-down corners.

"Ravish," said Ken. "I'm going to ravish you."

"Oh no, Ken, not that. Please, not that."

"I'll teach you what a woman is. Strip," he said, and when Barbie fell to her knees (actually her stomach, since her legs didn't bend at the knee) pleading, he pulled her up by her hair and tore off her blue dress with white Peter Pan collar and matching handbag. He bit the tips of her nippleless breasts.

"Help help help," cried Barbie.

"This is nothing," he said. "I'm going to invite all my friends over, as soon as Pammy can steal her brother's G.I. Joe. In the meantime take this." Ken put his two hands on Barbie's ears, and he pulled and he pulled till he took her head right off. He put her head on Ana's desk, positioning it so Barbie couldn't help but see what he did to her naked body. From the doll carrying case he took out a sewing needle, some matches, a ball of string, and a small Band-Aid. Before proceeding with his lesson he taped her mouth. The eyes of Barbie's disembodied head rolled in horror as he took off his clothes.

Afterward he ripped the Band-Aid from her mouth and put her head back on her body. He dressed but wouldn't let Barbie put on any of her designer outfits. "Cook my dinner," he commanded. Whimpering she went naked into the toy kitchenette Ana had set up in the corner of her room. She put a plastic turkey in the oven. Ken threw her a pair of shoes. He made her serve dinner with nothing on but black heels.

"Tell me the truth," he said, putting his face to the whole turkey, since none of the pieces came off. "Did you or did you not kill your brother?"

"I didn't, I didn't," Barbie squealed.

"Who is that baby in the pictures of you as a little girl?"

"That's a neighbor's infant. Mommy and Daddy always say so when we come to those pictures. Even before I ask they tell me."

"And you believe them? How come there's no picture of the neighbor? How come it's only pictures of you and the little boy, or you and him and Mommy and Daddy? Can't you figure it out? Are you so stupid? Pammy says you are. No wonder she doesn't want you to sleep over when Gertie and her other friends are there."

"No, no," cried Barbie. "It isn't true. Pammy made that story up to get back at me for telling her she was adopted. I said, 'You don't know. You're adopted,' and she said, 'Oh yeah? That's still better than you. You killed your own little brother.'"

"And didn't you?"

"No, of course not," said Barbie. "I wish I had a brother or sister. I hate being an only child, don't you?"

Ken nodded. "I would give anything," he said, "to have a brother or sister to play with. Pammy doesn't know how lucky she is." Ken was quiet in thought. "Why don't you ask them?" he said. "Ask Mommy and Daddy if it's true."

"Because," said Barbie, "what if it is?"

EIGHT

Dr. Wutzl read the cover of the latest *New York Review of Books*, then opened the back page. He looked at the letters, to see if there were any scholarly matters of import he had missed. His eye traveled down the length of a column till he came to the classifieds. As often happened, he became distracted by the personals. *Damn nuisance,* he thought but couldn't help wondering what DWFJ and GBM stood for. MJF, 26, he noticed, was looking for a *ménage à trois.* He did some armchair matchmaking (it was a form of relaxation, his own version of the crossword puzzle) and found BiWP couple, academics, seeking swing.

Really, he thought. He mused the possibilities till another boldface line caught his eye: "Elderly professor, vigorous scholar, seeks romantic involvement with woman 25-35." He snorted, then pondered what response such an advertisement might solicit. It was just an academic question, but when he finished imagining various scenes between letter recipients he was appalled at the amount of time he had wasted. He threw the paper down in disgust and rose from his seat with the air of one escaping a neighborhood gossip.

He went to his desk, unlocked the middle drawer (Mrs. Wutzl, he was sorry to say, was a bit of a snoop), took out a notebook, then sat back down. He chewed his pencil a bit, then absentmindedly scrawled a telephone number on the top of the page. He colored in the holes of the numerals, folded the page, put it in his left breast pocket. He didn't know why, since he knew the number by heart anyway. *By heart,* he thought with a sigh.

"Beloved," he wrote on the next page of the notepad, not quite realizing he was going to do so. "If only heart had a tongue, soul an ear, that I might speak and you might hear." He paused, proud of the little poem that had come unbidden from within. He began writing prose in a similarly intimate vein for a few paragraphs, then abruptly broke off, ending the letter he would never send, "Yours (truly), RufRuf." Was he mad, was he in his dotage, he thought, carrying on with this schoolboy obsession? He tore up the sheet, threw it in the wastepaper basket. The ancients were right, he thought. Love was an illness, a fever more insidious than most, for it was one its own sufferer did not want to be cured of.

He picked up a well-thumbed book, determined to turn to the matter at hand. Fingering the pages while looking for his marginal notes he jotted a few ideas for the magnum opus he was writing. Having a taskmaster who would accept no excuses, he felt himself under severe deadline pressure. A man at his stage of life who wasted time was a fool indeed; still, he spent much of it sighing about the authoress instead of squeezing the secrets from the book's breast.

"Death, hold back thy chariot charges a bit longer," he whispered, then smiling, jotted it down.

He turned the page of his notepad, took a deep breath. "How closely the *Bone* narrative follows Canaanite myth," he wrote. "That still doesn't help me understand the ending. Bone has been giving Anna drugs to induce orgiastic compliance. It is clear that the final pill contains a lethal dose of the aphrodisiac. If she takes it she will climax to death. This is clear, but Fleish chooses not to show it happen. Why? She has proven herself no prude in earlier chapters, conjuring scenes that might indeed have given the squeamish or fainthearted pause. But here, at the very climax of the book, she chooses to leave the ending ambiguous. What does this do? For one thing, it makes the reader her accomplice in imagining a voluptuous, horrible act. But does she actually accomplish this? Unfortunately, no. She can't quite bring it off, and in impotent rage she thrusts metaphor after metaphor at us, till at last she abandons all attempts for a successful union of reader and red." Dr. Wutzl paused, read back, found his spelling error, inserted the missing *a* with a caret.

"Can't one just as easily imagine a refusal of Anna's final participation?" he continued. "If so, then the reader becomes not partner in the act but savior, bowdlerizing author's intent because of his offended sense of propriety.

"Anna's lover, Matt, representing the death god Mot (as I've shown earlier), has already been chopped up by this point in the novel. Her salvation cannot, must not, come from anywhere but within. We have been prepared for self-destruction. 'The empty hand was dealt me,' Anna says to Bone some pages earlier [where? cite page]. When they shake hands it is clear that some sort of pact is signified. He holds out closed fists, tells her to choose. Then comes the final line. 'Anna pointed to his right and smiled.'"

Smiled, Dr. Wutzl thought. *Smiled. Why? Because she would escape in death?* It was maddening. Like Fleish, the come-hither looks signifying...what? Could she see beyond, could she really see beyond this old-man flesh? Did she know that in him she'd found her reader, a man who understood her, who would explicate her for the world? If only she'd let him in. "Let me in," he whispered. "Oh, Mabel, let me in."

All at once he laughed, having an idea that was so simple it was brilliant. What could be more natural, he thought, than for him to call her? He would explain he was doing a study of her novel. She would be flattered. After all, he was a scholar of some note, his critical works on Byron and Shelley were still assigned regularly in courses on the Romantics. Everyone knew he was working on his magnum opus, that that was why he had had to cut back on his teaching load. The anticipation in the academic community was almost, why...palpable. You could feel it throb when he was in the conference room. People wanted to talk to him about it but hung back. Great things were expected. He was a scholar nearing the end of his productive life. And when she found out that *she*, little Mabel Fleish from Winegarden, New York, was his topic, that he had chosen her, that he thought daily (nightly) about her, her book that is, that he was writing a book about her book, well, when she found that out she'd want to be as helpful as could be. They would meet to discuss it, it was only natural. She'd indicate what she liked, what she didn't like, in what he was doing. They would get together regularly after that, for more discussions. Of the book, and other things. They had so much in common. More than she knew.

He dialed her number quickly, listening to the familiar tune played on his touch-tone. (He had called before, just to hear the music of her number.) The phone rang, he heard her husky voice. He was just about to respond when Mrs. Wutzl knocked on his door and entered. He hated how she did that, not waiting for him to say "come in." He hung up and looked wide-eyed at her, like a boy with the last piece of cake in his hand.

"Who's that, dear?" she asked.

"No one," he said. "I was just trying the Hooks. No answer. They must have gone to dinner."

"Speaking of which." She gestured "after you," and smiled.

NINE

Mabel was sitting at her desk, pen in mouth, notebook in hand, looking out the window, and not writing. She couldn't think of a thing to write, except what was already written. Perhaps she was just a one-book writer, she thought. It wasn't that new scenes didn't keep coming to her, just they were for a book already written. Was she doomed then, like some Ancient Mariner, to tell the same story over and over? *Bone* was not the sort of novel that could have a sequel. It was done, finished, it was time to move on. It was never done, couldn't be finished; it was published, no longer hers.

She shouldn't have listened to Percy, that was the trouble. He told her to leave the ending ambiguous, he said it worked. And it did...for the reader. But the writer knew it was cowardice, a giving up after more than thirteen years. She didn't know how to end it, so she just did. And now there was nothing inside her but finished unfinished business spoiling.

She went to the file cabinet, took out a folder marked "Reviews." She read the one from *The Times*. It was short and mixed, and didn't do the trick. The recent *New York Review* piece helped, though it seemed to be about a book other than her own.

She turned to *The Brooklyn Wing*. The long, glowing review that had just appeared was not quite credible, even to Mabel. Especially to Mabel. Too much Local Girl Makes Good. And Mabel had the unfortunate inability to lie to herself. Or believe others' lies. Still, the three pieces must have boosted her morale somewhat. At least she was able to lift her pen and note the date.

She returned to the file cabinet, took out another folder, this one full of newspaper clippings that had caught her fancy through the years. The first one she pulled out was about a Jungian analyst raped in the mountains near Winegarden. She knew the woman slightly. Hers was an archetypal name, Wendy Wind, that Mabel didn't trust. Still, she seemed pleasant enough, a bit daffy but who was Mabel to judge? Wendy taught an intro. psych. course at the college. She had told Mabel at a recent faculty meeting that, based on her reading of *Bone*, she suspected the writer suffered from animus possession. The Demon Lover in Fleish's soul was trying to subjugate the Femme Fatale, and her novel was a battleground between masculine and feminine forces. Mabel nodded wisely and offered potato chips.

She now reread the article in which Wendy explained the odd circumstances of the event. She had had a dream, she said to the reporter, in which she was raped in the mountains. It disturbed her, so she "dreamtalked" to the "gods" involved, in an effort to find out what her unconscious was saying. It was necessary, she further stated, to make "obeisance to the images," so she went for a drive in the mountains. She came to a dirt road that she recognized from her dream. She got out, began walking, in order to "honor the images and make them flesh." It apparently worked. A guy came out of the woods. She responded as if he were a dream figure and tried to continue the Jungian dialogue. He raped her.

Dr. Wind sounded quite nutty in the article. Mabel didn't know enough about Jungian analysis to understand her thinking. She wanted to explore the event in which fantasy and reality merged in order to understand it. She began a story, then stopped. *God*, she thought. *Not another rape fantasy.*

Mabel feared her imagination, that dreaming of rape might cause it to happen. After all, her grandmother had spent a lifetime saying her stomach was in a knot, then died of an obstruction when her lower intestine tied itself in one. And her mother used to joke that if you could remember the name of the disease, then you didn't have it (and now she couldn't and did). So Mabel's fear might be neurotic, as Dr. Xavier said it was, but it was not unfounded.

She pushed the notepad away as a wave of nausea, not unlike morning sickness, came over her. Sex, shame, humiliation. Her own mind disgusted her. She reached into her pants pocket, took out a small notebook, writing in a tiny hand a thought she couldn't commit to the larger, more public, pad. "What to do with repugnant fantasy material—express it, or let it take over?"

She saw the words like small animals running in the snow.

Grabbing the large notebook she put herself on automatic pilot and began. "I was walking in a dark woods." Her eyes were glazing over as she dreamed awake. It was just starting to happen, finally, when all at once she felt herself being watched. Two eyes crawled on her spine. She turned, looked out the window behind her. In the middle of the sky, seeming to stand still, was a bird facing her. It was unlikely, she knew, but she couldn't get past the notion that it saw *her,* a woman at a desk at a window in a house. "Turning and turning in the widening gyre," she heard herself say as it flew in closer, "the falcon cannot hear the falconer."

As startled by the line of Yeats as by the animal she wondered if it were indeed a falcon. She had seen the same bird at other times, watching her like a great eye. One morning, when she was exercising, she turned and there it was, staring as she stretched.

She now grabbed the binoculars she kept by the window and turned the focus on the hawk. What was there about writing, she wondered, that gave it the shame, and the excitement, of nakedness? She struggled to keep the bird sharp. Exposure? Stripping off layers to reveal...revelations, of course.

She saw the jagged wings clearly, the haughty face. It seemed to stare back through the lens. Of course that couldn't be, but they did say hawks had sharp sight. It might very well see her, a woman pointing something, staring bug-eyed. She watched him watch, swooping, returning.

Was it a falcon, was it the same falcon? Truth be known, she could just about tell a peregrine from a pigeon, but somehow she recognized it. Horace had a falcon. And she'd been thinking about him a lot recently.

Horace, she thought, watching it circle. Horace used to say the hawk was his eye. If she were unfaithful he'd get her back. She shivered, remembering how she'd been walking one time after leaving Idi Masambe. She was plotting a story and liked to dream as she walked. When she came to a clearing she looked up. There he was—Horace's emissary.

It could have been another hawk, she now told herself. The one she was watching in the binoculars seemed darker, not so red. And there were many hawks in these mountains. One thing was certain though. This was a big bird, everything about it said hunter. Horace. Was he crazy enough to try to terrify her into bed?

Horace would be at the Halloween party, she realized. She'd be able to tell then if he were the one calling, writing. Sending flying spies. And if not? A jealous husband, an uneasy ghost, a spurned boyfriend, a demon lover. A figment of the imagination with scissors and glue. The usual round of suspects. She laughed.

She lived in dreams, that was her job, she thought. But when the dreams start living on their own.... And yet, wasn't that what a writer wanted, for her fiction to come alive? Make the images flesh and the Jungian gets raped. Wendy Wind went to the mountains, but Mabel traveled at her desk, trying to make characters people would discuss for years, *just as if they were real.*

She picked up her pen, crossed out "I was," read aloud, "Walking in a dark woods," reinstated "I was." A face flitted through her mind—that young fellow, the albino with the pastel eyes. He had a funny name. She'd forgotten it, but she remembered the way he looked at her. He had a way of sitting back, watching a person talk, that made her feel naked. As though he knew what she was thinking, and she knew he knew. Yes, those pastel eyes could really speak. There was something almost alien in those baby orbs.

She picked up her binoculars and searched the sky again. When she located the falcon it was just a dot. At least she assumed that was it, across the river, where the stone houses were.

She turned her sight on the houses, admiring the gray field-stones, the way the maple near the farmhouse was turning color. She slowly, nonchalantly, moved the lens to the building and refocused. Such quaint shutters. She tried to look in the windows. First she tried the ground floor, then the second, then the attic. Not that she could see anything. Or wanted to. But she had to see how much she could get away with.

What if someone catches me? she thought, and quickly turned the binoculars back to the maple. It would be hard to explain to a neighbor that she wasn't peeping. As a watcher watched, her perspective shifted from aesthetic interest to shamed outrage. She defended herself to herself. *Don't I have the right to look where I want?* From the corner of her eye she thought she saw a figure over by the tree. She refocused the binoculars, stared hard. It looked like a man. It looked like a man with binoculars looking back!

Terrified she stepped away from the window, threw the binoculars on the chair. Silly, she told herself. There was no one there. Maybe a birdwatcher. Or someone like herself, curious about alien interiors, not meaning to see anything but the night lamp.

But she couldn't shake the feeling that she herself was being watched. Her every move, even her thoughts, were studied. She shut the light, tried to work in the dark. *No one has the right to watch me*, she thought. "No one is watching me," she said aloud, for whose benefit she didn't know. She turned her back to the window and began again. "The sun was low in the sky," she wrote, "the air chill. I walked quickly, feeling the shadows gathering. He must have been—"

The phone rang. It was like someone screaming at her to get dressed. She dropped her pen and answered. She heard breathing. "Hello?" No one said anything, just breathed. She hung up, afraid silence might yet find a voice with which to tell her secrets she preferred not to know.

"I'm innocent," she said. She took the phone off the hook. She imagined putting it to her ear, hearing it breathe. Afraid of her imagination, she buried the receiver beneath a chair cushion. She didn't want to hear the recording click on, mechanical and dry, then come alive, demand things from her, talking in the busy-signal voice of the dead. "Leave me alone," she told the invisible listener smothered beneath the pillow. The wire curled out from under the blue cushion like a diver's lifeline. She had a terrible urge to cut it, but then they'd get her for sure. Because when you cut off the dead they had a way of severing other connections.

TEN

Ethel Wutzl, vacuum cleaner in hand, stood in the doorway of her husband's office, tsking. She stepped first to the window sill and cleaned it with a damp rag. This naturally led to the desk, which she tidied, just a bit, he'd never notice. Rufus was so funny about his desk. "Don't touch it," he said, as if she'd ever want to touch any of his silly old papers. "I'll take care of it myself," but he never did, so what choice did she have but to sneak-clean.

She took a neatly folded plastic bag out of her apron pocket. Putting on a pair of rubber gloves she pulled the wastepaper basket from under the desk, emptied it carefully. She took pride in her work. Interest. She didn't just turn the pail over and dump the contents. Instead she pulled out pieces, placing them carefully into the bag. Dirty tissues. Rotten apple cores. Used toothpicks. Assorted old-man mush. It was unpleasant, there was much in a marriage that was unpleasant, but really nothing Rufus could create disgusted her. After all, fifty-one years of marriage—well, in fifty-one years you get used to a lot of garbage. And this way no important paper would get thrown out.

Rufus was so careless, absentminded really. On more than one occasion he had accused her of throwing out his notes, said he was missing lecture material, students' reports, and of course that meant *she* had thrown something important out when she cleaned off his desk. Which was why he didn't want her to clean it. But it wasn't her, it had to have been him. Why, she just tidied the piles and dusted, same as she still did. Well, he wouldn't throw important stuff out anymore, not while Ethel Wutzl was around to help him.

Here, she thought. *Just as I suspected.*

The eight pieces of paper were clearly one page. Rufus had no doubt ripped an important something or other up, then forgot he didn't have a second draft. What was a wife was for, but to save the trash of a man's life. So she'd just put the pieces together, like so, a little tape here, some there, then, let's see.

She recognized her husband's peculiar habit of filling in the vowel holes of what he was writing when thinking. Mentally she reinserted the letters so she could more easily read the note.

"Beloved," she read. "If only heart had a tongue, soul an ear, that I might speak and you might hear. Do you think of me? Does my name pass your lips, does my image brush your mind? To learn that a shadow named Rufus Wutzl passed through your dreams even once would make me a happy man. Alas...

"I want more. It's not physical. Not at my age, although of course I'm still virile enough to want you, man to woman. But with my vast experience there must be more than that alone. I want to know you, to penetrate your mind as you have enveloped mine in your voluptuous phrases. I want your smiles, your laughs, for me alone. I want you to tell me about a book you've read, a thought you've had.

"Dearest, I want to be your friend. And/or lover. The intimacy I long for is soul to soul. Oh, darling, can't you see in me the inner bone of a man? I remember one time I asked you what perfume you were wearing. It was so innocent, so deliciously pure.

"'Perfume?' you asked. 'I don't wear, oh you must mean'—you giggled, and your laugh was the loveliest music. 'It's Desitin,' you told me. 'I get diaper rash from panty hose.' Surely you meant—"

But here the letter broke off, unfinished, though at the bottom he had penned in his most flowery hand, "Yours (truly), RufRuf." As if she wouldn't know.

Well, Ethel thought, trembling. *I don't remember telling him that about the Desitin. Still, Rufus no doubt meant to give that letter to me. Like all the others. Who else could they be for?*

Before she could answer her own question she began plotting a lunch extravaganza that would lay hearty and solid in his stomach all afternoon. That would be his reward, he justly deserved it, even if he never did give her that sweet note. It was the thought that counted. Fifty-one years of marriage and he was still as shy as a bridegroom. Of course it was meant for her. There was no one else. It had to be, it had to be.

She was about to go down to the kitchen when she noticed an impression on the top of the page in her hand. Why, it might well be an important phone number that Rufus forgot to copy. She almost ran to his desk (he would be home soon, hungry for his lunch), took the key from under his chair cushion (he thought she didn't know where he kept it, he thought she didn't clean *everywhere*). She opened the middle drawer, removed his notepad, riffled it quickly to see if the original of the impression were still there. When she was assured it wasn't she used the soft edge of a number-two pencil to shade the top margin of the recently repaired sheet. White numbers appeared in the gray. Before she could think clearly about what she did, and didn't, want to know she dialed. A sleepy voice answered. It sounded familiar. "Hello?" asked the voice. It sounded like a woman just getting out of bed. What lazy soul would be getting up at this time of the morning? "Hello? Who's this?" the voice asked. "What do you want?"

Why, it's that horrible Mabel Fleish, Ethel realized. *Sleeping till ten on a weekday!* Her bottom lip quivered. *Homewrecker,* she thought, slamming down the phone. *Hussy. Why don't you pick on someone your own age? Why don't you leave my husband alone?*

She put her head down on the desk and wept. Oh, the unfairness of it all, oh, the ravages of time. Ethel Wutzl nee Clopper had once been a beautiful girl. She had once worn short dresses (not so short, she had her dignity after all, and men treated *her* with respect) that showed off her legs. *I bet I still fit into that beaded flapper outfit,* she thought. She'd had dark curls, big eyes, a firm bosom. And there were plenty of men who desired her. But she wanted only Rufus Wutzl, Professor Wutzl then. She remembered how he would flirt with her in the English office, where she was secretary to the Dean. Why, she was nothing but a spit of a girl at the time, smart as a whip, cute as a button, gay as a lark. All the professors wanted her. But she had chosen Rufus, and would remain true only to him, that's the sort she was. True blue. His deep voice, his romantic eyes. The way he recited poetry, how impassioned he was about ideas.

She smiled at the memory, then wept anew. Wasn't there anything left in their marriage, the true marriage of minds? Her looks were fading, but Rufus, the man she alone knew, would be satisfied only with a woman he could talk to. He might momentarily desire another body, but he could only love a deep soul such as hers.

Ethel picked her head up. *No use fretting,* she told herself. *I'm not licked yet.* She made up to go that very afternoon to Miranda's Bookstore. Find something to read she and Rufus could discuss later. Something philosophical, provocative. About ESP maybe, but no, Rufus didn't much go for that. Poetry, a book of poems? Of course. Something by that nice Jewish boy who read at the college a few years ago. What was his name again? Albert, Alvin? Yes, that was it. Alvin Ginsberg.

It was a crisp fall day, and Ethel Wutzl already felt better for being out. She would have lunch at the Main Street Noshery (Rufus could have the bologna sandwich she left on the counter), go to Madame Tchernofsky afterward, make a day of it.

She entered the bookstore, pleased by the tinkling of the bell over the door. Such a cozy place, and the subjects were clearly marked in large letters. Not that she needed to read the signs. She knew the romances and gothics were by the register, the occults (where they kept ESP, spiritualism, as well as other serious works, goodness knows why) were in the back. But she wasn't sure where the poetry section was. She was about to ask the clerk when she saw the sign. Right across from contemporary fiction, how nice. She'd browse a bit. Oh, but what a nuisance—a young person was sitting in the middle of the aisle, blocking her way.

"Excuse me," she said, and the boy or girl—it was impossible to tell from the back these days—straightened for a moment, then returned to fingering some books. She was curious to see what was so interesting that a young person couldn't step aside to let an older woman pass. *Wouldn't you know!* she exclaimed to herself. *It's that witch's book.* Had to be a boy then, she figured, and who knew what sort of bad ideas it would put into his head. The young man was fondling all three copies, looking at the jacket, mumbling to the photo. Mrs. Wutzl shivered. *So that's what she wants,* she thought. *To excite strangers with her dirty thoughts.*

The fellow was wearing a sweatshirt, hood up. The sparse hairs that peeked out were flesh-colored. He walked to the front of the store and turned to look at Mrs. Wutzl (whose internal hmphing must have grown audible). She quickly grabbed the first book by Ginsberg that she saw—*Howl,* it was called. *Good,* she thought. *Something funny*—and got on line right after him. She couldn't help but notice he had taken all three copies of Mabel's novel.

"Christmas shopping early?" she said, to make polite conversation. He didn't reply. *Rude*, she thought, *but what can you expect from someone who reads that sort of trash.*

"*Bone*," the humorless voice said to the cashier.

"Bone?" the girl said. "Oh, you mean *Bone*. On the shelf." She pointed. The customer didn't turn.

"More."

She waited for other words. None came. Clearly the girl was uncomfortable. She tried guessing what he wanted. "You mean more than what's on the shelf? There are three copies, oh, you have them. Well, that's it. We reordered but they...do you want all three?" The hooded figure nodded almost imperceptibly. "You must really like this book," she said. She smiled, and met a stone face.

A skinny white hand held out the money. She took it. Mrs. Wutzl saw her shudder, as if the hand were deathly cold. The customer left quickly. The bell over the door tinkled long after.

"Oh hi, Mrs. Wutzl," the girl said. "How's Dr. Wutzl?"

"Fine," Ethel said.

"I'm Iris Specter. Your husband's advising me on my thesis."

"Oh yes, hello. Tell me, do you often have fellows like that buying up all your stock of a book?"

"Who? Oh, that guy. Yeah, he was kind of a creep, wasn't he? Hey, Miranda, did you see that guy who was just here?"

The bookstore owner was trying to make a space between Poe and Potok, and ended up dropping Porter. "No, dear. I'm sorry. I wasn't watching. What did he look like?"

"I don't know. Nondescript. What would you say, Mrs. Wutzl?"

"Sort of *faded* looking. Very unpleasant but hard to say why. Not quite human, if you know what I mean." Iris and Miranda looked oddly at the frail-boned woman, her large eyes magnified by her glasses. Ethel glanced longingly at the occult section. That was where they put the books about aliens, too. It seemed there were scientists from outer space who kidnapped decent people like herself and performed sexual experiments on them. It was just terrible, the things that went on. Not like when she was a girl.

"I mean, oh, it was like"—she felt compelled to continue when she noticed them staring—"like he could have been anyone's ghost." She herself seemed surprised after she said it.

"Oh, I don't know about that," Iris said. They all laughed, then the bookstore clerk and owner returned to the business at hand, their smiles fading.

"Hello, dear," Mrs. Wutzl said when Rufus came home. "Did you have a good day?"

"Tiring. Students, colleagues, all asking for advice."

She helped him off with his coat. "Something very strange happened today, Rufus. I went to the bookstore, to get a copy of Alvin Goldberg's *Howlers*—very interesting poems, dear, you should read them when I'm done and we can discuss them, here, let me help you with that. Anyway, there was a fellow there buying up all the copies of that Mabel Fleish's novel. A creepy boy. The cashier remarked on it. Said he made her flesh crawl. That's the sort who buys—"

"Yes, dear. I'm very tired just now."

"Oh, there's something else I wanted to tell you. I heard from Felix today. He's concerned about you. Says you're working too hard. Says for you to take it easy more, stay at home, don't go running around so much. Beware of redheads. He told me that. Felix said—"

"Felix? Felix who? Oh Felix. Really, Ethel."

Mrs. Wutzl's back stiffened. "Don't you pooh-pooh Felix. He's only looking out for you. Today's his birthday, you know. He's forty-six years old today."

"Don't be ridiculous, Ethel. A miscarriage doesn't have a birthday. He was stillborn. He never was a he."

Her mouth hung open a moment, as if he had hit her. "Don't say that," she cried. "You don't know. You didn't feel him kick inside you all those months. They killed him. I told you that. They gave me that stuff, frozen dream, twilight, I forget what it's called but they lied. They said it was a painkiller. The only pain it killed was theirs." She spoke from a memory trance, oblivious to her husband's attempts to distract her. "Now, now, Ethel," he kept saying. She didn't seem to hear him.

"It froze me," she said, "but it didn't keep me from feeling, just from moving. I remember everything that happened. I didn't right away, but it came back to me...later. Remember my nightmares? I saw what happened. My soul was hovering up there by the lights, watching. They took the baby out and he was pink as could be, crying lustily for life, I tell you. They put him down, and I watched.

I saw him turning blue. I screamed and screamed for them to attend to him. But stitch stitch stitch, as if that were the only thing that mattered. And meanwhile he was blue, Rufus. I saw him turn blue, and I screamed, they didn't hear me. Because I was frozen in their horrible twilight sleep that was no sleep at all, just twilight. I'd have saved him myself if I could have gotten up. We had waited so long, we had practically given up, and then we were so happy.

"The nurse, that big fat stupid old nurse, was right next to him and she didn't check him once. Finally I summoned all my psychic energy into a buzz and I flew in her ear. *Bzzz bzzz.* Her eyes, her mouth. She started swatting at the sound and that's when she saw him. He was blue, Rufus, blue as the dress I'm wearing. She yelled, 'Doctor! Come quick!' They tried to revive him, but it was too late. They lied, Rufus, I tell you they lied when they said he was stillborn. I tell you, I saw it all. I did, I did!" She collapsed into a sobbing mass of bluish curls.

Rufus Wutzl took his wife in his arms, held her head against his chest. She curved against him to accommodate his belly. "I know you did, dear. I'm sorry. Of course you did."

"Forty-six, Rufus. He'd have been forty-six today. Things would have been different. We'd have grandchildren around maybe."

"Imagine," and the old man closed his eyes for a moment, as if drawing the figure in his mind, himself at forty-six. "He might have taught at the college," Dr. Wutzl said. "We could have written books together. They'd call it the Wutzl Dynasty. Take my place in the department after I, you know."

"Don't talk that way, dear. I can't bear it. You're all I've got. You and Felix. He has such love for you. He's so respectful. If only you'd ouija with me sometime, you'd see what a fine son we have. I don't know why God took him. The ouija—"

He pushed her on to her own feet. "None of that, Ethel," he said. "If you want to pretend to communicate with the dead, by all means do. But don't tell me Felix is anything but nonsense Madame Tcherphonybaloney cooked up to steal your pin money. Spiritualism, table-rapping. Malarky invented by two sisters who produced strange sounds under the table by cracking their toe knuckles!" With a shake of his still-ample white hair he marched into his office, then belched loudly. Mrs. Wutzl looked shocked. "Speaking of balogna," he said, "you know it always gives me gas."

ELEVEN

"Fatso!" Ana yelled. "I don't even want to sleep over."

"Good. 'Cause Gertie and I don't want to catch your disease."

"What disease? I don't have a disease."

"I'm sure it's normal to go around killing babies. Listen, I have a little brother and I never killed him." Pammy smirked.

"I did not kill my brother."

"You did too."

"I did not."

"You did too."

This exchange went on for several rounds. Ana felt tears gathering in the back of her eyes, but she refused to cry. "You're just saying that 'cause you're adopted," she shouted, relieved as her tears dried up in hate. "Your mother's a big fat whore who never loved you. She gave you away like a pair of old socks."

"She did not."

"She did too."

"She did not."

At which point the door to Pammy's bedroom opened and in walked Mrs. Stein. "Hey, you two. What's all the yelling about?"

The two girls eyed her coldly. "You're supposed to knock before you come into my room," said Pammy.

"We were having a discussion," said Ana.

Mrs. Stein stared back, then shrugged, shut the door.

"I'm going home," said Ana. "I have a friend coming over."

"Yeah, who? Nobody likes you. Baby-killer!"

Ana picked up her Barbie case and walked out. *I'll never go back there,* she swore, not for the first time.

When she got home she went to her room and took out her diary.

"Pammy is a fattee and Gertie is to and I dont care if they dont like me caus I dont like them either."

She slammed the book shut, knowing she had made spelling mistakes but not caring enough to use the dictionary. A diary was a private place. In it one could write about secrets and not worry about Mrs. Blum marking the page all red. Spelling was Ana's worst subject. She didn't understand why ugly Blumbum cared more about the way she spelled words than what she had to say.

She reopened the diary. "Old Blumbottoms a big fat slob with stinky breth." Her handwriting was bad too, as Mrs. Blum had told her often enough. Ana took one of the galleys from her mother's book, which she'd found in the drawer with the scissors and tape. She cut out a sentence: "'Bone's articulate in the language of guilt,' Anna told Mat, 'a tongue I know well.'" The child pasted some of the words in her diary. "I know guilt," she wrote with her mother's print. "Anna cried."

TWELVE

Mabel and Ana went to the farm to pick out a pumpkin. The girl chose a misshapen one. "Honey, don't you want something rounder so we can make a nice jack-o-lantern face?" Mabel asked.

"You said I could pick whichever one I wanted."

"Yes, but I thought you'd pick a round one that—"

"Oh, pick your own pumpkin then. I don't care. Whatever you pick will be nice, whatever I pick will be 'Miss Shapen.'" Ana stomped back into the car while Mabel paid for the large orange squash that looked like it had melted and run down one side. She carried it over to the car, put it in the back seat.

"Shall we drive up to the orchard?" she asked. "Get some cider before heading home?"

Ana didn't reply. Mabel took that to mean okay. She turned left instead of right on the highway. It was a glorious sunny Saturday, late afternoon. The clouds were starting to turn pink over the mountains. When the stars came out, they would twinkle in that special fall way. It was the crispness of the air, Mabel remembered reading. Cold air for some reason magnified light. Or moved it around. Or something. In any case, it was too pretty a day to fight. "How's school?" Mabel asked. "Groovy," said Ana.

Mabel wanted to pass the pickup truck ahead of her. She looked in the rearview mirror. There was no one behind her. She looked in the side mirror, then over her shoulder, then in the side mirror again. She kept feeling someone was riding in her blind spot. "I have a problem, honey," she said, after completing the pass. "Maybe you can help me." From the corner of her eye she saw she had the girl's attention. "It's my costume for the faculty halloween party. What should I go as?"

Ana turned back to the window. "A witch," she said.

When they got to the house Ana went in without carrying the pumpkin or cider. Mabel lugged the heavy items herself. Anubis took advantage of the situation to jump on her. "Down, boy," Mabel said, trying to balance everything till she got to the counter. "Ana, call him." Ana did not call him. Nubi proceeded to dig his nose into her butt, taking tiny bites. She put her packages down and glared at him. "Bad dog," she said. "Watch out I don't take you to the pound." Whether it was the sound of her voice or the look in her eye, he put his tail between his legs and left.

Mabel began rolling hamburger patties for dinner. She put two plastic bags on her hands so she wouldn't have to touch the greasy meat. Percy came in, kissed the back of her neck. He hung up his jacket and sat on the stool watching her. He didn't mention the bags on her hands. Her method of making hamburgers, after sixteen years of marriage, no longer struck him as odd.

"Any more unusual phone calls today?" he said.

She turned quickly and stared at him, trying to read his face. "What makes you ask?"

"Threatening notes?" He poured a glass of wine. Mabel felt her eyes narrowing and tried to hide her suspicion. She returned to her chopped meat. "Dr. Xavier thinks your unconscious is writing home."

"Puh-leez." She laughed, relieved that that was what he was getting at. "I know the difference between fantasy and reality."

"Do you?"

Here it was, that funny feeling again, as if dreaming she might be a fragment of someone else's dream made her one.

She rolled three hamburgers, a big one for Percy, a medium one for herself, a small one for Ana. "Dinner for the three bears," she said, showing them to Percy. He laughed. She indented the tops, to keep the cheese from running off, and put the burgers up.

"How's Archetypes?" she asked, proceeding to wash spinach so she was unable hear what he had to say about the class. When she shut the water off Percy was still speaking. "...in detective novels. External mystery as metaphor for internal one." He paused. "Maybe that's what's happening to you?"

She flicked water at him. He laughed.

"Anyway, I'm trying to make a distinction between mystery and thriller. It's amazing how difficult the kids find it. Is it so hard to grasp? In mystery, something that was always there is slowly uncovered till it feels like an answer. Thrillers work on shock value. It's the difference between revelation and surprise. Gasp-horror is thrust at you, not unveiled *per se.*"

Mabel smiled. "We both make a living from fiction," she said, "but I don't think this way. My characters live on their own, I just follow with my pen, taking notes."

"I don't believe that. You'd have nothing but first drafts."

She paused. "Maybe," she said. She poured wine in her glass, offered Percy more. "Just, the characters *are* independent of me to some extent. I may have an intention, but they follow their own dictates, surprising me. And I want them to. That's what makes them live." She went to turn the potatoes, puncturing them with a butcher knife. "Part of making them come alive is having them stand against me. There has to be free will. You just hope it fits into your design."

A ghostlike image passed through her mind. She thought of the reporter she'd met at the police station. Long white hair, weird boy eyes. Was he thinking about her? Probably not. He was young and, despite his freakish whiteness, a charmer. She tried to remember what it was about him, for she was like a connoisseur of fine wines. When a man tingled her she liked to roll him around her tongue, taste the deliciousness of sensation, analyze the components of intoxication. With Kwestral it was the way he had of listening. It made a woman want to undress her soul. Compelled by the power of his listening, the intensity of his pastel stare, she would whisper secrets. He inspired a woman to dream. And sex was a dream.

"What are you thinking about?" Percy asked.

"My costume for the Halloween party. What are you wearing?"

"My tux and your cape. Come as a magician. Do my card tricks."

"Oh no. Spare us."

"You think that's too mundane? Have to maintain my dignity. What's more dignified than a magician in a tux? What about you?"

She shrugged. "I could use some help. Any ideas?"

"Go as a tramp."

She turned around. "You know," she said, a strange emphasis in her voice, "you and Ana have the same sense of humor. She told me to go as a witch and you tell me to be a whore."

"Hey!" Percy laughed. "I didn't say whore. I said tramp. As in bum, hobo, you know. But whore's not bad, if that's how you feel. I mean, not whore exactly but you know that long red dress you have, the slinky one? Put on that and a beard, go as a bearded lady. Cute—me a magician, you a bearded lady."

Mabel didn't answer right away, then said, "That dress is a bit risqué, don't you think? For a faculty affair?"

"That's never stopped you before."

She turned to look at him. He smiled back at her. Was she imagining a hidden sharpness to his words?

"What's the purpose of these things anyway? Fantasy. A time to act out your wishes. The darker the better, right? I say if you've got it, flaunt it." Percy took out salad ingredients.

Mabel spoke slowly, as if her words were the question on an oral exam. "Yeah, but it's rather lowcut, don't you think? And it has that long slit up the side."

Percy was holding a lettuce in both hands. "You've got beautiful breasts, beautiful legs," he said, squeezing the green head. "I don't mind their envy. Let them see my gorgeous wife."

"Not many men would feel that way, Percy."

"Not many men are married to you, Mabel."

She smiled but could not dispell the notion she was being set up.

That night she dreamed she was making love to a man whose face she couldn't see. She unzipped his fly, reached in, and pulled out a bone. It was still attached to him, it was warm, pliant, meatless. She squeezed it, excited by horror, till she startd to come. That woke her up. She heard Percy ask, "What's wrong now?" Had she moaned aloud? she wondered, annoyed at the lack of privacy in a marriage. She didn't answer. Hadn't she a right to her own dreams? "Why didn't you call me?" he said. Then: "No. Behind back, Hans. Didn't know."

Mabel felt overwhelmed with tenderness. It was his book, she knew, the one he couldn't get published, the one Hans Goobler, his previous publisher, turned down. No one wanted it.

Here they were, man and wife, inches from each other, lost in separate nightmares, miles apart. She wished she had a candle to light his face so she could look at it. *This is a marriage,* she thought. *One bed. Two dreams.*

THIRTEEN

He lived in a small dark room surrounded by books. All the books had his name. All the books had his lady's portrait. "How do you do?" Bone said. He removed an imaginary hat in the long, sweeping motion of a courtier. The room's many ladies smiled. They all had demon red hair. "Allow me," he said, removing a book jacket. The room was very small, the books very many. The walls seemed to be made of them. "I live in a book," he said aloud to the amusement of the ladies.

He took out his knife, carefully cutting Fleish's silhouette from the photograph. With a surgeon's skill he pierced her eyes, then put her picture on the lampshade. Light came through the holes. "You look," he said, "ravishing." The ladies tittered. "You look," he said, "almost intelligent. But of course you're not. No intelligent woman could write such lies." He turned his attention back to the naked book. Page 209. He read it, as he had read it many times before. With meticulous care he cut the letter o from the word no on page 209. He put it on a sheet of paper, already piled with o's and u's and w's.

"I don't want you to see this yet," he said, turning off the light. Mabel's eyes went blank. She did not see Bone rip the jacket from another book, tear out a page. She did not see Bone unzip his pants, unbutton his shirt. She could not see in the dark as well as he. Bone liked the dark. He liked the small dark room no one knew about, a place he rented over Patsy's Bar in Winegarden, New York.

Soon it would be time to put on his disguise. He could make himself invisible but preferred to save his magic for later. No one saw him come in. No one saw him go out. He stayed in the dark, in the hidden place, a rectangle of space, the door shut like a book cover closed. He knew how to bide his time, sleep among sheets lining his walls. Soon it would be Halloween. His costume would reveal the inner man, as a good costume should. The time was coming when they would stay in the dark. Together. He'd teach her, as he'd been taught, not to need the light.

FOURTEEN

The conference room on the third floor of Bibble Tower was festooned with orange and black streamers. Large picture windows faced the mountains. The spectacular night sky, Van Gogh stars twirling above sleeping humps of earth, was still the main topic of conversation—that and who had carved the lecherous grin on the jack-o'-lantern. English faculty members and their spouses, dressed as a variety of animals, ghouls, and lowlife, were busily downing drinks in hopes of getting onto more intriguing subjects.

Harvey Greene, a skeleton, wanted to ask Phyllis Blostein, a skunk, how her book on the New Critics was coming along. (He knew this would irk her, since she was suffering from writer's block; that would avenge him for the damaging review she had written of his Empson biography two years ago.) Percy Furnival, a magician, wanted to discuss deconstruction with Lana Loo, a Madame Bovary. (Ms. Loo was a teaching adjunct who had managed to write an extraordinary article, based on her thesis, on deconstructing genre fiction; Percy didn't want her to know he was picking her brains for his own forthcoming article in *Knickerbocker Review*.) Rufus Wutzl, a wolf, wanted to ask Mabel Fleish, a bearded lady, if she was working on a new novel. He wanted to tell her how thrilled he was to read the article about *Bone* in *The New York Review of Books*. He wanted to ask if she had meant Bone to represent her vision of men; he wanted to ask if Anna expressed her own passions; he wanted to ask on whom she had based the older professor, the one Anna has that first affair with; he wanted to ask if she could see in him the inner bone of a man. Ethel Wutzl, a flapper, wanted to make sure he didn't.

After his first drink Percy found himself out of sorts. Lana Loo was busy talking up the head of the department, who was dressed, as he was every year, as Hamlet's father's ghost. Percy didn't want to talk theory in front of Dean Hook with a girl who was practically a student. He stood at Mabel's side, listening to her answer questions about literature, her own writing in particular. She had pulled down her beard, saying it made her face itch, and now the black curls rested between her breasts in a most disconcerting decolletage. He marveled in the change publication had brought in her. There was a time when she stood in his shadow. Now he was in hers.

As pleased as he was with Mabel's local success, he couldn't help seeing his own failure in relation to it. He had been only twenty-three when he'd gotten his doctorate in English literature. It had been hailed an extraordinary achievement, particularly as it was followed by the publication of articles, then books, on arcane critical subjects, all acclaimed by his peers. Early on he'd been awarded a full professorship at Jones College. He had weighed that against the nontenured positions he could have gotten at more prestigious schools and decided to be a big fish in a small pond. He rarely regretted the decision. If he hadn't been teaching at Jones, he would not have met Mabel Fleish, the shy girl who stared intently when he spoke, who stammered in his presence, endearingly betraying her infatuation with her professor. Within two years they were wed.

Now look at her, Percy thought. He was ten years older than his wife. Some of his feelings bordered on the paternal: pride mixed with jealousy, envy with lust. Mabel gesticulated, pursuing her ideas. Professors stood around her like a bouquet of flowers, nodding in the breeze of her thought. She put one leg forward to emphasize a point. The slit of her dress fell open, revealing a long limb. David Copperfield caught the Ghost of Christmas Past swooning.

"You're a lucky man," Dr. Wutzl had said when he and Mabel first came in. The compliment was said to Percy but meant for Mabel. Percy knew he was a lucky man. He also knew he might not be lucky for much longer. Something was pulling Mabel away.

It wasn't just her affairs. He had known about them for as long as she'd been having them, at least since Seth died. Not that they didn't pain him. They did, to the point where he had to look the other way if he didn't want the marriage to end. It was something else—envy. Percy's star was falling as Mabel's rose.

More and more, Percy brooded in the dark, smoking pot, doing coke, telling himself it was okay as long as he wasn't addicted. When he was working on a book or an article he'd put the lights on, the dope away, scribbling like a demon till all hours. But then came the bad time, when he had nothing to do but wait. As book after book was rejected he fought hard to believe in his genius.

Mabel would listen to him play guitar in the dark, moaning that the avant garde wasn't avant anymore. She didn't say anything about the drugs he was taking, though she didn't do any herself. She just asked he not let Ana see. And Percy didn't say anything about the men she screwed. They each had their solaces.

He now walked to the bar, fixed himself another Bloody Mary. His wife was still talking to professors Hazel, Frank, and Zippo. If he had one wish regarding her infidelities it was that she wouldn't pick such losers. There was that hideous Peter McWiffle last year, whose politics, expressed in letters to *Sam's Corner Gazette*, bordered on the fascist. In counterweight to him was Idi Masambe, crying for revolution while making a good living as a fully tenured sociology professor. And what about that transient? Couldn't Mabel see Ryder Wood was no better than a tramp?

Of course there were also men like Frank Finger, a fellow so nice it seemed a disease. Everyone called him Frank Friendly. Always smiling, arm extended to shake your hand. You couldn't avoid a conversation with him. Sometimes Percy suspected he put shards in the road so he could help you change a tire. And what, after all, what was so nice about a man who fucked your wife?

Ryder, now that was an oddball. At least he didn't pretend to be anything else. There was something about him you just couldn't place. Like where he came from. He had a twang in his voice, but it wasn't Western, it wasn't Southern. He wasn't from the country, sure as hell not from any city either. Maybe he came from under a rock.

He had asked, and been granted, permission to audit Percy's class in Literary Criticism 101 the previous year. There he had revealed himself to be pompous and belligerent, not taking the subtle hints Percy gave that he was an auditor, which meant he was a listener, not a participant in discussions. Percy could have arranged to bar him from his class but hadn't. He knew Mabel was screwing him. He was fascinated as he would be by a snake. Ryder seemed to come from a place that people had forgotten about. Dark, wet. Things that were beautiful in an ugly way, like snakes, grew there. Yards abloom with flowers and trash. Rusted cars made sculptural by kudzu. It wasn't pristine, where Ryder came from. Its bald, barren mountaintops glittered with glass.

Percy added vodka to his drink, then guiltily took a splash of tomato juice. Lana Loo was standing alone at the window. He hurried over, spilling some of his Bloody Mary, and found himself licking his fingers as he said hello. Lana smiled, sipping at a clear bubbly drink that Percy suspected was plain Perrier. "I enjoyed your piece in *Knickerbocker*," he said. "I understand it was based on your masters thesis?" She nodded.

"Extraordinary," he went on. "Of course there were some elements I disagreed with. For example, you stress the importance of text but you don't deal with ambiguity of text. How do you tie that in with your ideas about—uh, hello, Harvey." Percy greeted the rotund skeleton of Dr. Greene.

"Fine article," Harvey told Lana, then lowered his voice and said to Percy, "I'm worried about Phyllis. I think she may be suicidal. She can't even talk about her book, let alone write it. All I said to her was 'How's it going this year, Phyllis? Any progress or are you still stuck?' And she glared at me, she literally glared, then turned on her heel."

Lana said, "Excuse me," and went to the women's room. Percy extricated himself from faculty gossip with difficulty. He'd have to pursue his discussion with Lana later. Meanwhile, he searched the room for his wife, finally spotting her in a corner with Horace Byrrd, the new teaching assistant dressed as a falcon.

"Great," he said. "More fuel for the gossip tanks."

He knew that Horace and Mabel had been caught skinnydipping in the mountains by Professor Hazel and his wife. Couldn't Mabel be a bit more discreet? Percy sighed, sinking down into a chair. He took out his pipe, tamped tobacco and lit it.

How lovely she looked in her red dress, her dark red hair pinned up, revealing the grace of her long neck. "Like a princess at a ball," he thought, "except for the beard." Well, at least Horace was attractive, even if he was just a kid, and a bit weird at that. He raised hunting birds, didn't he? One time Percy ran into him, and he had a crate of live rabbits in the back of his car. "Oh, the cute bunnies,"

Ana said. "Can I play with them?"

"I don't know," Horace said. "Are you allowed to play with your food?" He let one out, then and there. The rabbit ran off, but before it had gotten under cover a giant bird swooped down and carried it off. Ana screamed. "We all have to live," Horace said.

Percy took another sip of his drink and looked away. His eyes soon rolled back to Mabel and Horace laughing in the corner. Didn't she know people were talking about her? Didn't she care her own husband was sitting in the same room, watching her chat the pants off her lover? Didn't she realize that, after sixteen years of marriage, he could recognize her heat by the flash in her eye, the flush on her face? "How much more am I supposed to take?" Percy asked Bloody Mary who gave a silent red reply.

FIFTEEN

Costumed faculty members drank and eyed one another warily while a tape of *Appalachian Spring* played tinnily over the P.A. system. Dean Hook's favorite piece of music, it was heard at every faculty function. Only he was oblivious to the quality of the sound. Smiling, he surveyed his realm and tapped his foot, a jolly ghost remembering a country childhood not his own.

"It's good to see you, Mabel," Horace said, his voice cracking. "I've thought about you a lot. That time in the water..."

She took a sip from her wineglass, put her hand on his leg. "Shhh." She let her fingers rest there as she looked around. "I've thought about you too," she said, squeezing his quadricep.

Indeed she had. Every drive into the mountains she'd thought of Horace's hair, a gold helmet in the sunlight, how he'd flown his falcon for her, throwing the hawk from his arm as if flinging a piece of himself into the sky. The bird swooped, searching for prey, returning to perch on the leather glove. When Horace put the black hood over his tiny head Mabel had shivered. "Can I stroke his tail feathers?" she asked. "He can't bite me with his head covered."

"He can still claw you," Horace answered. "Irving's dangerous."

"How's Irving doing?" she now asked the feather-clad teaching assistant. "I see you're wearing some of his castoffs."

"Irving misses you," Horace said. "He misses your body beneath him. He misses flying overhead, seeing every mark on your—"

"Shhh, Horace, please." She laughed. "I still don't see how you could name that exquisite bird Irving."

"My father was named Irving," he said, as if that explained it.

They hadn't seen each other since June, when their discovery by the Hazels necessitated ending their liaison. The intervening months had brought about the publication of Mabel's book and an unexpected teaching position at the college for Horace.

The pair, oblivious to the conversing, carousing ghouls around them, now sat together at the Halloween party, catching up on each other's news. Horace's eyes, roving down Mabel's neck, betrayed his thoughts. "Take off that beard," he said. Mabel pulled the nest of dark hair over her head, put it in her lap. Her fingers played through its curls. "I read your book. It made me crazy."

"Shall I take that as a compliment?"

"Don't be coy. You know how I feel. All this time I've thought about you. I'm out of my head with wanting you. I'd never hurt you, only sometimes I want to take you—"

Her eyes glowed. She looked around. Percy was sitting in a corner by himself. He hadn't seen her with Horace yet, but even a man as trusting as Percy would soon spot the young man's excitement. Couldn't he control himself? There had always been an odd excitability, frightening and thrilling, about Horace. He was capable in passion of terrible excess. He bit, scratched, pulled her hair. Left marks on her body. She told him not to. "I'm a married woman." Which only made his actions more brutal. Afterward he was ashamed. "How could I do this to you?" He'd kiss the marks.

She looked around the conference room. Horace's eyes were burning as he told her of his fantasies. "Horace," she said, "people are looking. Percy's over there. I'm still a married woman."

He grabbed her hand, squeezed it till her knuckles cracked. "Do you think, I mean, hasn't it been—"

Something clenched inside her. "It's too dangerous," she said. "Foolish. Oh, Horace, things are different now." She remembered how he'd held her hands on the ground over her head. Watching her, staring into her, moving his body hard, deeper than she could bear. Pinning her beneath his penetrating eyes. *No,* she told herself. *You will not do this.* She looked at her husband. He was drinking too much. Probably wouldn't even notice if she left, and she'd be back...*no,* her conscience said. Horace stared intently. His hunger was delicious. She'd thought of him just that morning, when she'd been exercising. She'd been lying on the floor, rolling down her spine, looking out of the window. And there was that hawk again, hovering outside. *Horace*, she remembered thinking, *is thinking of me.*

"I can't," she said. "I've changed, I've decided to change."

"You'll never change." He was talking too loud. People were turning around.

"Lower your voice." She glanced at Percy. He still hadn't noticed. "I'm just not interested in this sort of thing anymore—sneaking around, lying, taking chances." She thought about the letters, the phone calls, she thought about Horace's weird demands.

"But you can't just end it like that. You owe me an explanation. I love you."

She didn't put it past him to make a scene. And she did feel as if she owed him something, as if memories of mutual pleasure weren't enough. Surely it made sense to meet him where they could talk openly. They couldn't sit together any longer. Faculty members were casting furtive glances their way, gossiping in corners, as usual.

"You go first," she said. "I'll meet you. You know where."

He gulped his drink, began to cough. Walked quickly out of the room, heading to the patch of woods on campus. It was not really thick enough for the things they had done there in the past, but they'd pretended it was. Horace obviously didn't care who saw them. He hadn't cared that Professor Hazel and his wife found them swimming naked. He hadn't cared that they saw Mabel in his arms, her red hair dark with damp, her skin bone white in the green-wooded light. Why should he? Mabel was only married to Professor Furnival, he had insisted. She belonged to him.

Mabel sipped her wine, thinking of Horace's hooded eyes. The hawk would circle the sky above them, diving down on small animals, taking them away from themselves before they knew they were gone. Horace and Mabel naked on the ground would look up at the flying hunter. "You see this tiny beauty mark on your breast?" Horace touched it with his tongue. "If he wanted to, Irving could swoop down, peck it off before you had time to take cover."

Goosebumps had formed on her skin. "Are you cold?" he asked, but it was June and the sun was strong, and though she shivered she refused the shirt he wished to lay over her. Stretched out on the flat hot rocks of the limestone cliffs she felt like a sacrifice. Irving could do anything he wanted to her. She knew it was really Horace flying above.

She finished her wine and took the beard from her lap, putting it on Horace's chair. The hairy mound seemed indecent, but she told herself the janitor would give it to a grandchild. She walked out of the conference room, rang the elevator. Lana Loo left the bathroom just then. Mabel gave her a guilty wave. "Great costume," she said, pushing past her into the women's room, as if that had been her plan all along. "You make a terrific Madame Bovary."

"So do you," said Lana.

Mabel waited in a cubicle until she thought it was safe to come out. Why did she feel so guilty, she wondered, when it was her intention to put an end to the source of her guilt, not provoke it?

The elevator came. She hurried in, willing the doors to close before anyone saw her. The woods weren't thick enough. She felt crazy. It was crazy to meet him there, even if her intentions were good. If anyone saw them they would misunderstand. Dr. Xavier thought she was crazy. Maybe he was right.

When the phone rang that morning she had been afraid to answer it. Every time the phone rang she worried it was Bone, though she was scarcely relieved, hearing it was Dr. Xavier.

"Percy tells me you're having problems," he said.

"Percy has his own problems."

"Tell me about Percy's problems."

"Don't you hear enough about them from Percy?"

"Why are you angry at me?" Dr. Xavier asked. "You left analysis right after I told you your affairs were a way of seducing your father. I think now you are trying to teach your father a lesson by leaving me. I represent your father. You never forgave him for siding with your mother when you had that abortion in high school."

"You're nuts. That's what I think."

Dr. Xavier sighed. "I'm just trying to save you from yourself. You have such a strong drive for self-destruction."

"Look, if it weren't for you I wouldn't be having any problems. I wouldn't have put my photo on the book jacket, I wouldn't have let them print a bio either. I was planning to use a pseudonym till you and Percy convinced me that that was paranoid. Now look what's happened. So *I'm* nuts?"

"You have to admit it's odd, not wanting the glory on a book you worked so hard to produce. I say you're trying to punish yourself. You feel you sacrificed your son for your book."

Mabel was silent.

"The book itself," Dr. Xavier continued, "saved your life. If you hadn't had that to devote yourself to after your breakdown, well, we know where you were heading. But *how* did it accomplish that? By enabling you to punish a mother for her son's death."

Dr. Xavier paused, sniffling a few times. As Mabel still didn't say anything, he went on. "I think I can talk in Freudian terms with you, can't I? You can handle it. If you can't, stop me." He cleared his throat. "The book is about a mother/son marriage," he said, "into which a father comes to punish the criminals. And how does he punish them for their sexual crime? He murders the son and enslaves the mother, using both sexually—"

"Oh, please," Mabel said. "Spare me, Dr. Xavier."

"And now the book is written, so you must invent a way to continue the punishment. What could be better than to dream up a threatening ghost who calls himself Bone? Your psyche is neurotic but always creative. You are still haunted by your son's death. You are looking for a father to spank you, as your own father did when he gave you a 'licking,' as he called—"

"Look, I'm hanging up. Having a conversation with you, Dr. Xavier, is not like talking to a real person."

"And what is real?"

"Real is that someone is calling me, pretending to be a character in my novel, trying to frighten me and doing a damn good job. I'm not one-hundred-percent sure that that someone isn't you. Are you trying to scare me back into analysis?"

"Who else tried to manipulate you that way?"

"Oh for chrissake! My father, my mother, my brother, and you. You!" She slammed the receiver, did not pick it up right away when it started to ring. After twenty rings she was furious. "Dr. Xavier," she screamed into the mouthpiece. "Leave me alone."

"Oh no, Annabelle," said the mysteriously familiar voice. "I'll never do that. I'm getting things ready for you. We'll play doctor then, Annabelle, but not Doctor Xavier."

Mabel hurried out of Bibble Tower. Despite her anxiety she was enjoying the night air. It made her skin tingle. The conference room had been stuffy.

She got to the woods outside Huller Hall where Horace was supposed to be waiting but couldn't find him. She walked on the gravel path, balancing with difficulty on her pointy shoes. She whispered his name. As she passed a great oak, an arm reached out, grabbed her. Before she could scream she recognized Horace. "Hush, honey," Beau had said, scaring her before making love. Horace pulled her to him, pressed her hard against the trunk. He moaned her name as his hands moved quickly over her, pulling up her dress. "Someone will see," Mabel protested weakly. "Oh please no, please." For a moment she thought she saw eyes glint in the dark. She pushed away, straightened her clothes. "I told you, Horace, that's finished. I'm not interested anymore."

"Then why did you come here? You know what happens to teases."

Horace reached for her again, but she eluded his grasp and ran into the darkest part of the woods. "Mabel, don't play games with me anymore," he cried. "There isn't time." She hid behind a tree, fighting the urge to giggle and the need to pee. There was a sexual excitement in her fear, something she remembered from games of Hide-and-Seek as a child. Part of her wanted to be found, to have the delicious relief of laughing aloud, of surrendering and being forced to pay. But she held herself back till, fed up and angry, Horace stomped off. When he was gone she shivered, as if her danger were still great. As if she knew she was not alone.

SIXTEEN

From the corner of his eye Percy saw Horace fly out of the room. A little later Mabel sauntered away. He went to the window and watched her cross the parking lot. She entered the stand of oaks and firs called Bryant Wood on maps of the campus but known to generations of students as Venus's Hairpatch. After that he couldn't see. "She is an unstable woman," he reminded himself.

Mabel had not taken well his suggestion that she return to analysis with Dr. Xavier. She said she was tired of telling that dirty old man her sexual fantasies, hearing him squirm in his seat as he asked, "So tell me exactly how these men take you. Anally, vaginally, orally? All ways at once?"

"That's neither here nor there," Percy said. "You know you have a history of nervous breakdown. Now you're getting phone calls no one else hears, letters that could be cut and taped to the page by anyone. Even you—"

"Or you!" Mabel exploded. "Or Dr. Xavier, for that matter."

"Why would he do that?"

"Because he wants me back. He's brainwashing you against me. 'Nag your wife, Percy, and I'll write terrifying notes. We're doing it for her own good.'"

"Oh come on."

"I'm not saying Xavier is doing it. I'm saying he could be."

"And why would I go along?"

Mabel looked around the bedroom, uncomfortable. "You could be pulling a *Gaslight* on me. For revenge maybe. Or, I don't know. I don't want to discuss it." For the time being he let the matter drop but remained perturbed. Did she really suspect him?

Percy knew about his wife's infidelities but assumed she didn't know he knew. Her knowledge of his knowledge would change things, and Percy didn't want to change things. But why was she being so flagrant, going off with Horace Byrrd in front of everyone in the department, unless she wanted him to act?

He stood at the window, wondering this, till he realized Dr. Wutzl was beside him, looking out the window too. *He knows,* Percy thought. The elderly professor—his wolf's nose having a splotch of pumpkin pie on its tip—must have seen Mabel enter the woods from the parking lot. "You're a lucky man," he had told Percy earlier. What he meant was "You're no man at all, just lucky."

Someone should teach Mabel a lesson, Percy thought. He sucked ice from his third Bloody Mary and exchanged commonplaces with the Wutzls. When Mrs. Wutzl wiped the pie off her husband's nose, calling him a naughty Woofy, Percy smiled, then frowned. Was it too much to ask, he thought, that he should grow old with Mabel, still as in love as the Wutzls obviously were—in their seventies, calling each other pet names? And here was Percy, only forty-six, standing alone at a faculty party while his wife fucked a teaching assistant.

A tear came to his eye. Percy pulled magician's silk from his pocket, forgetting how one kerchief was tied to another, red following blue following green, for ten hankies, as the Wutzls watched. "Very good, lad," Dr. Wutzl said. Mrs. Wutzl applauded lightly. Percy thanked them and hurried away.

Goddamn Mabel, he thought. He wrapped her cape tighter around his sagging magician shoulders and left the party. When he got into their car and turned on the lights he caught the green stare of an animal in the bushes. For a moment he imagined Mabel standing by the side of the road, her lowcut red dress slit up the side, her thumb out. He drove from the parking spot to the street, then hesitated.

Let her find her own way home, he finally decided. *Someone always gives a tramp a ride.*

SEVENTEEN

Dr. Wutzl watched Mabel enter Bryant's Wood. Just as he'd decided to follow her he turned and caught young Furnival's eye. "Lovely night," he said. "The moon casts a lovely glow."

Furnival nodded, looked at his watch. Mrs. Wutzl took her place at her husband's side. "Oh you naughty Woofy," she said, wetting her napkin with spit, using it to clean his snout. Percy laughed, Rufus gritted his teeth. The lad performed a paltry magic trick and left.

"Ethel," Dr. Wutzl said. "If I must tell you again not to call me Woofy, especially before my colleagues, I shall divorce you."

Her blue-white pincurls drooped till it looked as if she wore corkscrews in her head. She backed away from his fury and ran weeping to the ladies' room.

"I can't stand that old woman," Rufus said to himself. "I really can't stand her." He looked around. Professor Hazel and Dean Hook were conferring in a corner. They glanced his way. Professor Blostein was staring at him over her drink. Had they seen? He felt guilty. What would the faculty think of a distinguished professor who makes his wife cry? No one knew it was her own fault. He had tried to convince her not to come. It wasn't necessary for her to be there in a ridiculous short, beaded dress, showing off her knobby knees and varicose veins. Even when she was a flapper—did he remember the dress she was wearing tonight from their courtship or was that a trick of memory?—her legs had not been her best feature.

"I have to go to this absurd costume ball," Rufus had told her a month before, "but you can stay cozy at home. A hot cup of tea, one of your gothics. I'll fix you a nice fire."

"But I want to be there," she said, "right at your side."

Upon hearing this he pretended to become engrossed in his book. He swallowed hard, but the gagging sensation in his throat would not abate. He felt like a dog with a choke collar, and she was pulling his leash and pulling it. "Fine, fine," he said, but she still wouldn't leave his study. She stood over him, squinting to read the fine print on the page of a poetry book he had opened at random. She moved her head forward and back, bobbing like a pigeon as she tried to strike a balance between near- and farsightedness. He turned around. "I'm sorry, dear," he said. "I can't concentrate when someone's reading over my shoulder." She patted his head and walked out. He fought the urge to fling his book at the door.

Couldn't she let him alone for one evening? She didn't belong at the faculty Halloween party. His peers would be there. They all esteemed him. He wanted to aid the next generation of scholars with his advice, to be remembered as someone never too busy to help carry on the work of literature. He wanted to discuss ideas with Mabel Fleish, to tell her he was working on a book about her book, to slip her a note that would make things clear, to exchange secret words with her, let her know he understood Furnival was not man enough for her. He wanted to reveal himself. She would see him with new eyes. She would watch astounded as he unzipped his wrinkled flesh and out stepped a man as smooth, and hard, as a bone. "It is I, Rufus Wutzl. Professor Emeritus. Lover *par excellence.*"

Instead, when he approached her at the start of the party and started to say, "Hello, how are," he immediately found his wife at his side sputtering, "These hors d'oeuvres are vile. Don't touch them, Rufus. I'll fix you a snack later. Hmph, they should taste my salmon mousse, and it's not hard to make. You just take cream. Beat your own mayonnaise from fresh eggs..."

Dr. Wutzl nodded his head, not listening, but it was too late. Mabel had already walked off, and he hadn't had the chance to pull down her beard and kiss her lips (as he planned the moment he saw her hairy face). Too soon after that she was sitting with that horrible man, young Something Whatshisname, hardly more than an apprentice, a teaching assistant. Horace, Horace Byrrd. She could have been receiving instruction from an experienced scholar, a mentor who would take her and—

"I said, Don't you agree?" Ethel glared at her husband. "When

I get home," she said in a lower voice, "I'll fix you. A hot egg-milk toddy, with cream and brandy. That will wash these bad tastes from your mouth. Just wait and see if I don't."

She pulled her eyebrows together. Rufus thought of threatening storm clouds gathered on the horizon. Baal, he remembered from Mabel's book, was called Rider of the Clouds. For a moment he forgot to whom he was speaking, almost telling his wife this literary tidbit. Just in time he noticed Ethel's stormy brow, recalled her words.

"Sounds yummy, dear," he said.

Half an hour later Dr. Wutzl saw Horace leave the party. He was about to approach Mabel when she walked off. She rang the elevator before going to the ladies' room. He stood at the window, looked out, saw her wobbling across the parking lot. He decided to go after her, turned, and there was Percy Furnival. Fellow started up a tedious conversation about the beauties of nature, the mysteries of night. Then he had that fight with Mrs. Wutzl. Unbearable woman. Hard to imagine he had once murmured Pussy in response to her Woofy. So here he was, finally alone.

He knew he must act fast, before Ethel returned from her crying jag. He heard the bell ring, hurried into the elevator, and was out the building, rushing to Bryant's Wood like a lover to an assignation, before he realized he'd made up his mind to go. He might still find her there. Horace was no gentleman (Mabel was no lady). She might have had to slap his face, saying she was not that sort of woman (of course she was). The cad would have run off, leaving a disconsolate Mabel Fleish, her clothes in disarray from the struggle. Enter Rufus Wutzl. He would find her, comfort her, take her in his arms. Yes, if he hurried. Hurried.

The dark wood before him, the crescent moon, the stars, his furry paws and body and wolfish head. The night took on a transformative quality. Rufus Wutzl feared he dreamed, but his heart pounded with a young man's ardor. He had to stop, lean against a tree to catch his breath. Hidden from view he saw a strange vision.

A giant brown bird resting on one leg, then the other, appeared to be adjusting its crotch. Then it scurried along the path to the parking lot, got into a red Toyota. Rufus gazed for some moments after the strange spectacle, till finally he recognized Horace. The young man was already starting home. But where was Mabel? *Foul play?* Rufus thought, then laughed. He tried to catch his breath but couldn't stop laughing. The harder he tried, the harder he laughed, imagining the courtship dance of a huge falcon flapping over Mabel. Then, just as rain may take on snow in mountain towns in autumn, his old-man laughter mixed with tears. It wasn't fair, to be old when his heart was young. "Oh my Leda," he said to the haunted wood. "I am your Zeus, your swan, your swain, not that foul imposter," and again began to giggle. *Pagliacci,* he thought. *Laugh, clown, laugh.*

"Dr. Wutzl," said Mabel, appearing from behind a tree. "Are you all right?"

"My dear girl, I didn't see you. Yes, yes. I just felt like taking the air. Constitutional, you know. Ah, but you look lovely in the moonlight. Let me give you my arm. This path is treacherous."

Mabel took Dr. Wutzl's furry forelimb and accompanied him back to the party. "Good thing it's not a full moon," she said, "or I'd have thought you were a werewolf."

Dr. Wutzl grinned. The night again took on enchantment, but not of an unambiguous kind. Good and bad magic mixed, for here he was, alone with Mabel Fleish; yet, as if a witch had cast a spell, he found himself stuck, unable to say any of the things he had dreamed of. And as in a dream the moment passed too soon. Too soon he and Mabel were in the elevator, too soon the doors opened on the third floor. Too soon Mabel disengaged her arm from his.

"What will people think," she said, "when they see us entering the party together?" She smiled. Her dark eyes glowed, her red hair gleamed. Her swan's neck reminded Dr. Wutzl that it was he who had been ravished in the encounter, not she.

"Ah, my dear," sighed the professor. "If only what they thought were true."

"Where were you?" said Ethel, pouncing on him as soon as he walked through the door. "I was worried sick over you."

Rufus had not the time to say farewell to his lady love. Mabel was gone and he was caught in the steam of his wife's fury at the poor quality of the buffet being served "to distinguished professors, no less. I wouldn't feed this stuff to a dog, Woofy. Do you hear me? To a dog!" She stamped her foot.

"Yes dear," he said. "I'll just have a bit more balogna—"

"Don't you dare!" she threatened. "I refuse to be up a whole night listening to you fart."

"Ethel!" he exclaimed. "I believe you've had too much to drink."

EIGHTEEN

When Percy walked up to his front door he saw footprints tracking mud across the porch. He was annoyed with Ana, who knew to use the mudroom when her shoes were dirty. Then he remembered Ana was at a friend's house. *Maybe we've been robbed,* he thought, shrugging. He opened the door and out leaped Nubi. Percy didn't feel like coaxing the white shepherd in. His stomach was churning from too many drinks. He sat in the dark, not caring about the mystery of the mud, knowing what he was going to do.

"Fuck it," he said, and got his stash. Set up two lines of coke. Rolled a dollar bill thin. Inserted it into his left nostril. Sucked it up. Did his right. Sniffed deep, swallowed hard. Lit a joint. "I won't think about her," he said, thinking nonetheless how his wife had left the party to follow Horace like a bitch who smells meat. *I have that damn article to write for* Knickerbocker. *What did Lana say about deconstructing the—oh shit, what's that?* A large brown jiffy bag waited like a bomb on Mabel's desk. He knew what it was. His book on "The Relevance of Cigar Ash in Nineteenth-Century Detective Fiction" had been returned from yet another publisher, the humor of the title no doubt lost in the consideration (or lack of the same) it had been given.

"Just what I need," he said, throwing the manuscript on the couch. He didn't bother opening it, to read the enclosed letter that began: "Dear Professor Furnival, Thank you for..."

"Thank *you,*" he said, "for being too conventional to study convention. For being too dim-witted to know wit even dimly—"

The phone rang. He picked it up but didn't say anything.

"Hello? Hello?" asked the voice on the other end.

"Hi, honey," he said to Ana, angry at himself for thinking it might be one of Mabel's mysterious callers. "Having fun?"

"Loads," said Ana. "Listen, Daddy, I'm in big trouble. Could you please be a dear, Daddy dear, and bring over my Barbie case. I forgot it when I put it down to kiss Mommy goodbye."

"Sure," he said, though it was the last thing he wanted to do. "I'll be right over."

He took off his tux and put on jeans. "Some magician," he said. "Watch me make my wife disappear." He looked in the bathroom mirror. Put cold water on his eyes. Gargled. "This is ridiculous," he said. "They're not my parents." Hannah glared invisibly behind the shower curtain. "Just you shut up," he said.

"Dope fiend," she said. "You'll come to no good. Just wait."

"Look," he told the ghost. "I want to know something. How come you ignored me your whole life, didn't have anything to do with me while I was growing up, handed me over to servants to raise, and when I married called only to speak to Mabel—so how come now that you're dead you won't leave me alone?"

Hannah pointed a cold finger, shook it. "You'll get yours, Percival," she said. "See if you don't," and diminished herself to a cold water drip. Percy tightened the tap. He put on his jacket, shut the lights, closed the door, locked his mother in.

He went to the Steins, made small talk with Howard and Olga, declined a drink. Was his manner too wired, were his eyes too red? "I'm in a hurry to get home," he told them. "I'm working on an article for *Knickerbocker*, on deconstructing archetypes—"

"Yes, yes," said Howard. "Certainly if you must run."

The door shut behind him. Percy stood outside the Steins' house, looking at the sky. Though he had been anxious to leave, he was in no hurry to get home. He wanted to find Mabel sitting in the living room, terrified of her own ghosts, when he came back...if he came back. "Let her worry for a change," he mumbled.

He decided to go for a drive. He took High Mountain Road to the turnoff overlooking the small town of Winegarden. It was a star-heavy night. The lights of the town seemed a reflection of sky, as if Winegarden were the mirror of heaven. He sat at the overlook, smoked the rest of the joint, pulled the dark over him. He wondered if he could pinpoint the blank between streetlamps where Mabel was bedding. He hoped it was wet and cold, if there were sheets they were dirty.

When he tired of this game he drove down the mountain. Passing Mike's Tavern he decided to stop in. Squeezed his car into a spot behind the roadhouse. *Busy night,* he thought, opening the door to enter a holy cloud of smoke and noise. At least here no one would notice his eyes. The denizens of Mike's had stares as red as devils. He saw Iris Specter, a student in his Archetypes in Genre Literature class, at the same moment she saw him. She waved, inviting him to share her booth.

"Professor Furnival," she said. "Am I glad to see you! You're just the one to help me solve my problem."

A mutual solution? thought Percy. He smiled sheepishly and ordered a vodka and beer.

NINETEEN

The evening drew to a close. Dr. Wutzl spied Mabel by the bar, looking for someone. For him? His heart pounded. He hurried over.

"Hello again, Dr. Wutzl," she said. "I'm looking for Percy. Have you seen him? I think he's forgotten me."

It soon became apparent that the fool had left her stranded. What could be better? Rufus offered her a ride home, mentally rubbing his hands together, thinking the fates were conspiring to let him have his way. He scratched his furry torso. Percy Furnival was not man enough for a woman like Mabel Fleish. Soon she would know what it was to be loved by Rufus Wutzl.

Mrs. Wutzl was none too pleased when she heard they were driving Mabel home. "It's not exactly on the way, Rufus," she said. "And I have a headache."

"Why, that's no problem. I'll drive you home first, dear." *Oh goody,* he thought. *Thank you, Zeus, and the rest of ye gods.*

Mabel soon joined Dr. and Mrs. Wutzl, saying how kind it was for them to offer her a ride. "I hope I'm not putting you out."

"Well, actually, I have rather a bad headache, so if you—"

"No trouble at all," said Dr. Wutzl. "I'll drop Mrs. Wutzl off first and—"

"No, dear, I don't want an old man like you driving around the mountains alone."

"Oh, I'm not so old as all that," he said. He took his wife's hand, tried to squeeze it into silence.

"Really, an old man who, ow! Stop it, Woofy. You're hurt—"

"I'm sorry, dear. Just a love pat. Hush now. We'll both drive Mabel home. Come along."

When they got to the small white house they were surprised that it was dark and Percy's car was not in the drive. "Shall I go in with you?" Dr. Wutzl asked, his heart leaping at the prospect of entering Mabel's darkness. "You never know what you might find lurking in an empty house." He leered.

"We should be going, Rufus," warned Mrs. Wutzl. "You know how your rheumatism acts up in the chill night air."

"I'll be fine," said Mabel. "Thanks for the lift. I'm sure Percy will be along soon." Dr. Wutzl waited till she'd gone in and turned on the lights. He thought he saw the silhouette of a man by the window, but when he looked again the shadow was gone. *Probably that fool Furnival playing a joke on his wife,* he thought.

"What are you waiting for?" Mrs. Wutzl shrilly asked. With reluctance, he drove off.

TWENTY

Mabel smiled as the elderly couple drove away. *The Wutzls are really dear people,* she thought, *but what has happened to Percy?* She entered the empty house, turned on the living room light. The room filled with a hidden presence. "Percy?" she called. No answer. "Beau?" She began searching the house, peering into each dark room, calling the name of a dead boy. She did not turn on any other lamp. She didn't know how ghosts felt about light. She willed the darkness to take her away, refusing to shudder when she heard footsteps. That would be just like Beau, she thought, to come back after twenty years and tease her.

The floorboards creaked as she walked back down the stairs. She sensed him in the living room—there, behind the curtain; there, in the foyer closet. But when she looked the draperies moved emptily in the night; the closet, once opened, filled only with old coats. Still, she knew he was in the house, waiting. Her sense of him was uncanny, as if she smelled his smell. That's when she saw it, the envelope glowing eerily, caught in a moonbeam. She knew what it was. An invitation from death.

Beau's presence was as palpable as a lover's heartbeat in the dark. It made the shining envelope throb as she picked it up. It bore no postmark. Someone had entered her house to leave it. Someone was still there, watching. She whispered the incantation aloud, stumbling over the odd abbreviations:

> *Mght he woo hr?* *Wd he cd.*
>
> *Mght he screw hr?* *Mght be wd.*
>
> *Cd he wfe hr?* *Cd be wd.*
>
> *Wd he knfe hr?* *Mght be shd.*

Cd he hide hr?   *Mrk my wrd.*
Who wd ride hr?

"Horace Byrrd?" Mabel asked. "Are you hiding here?"

"*Rrrr,*" growled a voice in the corner. Mabel looked for Anubis but couldn't find him. A figure stepped out of the shadow, smiling like a skull. "By*rrrr*d," he said, "ain't got your bone. *Rrrr*yder Wood, girl." He bowed. "At your cervix."

TWENTY-ONE

"What are you having?" Percy asked. "Beer," Iris said. He ordered her another.

"Professor Furnival," she said. "I'm so glad to see you. I've been wondering and wondering about your last class. I didn't understand your point about the victim/heroine in gothic novels. I mean, I just don't see how she represents the Great Goddess archetype. How can she be a goddess when she's a sacrifice?"

The girl flipped her long black hair behind her shoulder, staring intently at his mouth. Percy thought he detected a gleam in her eye.

"Great Goddess," he said. His mouth was dry. He licked his lips, which only made them chapped and sticky. "She has a lot of manifestations. Life and death, you know. Eats corpses. Takes the dead into her mouth, births them from the other end. But what was your question again? I'm sorry. My mind wanders."

Iris had full, red lips. When she opened them she revealed white teeth that made her mouth look like an apple with a bite taken out. He leaned forward, then realized with a start he was falling into her mouth. He pulled back.

"Oh yes. Goddess," he said. "Sacrificial aspect. Sexual sacrifice. Ancient Sumerian cults ritualized temple prostitution. Prehistoric fat Venuses, faceless, with clearly marked vulvas, turn up in fields, graves. The goddess made to bear. 'Fuck,' you know, means to plant seed in a field. A farmer fucks the earth as a man fucks his wife." *And his wife fucks around,* he thought.

"Gosh, Professor, that's neat. So like when I'm fucking I'm not just me but the earth. And I—"

"Sometimes a sacrifice is made to demons, to keep them away. The Mother sacrifices herself to save her children. Inanna descends to the underworld to bring back her dead child. There's a mix of this kind of thing in the imprisonment of the virginal heroine in gothics. Rape of the virgin." He couldn't stop licking his lips. He knew his tongue was coated, his lips white. Iris's mouth was glossy. She had a wet smile. Perhaps she had something for chapped lips.

"Do you have any Vaseline?" he asked.

"What?"

Percy started to laugh. "For my lips. They're dry. Do you have anything moist?"

Iris stood up, felt the front of her hips. She put her hand into a pocket, pulled a cylinder from her tight jeans. "It's lip gloss," she said. "You can use it, though. It's transparent."

The gold lipstick case was more feminine than Percy felt comfortable with, but his need was great. He took the holder. The metal was still hot from Iris's pocket. He pulled it open, hid as much of the cylinder as he could with his hand, quickly smeared gloss on his lips. "Thanks," he said.

"Sure thing." She stood again, put the stick deep inside her pants. He saw it nestle near her crotch. She sat down and sipped her beer. There was an uncomfortable silence.

"What was it you were saying, Professor?"

He thought for a few moments, trying to catch his memory. "About the virginal aspect of the goddess?" She nodded. He went on. "I think my point was that the archetype is not just Mother but Daughter." Then he was off and running. *Must be speed in the coke,* he thought. That was okay. He liked speed. "It is in the latter manifestation that the romance heroine comes in."

Percy took a gulp of vodka. It was funny how much a person could drink and still have a dry mouth. He was looking at Iris, licking his lips, loath to ask again for her gloss. She lifted her hair off her neck. "So hot," she said. The upward movement of her arms raised her breasts beneath her skimpy shirt, showing him the possibilities. She smiled, it was a bedroom smile.

"Another aspect of the Daughter," he said, "is Virgin of War. Virgin only in the sense of unmarried, you understand. Holy harlot, if you will. That's why a temple prostitute stands for a virgin. No matter how many she beds she's still called virgin." *Mabel the Virgin,* he thought, but no—Mabel had a husband, even if she fucked everyone else.

"Why are you shaking your head?"

"Oh, was I? I was thinking about something else. Never mind. Actually, it was my wife's novel. You read *Bone*, didn't you? Recall how she played with the Virgin of War/Holy Harlot theme? Aspects of Anathe and Inanna in Anna. Take Anathe, for instance—you know, the Canaanite war goddess? She's vengeful, like Annabelle was at first. Remember that passage: 'She tried to hide Astarte'— Astarte, Inanna, Ishtar are all the same love goddess, you see—'She tried to hide Astarte under Anathe, but Ted saw through his mother's disguise. The hands she cut off and tied to her belt, tripping into gore, caressed and fingered her. She swooned from delight. Dismembered heads at her girdle had tongues wet with desire.'"

Iris shook her head. "I didn't memorize the book," she said. "Read it rather fast actually. Seemed trashy. I had some problems with the feminist implications of her acquiescence to bondage—"

"It's not for everyone perhaps. You're young. Mark my words, that book will be around when you're a grandmother."

"I'm sorry, Professor Furnival, I didn't mean to offend—"

"Not at all. I didn't write it. I'm just stating a fact. My wife has written a modern novel in an ancient genre—wisdom literature." Percy patted his chest, feeling for his pipe. He found his tobacco pouch in his jacket pocket. "Do you mind if I—"

"Not at all," said Iris, closing her eyes. "I love the smell of your pipe. I wish there was a perfume like it. I could just—"

"Have we covered Inanna in class yet?"

The girl shook her head. She watched him as if dreaming.

"For our purposes, Inanna—also known as Ishtar and Astarte— is a goddess of desire. But it is in Inanna's myth of descent that she figures in my lectures on genre fiction, particularly mysteries. You see, she also, oh, but you must not want to hear this now. Saturday night, Halloween. I apologize for boring—"

"Oh, no no. Not at all, Professor. It's fascinating." Iris's eyes were bleary, belying her words. "Desire, you say. A religion based on sex?" The girl leaned on the table. Percy felt himself falling forward again. He sat up straight, sipped his beer.

"As far as we know," he said. "The important thing for our class discussion is her descent to the underworld to bringing her son/ lover back from the dead. Sacrificing herself, switching places with him. You hear resonances of this ancient Sumerian myth in gothic romance. The virginal heroine imprisoned in a dungeon corresponds to Inanna in the underworld turned into meat—which can only mean forced to perform temple prostitution. At least, that was the thesis of my book *The Mysteries of Inanna/The Mysteries of Pulp.*"

Iris took out a pen and paper, jotted down the name. "I want to read that," she said. "Who's the publisher?"

"A small literary press, Academy of the Mind, ever hear of them? You can order it direct. What was I saying? About Inanna bringing her son/lover up from the underworld through her own transformation into meat?" Iris seemed to nod, though she might only have been falling asleep.

"When Inanna," said Professor Furnival, "reawakens from her meat stage she sees Tammuz—"

Iris stifled a yawn. Her eyes teared. "Ooh, listen. It's my song," she said. She pulled his hand. "Come on, Professor Furnival. Let's dance."

Percy allowed himself to be led to the dance floor. He stood awkwardly while Iris gyrated around him. It was dark, the room crowded with couples. He began to bounce to the beat. Iris wiggled her hips, moved her arms like snakes, writhing like a belly dancer in a style that was different from the jerking fashion of the others. Percy stared at her, mentally taking off her clothes. Pulled her head back, planted kisses on her neck, planted himself inside her. Her body arched. She was moist. Dark. He grew inside her wetness. The song was over. The music stopped.

"No more," he said. He returned to the table, drained the last of his drink. "I have to get going."

"Oh, Professor, don't go. The fun's just beginning."

He saw the invitation in her eyes, she was beautiful, but he could not respond. He felt foolish. It was as if, in the last minutes, he had lost something more than he gained. "Another time," he said. "I have something to take care of." Without knowing when it happened he had come to a decision. He would have it out with Mabel. Tonight. Tomorrow he would be a happy man. Or a free one.

TWENTY-TWO

"Ryder!" Mabel dropped the note. It fluttered like a fallen angel. "What are you doing here? I thought, that is, you startled me. How are you? I didn't know you were here."

"No," he said. "You didn't."

"Well," she said. "Nice to see you. I'll uh, I'll fix us some coffee."

"Don't bother," he said. "We should be going."

Her heart stopped for a minute, then raced to catch up with itself. "I can't go anyplace now. My husband will be home soon."

"That's why we need hurry. Come on."

She gripped the table as if intending to hold it if he tried to pull her. "I can't go with you, Ryder. I don't know how you got in here. Or why you've been calling me, leaving threatening notes. You just better stop it, hear me?"

The man opened the crack of his smile, his chuckle was mirthless. "You know you called me. You sent rays of rapture searching for me, telling me to come. I know what you want. That bird in the woods tonight, you thought he had it? It's me that's got your bone—you got mine anyway, and I'm fixing to get it back...by giving it to you, imagine that! Come on, let's go where I can give a bitch a bone." He motioned with the bulge in his pocket. "Is that a pistol in your pocket?" he said in a mocking Mae West voice.

She looked from his face to his pocket and back again, figuring the chance she had to make a run for it. She was wearing high heels. If she kicked them off and ran barefoot, she might make it into the kitchen before he caught her. She wouldn't get much further, and it could make him mad, he was already mad, but it might set off some hunting instinct as when you play rough with a cat. No, her best chance was to stall for time. Distract him. Percy would be home soon. He had to be.

"Well, sure, Ryder. But I can't just go off without any clothes. Let me pack a few things."

"Oh no." He laughed. "You won't need any. Hotter'n hell where you going." With a shock it came back to her—his habit of speaking like a hick from time to time, making fun of fun. It used to excite her, part of their play acting, but this was different, this was out of control. Out of her control.

"Put your arms out now," he said. "On second thought, turn around. Put your hands behind you." She moved away till she was in a corner. He grabbed her hands, pulled them back, turned her around. Thinking furiously how to slow things down she spied the letter-opener on the table, but before she could make a lunge for it her arms were tied.

Still facing the wall she felt him push his crotch against her. He was hard. *Good,* she thought. *That will slow him down.* Then she shuddered with realization. The rod nuzzling her buttocks was cold. It was a gun. Her mind raced desperately, looking for a way out, like a small animal looking for a hole. "Ryder," she said. "Mmmm, honey, that feels good. Let's go upstairs first. We'll have time to get on the road."

"I thought you said your husband's coming home?"

"No, no, I was wrong, I-I forgot. He has a meeting tonight. He won't be home till late. Much much later. We have lots of time. Come, let's go upstairs. I can't wait any longer."

He pulled her arms up in back till she cried out in pain. "Lies," he hissed. "I'm going to teach you what it means to write the secrets of my soul. Learn the hard way what you set in motion when you put me on paper. School's about to begin, and you're teacher's pet, a real eager beaver, ain't you?"

"Ryder, I didn't write about you. I don't—"

"What you call me?"

"Ryder, I didn't—"

"What was that?"

"Ryder, stop it. I—"

"Can't hear you. Don't know no Ryder, you see a Ryder?"

Mabel knew what he wanted. She refused to do it. She had to figure out if it would work for or against her. She walked as slowly as possible. He pushed her. She twisted her ankle on purpose, crying out, "Oh Ryder, I can't walk." He thrust the nozzle of the gun deeper inside the crack of her buttocks.

"Annabelle," he said, "I could just put it inside you right now, blow you"—he laughed—"to Kingdom Come. But who's this Ryder? Another of your men?" He tsked and shook his head. "Insatiable. Well, we'll see about that too, won't we? Now march! Like the captain says to me, he says, March, I march. He says, Jump, I says, No, Sir! He pushes me out. Screaming. Falling. Flying. Laughing to Kingdom Come. He says, Airborne, I says, Yes, Sir! He says, Jump! I jump."

Ryder's laugh spiraled. He convulsed forward, gagging from an excess of humor, elbowing her with the gun to enjoy the joke. "He says, last thing he says, Airborne, he says to me, Airborne! And I'm airborne all right." The laugh gurgled as if down a drain, then stopped. Ryder stiffened, like a soldier whose superior has just entered the room.

"Yes, Sir!" Ryder saluted Mabel with his gun. "Yes, Sir! Now, march, I says march. Hear me? Yes, Sir! Hup."

She marched, he kept step with her, keeping the gun nosing inside her buttocks. *Where's Nubi?* she thought. "Ryder," she said over her shoulder. "My dog has to be fed. Please. He'll cry. He hasn't been fed since morning. You like dogs. You told me so."

"Don't worry about him, Annabelle. That Ryder fellow fed him. Goddamn good dog, Ryder told me. Ryder and him made friends just like that. So don't you worry. Get in the car now. I promise I won't do nothing you ain't going to like. Deep inside. Hey girl, I'm your dream man, remember?"

Mabel entered the ancient Volkswagen with difficulty, her arms still behind her. He tied her with the seat belt. She looked out the window, a last glance at her home. She saw the ghost of Anubis smiling in the yard. *Help me, you dumb beast.* But the white mutt seemed to lack ESP. All he did was offer his paw to an invisible master.

The pale man slid beside her in the car and turned the key. *This is it,* she thought, *how my story ends.* An odd calm came over her— as if she were a criminal finally caught, forced to pay an overdue debt.

Ryder drove onto the road. The few houses that lined it were warmly white against a star-laden sky. Silent witnesses at peace with themselves, they glowed pure as candles, lighting the way for the Bug. *It is so beautiful,* Mabel thought, *the cornucopia of stars. How odd to be killed under such a fat sky.*

Ryder looked in the rearview mirror. Percy's car was pulling into the driveway behind them. "Just in the niche," he said, "of time."

TWENTY-THREE

Percy opened the door. It wasn't locked. He called Mabel's name. She didn't answer. He couldn't believe she wasn't home. It was past midnight. How could she still be screwing that grad student?

He started to turn around, to go back to Mike's Tavern, to Iris's snake arms. Instead he shut the light and sat in the dark, smoking a joint. "Shit," he said, closing his eyes. He looked down, staring some moments without seeing. Then he noticed a piece of paper on the floor and realized he had seen it, without seeing it, all along. He picked it up, turned on the lamp, and read:

> *Mght he woo hr?* *Wd he cd.*
> *Mght he screw hr?* *Mght be wd.*
> *Cd he wfe hr?* *Cd be wd.*
> *Wd he knfe hr?* *Mght be shd.*
> *Cd he hide hr?* *Mrk my wrd.*
> *Who wd ride hr?*

Who would ride whom? The ominous question vibrated in his brain like a word he couldn't remember, couldn't forget, a déjà vu recalled as it was happening, not before. The poem circled, refusing to land. Suddenly Mabel's absence seemed to be more than evidence of infidelity.

That's when he remembered: He had shut all the lights before going to Pammy's, he had locked the door, but when he returned just now the lights were on, the latch undone. "Mabel?" he called into each room of the house, as if she might be hiding. She didn't appear. If only he could think straight. If only he hadn't just smoked a joint. What should he do? What did one do in a situation like this?

Could he ride her? Mark my word. Who would ride her? He looked up Horace's number, called him. A sheepish Horace Byrrd said he hadn't seen Mabel since the party. Percy coldly thanked him and hung up. Was he lying? He drummed his nails on the desk, called the police.

"Is your wife eighteen years of age or older?"

"Of course," said Percy. "What do you think I am?"

"How long has she been missing?"

"Well, I'm not sure she's missing, but there's this note. Also, the door was unlocked and the lights were on when I came home. I guess it's a couple of hours."

"To be officially considered missing, an adult eighteen years of age or older must have disappeared twenty-four hours prior to any investigation by police. May I suggest, if your wife has still not turned up by this time tomorrow, you call back?"

"But there's this note. I'm worried. Do I have to wait?"

"We can't do anything for twenty-four hours. If she hasn't turned up by then or made her whereabouts known a uniformed police officer will come by your house and take your statement."

Percy shook his head, willing himself to awaken from this dream. "I see," he said. "Okay then. Tomorrow. Probably she'll walk in any moment." He laughed uncomfortably and hung up.

PART TWO

TWENTY-FOUR

Kwestral faced the mirror. *Row,* he told himself. His arms reached, his abdomen pulled, his legs braced. It had been well over a month, and still he couldn't get Mabel Fleish out of his mind. Neither had he worked up the nerve to call her. A few times he'd actually dialed, but when she picked up he found himself unable to speak. That she had a voice, an existence, a telephone number, that he could dial it and actually speak to her felt too much like a dream. As if he'd made her up.

He no longer remembered what they had actually said to each other that day they'd met, what he had since fantasized. In the back of his mind he recalled initial disdain. When and how that had changed he didn't know. He knew he'd been mildly impressed when he first read her book but critical too. Still, it had stayed with him. She stayed with him. And he read the book again, looking at her picture, thinking about their meeting, her mysterious quest for the truth behind death.

Every sentence he read now was multilayered till it was like poetry. He wanted to ask what she'd meant there, what she'd intended here. He wanted to tell her, also, what he'd learned about her dead friend, to ask what that meant to her, what everything meant to her. Did she even remember him, Herm Kwestral, he wondered, but why should she? He was nothing. A skinny albino reporter for a Brooklyn rag. And yet, how could she not when she dwelled in his mind like a resident muse? *Row, row,* he demanded, going over the reality again, forcing himself to stick to the facts. When was it he'd begun to love her, he wondered, the mystery woman a million miles away?

They had gone to a coffee shop together, and she had ordered

a spinach salad. "Two eggs," he told the waitress, "hardboiled."
That made her laugh. She had a surprising laugh. Hearty. Virile.
Manly even. The deep *ha ha* contrasted excitingly with her delicate
bones. Like a bronchial cough in a child's chest. Her shoulders
shook till the laugh seemed almost a sob.

"I can help you," he said, "if you let me. I work on *The Brooklyn
Wing*. I have access to their files."

She smiled, seeming to mock him. "And still so young."

"Not as young as I look," he retorted. "Inside me is an old man.
My life's just a case of my body catching up."

He winked, then realized he had just winked at his own
reflection in the gym mirror. He looked to see if anyone else using
the machines had seen him.

Rowing, rowing, never getting anywhere. God, this was a pain.
He scrunched his face, pushing himself, trying to make wrinkles at
the same time. Too damn young, too damn white. At *The Wing* they
called him The Kid. Twenty-six, hey, it wasn't ancient but it weren't
no kid. Last week the liquor store owner proofed him. Almost
thirty, man. Maybe that was the turning point. Why rush it
anyway? Would he have accomplished anything by then, published
a novel? Or would his head still be clogged with obit *obiter dicta*?

Manhood waited on the other side of thirty, far away and
desirable, terrifying as failure. What had he done in twenty-six
years that he wanted the next four to fly? Christ, he was still living
with his mother.

Flinging back his long white hair he conjured the face of a moist-
lipped woman. *I'm going to call her*, he told himself. *Today*. As if
she held the key to his manhood.

When he'd finished his workout and shower he asked the
attendant, a middle-aged black man full of hate, to open his locker.
"Charlie"—that's what people called him, but Kwestral suspected
it wasn't his name—sneered. *You think I'm just a rich white kid
with nothing to do but play*, Kwestral longed to say. *I'll have you
know I work hard. Harder than you, standing around smelling
sweat, doling out shampoo. I'm a writer, man. Free-lance, like a
knight. And I've been working hard since I was fifteen and my dad
was murdered saving a whore, so don't look at me that way. I'm a
man, too.*

He stood by, saying nothing except thanks when "Charlie"
threw the door open with an angry clank. Damn, Kwestral thought,

searching his pants pocket. There was no change—must have fallen out when he was getting undressed. He shrugged, put on his clothes. He'd lost his nerve by then anyway. Mabel Fleish, he thought. A man would do anything for such a woman...except ask Charlie for change of a buck. *Maybe I dreamed you. Maybe it's best to keep it that way.*

"Lambchops for dinner, honey."

Herm was heading up the stairs. "Great, Ma," he called. "I have to make a phone call first."

Mrs. Kwestral stood at the bottom of the staircase. "They'll get cold. Can't it wait?"

"Nope."

"Herman! You get back here. This minute. We are going to have a nice family dinner, just like we had when your father was alive. You've got a whole night to make your call."

Kwestral slammed the door to his bedroom, pretending he didn't hear her. His father's police hat sat on his dresser. The visor gleamed sharply. He gasped, grabbed it, put it in its box quickly, afraid his mother would catch him. Had he really left it out, exposed, all day? Had she noticed when she made his bed? "Okay, okay. I'm coming," he yelled down as she continued to nag. "Don't blow a gasket."

He ate his dinner sullenly, didn't clear the table. "I have work to do," he said when he was done.

"That's okay. Run along, sweetheart. I'll clean up."

He walked up the stairs, feeling rotten, feeling also a tingle of tension in his groin, an uncomfortable sexual buzz. More like anxiety than longing. Hard without desire.

He went to the bathroom and masturbated pleasurelessly, just doing his job. Then he picked up the phone.

He took a deep breath and dialed, determined not to hang up, no matter that she wouldn't remember him after so long. A man answered.

"Mr. Fleish?" Herm asked, his voice squeaking.

"Who is this?" the tired voice asked.

"Uh, you don't know me. I'm a friend of your wife's. She—"

"Who is this?" The voice didn't sound tired anymore.

"Who is who?"

"Where's my wife? Who are you?"

"I told you. You don't know me. I met your wife some time ago. She was asking about someone. I told her I'd dig up—"

"Dig? What do you mean, dig? Where, you bastard?"

"Hey, what's the matter with you? I told her I'd try to dig up information. What's going on? Something wrong with you?"

"With me? You, what are you, some sort of crank? Nothing better to do than call the families of missing persons and talk to them about digging—"

"Whoa! Missing persons? Please. I haven't spoken to your wife in a long time. I don't know what you're talking about."

Kwestral heard a sigh. "I'm sorry," Mabel's husband said. "I assumed you knew. Mabel's been missing since Halloween."

"Gosh," said Herm. "No, I didn't. It didn't make the Brooklyn news. I just—"

"Why was it you called again?"

"Your wife. I met her at the police station about a month or so ago. She was trying to find out about this guy whose body was found in an abandoned house. An old boyfriend."

"Great. Another old boyfriend."

"It was a long time ago. Twenty years."

"Oh, I see. Yes, I'm listening."

"The thing is, well, your wife thought the body was that of a kid named Beau Barbon. That was her boyfriend. I told her I'd check the clips in the morgue, I'm sorry, in the file room here at *The Wing*. Where I work. I'm a reporter. I cover crime, write obits for, oh, I'm sorry again. I didn't—"

"Forget it. So what did you find?"

"The body was that of another sixteen-year-old. I mean, they don't give the names of minors in the news, but I got access to police records at the precinct. It was complicated but I know somebody in Crime Analysis who let me take—"

"Yes, yes, I see. So what did you find?"

"Oh, yes. I'm sorry. Let's see. The kid's name was Larry Lazar. Your wife ever mention him to you?"

"Not that I can recall."

"Anyway, her interest was in this guy, this Beau. I thought she'd want to know he was still alive...as far as I can tell. She seemed pretty broken up about his suicide, what she thought was a suicide. I mean, considering the time that had gone by and all."

"I see. Well, thanks. It was nice of you to go to the trouble."

"Not that it will help her now, I mean, I uh...hey, I also looked up real-estate records. Found a Mrs. Barbon who sold her Brooklyn house that year. Don't know for sure it's the same one, but I got an address in Louisiana where the owner of the Brooklyn property could be reached. It's not current, of course. A lot can happen in twenty years, but I thought Mabel, uh, Mrs. Fleish, would...I guess you don't care—"

"No, actually, I mean, thanks and all for your help, for my wife, but I don't like to tie up the line."

"Sure, of course. Listen, I don't know what I can do, but if there's anything. I mean, I didn't know her—"

"Don't."

"Don't?"

"Don't. Not didn't, if you don't mind."

"Oh, I see, sure, I'm sorry. I didn't mean...just, I want to help. Is it okay if I keep in touch?"

"Sure." The man sighed. "I'll take whatever help I can get."

When Kwestral hung up he was shaken. He pressed the tips of his fingers against the table, looked at the pinkening tips. Terrible images played in his mind. He kept pushing them away, they kept coming back. *Row, row.* The muscles in his arms clenched, released, clenched. He longed to feel the hard poles in his hands, something he could squeeze that would take his pain, convert it to sweat.

He listened to himself breathing shallowly, forced himself to deepen each inhalation as if he were smoking air. He looked at his watch. Monday night. The gym was open late on Mondays. He grabbed his bag, ran down the steps, headed out the door.

"And where do you suppose you're off to?" his mother called.

Herm slowed but didn't stop. "I'll be home early."

"What about your assignment?" she asked as if it were something for school.

"I'm working on it, Ma. I need to clear my head." He met her, will to will. *I'm not a child,* he wanted to cry.

"Instead of the table. Listen to me, Mister. I declare sometimes you act like you're as mad as sin, and I'm not about to—"

"Ma!" His voice cracked, as if he were still fifteen. He turned, let the door slam behind him, hurried down the path, ran down the path, not stopping to turn on the Sure-Lock Homes alarm his father had had installed before his death.

"Remember, son," his father had said, showing him how to turn the key, "you must put it on every time you go out. Mother's a defenseless woman without us there to protect her." *She can lock it herself,* Herm now thought, slowing down. He saw his father's visor in its box, gleaming a sharp reprimand. He saw images from Mabel's book, his mother at their center. He turned around, went back up the path. Found the key, inserted it in the lock that safeguarded the house. He twisted, pulled. *Okay, Dad?* The lock was resistant to turning as he worked it. *I'll oil it tomorrow,* he promised. He pinched the mechanism, making his fingertips hurt before letting go.

Kwestral was filled with déjà vu, sitting at the rowing machine again after such a short time. It felt like something prescient, something from a dream, only he couldn't remember what came next.

Reaching through dream space he leaned and pulled, forcing himself to pick up speed. He cut through the thickness of dream with the blades of his hands, driving all thoughts from his mind except rowing. He was a soft machine, a sweating piston. He made himself over into the image of a mechanism, rowing harder than he ever had in his life. As if the mere expenditure of energy could save her.

Merrily merrily, squeaked the seat of his little toy boat. And the thought popped into his mind unbidden: Why would a woman want to investigate a death that had happened twenty years ago right before her own disappearance? *To get to the other side?* asked the comic in his soul.

There's a story here, he thought. He felt like a vulture picking through dead meat, but he couldn't help turning over the possibilities. A woman writes a mystery novel, then disappears mysteriously, as if from the pages of her own book. The setup cried for a writer, but was it a novelist or an investigative reporter? He saw himself pursuing the story, writing the book, though he still wasn't sure if the account would be fiction or non-. He saw himself heaped with praise. Then felt himself heaped with shit.

Mabel Fleish was a woman, a real woman in trouble, he told himself. And he would reduce her to a setup, a character. He really did want to help her, he protested to himself. His motives were honorable, as honorable as his father's maybe, who still might have been thinking of a detective's badge when he went to help that prostitute held at gunpoint. If Herm got a book out of Mabel's plight, she wouldn't begrudge him that. Not at the expense of her life. After all, she was a writer. She knew one's life was one's material. And she knew she was a character, too. She acted a part, the woman escaped from the pages of a mystery. Played herself that way, as caught in an image as her own reflection in a glass. Some writers dangled cigarettes from their lips, some held drinks in their hands (or wore hats on their heads, Herm thought with a blush). She was the type who felt she had no substance without portraying herself as strange sex.

He tried to recapture his sense of her. The sparkle in her eye—complicity? The half smile that seemed to say, "I *am* Mystery. Enter me." And he wanted to, he wanted to now more than ever. For it seemed to him he had just learned what mystery was. A woman who disappeared. A woman who asked questions, set tasks, and vanished. A woman whose love had to be earned. A woman from a dream.

Machines don't dream. Machines don't get tired, don't sweat, don't chafe. And a time came when Kwestral did all those things and could do no more. He put his head down, let go of the oars, feeling the blisters on his hands with relief. He breathed deeply, taking in the stink that was life. He dreamed of a woman from a mystery novel. A woman who disappeared.

TWENTY-FIVE

Dr. Wutzl didn't know what to do with himself. From hour to hour he sat in a chair, looking at the table. His hands hung at his sides, as if they'd been cut off a corpse and sewn on his sleeves. His legs were carved posts stuck inside his pants. They obeyed his commands, carrying him wherever he wished to go, but as he wished to go no place, they waited like twin butlers with nothing to do. When he looked in the mirror the face that looked back seemed a mask. Instead of a wolf it was now Father Time. Tick tick tick. Minutes passed, hours passed, days passed, and still no word. He felt useless, tired, he couldn't sleep. His earlier fantasies of Mabel haunted him. He worried that they might indeed be happening to her, that he had caused them to happen. Like a father obsessed with his daughter's sexuality the repulsive images assaulted his imagination.

He ate without tasting the excellent meals his wife prepared. Could hardly bring himself to swallow more than a bite of cake, and even that had the texture of ash. When he found he could button his vest to the bottom the discovery brought no pleasure. English Romantics had nothing to say, poets and essayists could not comfort him. The only thing he looked forward to each morning was getting to the school at half past nine. He parked himself outside Furnival's office, waiting. "Any news?" he asked. "Nothing," said Furnival.

Day after day.

"Why are you worrying yourself sick over that girl?" Mrs. Wutzl asked. "She probably ran away with the milkman. You know the type. There are stories in the paper all the time about—"

"I won't have you talk that way," Dr. Wutzl said. "She's a gifted writer, a lovely person. I just know in my bones she's in trouble. Don't you have any compassion, Ethel, any womanly concern for one of your own sex?"

"Hmph," said Mrs. Wutzl. "We are certainly not of the same sex, Rufus, and if you think we are, that shows how much you know." She turned on her heel, leaving a confused Dr. Wutzl staring after her.

Almost a week after Mabel's disappearance the English department of Jones College was buzzing with the news. The police had questioned not only the immediate family but Rufus and Ethel Wutzl (she had told them what *she* thought, and they found it very interesting), Horace Byrrd (his alibi was watertight, his landlady backed him up), Iris Specter, other members of the faculty and student body. The police seemed to agree that, given Mabel's well-documented history of marital infidelity, it was likely she had gone on a fling.

"But she wouldn't do that," Furnival said to Dr. Wutzl. The pair sat in Percy's office, commiserating. "I told the detective she's never left me before. She wouldn't do that to Ana. She was, *is* a very good mother. Her infidelities, look, I won't pretend not to know about them, but they were hour-long assignations, never anything like this. It's been four days without a word."

"Unfaithful? Mabel? I never heard anything so absurd. There, there, lad. I know how you feel, believe me, I know," said Dr. Wutzl. "And what did the detective say?"

Percy picked his cold pipe from the ashtray, sucked it though it was out. "The man's an imbecile. Tried to out-professor me, all dressed in tweeds, wearing ridiculous dark sunglasses. What was most offensive was his boredom. He acted so sick of the whole thing, as if he's been through this a thousand times and Mabel's case is no different than the rest. I'd take the investigation into my own hands, but what can I do? Grinn, that's the man's name. Detective Sergeant Grinn. He shook his head and said, 'The letter you showed us is being analyzed. The one you told us about is too.'"

"What's this?" asked Dr. Wutzl. "Have you received letters?"

"I mentioned them to you, didn't I—how Mabel kept telling me she was getting notes and phone calls from a man calling himself Bone? Oh, why didn't I listen to her? I was deaf. I was blind."

"You didn't know, lad, you couldn't help it. So what did the detective say then?"

"He had the nerve, the audacity, to quote me to myself—getting my meaning all skewed."

Dr. Wutzl looked at his hand, wondering how it had come to rest palm up on his thigh. "What did he say?"

"What? Oh yes. Something like, 'As you said, Professor'—he has this way of saying 'Professor' that is both obsequious and sarcastic. 'As you said, Professor,' he says, 'your wife could have written those notes herself. You told us she had a history of mental breakdown. Perhaps it's that. Or she may have written those notes to make it look like she was abducted so she could go off for a few weeks with a lover. You never know with an unstable character.'"

"Did he really? What did you say?"

"I said, 'Don't call her an unstable character. This is my wife we're talking about. She had a nervous breakdown years ago, after our daughter accidentally killed our son. Do you blame her? Can you imagine what that was like?'"

"Good for you, lad. The police need to learn respect."

"That's nothing. He said, 'Hold on there, Professor. I'm just repeating what you told me.' Imagine! 'There's no reason to lash out at me. We're doing what we can.' I almost leaped out of my chair to strangle him. Then the strangest thing, Dr. Wutzl. A cold detachment came over me. I looked at him and said, 'The man is just doing a job. If I want to find Mabel I will have to find her myself.' I feel like, I don't know, you might laugh but I feel like a literary detective. How to explain? It's as if there are clues right under my nose. I sense them all around me, but I can't find them. I'm rereading *Bone*, looking there first. You've read it, haven't you?"

"Well, uh, yes. When it first came out. Different from what I'm accustomed to—Romantic poets, you know—but I thought it excellent. Someday when I've time I shall read it again."

"And then there are the notes Mabel showed me. There's the one I found, of course, the night, the night I came home and she, that is, Halloween. But there were others. She must have saved them. She saves everything. I'll find them. They're the best clues."

Dr. Wutzl sat back, all but unaware of how his feelings had changed. He looked out the window. Students were milling about, heading to class. Poor Furnival, he thought. If Felix had lived he might have been like him, brilliant theorist and all. And Mabel, why, she was like a daughter. He couldn't be more upset if they were both his flesh and blood. His concern was fatherly, all the more tragic because he was not in fact next-of-kin.

Percy put his pipe in the ashtray. "So that's it, Dr. Wutzl," he said. "I told the detective to call if anything came up, anything at all. He told me to carry on with my life. 'It may take a while before we have something to go on. A long while.' I saw Harvey the other day—was it only yesterday? Hard to believe it's only been a day. Anyway he offered me time off. Nice of him. I don't think I shall take it though. I need to keep busy."

"I believe that's wise," said Dr. Wutzl. "Work is what you need, and plenty of it. Bury yourself in it. Oh, and by the way, I've been meaning to ask you, Mrs. Wutzl and I would be pleased if you would come to dinner. With Ana, of course. Mrs. Wutzl is an excellent cook. There's no reason to sit alone, worrying."

"That's very kind, but I don't think.... I want to be by the phone, in case, you know, in case..."

"Oh yes. How stupid of me. Some other time then. Well, if there's anything I can do..."

"Thank you. Just talking to you has been a great help."

Dr. Wutzl walked back to his office. He sat at his desk. The noon bell rang but he didn't hear it. He was stimulated by his discussion with Furnival. He took out a leatherbound book he had bought for his memoirs. The first page was still blank. He wrote the date in his most flowery script, resisting the urge to fill in the vowels. He wanted to try something different from the academic prose for which he was famous. In the past months he'd written a bit of poetry, and now he thought he'd try his hand at a personal narrative. He had such deep feelings about Mabel Fleish's disappearance, her husband's heartbreaking search.

In the center of the page he penned the words "The Case of the Missing Author by Doctor Rufus Wutzl, Ph.D." The letters were scratchy. His fountain pen was running dry.

"Percival Furnival," he wrote, "literary detective, sat in his office, mulling over the notes of his latest investi—"

The telephone rang, startling the good doctor from his task. "Damn," he said. "Hello? Who is it?"

"It's me, Woofy. I was just—"

"Me? How many times have I told you, Ethel? It is I. *I*, do you hear me? A reflective object takes a subjective pronoun. It's not fitting for a college professor's wife, a distinguished professor emeritus, I might add, to use ungrammatical—"

"Oh pooh. I just called to find out what happened to you. Lunch is waiting. I was worried."

"I won't be home for luncheon. I'm sorry. I'm busy here at the office." He heard a sniffle. "Oh, don't carry on. I am at the end of my rope. I'm hanging up."

"Rufus, don't!" screamed Mrs. Wutzl. "I know how upset you are about this Mabel Fleish thing, but it's not worth killing—"

"What? What are you talking about?"

"I thought you said you were hanging at the end of a rope?"

"Oh balderdash and consternation. Well, my inspiration is gone now. I may as well come home and eat. I'll see you shortly."

"Yes, dear," said Ethel. "You won't be sorry. I made a lovely veal stew with juicy marrow bones. I know how you love to suck the marrow from the bone so I—"

Rufus Wutzl hung up the receiver, inserted his hands into the sleeves of his coat. He watched them lock the journal in his desk drawer. On his way to the stairwell his legs took him past Furnival's office. His head poked in, just for a moment, to see if there was any news. The young fellow was deep in thought, flexing his fingers, apparently oblivious to Dr. Wutzl, who turned to leave.

"Have a good lunch, Dr. Wutzl," Furnival said suddenly.

"Oh, Furnival my lad, I didn't know you saw me."

"I see everything," Percy Furnival said, "but I must learn to see past it all to the obvious."

TWENTY-SIX

"Who would ride her?" The poem jangled in Percy's mind. He recited it while driving to the college, dreamed about it at night. He tried to find a hidden subtext to the words, as if they could stand for other meanings. Like an insidious commercial heard from a passing radio the poem went around in his brain. If for a moment he forgot, he was conscious of having forgotten. *What was I thinking about? Oh yeah. Would he knife her? Might be should."*

It was early November. Percy could smell snow in the air but none had fallen. It smelled meaty. Like the deer that time he went hunting with Jon and Howard. He remembered the animal so clearly it was like a photograph of someone he knew—a woman crouching down, baring her behind to take a piss in the woods, turning, seeing the camera aimed at her, her surprise caught as she was shot. The terror in those large womanly brown eyes, the tensing of her haunches. Flying into the air, bounding off, and part of him crying, "Run, get out of here," and the other part crying, "Give it to her." Stumbling, running ahead, heavy in her meat but still moving. Jon yahooed. "What a shot!" The men ran forward, following the blood. The smell of the blood. Excitement pounding through him. They followed the red snow. Bright at first, turning muddy as they tracked her. And there she was, lying down. They came with their knives, hacked her through—too heavy to carry out any way except in pieces, they said, but Percy wondered if killing a doe was a crime. The thrill, the heat of her blood. He would never do it again. Like violent sex it pulsed dirty long after.

Mabel had been missing for almost a week. Everyone thought there was hope if it didn't snow. Percy didn't know why—maybe they were hoping for different things. A body would suffice for some; he wanted to find her soul.

Despite his resistance to it life was resuming its rhythm. Meals had to be shopped for, cooked, eaten; classes taught. Laundry piled up, mail arrived each day. He and Ana were wary around each other, as if the slightest remark could touch off tears. The girl asked surprisingly few questions. Percy almost wished she would say something, get it out—it couldn't be good, holding everything inside. But he was holding everything inside too, and mutual reticence made it just a bit easier for him.

People spoke to him, he answered. Sometimes he laughed. His laughter had an edge to it. On the other side was hysteria. The worst moments came when, in the middle of talking, teaching, eating, he had to stop to ask what was wrong. He remembered instantly—it was only for a second that he forgot, but he could never forgive himself that second.

People were kind till he couldn't stand it. Gigglers hushed when he passed, as if he were a hearse. Mabel was in the middle of every conversation, not mentioned but palpable. Everyone was uncomfortable around him. Except Dr. Wutzl. The old man was proving to have qualities Percy had never before noticed. He wasn't afraid to listen. He heard what Percy had to say without denying it. "Nonsense," Dean Hook, Phyllis Blostein, Harvy Green had said in chorus when Percy, early on, made the gaffe of mentioning his fears. "Mabel's fine." But Dr. Wutzl had nodded and taken in Percy's words.

He had a way of showing concern that didn't offend. His interest was not that of gossips who presented Percy daily with their thoughtfulness: Have dinner with us, how's your lovely daughter?—all the while noting what to tsk later. It was clear the old man felt paternal toward him and Mabel. A good-natured, gentle soul, he didn't mind if Percy repeated himself, going over the same ground yet again. He was always willing to listen to the distraught husband's latest theories.

"What do you make of this, Dr. Wutzl?" Percy said that afternoon as the pair sat in the older professor's office. He took out of his wallet a copy of the poem he'd found Halloween night. He had mentioned it to Dr. Wutzl but hadn't yet shown it to anyone but the police.

Dr. Wutzl read it, put it down on his desk. "Chilling," he said.

"Especially the way the final question goes unanswered."

Percy nodded. "Yes, there's something, I don't know. A queer power to it. Not just circumstantial, though the fact of her disappearance adds to its effect. And Bone's signature on the other letter, as if a character from a novel could take on independent life." Percy rubbed his head, then left his hands buried in his hair. "If only I could answer its question with anything but Horace Byrrd. I've been over it again and again, and yet Byrrd says he was home, that he left the party, met Mabel in the woods, she turned him down, so disgruntled he went home. The police have searched his place, the woods, his car. Nothing. He *was* home when Mabel got back to the party. At least his landlady says she met him, she showed him all the broken eggs trick-or-treaters had thrown on the steps. You gave her a ride back...oh, I don't know. I'm going crazy, rehashing the same old stuff."

He smoothed the plush of his chair. "It's more than just the poem," he went on. "I sense there are clues all around. Especially in her novel, do you know what I mean? I'm reading *Bone* again. With a magnifying glass, so to speak. Trying to see beyond plot, beyond what others have said. It's damn hard to see it fresh when that pack of critics has been through it, muddying the tracks with theories. How am I supposed to find what I'm looking for? They've stepped on all the bits of evidence, explained them away. I'm seeking oddities, Dr. Wutzl. Dead ends that stand out as discrepancies. That's where she's hiding. I sense it strongly. Illogic, my dear Dr. Wutzl, is the road I must take."

He waved his finger in the air, then clenched his fist. "But when I suggested such an approach to Grinn—you know, the detective on the case—he looked at me as if I were mad." Percy shook his head. "Or trying to sell him Mabel's book."

"Well, madness *is* where illogic leads," Dr. Wutzl said.

"Touché," said Percy, mirthlessly.

Wutzl took out his pipe and tobacco, offered the younger man his pouch. The pair filled their bowls and tamped. "My boy," said Dr. Wutzl, "the police can study tire prints without you. Your field of expertise is literature. That is where you must look."

"I'm glad someone understands that. The police act as if I'm crazy, obsessed with a woman who happens to be my wife."

"Pah! What nonsense. Don't they know, 'The proper study of mankind is woman'?"

"Man."

"Pardon?"

"'The proper study of mankind is man.'"

"Well now," said Dr. Wutzl, "what's proper about that?"

Percy was beginning to see Dr. Wutzl as the father he'd never had. His own father died when he was in high school, but Hannah had stood between them long before that. Now Hannah was dead, and Rufus Wutzl's bulbous head with its abundance of white hair inserted itself in the few memories Percy had of his father.

Once, he recalled, his father came home from the deli where he stood all day slicing pastrami and gave him a candy bar. "Shhh," he whispered. "Don't let Mama know. Save, for after dinner." He grinned just like Dr. Wutzl after he had finished a piece of rhubarb pie. At the time young Percy thought only that his father was a coward. Which he was. But he was also kind.

A Russian immigrant much older than his wife, Sol Finklestein had let Hannah Furnival have her way in most things, even in giving the boy her last name. "Just remember you have me to thank you're not Percival Finklestein," she said often to her son. "He ruled me. Hid his papers from me, wouldn't let me read his will. We're struggling now because of him." Death was the old man's fault too. Percy nodded. It was easier to give in than to hear Hannah's tape go around and around: "What? You didn't think he ruled me? What? You didn't see how he hid his papers, locked them in the drawer? I didn't have a decent dress to my name. You'd be Percival Finklestein if it was up to him. You have me to thank..." Percy nodded, opened a book. He had learned to read and have a conversation with his mother at the same time.

"Daddy, didn't you hear me?" Percy's eyes focused on his daughter, standing with her hands on her hips.

"I'm sorry, darling. I was daydreaming. What did you say?"

"You're getting to be as bad as Mommy."

Percy frowned. "I have things on my mind. What is it?"

"Nothing," Ana said. "Maybe the only way to get attention around here is to disappear."

"Don't you say such a thing." He lifted his hand but stopped short of slapping her. The girl began to sob. "I'm sorry, honey," he said, taking her on his lap. "It's okay. Shhh. Don't cry."

"Oh, Daddy," she said. "Why won't she come home?"

He pushed the hair back from her face. "She wants to, Ana. You know how much she loves you."

The girl sniffled into her father's neck. He put his arms around her. Her bones were thin as a sparrow's. He wished he could save her, from everything. He wished he could stand guard before her consciousness and fight off all her dragons.

She raised her head, looked him in the eye. "Do you believe in wishes, Daddy?" she asked.

"Yes, honey. I do." He tried to smile.

"So do I, Daddy." She cried harder than before. "I remember how Mommy always saved the wishbone for me. She cleaned it, let it dry, gave it to me to make a wish. And if Pammy wouldn't make a wish with me Mommy would. 'Think hard, Ana,' she said. 'Make a good wish. Make sure it's a wish you want to come true. Sometimes the worst thing about wishes is when they come true.' Oh, Daddy, do you think I made a bad wish? Maybe by accident I wished she'd leave me alone and—"

"Shhh, honey. I'm sure you didn't. Mommy didn't mean that. Nothing you wished for made this happen." Percy tried to comfort his daughter, wondering what in the world Mabel had in mind, telling the child such a thing. "Oh, sweetie, don't cry. Say, how'd you like a new outfit for your Barbie? Or a new Ken?"

"No!" she yelled. Percy stared. Ana lowered her voice. "Who's got time for dolls anymore?" she asked. "What with all that's happened I hardly get to finish my homework."

"I know," Percy said. "I just thought. Maybe you, would you like to see Dr. Xavier, talk things out..."

"Oh, Dr. Xavier! Who's Dr. Xavier, a god?" She pushed away. Percy, surprised at how much she sounded like her mother, became lost in one of the blanks of time he kept falling into of late. When he regained consciousness of his surroundings he found he was setting the table and his daughter was upstairs.

The mail kept piling up on Mabel's desk. Some days after her disappearance a box of slides had arrived. Days after that Percy still hadn't opened it. On their last hike, Mabel remarked they had finally finished the roll of film that had been in the camera a year. "Remember when we first met, how we used to take pictures all the time? We were each other's child." Ana walked between them on the trail, her head cast down. Percy didn't answer. "Is it that we trust memory more now," Mabel asked, "or that we care less?"

"Oh Mabel," he wished he had told her. "I never cared less."

He was alone in the house. It was after three but already getting dark. Ana had band practice and wouldn't be home till five. Percy sat in the gloom, near Mabel's desk. He was sinking into a black mood and knew what the consequence would be. He had not smoked pot or done coke since Halloween. He'd hardly drunk a beer. He had to be ready in case she, or someone, called. But now, alone in the November dusk, he heard his stash calling from the basement freezer. Its voice was high and tinkly at first, gay as a scotch on the rocks.

A drink wouldn't be so bad, he thought. Not as bad as a joint. Or a line. He looked at the white refrigerator, gleaming like a tooth next to the cellar door. "No, I can't," he said.

The cold voice became a whistle. *Perrrrssseeeee.* He licked his lips. Snow—there wasn't much, it didn't take much. He was frugal; things could become crystalline with just a few flakes. A touch on his gums, he thought, and his mind would turn to ice. He might see Mabel in its frozen mirror.

Perrrrssseeeee—the invitation of snow offered a taste. He got up, walked into the kitchen. Touched the cellar door. The voice filled his head with promises: cold clarity, numb vision. He could think clearly, if the pain would just stop. He would find her, if he could just think.

He took his hand from the knob. Opened the kitchen freezer instead, put ice in a glass. Ran water in the sink, filled the tumbler. Sipped water, kissed the glass. It numbed his lips. He rubbed them with his finger till they burned. Kissed the cold glass again. Again.

Water dripped from the tap. Hannah, he thought. Each splat had her voice. "You are a failure," she said. "Your wife ran away."

"She didn't," he told the sink. "I wish she had. It would be better than this, don't you see?" He put his hand under the drip. If Hannah were alive would she cry? She had loved Mabel...as much as she could love anyone. The water was cold. Too cold for tears.

Hannah was a snow queen. She couldn't help it. When she tried to be warm it was worse. She squeezed Percy's shoulder. His neck ached for a week. She kissed Percy's cheek. He had to wrench his head free of her. She held his face to hers, her nails poked him, her fingers mushed his lips. "My boy," she said. Her eyes glittered with pride. They both knew she was acting.

Percy opened the refrigerator—empty. In the freezer—nothing but cubes. Downstairs, the freezer was well-stocked. He shut the door. Dr. Xavier said Hannah force-fed him. Was it true? Percy asked her once. She denied it. Then why did he always feel stuffed? *Ungershtuft,* his father used to say. He almost recalled pinched nostrils, gasping for air. Food in a mouth struggling to breathe. Gagging. Was this memory or imagination? "Don't make a mess," she'd yell. Percy was a fastidious man. His desk was orderly, his pencils sharp. The mail on Mabel's desk was neatly stacked.

Perrrrsssseee. The voice came up from the floor boards. A tiny voice in a vial, wrapped in foil, hidden in a white box in the basement, buried beneath ice cream and frozen deer meat, his share of the kill...untouched.

"Percy!" The snow queen stamped a foot as tiny as a flake. He took an ice cube from his glass, put it to his temple, to his lips. He sucked moisture as if from a stone. He did not put the whole cube in his mouth. Water dripped from his fingers. His lips chattered. He opened his shirt. Lowered the setting on the thermostat. Licked the cube and thought of his wife.

He carried his glass to Mabel's desk. The slides caught his eye. He spit the ice cube into his glass but didn't open the box. He put it in front of him. In the basement, a box of frozen meat. On the desk, a box of frozen time. He laughed, thinking how his house was a box, each room was a box, how he sat above a box, beside a box, looking at a box, trying not to think of his mother in a box, his wife in a bag. He put his hands to his face, rubbed it hard as if to erase it. Six days. Not even a week. What had he brooded about before? His career, his brilliant theories? Waste of time, locking himself away in the dark, indulging his melancholy, away from Mabel. How horrible his moods must have seemed to her. Even Anubis knew to avoid him then.

"Nubi," he called. The white ghost pattered over. Percy buried his hand in his fur. The dog tried to pull away. *My hand must feel like death,* Percy thought, holding the animal to him, patting his side, forcing him to lean against his shins. Anubis whined. "Don't be a baby," Percy said. The dog's hindquarters trembled. "Okay, go, you coward. Go!" He stopped petting him. Nubi returned to his spot by the radiator. Percy went to the kitchen, raised the setting on the thermostat, rinsed his glass. When he returned to the desk the dog was sleeping.

He tore open the plastic wrapping of the slide box. The loupe was in the top drawer. He turned on the lamp, held the first photo to the magnifying lens, placed it to his eye. A tall flame-headed woman smiled. Pink and white laurel. It was spring.

As painful as he expected. Percy took the shade off the lamp, used the naked bulb to shine through their merriment. That was the day they picnicked on Mount Weinberger. How much younger Ana looked. Just a few months ago, but she had more baby fat, less height. He hurried past closeups of flowers, shadows on rocks, till he came to a photo of him and Mabel kissing, Ana in front. He remembered how he put the camera on a boulder, set the timer, ran to take his place. Thinking back, he smiled.

He squeezed his mouth till he unmolded its grin. Glanced at shots of moss, of stumps, of mushrooms. There was a photo of Candle Falls. Ana must have taken it. He was laughing at a joke he couldn't remember. Mabel was telling Ana something. She was pointing, her lips scrunched in an *ooo* sound. You? Was she saying "you" to Ana? Percy listened hard, trying to hear. You need to check the light meter? You have to wind the film? You mustn't, you should?

He continued through the box. How quickly the seasons passed. Summer now. Murr Lake was turquoise. The birches were naked women, green-haired and graceful. People wore bathing suits. Mabel in her bikini didn't look like someone's mother. Percy swallowed hard. The thought of her, the taste and smell and feel of her. Other imaginings clashed against his longing. Of flesh not so round, of bones shining through.

Why was he doing this to himself? He put down the loupe. What earthly good was it to look at what might be the last pictures of Mabel alive? *Perrrrsssseee*, called the voice in the basement. He ignored it, picked up the loupe.

Autumn—already? What had happened to the rest of summer? He felt cheated. What about the time they drove all the way to the beach? There were jellyfish, he didn't want to get salt and sand in the camera. And the time in the Adirondacks when they camped for two weeks? The island where they pitched their tent was in the center of a lake, it rained and rained. The lake was beautiful but the canoe was always wet. The camera stayed in a waterproof bag.

As the pile of unviewed slides dwindled he grew to despise the shots of flowers that would bloom each year, stalks, mountains, clouds, lakes. There were so few pictures of Mabel. Gone, and there would be no more. "No," he said aloud. "She'll come back. We'll take pictures every moment. I swear. I'll invest in Kodak." He laughed humorlessly. "I can take it," he said, looking at autumn, and it seemed as if he were making a vow. "I can look at these pictures. Our wedding. Our honeymoon. The times she was pregnant. When Ana was first born. Seth nursing. I can take anything only please, please if she's okay, I..."

He refused to weep. He turned to the next slide. Ana and Mabel eating apples. He tasted the tartness. Smelled apples in Mabel's hair. Her lips were red. He knew they were chapped, but she looked beautiful, laughing, always laughing. The cool mountain air, the bright sunlight. She and Ana, she and Percy, laughing. What was so funny, what could possibly have been so funny that they laughed and laughed? Their joy mocked him. Was it really so much fun, eating apples? Leaves were falling everywhere, gorgeously dead, the family oblivious to their hidden meaning. Now he was angry, he had never been so angry. He wanted to slap her, to slap all of them. Especially himself. What right had they to laugh, to be so happy, so stupidly unaware? It couldn't have been more than a week or two later...

His hands shook as he held the next-to-last photo. Mabel was not in it. He was disappointed, almost put it down without seeing, but he had an eerie sense of recognition. He looked again. A house, a shack really. Made of stone, crudely, as if by an eccentric. A hermit's hovel in the woods? It looked almost like those tiny roofed houses people put over wells. The angles were off, dry stalks poked out of the dirt between the rocks. Percy rubbed his temples, looked at the photo again. Again, déjà vu.

Where had he seen this house? He didn't remember driving up the dirt road he could make out to one side. He didn't remember the day, a gray day. Patches of snow—it hadn't snowed yet this year. He took his eye from the loupe, trying to think.

He looked at the number on the slide's frame. One. The next— also of the house—was two. They must have fallen out of sequence. These pictures were taken last winter. Or very early in the spring. He tried to remember. Had he and Mabel hiked somewhere, found the strange house, taken pictures of it? He couldn't recall. No, she must have been alone, but if so, why did it seem familiar?

He went to the glass cabinet where he kept his inscribed copy of

Bone. Mabel had scrawled on the first page, "Percy, my brother, my spouse. 'Marry and you get a best friend for life.' For once my mother was right." He turned quickly to the chapter where Anna was taken to Bone's house, a page near the middle of the book. "The walls angled oddly, and there were weeds growing between the stones. It was tiny, as if a troll might live in it. Bone made her duck down to squeeze through the door."

Percy held his breath. Hackles rose on his neck. This was it. The house in the photograph was the house in *Bone.* A place Mabel had been.

"So what?" he said a moment later. "It doesn't mean anything." But he couldn't rid himself of the notion that if he found this house he would find Mabel. He shook his head at the illogic of the thought. Then wondered if it were illogical enough. The place was real. Mabel, like Anna, was missing. Someone calling himself Bone had threatened her. If the place was real this Bone person might know about it. A madman might feel compelled to act out a sick fantasy in such a place.

Percy got up, sat down. "I'm losing my mind," he said. "I'm mixing up fantasy and reality, thinking someone else would too." After all, he knew that Mabel's fiction often had a rundown house or a deserted barn in it. She herself joked about her gothic imagination. Abandoned ruins figured strongly among her im-ages—representing the emptiness of her childhood, he'd always thought.

He took out the slide projector and put the two slides in a tray, projecting them one at a time on the wall over the couch. The second slide had a shadow reaching toward him on the right. The more he looked at it the more certain he became it was the shadow of a man. Percy stood to the side of the projection, trying to peer around the corner of the house. He was sure now that the shadow belonged to the man who had stolen his wife. He knew it with the illogic of genius. A man who called himself Bone was Bone. There was Bone's shadow, there was Bone's house.

Percy put on his coat, went to his car. He had a plan. He would drive around till he found Bone's house. He would free Mabel, murder Bone. No court would send him to prison for killing his wife's abductor. He and Mabel and Ana would live happily ever after. He did not think how Ana would come home soon to find an an unlatched door, an empty house, a strange ruin projected on the wall, an open box of slides with the most recent pictures of her mother. He was sitting in the car, waiting for the engine to warm up, when he remembered. He shut the engine. "I should call Dr. Xavier," he said. "Something is wrong with me. Something is very very wrong."

He came inside, turned off the projector lamp, let the fan blow to cool the bulb. He took the two slides from the tray, put them in the box, went to hide it in Mabel's bottom drawer, under a pile of paper. That's when he found the buried folder. He took it out, opened it quickly. In it were letters. His heart drummed when he saw they were from Bone. The first said, "Mthr, dghtr, sistr, wfe: I'll git you back if it takes yr life. You had no rt to rt such lies. I'll cut the truth betwxt yr thighs—Bone."

"Mabel, please be all right," Percy whispered. "I'll find you. Just hold on. I swear I'll find you." He glanced at the clock. It was 4:45. He had to read quickly, before Ana came home. The next envelope bore a *BB* in the upper left corner, just as the notes from Bone did. It was signed Beau and was a sophomoric love letter threatening death if "Maybelline" weren't true to him.

Percy used the loupe to magnify the *BB* in the corner of Beau's letter and on one of the Bone envelopes. He looked at the shapes, where the pen was pushed hard, how the periods were made. One had been written with a ballpoint, the other with a fountain pen. It didn't seem to be the same writing, but twenty years...

He started to read a newspaper article about a boy's death in an abandoned house when he heard Ana on the path. Quickly he hid the folder in Mabel's drawer, along with the slides. He would show Detective Grinn the slides and letters the next morning. At last there were clues.

TWENTY-SEVEN

Ana put down her trombone, hung up her coat. She said hello to her father. He was busy looking through the mail and hardly returned her greeting. She went upstairs.

Barbie was weeping in the crib from which Tootsy Wootsy had been evicted. "There, there," Ana said. "Shhh, honey. Don't cry. Are you cold?" Barbie nodded. Ana put a sweater on her. She wrapped her in a doll blanket, kissed her again, lay her down to sleep. The blanket covered her from head to toe till she looked like a flannel mummy. "You'll be okay now," Ana said. "Mommy loves you. Mommy wishes only good things for you."

"I love you, Mommy," said the muffled voice. "I love you more than anything," and then she was asleep.

In the other corner of the room grumbled the pink doll case. "Let me out of here," yelled Ken. "You just better get me out of here. You're asking for it and I'm going—"

"Shhh, sweetie," said Ana. "I'm doing this for your own good. Try to get some sleep."

"Sleep! I don't need to sleep. It's dark in here. I can't see. Where's that bitch Barbie? My arms and legs are tied with these damn rubber bands, but if I ever get out of here, I'm—"

Ana covered her ears. She sang a little song. She said a little prayer. "Now I lay me down to sleep."

"I'll lay you all right, you twat—"

"I pray the Lord my soul to keep."

"I'll keep you too, locked up in the dark like you're keeping me. Only I'll take all your clothes, make you—"

"If I die before I wake."

"If! You mean when, don't you?"

"I pray the Lord my soul to take."

Ken's voice became high and mocking. "God bless Mommy, God bless Daddy, God bless all the sweet little children of the world and the president of the United States and you make me sick."

"Shhh, Ken. I'm doing this for your own good." She didn't listen while Ken continued ranting and raving. She sang a song about a tender shepherd who watches over his sheep, while she put the doll case in the back of her closet, setting several pairs of shoes on top of it, closing the door, trying to lay her demons to rest.

Daddy was fixing dinner. He took two chicken pot pies out of the freezer downstairs, put them in the oven. "Daddy?" she asked. He looked up. "I have a question to ask you. I tried to ask you before but, I don't know. It's a serious question, and I need a serious answer."

He was smiling and trying not to. It made his face twisted. "What is it, sweet potato?"

"I have to know the truth. Pammy told me something. About me, about how come I don't have any sisters or brothers. Why I'm an only child. Was it something you wanted or—"

Daddy's face got twisted again. She saw the pain come over it. She heard his secret voice, the one he didn't know she heard. He went to the sink, rinsed his hands. "I'm listening," he said. "I won't lie to you, Ana. Whatever it is, I'll be honest."

Ana bit her nails. "Well, Pammy said something and I don't know if I should believe her, but"—she put something into her pants pocket, quickly calculating the risk of her question, the value of its answer—"am I adopted?"

Daddy turned quickly. His face untwisted into a bright smile, the first she had seen all week. He opened his arms and she entered them for a hug. "No, honey," he said. "I can honestly say you are not adopted."

"Well," said Ana. "That's a relief." She put her hand to her back pocket, crinkled the picture of herself and the baby, pushing it deeper inside.

TWENTY-EIGHT

The Case of the Missing Authoress
by Rufus Wutzl, Ph.D.

Percival Furnival, literary detective, was sitting in his office, mulling over the notes of his latest investigation when I decided to look in on him. It was the most dastardly crime he had to research, for it was his own wife, the beautiful red-haired novelist Mabel Fleish, who was missing. I was nonplussed to find him closeted with an odd pair: a middle-aged man in sunglasses and tweed jacket, eating an ice-cream cone, and a young albino, head buried in a book, scribbling notes. "I'm so sorry," I said. "I see you're busy—"

"Not at all," Furnival said. "I'm glad you came. I'd like you to hear what Detective Sergeant Grinn has to say. And this is Herm Kwestral, a reporter for *The Brooklyn Wing* who has taken an interest in the case. You can talk freely in front of Dr. Wutzl, Detective. As a matter of fact you may find it interesting to know that he is the husband of the aforementioned woman you—"

"Eh? What's this?" I asked.

Grinn licked his mint ice cream in a most offensive manner. There was something rather cowlike about the way he coated his tongue with the green substance. All the while he watched me closely through his glasses. They were the darkest lenses I'd ever seen, and the effect was of gigantic, all-seeing, eyes. He took a long pull of frozen cream. "I interviewed your wife Friday," he shot at me.

"Ethel? Are you sure?" I was surprised to hear this. "A police-man stopped by the house when Mabel first vanished. He spoke to both of us. Is that what you mean?" The detective shook his head, proceeded licking and not talking till I broke the wet silence. "Why would you want to talk to Ethel?"

"Why indeed?" He bit off the tip of his cone, sucked the remains of the scoop out the bottom.

"Well, uh, I'm sure I don't know." And indeed I didn't, although I admit I felt mildly discomfited to think of the things she might have said. Ethel can be an unreasonably jealous woman, and is furthermore inclined to judge people by her own unscalably high standards. "My wife hardly knows the woman in question," I said. "I suppose you must talk to a lot of people, although I wouldn't think you'd need to question her twice."

He popped the last bit of cone into his mouth, wiped his hands on his pants, and assumed a professorial attitude as he studied me. "Have you known your wife to frequent a certain Miranda Bookstore?"

"Well, uh, yes. Upon occasion. They have an esoterica section that she...excuse me, Furnival, what is this about? Do you know what he's driving at?"

"Allow me, Detective. Dr. Wutzl is somewhat confused by the goings-on here. It seems, my dear friend, your wife has been telling everyone about a certain unsavory fellow who bought all the copies of Mabel's book just before her disappearance. He even asked for more copies. The police want a description of this man, but your wife can recall neither his appearance nor the exact date of the occurrence."

"That figures."

"The cashier, a student I believe you know, Iris Specter? Unfortunately she can't quite remember the event, although she thinks maybe she does. Anyway, the police want like to locate this avid reader."

"I hardly think buying your wife's book makes him a likely suspect. There is a right to privacy. It seems odd to me."

"Exactly," interjected Grinn. He took out a leather-covered notepad and flipped pages. "Ah, here it is. '11/6—Mrs. Wutzl says Fleish is a well-known tramp.'" He looked up a moment. "Excuse me, Professor. I'm quoting. In summary she accuses your wife of having written a trashy novel to attract a trashy type, and says that if she didn't actually run away, then she's getting what she wants anyway."

Furnival's face didn't betray emotion. He maintained a stoical silence, but I could not. "Ethel said what?" I exploded. "I'm sure she didn't say that. You misunderstood. She didn't mean it the way you've taken it." Something suddenly struck me strange about this Grinn fellow; his manner was not at all as I'd imagined a police detective's to be. He snapped his notepad shut, put it in his back pocket. In doing so he revealed the bulge of a revolver in a shoulder holster.

"Watch out. He's going to shoot!" I cried as he pulled a Snickers from his pocket and commenced unwrapping it. He offered Furnival and me a bite. We both declined the inferior chocolate.

I felt a bit of a fool, nonetheless I still had my suspicions. Why hadn't Ethel mentioned this interview with the police to me? I wondered, pondering the mysteries of womankind. For that matter, why had she refrained from telling me about the incident in the bookstore? Faintly a bell rang in the distance, but I could not locate the memory of which it tolled.

I returned from my momentary reverie to attend the words of the young man accompanying Grinn. He was a most peculiar-looking fellow, and so I had averted my eyes from him. I never know quite what to do when confronted by such a person. I mean, to look or not to look is the question. I didn't wish to make him feel self-conscious, and yet not looking, which is how I had decided to respond, called even louder attention to the fact that he was as white as Alice's rabbit. He had long white hair, pink-rimmed eyes, and conveyed the impression that his feet and hands were too big for him. He had been bent over his book, taking notes on all that was going on, like some madly compulsive student in a lecture hall. I had the feeling he was trying to be as unobtrusive as possible; that, in fact, he was trying to disappear behind his notes as down some hole. But now he was speaking. He had a surprisingly low voice. In fact, it didn't sound like his real voice at all, and I felt hackles of suspicion arise anew on my neck.

"—wasn't Beau Barbon, after all. Larry Lazar was the name of the dead boy. I thought it seemed strange—"

"Yeah," Grinn interrupted. "Any idea why your wife would want to know about a death that took place so many years ago?"

"Hold on," I cried out, sure I had found the chink in the so-called officer's armor. "Furnival, I believe this man is an imposter. Allow me to question him, if you will." Percy Furnival turned the case to me with a gesture of his hand. I confronted the so-called detective. "From whom did you get this information about my wife? I mean, how did you know to ask her about the incident?"

Grinn sighed, looked at Furnival, then turned to me. "From my wife," he said, busying himself with taking out his notepad again.

"Aha! I knew it. Furnival, I tell you this man is no more a detective than I am a hot-air balloon. Grinn is a *nom de guerre,* you see, a pseudonym. My wife knows, or knew, a Mrs. Grinn quite well. They are all disciples, I'm ashamed to admit, of a certain Madame Tchernofsky, a well-known charlatan spiritualist who practices table-rapping. You are a liar, 'Detective Grinn,' and I dare say so to your face. I remember quite well my wife telling me that Mrs. Grinn passed away a month ago." I put my hands on my knees and began to rise from my seat.

Grinn turned his black lenses on me. "I'm well aware of my wife's death, sir," he said, staring till I realized my gaffe. The death of Mrs. Grinn in fact no way negated my wife having mentioned the incident to her and she to her husband some time before. I had made a terrible *faux pas.*

"I-I'm dreadfully sorry. I just—"

Grinn looked away and munched the remainder of his chocolate bar.

Furnival's eyes twinkled. "I see you are beginning to read between the lines," he said to me. "Now you must learn to read the lines as well." He turned. "As you were saying, Detective?"

Grinn continued chewing. He didn't resume speech till he had finished, swallowing hard. At which point he said, "Does it seem an odd coincidence that your wife disappeared right after coming to ask the police about this Barbon character?"

Furnival said nothing. The detective maintained his own silence. I felt as if he and Furnival were locked in some sort of battle where non-speech was the weapon. "Go on," I said finally, exasperated by the long pauses. "What have you found out about Barbon? Surely you must know his whereabouts? Have you found him?"

Grinn stared through me. "There's not much information readily available on non-criminals. The price we pay for freedom. What exactly is your interest in all this, Doctor, if I may ask?"

"I, uh, I'm a concerned friend. I just want—"

"You don't have to answer that," Furnival said, then turned to face Grinn. "I resent your implication. I wish you would spend more time searching out logical suspects and less time intimidating upstanding citizens like Dr. Wutzl."

Grinn snapped his notepad shut, put it in his hip pocket. "I'll be in touch," he said and walked out, the suede elbow pads on his jacket continuing to stare at us from the back. The albino reporter glanced up hurriedly from his own notebook, looked around nervously, and waved bye-bye. "What a pair," I said when he was out of earshot.

Furnival wanted to learn what I'd deduced from what I'd heard, but I was so confused. Larry Lazar, Beau Barbon. "I can't see how these names of high school acquaintances tie in with the disappearance of your wife."

"Nor can I."

"Who is Beau Barbon anyway? The name rings a bell."

Furnival smiled. "You have a most remarkable memory, Doctor. Was it yesterday that I mentioned finding the file with letters from 'Bone' in it, and also one from this Beau fellow, plus an article about a dead boy? Do you recall any of that? The significance of the matching names could be coincidence or even subliminal associative psychology, I suppose."

"I'm afraid you've lost me there. What are you saying?"

"Reality and fiction, my dear Doctor Wutzl. Beau Barbon, a real boy in my wife's past. Bo Bone, a character in her novel. There's a striking similarity, don't you think, in the sound of the names? Or do you subscribe to Grinn's school? Discard all but the most physical evidence?"

"Uh...hum." I cleared my throat. "I see." Generally I take little offense at Furnival's remarks. Brusqueness is his manner and I knew, in this case, he meant it not unkindly. I lit a pipe. Furnival put the fingertips of both hands together and did spider push-ups. He sank into a gloomy silence, which I was loath to interrupt. "I say, Furnival," I said after some time. "I came to remind you about tonight."

"Tonight?" His face was clouded with dark thoughts.

I affected a cheer I did not feel, laughing heartily. "I can see it's a good thing I did. Remember, Mrs. Wutzl *insisted* you join us for dinner. Your daughter too. Don't try to back out now. Mrs. Wutzl would not hear of it. Believe me, you won't regret it. She is a veritable *chef de cuisine.*"

Furnival smiled. "I wouldn't miss it for anything," he said.

"We'll be there promptly at four-thirty, as you requested."

Leaving, I turned to shut the door behind me. Furnival was sitting back in his chair, smoking his pipe, seeming to read the tobacco clouds that billowed above him.

As good as his word Furnival and his daughter appeared at four-thirty. "Looks like rain," I heard him remark, making conversation with that inestimable housekeeper and cook, my wife. She took their wraps and led them into the parlor, where we had wine and hors d'oeuvres while she finished preparing our feast. Then she called me to the kitchen to carve the bird. Together we came to the table, where Furnival and Ana were already seated.

"The turkey is so succulent," said Furnival. "I don't much care for turkey but this—" He waved his fork in the air.

My wife was greatly pleased, for she prides herself on her cooking. "It's nothing," she said modestly. "I just prepare a special stuffing with wild rice and mushrooms. And of course I use a fresh-killed bird. From Tooly's Poultry Farm. Do you know it? And then when I cook it the secret is to drench a cheesecloth in melted butter and fat from the turkey, which has been cooking for an hour already. Lay that on the breast. That's how I keep it plump and juicy. No one likes a skinny breast."

"Er...yes, dear," said I.

"Oh, Rufus, here's a drumstick for you. I know how you love a tasty leg." I thanked her, for indeed I am a leg man and this one was delicious—the skin crisp, the meat moist. I tore at it with my teeth, which, unlike the teeth of many men my age, are my own.

"Furnival," said I, pointing the drumstick at my guest. "Have you figured out anything new about the case?"

The man looked uncomfortable. I quickly perceived he was casting his eyes on his daughter, signaling subtly that he would prefer not to discuss anything in front of her. I hit my plate with the turkey leg, thereby creating a diversion. "Mmmm. Leg. Errruff," I said, growling for the child's amusement. The girl giggled as I took an oversized bite.

"Oh, Rufus," said my wife. "How funny you look with that big bone in your hand. You look like"—she searched the room for an apt analogy—"like Fred Flintstone."

I turned to my male companion, a literary fellow like myself, and in my eagerness to show my wit I spoke with strands of dark meat hanging from my mouth. "I thought she might at least say Henry the Eighth," I joked, then swallowed.

Furnival stared into his plate. "I believe I've had enough."

"Oh, but there's dessert yet. No one leaves this table without tasting my chocolate cream nut mousse," said Mrs. Wutzl. "With homemade nonpareils."

Furnival groaned.

After dessert and coffee my good woman suggested we "go into Rufus's study for a pipe and some brandy. Ana can help me clean up. I'll give her some recipes. No doubt she'll want to start cooking for you, Percy. She's just at that age where a girl loves to give pleasure to a man, isn't that right, Ana dear?"

My wife proved herself to have an astute knowledge of adolescent feminine psychology, for the girl was already stacking dishes. As Furnival and I headed out for a smoke, I heard her say, "These recipes are simple but tasty. Just remember, The way to a man's heart is through his stomach." I was pleased to know the girl was receiving instruction from an able teacher.

Furnival and I filled our pipes. We stood, looking out the window. He declined my cognac. "I haven't been drinking," he explained. "I have to be ready, you know, at a moment's notice."

"Like a fireman, eh?" I said. Furnival did not laugh. I saw he was distressed. "Things not going well?"

He shook his head. "The police disregard all the clues I uncover. They won't or can't investigate the case properly, so I've been doing it, yet when I turn over evidence, I am only ridiculed for my efforts. I shall have to do more than research from now on. I shall have to find her myself. I am not a violent man, I don't even have a gun. I borrowed Jon's once when we went hunting, and I suppose he'd lend it to me again, if.... I don't think I will though. I am more at ease with a pen than a gun. When it comes to brains I have no doubts about my superior ability. But when it comes to brawn, to bringing about a physical resolution, well, what will I do if I find her? The police won't help me, so I'm apt to be alone."

His voice trailed off. We stood in silence some moments. Far away in the mountains we heard thunder.

"Rip van Winkle bowling with trolls?" I ventured to joke. Furnival said nothing. I drew on my pipe and continued gazing out the window. Thunder rolled across the sky. "Shall we ever understand the divine mysteries?" I asked. A poetic mood seized me. "Even now, you can hear the great Baal. 'O mighty Baal,'" I intoned. "'O Rider of the Clouds.'"

Furnival turned. "What did you say?"

I grew embarrassed, for it suddenly occurred to me where I had gotten that line of poetry. It was the epigraph to *Bone*. I feared my friend might err in his assumptions, believing I spent much time thinking about his wife, when, if I thought of her at all, it was solely as the authoress of a novel that I was contemplating analyzing. After all my years' studying poetry the poetic line naturally planted itself in my mind. Then, upon hearing the thunder I found it sprouting from memory as from a fecund soil. I was as surprised as Furnival at the quote revealing itself after so much time underground.

"It was just a line of poetry. I was reading Canaanite mythology last night before bed and—"

"Dr. Wutzl, please. Just repeat it."

I took a breath. "'O mighty Baal. O Rider of the Clouds.'"

"Dr. Wutzl," exclaimed Furnival, standing up, staring like a madman. "You have stumbled upon it. The answer."

I'm afraid the wine and cognac and heavy meal addled my thought processes, for I had to ask, "What is the question?"

Furnival did not respond. I saw ideas race across his brow. He asked to use the phone. "Damn," he said after dialing. "The line is busy. Listen, Dr. Wutzl, I must leave you in charge of little Ana for a while. I'll be back shortly."

With no further explanation he grabbed his coat and hat and was out the door, leaving me to explain to a confused Mrs. Wutzl and an upset Ana where the strange fellow had gone. But such is his style of investigation when he is hot on a new scent.

He returned an hour later, fuming. He took off his coat and dropped it absentmindedly on my wife's antique damask chair. She hurriedly picked it up and hung it over the bathtub. (As the thunder had forewarned it began to rain not a moment after Furnival left the house.) Ana wanted to sit with her father, but he brushed her off in a most insensitive manner. He asked to speak to me in private.

"That was rather rude of you," I said, for I cannot bear insensitivity, especially to the weaker sex.

He appeared not to hear me. I offered him tobacco but he waved it away. "Why did you run out like that?" I asked.

"Listen to this, Dr. Wutzl," said the hawk-nosed professor.

Might he woo her?	*Would he could.*
Might he screw her?	*Might be would.*
Could he wife her?	*Could be would.*
Would he knife her?	*Might be should.*
Could he hide her?	*Might he could.*
Who would ride her?	*Ryder Wood.*

"My dear fellow," said I, "this is no time for poetry. Why did you run out of my house an hour ago? Your daughter was—"

Furnival laughed. "Don't you see? Ryder Wood is Bo Bone, not Horace Byrrd. Do you remember Ryder Wood?"

"You mean Bryant's Wood? On campus?"

"No, no, my good man. Ryder Wood is not a forest but a vagrant. He used to stay in town, left suddenly last year. Fancied himself a poet. Mabel went out with him for a while."

"Your wife—" I exclaimed.

"Look at how his name fits the rhyme scheme. And the pun: Who would ride her? Ryder Wood. Metrics dictate the answer. 'Mark my word' is a false lead, do you see? He set us on the trail of a foul bird, that we wouldn't look in the true wood. Tell me, Dr. Wutzl, as a man of literature—do you think all this—rhyme scheme, pun, rhythm—could be coincidence?"

I paused, took a deep breath, considered the facts as Furnival had laid them out. "No," I pronounced slowly. "I think it unlikely that a rhyming pun should fit perfectly to the metrics of a poem, answering its question, without intention."

"Ha! Exactly." Furnival sighed, then sat back. "But the brilliant Detective Grinn begs to differ. 'Don't meddle in our investigation,' he said. 'Police work is not poetry.' Oh, why do I bother with him? The man has probably never read a poem, he has no ear for it. Can't hear the rhyme. Has no rhythmic sense. What could better fit the needs of a madman such as Ryder Wood than to act the poet in a bizarre crime? I ask you, Dr. Wutzl, is not notoriety a form of fame? And there's also the character of Bo Bone himself. Do you remember him from my wife's novel?"

"A tad," I said. "Bo Bone was the villain who abducted the protagonist, wasn't he? Anna—like your daughter. Funny, I never thought of that be—"

"Both Bone and Ryder are fair men with flesh-colored hair. Thin, tall, eerily nondescript. Am I accurately describing them?"

"Yes, but many men fit that description. Nondescript—"

Furnival raised one eyebrow. "It's not just a physical portrait. It's the mood such a character evokes. An absent presence. Something ghostly. I believe the term *au courant* is soul-murdered. Look, I won't mince words with you. We both know my wife has had a number of affairs. Examine the other men she's been with. Horace Byrrd?"

"Really, I—"

"Peter McWiffle? Idi Masambe? Sheppard Sch—"

"All those? I'm shocked at—"

"I'm not trying to shock you. I'm pointing something out about my wife's attractions. These men are all different physical types. Horace Byrrd, with his gold helmet of hair, is not anything like the bleached-out Bone. Neither is Peter McWiffle, who's a giant redhead. Masambe's African. Shep Schooner is fair but you would hardly describe a one-legged man as nondescript. Do you see? Unless there was someone else in her life that I didn't know about, Ryder is the only one who fits Bone's description."

"Hmmm, yes, I see, sort of."

"Dr. Wutzl, please sit down. What I have to say may astound you." I did so, wondering what the literary sleuth could say that would be more astonishing than what he already had.

"I think," said Furnival, watching me carefully, "my wife has been captured by a figment of her imagination."

I gasped several times. "What? Furnival, that's preposterous," I cried. "You're mixing up reality and fantasy. You told me you think the Surrealists were full of hooey, that you have even less respect for Magic Realists, who aren't even original. Are you going back on your primary ideas about—"

"I think," said Furnival slowly, "that a character from her novel has escaped and is acting out her fiction. I have to find her before they get to the end of the book."

His mind somewhat eased by our discussion, Furnival went into the parlor to collect his daughter and coat. He thanked my wife for the delicious meal and started for the door.

"Wait," Mrs. Wutzl called. She went into the kitchen, returning with a large bag and a small one. "This is for you." She handed Furnival the large one. "Leftovers. Put the turkey in a pan with a cup of bouillon—I gave you a chicken cube in case you haven't any. Heat it with the cover on. The candied yams need to be put in a Pyrex and baked at, oh, three hundred for twenty minutes, covered. The sweet potato pie is good with whipped cream. So's the mousse. Do you know how to whip cream?" Furnival nodded. "Good."

She turned to Ana. "This, darling," she said, "is for you. And I hope you'll come visit me sometime."

The girl took the small bag. "What is it, Mrs. Wutzl?"

My wife smiled. "I know how you children are about these things. It's the wishbone. Just let it dry out on the sill for a few days, then you can make a wish and break it."

Ana lowered her head. "Thank you," she mumbled. The pair went out into the miserable night. I turned to my wife.

"That was a wonderful meal," I said. She smiled sweetly, looking like the bride I remember from long ago. "You have quite a way with children," I continued. "It's a shame you..."

"But we've been happy, haven't we, Woofy?"

I squeezed her hand. "Immensely."

TWENTY-NINE

She sat in the dark, telling herself a story, hoping the transformation of events into narrative might give the illusion of meaning, a purpose toward which everything raced. She refused the paper and pen he had left her, like a horse refusing to take the bit. It was what he wanted, and that was reason enough not to give it to him. For the time being she wrote in her mind, knowing he had not yet found a way to penetrate her there.

They drove through a night aglitter with stars, she mentally wrote, remembering how she had tried to keep track of the roads. The trick was to do so without appearing to. "This is crazy," she said to Ryder. "You don't have to take me away. We can see each other on the sly. Like last year."

He didn't say anything. He didn't turn to her, he didn't part his lips. In no way did he acknowledge he was more than a driving machine. Mabel glanced around. They were taking forty-four/fifty-five through the mountains. She continued bargaining. "Like this, you're committing a crime. People will miss me. Cops will look for us. But if I just stay home, then...remember the fun we had?"

His mouth fell open like a gate, emitting a creak. She was aghast. He looked at her. He did not watch the twisting road.

"Oh, we'll have fun," he said. "Lots of fun."

"Look out. Ryder! The Hairpin. You're going too fast."

He turned his eyes forward. The car cried, shuddering as he took the five-mph turn at thirty-five. He laughed. "See, wasn't that fun?"

Mabel wriggled her hands behind her. Ryder had to be stopping soon, they couldn't drive forever. If she could free her hands, then she could surprise him. Hit him in the face. If only she could get her hands loose. The key element was surprise.

He drove off the main road. She didn't recognize the turn. He seemed to know the back roads. Her sense was that they had been going west, then north, and now she thought they were going east. The roads wiggled around the mountains. The moon was on her right, then it was behind her. "You really know this country, don't you?"

He didn't answer.

"I admire a man who knows his way around," she said, flirting with death, having gotten her way with it before.

Ryder maintained a stiff silence.

"We could just pull off here, you could untie my hands and we—"

He faced her. "You seem to think this is all sex," he said. "There's more to it than that. You figure you can do anything you want 'cause you're a writer married to some highbrow professor, and the two of you sit and shit intellectual crap at each other. You figure you can examine me under a microscope, write it all down, and make a fortune, saying whatever you please. You twisted my life around to make a better story. I'm not your doll," he said. "I'm not your puppet."

"I know you don't believe me," she said, "but I wasn't writing about you. I'm sorry it seemed that way. I was writing *Bone* before I ever met you, Ryder."

They were on a dirt road. He stopped the car, turned to glare at her. "The sooner you remember my name," he said, "the better. Bone. B-O-N-E." He took his hands off the steering wheel. He stroked the gun between his thighs.

The road they were on was so steep and full of holes it would have been easier to walk. When they reached the top it leveled off behind a house. Mabel, with a start, recognized the place. All at once she knew where she was. She hid her glee.

He opened her door, undid her belt, helped her out. It had been hot in the Volkswagen, and at first the air was refreshing. But as she waited for him to undo the padlock on the house she grew cold.

Instead of working steadily, seeing how the woman hopped from foot to foot, trying to get warm, Ryder made conversation. "Know this here spot?" he asked.

She shook her head, fighting back tears. Had she given herself away so soon?

Ryder looked up at the malevolent stars. "Recollect the moon," he said, "the day we made night?"

For a moment she remembered a moon, a boy silver in its light. Then she remembered a man, and a moon that wasn't there. How stupid she was. How could she have forgotten? She had been with Ryder that day—a gray day, the end of winter. They had driven into the mountains, looking for a place to yowl. They had a blanket with them, left the car below and hiked up, coming upon the house the back way. She'd known it was there, having discovered it some years before with another lover, a fellow who loved to ride horseback before womanback. When she and Ryder saw it they knew it for perfect. A perfect ruin, thrilling in its decay. They were alike in many ways then, but to her it was all a game.

He'd broken open the door, they'd gone inside. It was her idea. She remembered that too now. She had the kind of mind that dreamed nightmares and rituals. "It's dark. It's night," she said. "There's a full moon, okay?" She spread the blanket on the floor in the center of the room.

He stripped to the bone, laughing. That was the thing about Ryder. He was quick to join whatever fantasy she dreamed. "You're my fat-nippled goddess," he said, "swollen with milk." He gently bit her neck. She smiled, cupping her breasts like terra cotta in a grave. "I'm a hunter," he said, his words exciting her beyond all reason, "and you are my meat."

The door was tiny. Mabel had to crouch to get through. The night of the abduction, when was it—a week ago? Just a week? It was dark till Ryder lit a lantern. Darkness had been considerably less frightening than what next assaulted her eyes. A nasty bit of work at center. Dangling harness, system of pulleys, ropes threaded through eyehooks in the ridgebeam. On the far wall a winch. The strangely human harness hung in wait, a sick promise.

Terror orgasmed through her and for a moment she knew this had to be a dream. She shut her eyes, opened them. All was as before. She saw how the room had been prepared for her—leaves and animal droppings swept out, two small windows shuttered and barred. On a table near the wall was a jar with an arrangement of dried flowers and foliage. Under other circumstances she might have found it quite lovely. Ryder had always had an artist's touch.

"A remarkable piece of apparatus," he said, closing the door behind her, "ain't it?" Déjà vu tickled her mind. There was something familiar about his words, but she couldn't place them. Surely she'd not have forgotten such a setup. Her fantasies were just that, fantasies, and this was more than real. Though she was cold, she began to sweat. She could smell her own stink of fear. Bitter, like grapefruit.

The harness, red body with white slings, was made of a light fabric. It reminded her of a bag she had—very durable, said to be parachute material. Yes, she thought, looking at the ropes, remembering that Ryder liked to skyjump. He'd told her how it reminded him of a time. A time when he'd felt almost alive. She had been struck by the phrase. *Almost alive.* She had gone with him once to a small airport near the college but refused to participate. "You just like to watch, huh?" He tried to cajole her into it, then gave up, shrugged. "Some other chance then," he said. She thought he was crazy and said so. "You're going to leap out of a plane, putting all your trust in a bit of cloth." He grinned, showing off his gap teeth. "There's got to be trust, now ain't it so? Someone puts you down, you got to believe she'll bring you up. Someone lifts you up, you better hope he'll let you down—easy, so you're spread-eagled in the sky, riding wind." That was when he'd explained about the time he'd felt almost alive. War stuff, he said, "but you wouldn't know, little-bitty girl like you. That's a man thing, ain't it?" She was no little-bitty girl and hadn't been for a long time, but when he'd stroked her cheek it thrilled her with insinuation. Yes, it was a man thing. Things men do. Women would never. And men would, and did. And women were just little things, bitty girls, and men did terrible crimes. To them. "That was a time," he said, "and nothing's been as exciting since. Now everything's dead—except jumping out of a plane, pulling at the chute." He looked up from checking a cord, saw her watching him. "And laying with you, of course," he said, giving her a slight bow.

Staring at the harness, remembering, she felt mesmerized. "I have a feeling I'm not going to like this," she said softly, so softly she was surprised when he responded.

"Oh, you don't know. Come on, try it on. I'll need to make some adjustments."

She didn't come closer. He went to get her. He took her arm in a gentlemanly way. "Now Annabelle, you know I wouldn't do nothing to hurt you. This is just what the doctor ordered. Balm of

Gilead on your soul." Fascinated despite her fear she allowed herself to be led forward without quite realizing it. When she caught herself she heeled down, shook off madness like a dog water. "No," she said. "This has gone far enough. Too far. This is sick, Ryder—sick." She turned to him, almost expecting him to agree. He smiled, so that for a moment she hoped he'd reveal it was indeed a joke. Then he stroked her cheek, snailcrazy slow, traveling his finger down her neck, slow slow, almost stopping but no, continuing along the fullness of a breast. With her hands tied behind her she couldn't prevent his wandering.

"Now now," he said, hushing her. "I don't think it's sick at all. It's ingenious, if I do say so myself. You just don't get it yet. But you will. Someone has to pay, you know. Something's stolen, someone pays. I can't get back what you took, but you can give me something in return." He smiled broadly. "It'll be like Christmas. An exchange of gifts."

"Stolen?" She shook her head. "I never stole anything from anybody."

He gave her a conspiratorial wink. "We don't have time for all this. The sooner we get started the sooner we'll finish." He held the harness open, as if expecting her to slip in, like someone trying on a beautiful mink vest. "It's for you too. Can't let it fester. Got to extract that guilt."

"Guilt," she echoed. She thought she was asking a question but it came out a statement.

He nodded proudly, like she was his prize student. "Guilt is never to be doubted." Again a thrill of recognition shivered through her. She must have done this—with someone, somewhere. Maybe in a different life, for she had no recollection of it in this one; still the feeling would not subside. The familiarity of his words. Ryder clicked his tongue, shook the harness at her, as you might at a dumb animal accustomed to being ridden. She didn't move, but she could taste a recollection. It was one of enjoyment, of pleasure, despite her palpable fear. The acrid terror stink on her skin—there was no doubting this was happening against her will; but neither was there any doubt that something else was rising to meet it. The enjoyment she seemed to recall was not physical. At least it didn't strike her so. It was more an intellectual pleasure, but how could that be? A pleasure centered on her eyes, her head, the cauliflower organ inside. Was Ryder hypnotizing her with those snake eyes of his, tricking her with imposed memory? She knew she was suggestible to the promise of strange knowledge. Was he using her quail sense of self to trap her?

Ryder dropped hold of the harness. She watched it swing. "Let me introduce you," he said. "I think then you'll agree. It's the only way." He seemed to be flirting with her, and she had glimmers of the old Ryder, the one she had fallen for—before she knew he was quite mad.

He brought her into the center of the room, pointed up the rope, along the ceiling, over to the winch. Near the handle was the table with the autumn display. She saw in its center a bright red cone. One you saw everywhere on bushes in the fall. He pulled her down slightly so she could see under the table. There was a tape recorder, paper and pens, several books, including (she was alarmed to notice) a copy of *Bone*. "That's the Designer," he said, and her heart thudded again with familiarity. She was looking at the table, the objects under it, wondering which he meant. She didn't notice what he was doing till it was too late. He had deftly wrapped the harness around her torso and now, though she struggled to get away, he held her easily in place with one hand and zipped her into the sling. By the time she realized what he was doing he was already done.

She twisted about, trying to wriggle free, but that only served to prove how trapped she was. "That was a lousy trick," Mabel said. "You fooled me, showing me one thing and attaching me to another."

He came close, she thought for a moment he was going to kiss her, but he only pushed the hair behind her ear. "You look good enough to eat." For a moment she feared he would, that he was that insane. And truly she felt like a carcass, hanging there, heavy in her meat. He licked his lips, she could hear him smacking them near her earlobe. He nibbled it gently, for he knew her weaknesses. She had instructed him on her likes and dislikes in different circumstances. She shook off his mouth, moved her head as far away from his lips as she could, and was relieved when he desisted in chomping on her fleshy lobe, for if he'd wanted to he could have in fact bitten it off. His mother, she remembered, had kept her teeth in a glass, she'd made him brush them morning and night. If he didn't do a good enough job she exacted a horrible price, something to do with the teeth and the well. Ryder couldn't quite talk about it. In some ways that was more chilling than any detail he might have supplied.

"I could have strung you up by force too, Annabelle, now couldn't I, girl?" he said. "And if I have to I will. But maybe we won't have to do any of that, you know that man/woman thing you, what is it you said to me that time? you abhor. Abhor. Good word. I love that word. Why shucks, old hillbillybos like me don't know good words like that. Sure glad you taught me. And now I get to return the favor. Soon we'll see who's the horse"—he smiled lovingly—"and who's the whore." He gave her a shove, like someone sharing a joke with a pal, but she was unprepared for it and, though her feet were on the ground, she was thrown off balance and just swung.

"No time for fun and games right now. Soon, sugar pie, soon enough, but come. Let me share this with you. I really think you'll admire it, be proud of me. Proud to take part in it—when you see how it goes. Let me introduce you to the rest of the gang, ha ha. See, this here now, where you are, I call this the Bed." She looked at where he pointed, at the floor beneath her, but didn't see anything bedlike. "Oops," he said. "I forgot. Don't peek."

He made a goofy hick face. She had forgotten how much he held it against her "for having it easy" when he'd grown up someplace hard, with someone who exacted a price for every mistake he'd made. Now it came back to her, his resentment, his playing country mouse to her city. As if she'd been a Brooklyn princess when he was starving in some hole.

He left her standing in the middle of the room and went behind a curtain she saw hanging in a corner. He wasn't gone long, but she shook off the bit of empathy she'd felt for young Ryder, took those moments to test the limits of her rope. She had some slack, enough to walk a few steps. It seemed she could wriggle her hands, might free them eventually. She tried to will her wristbones smaller (as she had read once that Houdini did). She would work on that later, she figured, when he was busy with something else. Surely there'd be a time when he would sleep. Unless he meant to finish with her sooner than answer such bodily needs.

He came back, dragging a mattress, which he positioned just in front of her. She offered to step up onto it but he said don't bother. He went to the wall and unhooked the winch, turning the crank so that she was lifted a foot off the ground. "Ohhh-whoaa," she said, the sensation of being hoisted like a sack, unable to control the spin with her arms, filled her with renewed terror. She wondered at her own madness, that just a moment before she'd been feeling pity for the boy he'd been. It was true he'd been abused as a child, but one didn't have to cozy up to someone pulling wings off a fly.

He set the crank and returned to the mattress, which he pushed beneath her feet, measuring with a tape so that it was centered just so. She spun lazily above it, craning her neck to keep him in view so he wouldn't pull any horrible surprise. He took hold of her waist, turning her to face him. His eyes penetrated hers as he stared into them.

"I think," he said, "you see the possibilities."

Then he turned her around and untied her hands. Surprised into not reacting she thought he was about to let her go. Instead he pulled her arm through the loop of the harness and adjusted the shoulder strap, did the same for the other. Now she could use her arms to shift her weight, but before she had a chance to do so he brought her hands in front and shackled each wrist to a length of chain. Looping nylon cord through hooks in the bands, he tied them above with professional skill. Her hands were bound to the harness rope on some sort of slip. He was humming tunelessly, like a man working on his car, oblivious to her questions, to her trying to move around, trying to free her hands from their bracelets. She was like a small animal leashed in a yard for a child's amusement. He busied himself with tightening and loosening ropes, making adjustments, ignoring her all the while. When he worked behind her, swinging her around to do what needed to be done, he held both her legs between his own so she couldn't kick him. When that grew cumbersome he tied the ankles so she just hung there, pointing down. He pulled the cord from her hands along a swivel-pulley attached to a second winch and coiled it. He tested the device, raising and lowering her arms, still humming. Then he stopped. Looked at her. Her dress was bunched up between her legs. This seemed to bother him. He ripped a seam and pulled the red material down straight. Stood back and admired his handiwork. He wiggled his fingers like a bug, smiling as if this were harmless fun, going, "Cootchy cootchy."

He knew she despised being tickled, that her brother used to torture her, holding her hands in one hand, going at her neck, her underarms and belly. She felt indignant that he would do this to her, on top of everything else. Anger replaced fear. "Cut it out!" she said. "Hear me?" She hung a foot off the ground, her arms manacled and tied above her head, her ankles bound, she was alone in a secluded shack in the mountains with a nut. "Don't make me mad," she warned.

Perhaps he'd tired of the tickle-game, perhaps he had other plans. Whatever the reason, Ryder backed off. But Mabel, surprised at her success, tried to go further. "I've had enough of this," she said. "I want you to get me down from here. Untie me. I mean it!" She was using her best mother-scolding voice, but it was starting to sound tinny. She was reminded of the times she'd tried to discipline her daughter and found herself losing confidence in her authority.

Ryder went back to the winch. He was still humming while he practiced using the two axles to make her dance. With a start she recognized the lively tune. He lifted her body and lowered her arms so that she held them in front of her. "Once I had strings," he was singing, "but now I'm free." Pulling on the ropes without resorting to the winch handle, he got her to swing back and forth like a child going for an airplane ride. "There are no strings on me." With that he loosened the setting and let her drop to the mattress. It didn't hurt but it scared her. *You see the possibilities.* He lifted her up, higher this time. "Airborne," he said. She began to scream.

Once started she couldn't stop. "Shhh," he kept saying, "shhh." But she wouldn't shhh. "I didn't mean to scare you none, just you know—show you the ropes. Yuka yuka." He hit his knee, having far too good a time. "Get you your little boneriding hood," he said, "if you won't behave." He went to retrieve something from the curtained corner.

It was a sack made of a heavy, soft material, velvet with the density of leather. She saw him setting the eye slits forward on his thigh. Then he opened the neck and tried to slip it over her head. She struggled, twisting about. "No," she said. "No, I promise. I won't scream anymore."

He stood back, looked at her, there was a brightness in his eye. "That's a good girl then," he said. "We'll let you have your way...for a time." He loosened the winch, slowly this time, and let her get on her feet. He played out the rope to the last coil. "Come," he said. "Let me finish showing you around."

He untied her ankles and took her arm, strolled her to where the curtain hung. She could not get close enough to raise the fabric, but she could just make out some bulk behind it. "You've seen the Bed. You've seen the Designer," he said. "And now I'd like you to meet the Harrow." She nodded, waiting for him to lift the curtain. He didn't, he waited, watching her. "Well?" she said, encouraging him slightly, as if to say, Go on. "Well," he said. "Let's save that for another day."

She was optimistic for a moment at the thought of another day. Then fearful of another and another.

Ryder accompanied her back to the Bed and told her to make herself comfortable. She sat crosslegged, her wrist chain gathered in loose links in the hollow between her legs. "I guess you must be wondering what all this is about." He sat down at the table.

Surreptitiously, she was trying to take in her environment, to figure out how she might escape. There might only be a second when he let down his guard and she must be ready. All at once it struck her how ridiculous this was. She started to laugh.

"What's so funny?" he said with a half smile.

She shook her head.

He smiled again, broader. "Come on now. You wouldn't want me to *pull* it out of you?" His smile was so pleasant, the camaraderie in his voice so sincere, that it took Mabel a moment to realize he wasn't joking.

"It's just, I mean, this is all so"—she looked around, lifted her hands, rattled her chain, let them drop back into her lap—"it's so, I don't know. Like out of Kafka. I mean, I'm being punished, I don't know my crime, there's no trial. It made me laugh for a minute, but it's not really funny. Like Kafka."

"Kafka?" Ryder said. "Who he?" He gave a goofy grin. "Oh, I get it. One a them there book jokes. Like 'In the Penile Colony,' huh?"

She didn't say anything. Bed, Designer, Harrow. Of course. He wanted it both ways—playing the hick, acting the intellectual. Harrow, it occurred to her, a Harrow had teeth. She looked fearfully at the curtain. "Well, you're right about that, I guess," Ryder was saying. "It is all about sentences. One kind or another."

She nodded, though she had no idea what he was talking about. "You took my life sentence, stole it, made sentences with it, so now you must be sentenced, see? But what I can't figure out is"—he scratched his temple and gave her a long look—"just what to inscribe."

"In the Penal Colony" was coming back to her now. She recalled the Harrow in the story was set to write with needles on the prisoner, who was shackled to the Bed. She looked at the curtained area in the corner. Behind the fabric was a cylindrical thing, about three feet long. She could make out bulk, but it didn't look like Kafka's Harrow. It didn't seem a contraption with needles.

"I thought and thought," Ryder was saying, "how to *sentence* you. Be generous? But you are, to a fault. Obey your superiors, respect your inferiors? Be just? Be Justine, how about? Then I got it! Be chaste. Because you were, and now you're caught."

"Chaste?" Mabel asked.

"Chased," he replied.

She didn't comment, her mind working furiously to figure out what was going to happen to her, what she could do. "Hello," Ryder said, "Hell-ooo." She looked up. "You still don't get it, do you?" She shook her head. "It's simple really. Perfect. I figured out a way you can pay me back. For stealing. We're going to write us a book, you and me. You will be my research, my paper, I will be your pen. Your pen is going to write on you. Your pen is going in deep, baby, deep. Your pen is going for the red ink, you know." He stood up and went to the winch. He turned the crank and against her desire Mabel found herself standing, then rising off the ground.

She felt like crying but was too afraid. "Why are you doing this to me?"

He picked up *Bone*, flung it at her so that it hit her pubis and fell open. "You still don't know?" he yelled. "That's me in there, trapped. You took my material. With your hootchie-cootchie ways and your soft soft skin, that lying mouth, so wet, so knowing. Oh, and your liquid eyes. Now Ryder, now honey, it's all right, it's over. Tell me, tell me. You'll feel better if you let it out. And I told you everything. I spilled my guts and there you were, ready to lap it up like a pussy, weren't you? You suckled me of my milk. You swallowed it, gulped it, begged for more. Sucked the marrow from my bone. I told you everything, and you took it and stole it and told everyone it was yours. But it was mine, and you know that and I know that. That was my book, made trash. My book would have told the world something. The children in their holes, the ones in the mother well. I'd have saved them but all you did was look for meat to put on your table, so you and your *professor* could sup. Well, honeygirl, that was my bone. You gnawed on my bone, so now I'm going to gnaw yours." His mad eyes glared. She had never noticed before but they were the blue of newborns, the blackish blue of changing eyes, unfocused, not quite real.

"I'm writing a book," he said. "Didn't know that, did you? Yeah, well I am. You're not the only one can write. I'm not some ignoramus country bumpkin like that Bone in your book. I might call it Marrow. You know, like the heart of the bone. What you think?"

When Mabel didn't reply, just hung there, watching through the holes in her face, he went on. "There's something inside me, something that's got to get out. And you, this is where you come in—you are going to help me. We'll find it in you, the stuff you stole from me, oh now, let's talk about your father's bone, let's talk about your brother's bone. Know what I mean? Know what it's like in a hole, buried like a potato eye, things crawling, wet, dark? I done told you but telling's not enough. What's it you always say to me— show, don't tell? I bleed on the page and I give it to you, you twitch in your seat, just wet at the opportunity to steal my soul, tell me it ain't worth a damn. Show, don't tell. Well, now you'll learn. The hard way. I done told you, but it don't sink in. Guess I'll have to show you, my little dollie. My puppet." He rattled her chains and set her to bouncing.

"Yeah, dance for me now. You want to know all about it? I'll tell you. She kept me in a well of darkness. Brought me into the light when it suited her. She put words in my mouth with which to accuse me of accusing her. Then left me in the well, and I was there till you conceived me. I didn't exist. I remember nothing from that time. You started thinking me in that wet dirty mind of yours, plotting your plots, drawing me out of your wet dirty mind, and it was hot and moist and you were squeezing me to come, let me hold you, let me comfort you. I thought you wanted to succor me, become my mother well of inspiration, but I was the sucker. All day sucker, but now it's night. You better get to work on that bone, you got a lot to learn. That's my brother you're talking about, you little prick, she said. Priests don't do that sort of thing. I didn't tell you that part, now did I? You call him Father, she said. He'll teach you what happens to liars in hell. He taught me, he'll teach you. Mother is the root of all evil. Tear it out by the root. Know what happens to liars in hell?"

Mabel was transfixed, removed from her terror as if at a movie.

She waited for whatever came next.

"I said, know what happens to liars?"

She realized then that he was talking to her. She shook her head. "I don't know," she said. "I don't know I don't know I—"

He smiled, and the gap between his lips opened like a grave. "Swallow your marrow like a Frenchie gulping snails. Need a practice session first? Fine, let's play a game. You'll like this. You invented it. Page 209. Remember page 209?"

She said nothing.

He went to where she hung; gently ripped her dress along the seam till it was easy to remove. Folded it, laid it across the table, straight. He stripped her as a lover might, except she struggled to make it difficult. With a wink he acknowledged she was prolonging his pleasure. As if it were intentional, a game lovers play, tease and beg like a dog with a bone.

For a moment he was between her legs, retrieving the book he had thrown at her. She contemplated kicking him in the head. The thought of him unconscious on the floor while she hung above, dying of starvation, was not enough to stop her, for truly she'd pay any price for revenge. But he moved fast, darting in and out, resuming his seat before she'd a chance to act.

He held her book up. "You took my soul, made a dirty bone of it, when it was mine to begin with, when it was meant to be so much more. So now get ready to ride your dirty bone." He gazed at her hanging in her meat. "Let us open our book," he said, "and begin to prey. That is, I'll prey, you be prey."

He forced her into position with adroit twists of the ropes. He held up the hood. "You understand about this, I think. The need to improvise?" He put the sack over her head, pulled tight the cord in the grommets, swung her helpless as a convict.

Naked, cold, frightened, humiliated past shame. Expecting what must come. A naked woman on a rope. Available to all, unable to refuse. Refused. Made refuse. He held her in that position, looking at her, laughing, greedy to take in all her parts and make them ridiculous. Spinning her, looking, looking with dead eyes and laughing mouth. Then he stood behind her. *This is it*, she thought. Soon it would be over, it had to be done and over. But instead of the shove, the grunt she tried to prepare for she felt an insect crawl up one buttock, across her back. She twisted like a dog with something tied to its tail. Trying to see, unable to see. A feather, she saw at last. *A plume!* He was writing all over her with a fucking plume like Cyrano de Bergerac scribbling love letters past the tip of his nose.

She tried to read with tactile sense what she couldn't visually but found herself illiterate to his mad-poet touch. When he was done he read it to her. "The only way to win a woman's heart is by tormenting her." She said nothing. "Know who wrote that?" he asked, twisting her about on her leash. She moved her head slowly from side to side, hypnotized by his rhythmic snakedance. "Guess," but she just stared, as if she recognized him from long ago. Bleached as a bone.

"A literary lady like you not familiar with the works of the great Sade? Annabelly, that's okay hon, I'll teach you *everything* I know."

He went to build the fire. He made it hot, he made it roar. And she hung there, displayed, drying in the hut like beef jerky all night as he wrote in his notebook, looking up now and then to gaze with fixed attention, as if she were a still-life and he a painter. When daylight began to snoop at the windows he loosened her bonds. She fell to the Bed, groaning with relief, and slept like someone escaping hell, carrying secrets on her back only the dead could read.

THIRTY

Dr. Ana stroked an invisible mustache, eying the two patients who sat on her blotter. She sniffled, remembering Dr. Xavier, who had also picked his nose when he thought no one was looking and had asked Ana to play with his dolls. "What is the dolly's name?" he'd asked. "Is that the daddy dolly? Where is the mommy? Where is the sister? Where is the brother?" One time, when she'd had the baby doll crawl to the bathroom, Dr. Xavier became very excited. "Why is the baby going there?"

"To take a bath," Ana had said. Her parents were in the room too. They had been having a "discussion." Daddy'd said, "I didn't mean it that way. I just asked why you weren't watching them. I wasn't accusing you." Mommy began to cry. That was when Ana decided she'd had enough and went to the dollhouse to play. Ana pretended not to notice when Dr. Xavier motioned to Mommy and Daddy to watch her. "Is the baby going to take a bath," Dr. Xavier had asked, "by himself?" Ana didn't look up when answering. She sighed. "I suppose I'll have to wash him, won't I?"

Dr. Ana's eyes were now unfocused. Then she noticed the fashion dolls sitting unfashionably splay-legged on her desk. "What is the problem?" she asked.

"He's so mean to me, Doctor," wept Barbie.

Ken widened his eyes, as if to deny his wife's charge. Dr. Ana turned to him. "Why are you so mean to her?"

He relaxed his face, letting his eyes shrink back to normal. "She likes it," he said.

"Is this true?" Barbie hid her face in her hanky and nodded. "So why do you cry?"

Barbie sniffled a few times. "I don't *really* like it," she said. "It hurts, and he's always yelling at me, making me cry."

"But you just nodded when Ken said you liked it?"

The doll's blue eyes grew large with real tears. "I can't explain, Doctor. It's just, I like it when he makes me do what I want to and can't. And when he loses his temper it's scary, but it's exciting, it makes me laugh inside. I don't know why, but it's like I'm powerful, I'm the one who makes him hit me. He doesn't want to, he says all the time how he doesn't want to but I'm making him. He's only giving me what I really want, but I don't really want that, I just kind of do. Oh, what's wrong with me? Am I crazy?"

Dr. Ana shook her head sadly. "I'm afraid," she said, "you're sick. There's only one cure." She twirled her mustache. "We'll have to take you far away and leave you there, where no one will know where to find you. To a hospital for injections in your tushy."

"Oh no," cried Barbie. "Oh yes," said Dr. Ana. "I'm sorry, but there's no other way. We'll take off all your clothes and tie you to the bed and take your temperature and stick you with needles. Oh, don't be such a baby. After all, Dr. Levine gives me needles when I'm sick, and he puts that disgusting thermometer up my butt too. I used to hide under the table, and he'd pull me out, even though I kicked and screamed and even bit him. One time Mommy sat on me to keep me still while he stuck a needle in me. She only got away with it because Daddy wasn't there. He'd never have let her do that."

Dr. Ana paused for a moment, trying to understand how the horrible monster who had sat on her so the doctor could hurt her was also the mother she missed. "I don't cry anymore," she told the dolls. "Never. I'm no baby like you. You have to learn to grin and bare it. Bend over," she said, lifting Barbie's skirt.

"Can I watch?" asked Ken. "Of course," said Dr. Ana, sticking a pin into pink plastic. "Ow!" yelled Barbie. "Shhh," said Dr. Ana. "*Eeeeerrrrrrrr,*" cried the ambulance siren.

Before she could say boohoo Barbie was in the hospital, her clothes were torn off, and she was put naked into Tootsy Wootsy's crib. Dr. Ana took down the lace canopy and attached Barbie's arms and legs to the posters of the bed, using rubber bands.

"Now you must jump on her stomach," she told Ken.

"Yes, Doctor."

Ken took off his shoes and began jumping on Barbie's belly. The fashion dolls groaned and humphed with each landing. "Oh oh oh," cried Barbie. "Oh, it's happening. Oh, it's coming, it's aaarrrgh"—and with that final yell a stuffed animal, a small black and white skunk, poked his head from between her legs. Dr. Ana pulled him out by his furry ears. "It's a boy," she told the whimpering doll.

"A boy!" said Barbie. "Oh, I'm so happy. I always wanted a little boy. What should we name him?"

Ken smiled proudly. "Let's call him Seth."

"Seth," Barbie said. "Oh, how I love my Sethy Sethy Seth."

"Cootchy cootchy coo," said Ken, tickling the skunk under the chin. He bent over his wife and kissed her. Dr. Ana put the furry doll in Barbie's arms.

"Darling," said Ken, "I'll never be mean to you again."

"Oh, Kenny." Barbie lay back, wanting to sleep now. Dr. Ana moved the skunk to Barbie's titty, where he lapped milk with his little pink tongue just like a kitten. Ken smiled, holding her hand.

"And they lived happily ever after," said Ana softly, scratching her cheeks where the tears tickled.

THIRTY-ONE

The Albino Detective Series

The Simple Act of Vanishing

by Herm Kwestral

Chapter One

"Letter from a Corpse"

I was looking at a flock of birds. In the center was a white one with a long, crooked neck. Almost two-dimensional in profile, it had a sharp beak, wings stretched out like a cape. It could have been a heraldic emblem on a coat of arms, but this bird was alive, zooming toward me, not flapping its wings or turning its head, just growing in magnificence and size. When it seemed about to hit me I lost my nerve and ducked. Raising my head I saw the bird had fallen at my feet and was impaled on a flaming torch. That someone should do such a thing made me cry. Then a child pulled the torch from the bird's breast and put a blazing arrow in its claws. It flew off. The whole thing felt less like a dream than a visitation.

So that's how it began, with a dream. But no, it started the way it always starts, with a woman. Maybe even earlier than that, with the murder of the Latoch family. That was the grisly crime I was covering for my paper, *The Brooklyn Wing*. I was sitting in the Sixty-Third Precinct station house, waiting for further splatters of newsjuice, when in she walked, Mystery Incarnate, curves like the Interboro Parkway. Dark red hair, what they call auburn, and who has auburn hair but a character escaped from a detective novel? All in all, a smoky woman—smell of burning leaves, walk like a curl on the end of a cigarette. Her voice was husky when she asked for help.

Sergeant Braithewain either had nerves of steel or someone'd stolen them. In any case he was impervious to charm and said he was too busy to help. She wasn't a woman used to being turned down. You could see it in her eyes. Then I saw something else. Tears, the genuine article (as they say). These were more exciting to me than the latest bits of carnage revealed by a coroner.

She turned, heading out the door...and my life, if I didn't act fast. "Maybe I can help," I said. "Tell me your story."

And she did, only I still don't know if it was one of love or deception. We went to a coffee shop. She told me her sixteen-year-old boyfriend committed suicide when she was a kid. Now, twenty years later, she'd gotten a letter from him, and it wasn't the first since he'd died. My face must have betrayed my thoughts, that she was either a joker or plain nuts.

She smiled. "I know," she said. "It sounds crazy, but after his death a letter came. It must have been mailed before. Maybe he wrote it while he was in that house, waiting to...you know. In retrospect it had to have been a suicide note."

Her name was Mabel Fleish. This alone would have interested me in her case. She'd written a novel that, even as we spoke, was waiting on my nighttable for a late-night read. But it might have sounded like flattery to tell her that, so I didn't.

"Why do you think a corpse is writing to you now?" I asked.

The note she'd just gotten was signed *BB* and the boy's name was Beau Barbon. *Voilà!* But of course. That was the way the woman's mind worked. She told me this while fumbling in her bag. Why is it women can't go out without packing a suitcase? This voluminous leather satchel was full of books and papers and tissues, God knows what else she found essential to her existence— but believe me, if that stuff was so important she couldn't live without it she'd be in serious trouble: It took ten minutes to find her pen. She wrote her phone number on the back of my card. If she'd told me what she was looking for I could have pulled my own pen out in five seconds. I always carry a penlight in my back pocket. Two real essentials in a writer's life—a light to illuminate the muse's path and a pen to jot down her musings.

At work over the next few days, whenever I had a chance I did preliminary research in NEXUS, then went to the morgue, which is surprisingly well-stocked when you consider *The Wing*'s only a small local tabloid. But it's been around over a hundred years. Walt Whitman used to write for it (I remind myself on days when hack hackles are rising).

Barbon didn't have his own file, of course, but there was one on a series of crimes in Flatbush in the Sixties. Missing pets, dead dogs and cats with symbols cut into them. She'd given me the address of the house in which the body had been found, and the date of the death of course. What I found interesting was that the marks on the boy's body matched those found on the animals. Police had speculated the existence of some sort of cult, then the incidents stopped; so did the public investigation, and the news coverage.

It's not just luck that I'm friendly with cops at the precinct, it's necessity. I asked if I could peruse their files on the case. They didn't say yes or no, just managed not to notice what I was doing one afternoon in the Crime Analysis office.

So, as far as the dead boy went, I discovered, suicide was not ruled out—he was said to be a gloomy sort and there was no sign of a struggle—but the location of the tattoos, on back and buttocks, called for the existence of an accomplice. I thought Fleish would find this interesting. And I thought the other thing I learned would be even more interesting. The dead boy wasn't Barbon. His name was Larry Lazar, and since he was nothing but a kid, sixteen and morose, I couldn't find anything more about him.

I meant to call her the next day, but suddenly everything at work was due yesterday. I had obits to write, murders to recount. Death was having a Brooklyn beach party, and I figured a corpse twenty years dead wasn't about to walk away. More than a month rolled by before I finally had a chance to think straight. *If she's getting correspondence from a corpse,* it hit me, *someone better tell her that the body ain't lying down.*

So I called, disappointed but not surprised when her husband answered. The jacket copy of her book said she was married, had a daughter, lived upstate. I'd read that, studying the author's photo more times than I'd read her novel—twice by then. Nothing stimulates reading interest so much as acquaintance with the author, no matter how slight. I was looking for something, I don't know what. I'd stare at her picture, part of me trying to see into her, part of me trying to remember her. She'd become a figure in my mind—know how that is? I was no longer sure where I left off and she began. Then her husband told me something that made me feel I really did dream her. Mabel Fleish had disappeared.

The wind was knocked out of me, I saw stars, I heard bells, I felt like someone had punched me in the solar plexus and I never even knew where that was before. Yeah, suddenly I knew I was a little in love with her, and maybe that's like being a little pregnant. But even then, while I pumped the good prof for the facts, a thought kept circling. Why would someone ask the police about an old crime right before disappearing? There was a story here. And I could smell the faint, intoxicating perfume of deception.

She'd been on my mind so much the past month that telepathic narcissism caused me to believe I was more than a minor character in her life too, but I was nothing, someone who bought her coffee and listened to a story she might have been making up as she went. Maybe she didn't figure anyone would know about her search at the police station. Maybe she didn't figure on a guy like me, who's read all the books and knows the damsel in distress turns out to be the dame with an angle. It was the angle I couldn't quite get. I turned the puzzle around. The pieces still wouldn't fit. All I knew was that this case was more interesting than murder and mayhem in Midwood. I decided to pay a visit to the upstate police.

The police station was attached to the firehouse, a small municipal box in the center of a parking lot. I'd called ahead, so Detective Sergeant Grinn was expecting me. I had no trouble getting into the squadroom, which was as desolate as bureaucracy can make it, and that is desolate indeed. Two men sat at separate desks, ignoring each other. One read a paper. The other was wearing glasses so dark I'd have thought he was blind except he was playing solitaire. He played a standard seven-card, red-on-black game. He was fast, cocky, careless. Almost missed the chance to open a closed ace. That would have cost him. I showed him the move. Without thanks he finished.

"Ever do a four-card lineup going for fifteens?"

He nodded. Didn't say anything but showed me a variation, playing four cards in the hand.

"How about this one?" I demonstrated seven cards open, building on multiples of ten. I could tell he was impressed. "You've played a game of solitaire or two in your day," he said.

"Skills of a lonely childhood. Someday I'll teach you cat's cradle, using hands, feet, and the knobs of the dresser drawers."

"Kwestral," he said, "I've been expecting you. Listen, you didn't come to teach me card and rope tricks."

I told him I was researching the Fleish case.

"What's in it for you?"

I didn't like his tone. I'd come all that way, taught him my solitaire games, and he just saw me as stealing his meat. I cracked my pinky knuckle *loud* in his direction. It produced a piercing sound that drove people crazy and was the equivalent of saying, "Fuck you." I watched for a reaction. He bent his wrist, making a resonant pop. I pressed my palm against my chin, cracking the upper vertebrae of my neck, first in one direction, then the other. Grinn laced his fingers together, pushed them back, getting at least nine good knuckle pops out of it. All at once I heard a newspaper being thrown down. The cop at the other desk marched out of the room, shaking his head. "What's the matter with him?" I said. "Squeamish," he said.

Grinn and I continued our routines, admiring each other's technique. He had a fancy little fingertip twist I'd never seen before. I almost peeled off my shoes to show him what I could do with my toes. That's the thing about knucklecracking—real knucklecracking. It's a virtuoso performance each time, like Houdini untying himself underwater. People don't get it. I figure I'm the Lord Byron of knucklecracking. I keep trying to get across what there is in it that makes me want to twist past the limit.

When Grinn and I finished I told him about Fleish's research into the death of Beau Barbon right before her own vanishing act.

"Mabel Fleish might like to make it seem she's been kidnapped," I said, "even murdered. So she can assume another identity, another life." That had the effect I'd hoped for. He decided then and there that I wasn't just some annoying fly, that it was to his advantage to share information with me as well.

"Contrived disappearance," he said, "would go along with some of what I've learned about her." He told me she had a less than sterling reputation with the townfolk, then showed me copies of poems written by somebody pretending to be a character in her novel. I read them, twisting fingers for tiny snaps like hors d'oeuvres.

I didn't like the setup. It was too literary, like Pirandello was the God of her universe. But I didn't say that. It didn't matter. We had reached the same conclusion. Mabel Fleish just might be the author of her own disappearance. Chances were that if we found Barbon, recently returned from the dead, we'd find Fleish.

Trouble was we didn't know much about him. I'd already found out that he and his mother had moved to his grandfather's house in Louisiana right after Lazar's death. At least that was the forwarding address Mrs. Barbon had given twenty years before.

Grinn said he'd contact cops in New Orleans and let me know if he found anything. I told him I didn't know what I'd be doing, but if I learned anything more I'd keep him informed. I went home, decided to let things slide, concentrate on the death that crossed my desk, not any I had to go looking for. But I couldn't. I called Furnival, told him I'd met Grinn. The prof didn't want to face up to the meaning of his wife's infidelities. He insisted, in his superior academic manner, that Grinn and I were unable to see the forest for the trees. Kept referring to Poe's "Purloined Letter," thinking I hadn't read the Dupin story in which the searched-for document is right in the middle of a bunch of notes, overlooked by the police because it was in such an obvious place. He said we were so busy trying to unbury clues that we couldn't see what was right under our noses. I tried not to let him infuriate me. I understood what he was going through, although his attitude was hard to bear.

"It's not the disappearance *per se*," he kept telling me. "It's not the infidelities *per se*." What is it *per se*? I wanted to ask but didn't want him to go on another lecturing jag full of arcane illogic and literary correspondence to her novel. I decided I'd keep in touch...but not too often.

When I called Grinn the next day he told me his contacts in Louisiana had dredged up the following: Barbon graduated from public high school in '69 and was drafted, served as a paratrooper in Nam, was committed to a vet hospital in '79 after some violent episodes.

"Well, that messes up our theory," I said. "How could they be together if he's in the bin?" Grinn didn't have any answers.

I knew I'd have to go to Louisiana myself. I let him know as much, in a roundabout way. No cop could research the case the way a reporter could. There were too many rules, prison bars around them. What they could do, what they could not. Legal tangles that drive cops to drink. Search warrants, Miranda rights—I didn't have to worry about any of that, and paperwork didn't scare me either.

But I kept asking myself why I cared, why some strange woman's running off felt like a personal betrayal. When I first heard the news about her disappearance I felt sick, imagining the possibilities. I couldn't stop imagining them. Which was a good thing, I suppose, because it was then, thinking around and around, that it occurred to me: She'd pulled a *Postman* on us, on me and Grinn and most especially on her poor besotted boob of a husband. Once the idea popped into my mind I knew it was true.

My feelings kept riding up and down like a boat on waves. There *was* something dirty about her, I had known it from the start. She was ready to sacrifice anyone to the god of lust. So, how can I explain that I felt compelled to take the raw material of her and create someone else? I made her an artist of sensitivity, a woman with poetry in her soul. I fell in love with my creation, then I just fell. Now I was floating up on waves of realization. That woman had played us all for fools. I had to find her. She'd stolen my manhood.

I started having another dream around then. In it I saw myself breaking into a motel room. The harsh dirty sunlight uncovered her, naked on the bed. She pulled up the sheet. The man started to get up. "Wait," I said, and shot them both with my automatic. Camera. Because a damsel in distress had no right to call out the knight in me. Because in Louisiana I found—

"Herman," a shrill voice called up the stairs.

Shit, Kwestral thought. *Already?* Thursday nights were Mrs. Kwestral's bridge nights, her evenings with "the girls" the only time, it seemed, he managed to do any of his own writing. She didn't understand how vulnerable he was when writing, how her voice was like a blade running through him. It sent a physical shock to his system. Writing was suspension in a dream state, he wanted to explain. Her presence was a perpetual shark in the floating fantasy.

Row, row, he now told himself, as if he could somehow finish what he was working on when he knew she was there. At any moment she would stomp up the stairs, throw open the door, offer her lips, saying, "Hi, hon. What you doing, writing? Good. Just wanted to tell you Mommy's home." The smell of her cologne would linger, staring over his shoulder, sweetening everything he wrote. And she'd barge in again. And again. "I wanted to tell you..." "Lil Ropoff asked if you'd..." "Did the plumber..."

Do Not Disturb signs meant nothing to Ida Kwestral. All the locks in the house had been removed when Hermie was a baby, at the same time that his father had installed the Sure-Lock Homes system, leaving the outer doors safeguarded, the inner ones vulnerable. When Herm told his mother he wanted to reinstall the lock on his door his mother changed the topic to the Sure-Lock Homes system—how far ahead of his time Daddy was to install the alarm and locks—so that requesting a change seemed infidelity to his father's memory.

He envied the problems of starving writers alone in their garrets. He could move out, he had money enough, that wasn't the problem. But his mother, the one time he'd broached the subject, took it hard. "What will the girls say? It would be one thing if you married, and even so, this is a big house, there's room for a wife, children, you wouldn't even notice me. But on your own, who would cook for you, clean? I know you, you'd live in filth, eat potato chips for dinner while I'd rattle around like a pebble in a skull. Oh, your father would cry his eyes out if he knew."

Though he didn't want her to die he entertained fantasies of her death. If only she could be dead a year, come back for a month, die for another year, like a tulip. *Mom-in-the-Box*, he thought. How easy to push her away, knowing that if he cranked the handle she'd pop up, smiling, grocery bags in arms, promising to make his favorite dishes, sit back, hon, relax, it'll be done in a jiff. Eternity was just too long to wish someone away.

There was no putting it off, he realized. Maybe if he went down, talked to her, she wouldn't come into his room and try reading his screen. She seemed to think his efforts at narrative were term papers he wanted her to proofread for spelling mistakes.

With a sigh he backed up what he'd written. After she went to sleep maybe he'd get to the Louisiana part of his story while it was still fairly fresh in his memory. He didn't know where, if at all, the meeting between him, Grinn, and the two profs fit. He turned off the computer, saying, "Later, Luz," having femininized the receptacle of dreams. The sound of the wires going dead, the feeling of having killed someone, sickened him momentarily. But electrical death, he forced himself to believe, was not eternal. *It will wait,* he thought, and that secret, exciting as a woman, enabled him to go down for milk and cookies with Mom (whose heavy tread he could already hear approaching the stairs).

THIRTY-TWO

The desk sergeant did not return Percy's greeting, he just buzzed him in, then went to other business. Percy tried to seem equally nonchalant as he walked by, but there was something about the presence of so many cops. It made him feel he might reach out and take the gun of the one in front of him—not to shoot or even point, merely to twirl on his finger and give back.

There were three desks in the squadroom. Detective Sergeant Grinn sat closest to the door. Every inch of his desk was covered with paper. The chaos would have driven Percy crazy. He was the sort of man who had to straighten table settings before he could eat. Grinn was sucking a thick shake through a straw. He pulled hard. His cheeks were drawn in, making death's-head hollows beneath the bones. That and the large black glasses he wore made him seem a giant insect. Percy wasn't sure if Grinn were older than he, but he seemed to be. He looked tired. Sick of everything, his job, his life, and Percy. Especially Percy.

Percy took out his notebook. He had a list of items he wanted to discuss and was determined not to let Grinn intimidate him. He took the top off his pen and asked how things were going.

Grinn took the straw from his mouth. "I told you I'd let you know if anything turned up." He resumed sucking. The skin in the hollows of his cheeks played like tympanums. Chocolate oozed down the sides of his cup onto the papers below. Percy fought the urge to pull the container away from the messy cop and sponge his desk.

The phone rang. While Grinn *unhunh*ed and *mmm*ed Percy looked out the door. Two cops walked by carrying a cake. A small cop passed, holding a manila folder. Another cop ran by with a gift box.

"What about the clues I gave you?" Percy asked when Grinn hung up. He could make out an offkey version of "Happy Birthday." The voices were tinny. He tried to smile. Grinn raised his eyebrows.

"Such as," Percy said, interpreting the detective's gesture, "the slides of the house where my wife's being held. If you have pictures of a place there must be ways to find it."

"If that's the house."

"It's worth pursuing, isn't it? Remember that passage from her book? Don't you have a copy of *Bone*?"

The detective shook his head. Percy had the uncomfortable feeling that Grinn thought Mabel's disappearance a publicity stunt. "I'll bring you a copy," he said. He began to recite from memory. Grinn slurped greedily at the last of his shake. "'The walls angled oddly, and [*slurp*] there were weeds growing between the [*slupslup*] stones. It was tiny, as if a troll might live in it. Bone made her [*shlurrrp*] duck down to squeeze through the door [*ahhhh*].'"

The detective continued making obscene noises as he sucked up sweet foam. Percy was sure he was doing it to get a rise out of him. He refused to react. He looked at his notes. "What about the shadow in the picture?" he said. "It's a man, don't you think? It could be the man who calls himself Bone."

Grinn licked his lips. "It's a picture of a house. Any house. I told you that already. And that shadow could be from a tree, for all we know. A wood stump or something."

A tree, Percy thought. *The man can't see the forest for the trees.* "Okay then," he said. "What about the letters from Bone? Particularly what I discovered about the last one. Have you found Ryder Wood yet?"

"We're looking."

Percy gripped the pen tightly in his hand till it felt like a knife. He forced his fingers to relax. "Looking where?"

"We have some leads."

"Like what, for instance? If you don't mind my asking. I mean, it's just my wife we're talking about."

"Exactly," said Grinn. "That's why you should leave the detective work to us." He tossed the paper container in the trash can across the room. It first hit the wall, leaving a chocolate stain that in a few days might pass for blood. "Look, *Professor,*" he said with sarcastic emphasis, "do me a favor. Don't try to solve mysteries and I won't write them, okay? I'm sure this is very exciting for you and all, but it's my job and I know how—"

"Then tell me how. I want to know. Because you don't seem to be doing much of anything." More cops sauntered by. Old cops, young cops, male, female, black, white. It seemed like a Halloween party where everyone had come dressed as a cop.

"You don't value my leads," Percy said, "so I want to know exactly what you're doing instead. I want to find my wife before worse happens to her than already has. Do you know...can't you understand what it is to lose your wife this way?" Percy threw his hands up and his pen flew across the room. He got up to retrieve it. When he sat back down he saw a vein in Grinn's forehead pulsing.

"Look," the detective said, his voice forcibly calm. "I know what you're going through. I know exactly what it is to miss your wife, to worry, to fight to save her and...and to lose her anyway."

Percy could scarcely listen to the detective's platitudes. Empty mouthings. Everyone came up with them. How could anyone know what it was like? Certainly that anthropomorphic mosquito didn't know. Having someone "pass away" of natural causes was not the same as having her vanish. One could eventually replace the images of death with the images of life, but one could do nothing with the imaginings of what had happened—what still might be happening—but imagine them. Over and over. Torture by the sadist who lives in your soul.

"Taking it out on me won't help," Grinn said. "You want to know what we think? Okay, I'll tell you. I'm not going to mince words either. It's almost certain she ran off with someone. She most likely set this thing up with a lover. Letters, phone calls, the whole shebang. To hide the fact that she was planning—"

"No!" Percy yelled. "How dare you—"

"You want to hear what we're doing, then listen. Or get the hell out. I have work to do. Your wife isn't the only missing person around here. We have a kid's been lost since biking with friends Saturday. A teenager last seen leaving a dance. This isn't a babysitting agency. I'm not paid to hold hands with grieving husbands." The vein throbbed bluely. Percy watched it instead of Grinn. It beat a Morse code from the detective's brain.

"You people," Grinn said suddenly. "You may not believe this,

Professor, but I also know how to read. I read the letters in the file you gave me. I read that article about the dead kid. And I was more than interested to hear that your wife showed up at a Brooklyn stationhouse right before vanishing. That seemed suspicious. Even more so when it turned out that the boy she was looking for wasn't dead."

Percy wondered if Grinn's head would explode from that vein pulsing, he wondered if he could make it explode, filling it with hate. Grinn was just repeating what Kwestral had told him, as if that had anything to do with anything.

"What to make of it all, I don't know," Grinn was saying. "I suspect it ties in with the murder of the Lazar kid twenty years ago. That's what I'm doing, trying to figure out how it ties."

"I thought the boy who died was a suicide."

Grinn leaned back, seemed to relax. "I went to the files," he said. "Read old forensic reports. I just don't believe it was done unaided. It's a hunch, but there were marks on the body that had to be made by someone else. With a pen knife. Nice, huh? Now, I'm not saying your wife was in on that, or even that this Barbon character was. But you tell me why your wife felt compelled to open up a case that had been closed for twenty years."

"And you tell me why she'd alert the police first if—"

Grinn shrugged. "Guilt works in mysterious ways. Maybe she wanted to be found out—"

"Or found. She wants to be found. She—"

"—to pay for her crime. Maybe that's the source of her infidelities too and—"

"—she's never been unfaithful. She just fucked around—"

"Oh, come on, Professor. A smart man like you. Look, I've talked to lots of people in this town, they all say the same thing. Mabel Fleish did you dirty every chance she got. And if you don't know it, you're the only man in Winegarden who—"

"Who says it? A bunch of envious gossips with—"

"All right, I've had enough of you." Grinn took off his jacket, exposing, as if by accident, his gun holster. "I don't do marriage counseling. You wanted to know how the investigation's going. So now you know." He interlocked his fingers, pressed them back, cracking eight knuckles at once.

"Wait," said Percy. "What about Barbon anyway? Kwestral

told me you found out he's in a psychiatric ward. That's a dead end."

Grinn relaxed, musing. "At first that stymied me," he admitted, "then I found out he'd been released two years ago—a.m.a."

"By the American Medical Association?"

He almost smiled. "Against medical advice. And guess," he said, "who took him out."

"Mabel Fleish."

"Ha ha, funny. A comedian. No, it was Mrs. Lazar. Interesting?"

Percy shook his head. So what? So Larry Lazar's mother took Barbon out of the hospital. What did that have to do with Mabel?

"I can't say yet how the pieces hold together."

"That's just it. They don't. You're going off on a tangent."

"We think this tangent will lead to your wife."

"You think Mabel knew this stuff? You think she planted the notes from Bone, told me about phone calls, so she could run off with Beau Barbon because when the two of them were teenagers they killed a boy together and somehow this ties in with the murdered boy's mother? You're crazy. What are you saying? My wife wasn't a schemer. She could never have thought up this outrageous—"

"Your wife's not a schemer? She's a writer, isn't she? Spends her time alone, plotting ways to manipulate people. Readers, characters—doesn't matter who she plays with, whether they're flesh or paper. She sits there at her desk, dreaming up disguises. Man, woman, old, young. You think that's not *her* hiding behind her words? Invisible woman figures no one sees her behind her lies, but hey, I've got X-ray eyes." He adjusted the bridge of his glasses.

"That must explain it," Percy said. Grinn didn't acknowledge the dig. With a flash of insight Percy suddenly knew that was because Grinn wasn't joking. Dark lenses covered his mad vision. The man was strung out on bitterness.

"You think I'm a dope because I'm a cop," Grinn was saying. "You think someone who never went to college is a moron. I didn't get to be a detective watching TV. Listen, I educated myself, and I did it on the streets as well as through books. I read plenty but I also—"

He didn't know what to do, how to get the cats Grinn was releasing back in the bag. He knew one thing though. When Grinn remembered this conversation he was going to blame Percy for it.

"I know the stink of death," Grinn told him, "and that's not something you learn in a book. Think of the most horrible things you can, and that's not half of what I've seen, what I've had to *touch*." He held his hands out, as if importuning Percy to understand...as if they held visible proof. "You can't even imagine what I know. I see a person, I see a corpse. And it's my conclusion that what we are is meat. You, with your smart ideas about how you're going to solve the case and prove me wrong, how you can do it because you're a professor and I'm a cop. Look, you're not giving me a grade on this one."

Percy had never expected such an outburst. Grinn had always been taciturn, superior in his silence. Now he could see he was a man on the edge, someone who shouldn't be working, certainly not police work. He had a chip on his shoulder, a chip with *Professor* Furnival's features. "You think I'm a dope," he kept saying. "You think I don't know how to read. You think I'm not as smart as you."

Percy didn't know what to do. All he knew was, this was the man in charge. A man with a gun. And the right to use it. "Look, I never meant to criticize you. I just thought—"

Grinn couldn't hear past his own ranting. "Your wife, maybe she's dead, maybe she's not. But you know what meat likes to do before it rots? Have itself a party. So"—he took his head in his hands, twisted it, cracking his neck—"let's talk literature, *Professor*."

"Sure," said Percy, stalling for time. Should he speak to Grinn's supervisor? Would it help or hurt to do so? He didn't want to become embroiled in department politics. He had a feeling the police looked after their own. "Isn't your gun heavy?" he said, surprised to hear himself. "Why don't you take it off? Clearly, I'm no threat." His words were wind. Grinn could no more hear them than he could admit there were clues he was overlooking. With a gun he was a man who had super powers. Without it he was just a sick and tired old man.

Grinn rested his head between index finger and thumb, pointing to his temple. "If you think about it you'll see a detective's the perfect reader," he said, growing philosophical. "He reads what the writer never meant to reveal. She thinks she's covered everything with her cleverness, but false mustaches don't fool me. And it's a tiny step from thinking to doing."

Percy opened and closed his mouth several times before he could respond. "If you feel this way," he said quietly, "then why don't you study her book? She's being forced to act out a fantasy she may have set in motion but which—"

"I *am* reading her book, one she didn't know she was writing. How I see it is, she dreamed the fantasy to begin with. There's no reason to believe she's being forced to act against her will."

"Thoughts are not deeds."

"Yeah, then what are they? I don't teach English classes, but I know 'to wish' is a verb." Detective Grinn got halfway out of his chair. Percy continued looking at his notes. The letters swam together. For a moment he saw the Bone poems, how they were all cut from the same book. He heard the sound of laughter and saw two cops eating cake from paper plates with pictures of cartoon police dogs. They held a piece out to Grinn, who reached to take it. His glasses slipped down for a moment, just long enough for him to wink. But his eyes looked so tired Percy thought it must be a tic.

THIRTY-THREE

Mabel sat in the dark, hooded and alone, listening to the wind blow. She pulled the ratty blanket Ryder had left tight across her back. She remembered how he had gone to a dark corner of the room before leaving the first morning. He pulled out the blanket, spent some time draping it around her shoulders. It kept slipping off. "Can you hold it on?" he asked. She didn't feel like answering. "Come on, it can't be that bad." He took out a knife, held it up like an artist measuring perspective with a paintbrush. She grabbed hold of the blanket with her chained hands, to show that yes, she could hold it on, only please please don't cut her. He pulled the blanket away, made a slit in the center, inserted Mabel's head, creating a poncho. "That suits you fine," he said.

There was no wood in the fireplace. Ryder brought firewood in with him when he came. He liked to make the place warm, but only at night. The smoke was less likely to be detected then, she figured, passersby rare.

He fed her well—when he was there—but when he wasn't he put the hood over her head, tightly tied, so all she could have was liquids through a straw. She'd already had all the soup in the thermos when it was cool enough to suck up but warm enough to be a comfort. He left cans of Ensure and plenty of water. Wine, beer, hard liquor too—as if she would drink any of that. Even eating seemed to have a strange effect on her. It made her drowsy and oddly sexy. She thought the food must be drugged, but she couldn't stop eating it. When he wasn't around there was nothing to do. And when he was, eating seemed to put off the inevitable "experiments" and "writing exercises" he dreamt up.

Her stomach growled. How could she be hungry? She'd just had a whole can of chocolate Ensure. Trying to forget food she looked at one of the windows. She could make out brightness through the slats. Thin blades of sunlight penetrated the hut, crisscrossing in its center like ceremonial rapiers. Wind was blowing around the cabin like an animal looking for a way in. Cold and sunny, the kind of autumn day she loved...but not here.

A bitter bile rose in her stomach. She tasted the horror of the past nights, the metallic afterbite of irony. For, here she had finally decided to be a faithful wife and had fought off Horace's advances despite her desire, only to find herself imprisoned by a creature from her past. A creature that insisted she was his creation and he hers, that he was the evil in her soul.

It was madness, it was all madness. She knew it, but she didn't know what to do about it. He was in control now, making her his partner on the assault against her sanity, forcing her to play out scenes from her book...with revisions.

He kept saying she'd created him, that he hadn't existed till she called him from the well. Maybe in a sense she did, or created his madness. Was she then responsible for the crime against her? Ryder argued that she was. "That's nonsense," she said aloud, continuing the disagreement they'd been having. It would almost be a relief when he returned, to have someone to set herself against instead of battling within this way.

If only she knew what he wanted, what he really wanted, if only it was something she could give. She thought for a while it was sex, although he didn't approach her in an overtly sexual way. He teased her, he tormented her, but he didn't screw her. At first she was relieved for, despite a certain amount of pleasure she'd taken in games of powerlessness, she'd never relished actual rape. However after ample time spent assessing her situation she'd begun to think sex might be her only way out.

"Ryder," she had said, "you can take these things off my wrists now. We don't need them, do we?" She smiled in her shackles and tried to look seductive although she felt unwashed, stinking from days of fear. "I like to use my hands," she went on coyly, "when I'm making love."

He looked at her, the skin pulled taut beneath his cheekbones, vibrating like a drum. "Making love," he said. "Making *love*? Is that what this is about for you? You really are a sick woman if you think this is love." Shaking his head, chuckling to himself, tapping

his foot with angry energy. "Making lust at one time. Making
litacha now." He gave that annoying goofy smile, showing off his
hick pronunciation to mock ambition, only the more so revealing
its hold over him.

He wanted to collaborate with her on a book. To that end he
hung her up and dropped her down, made her arms and legs dance
puppetlike, all the time getting angrier, screaming that she was
holding something back. And she was—her sanity.

But of course there was more to it. For though he left pen and
paper within her reach, and though she wrote continually in her
mind, she never wrote anything of substance down for him. It
wasn't simply her dislike of someone (including Percy) reading over
her shoulder, her inability to work that way—though it was true
she had to feel free to edit, to keep what she wanted, discard what
she didn't. She couldn't let go, knowing that as soon as he came in
he'd head to the pages, read what she'd scrawled. But there was
something else, she *was* holding back. He wanted her to make a
beginning, something they would then follow through together. He
squirmed around in front of her, trying to get her to understand his
need. Wanting her to dream her dirty dreams. He didn't seem to
understand, and she couldn't explain it, but she was having one of
the worst cases of writer's block in her life. The thought of picking
up a pen and actually writing the words that passed through her
mind made her sick. As if the things being done to her were fantasies
of a nature too shameful to divulge.

She got up and paced the room. She couldn't reach the winch
handle or the curtain that hid the Harrow from view. He left the key
to her wrist shackles just out of reach too, on the far end of the table.
Alone, she couldn't help wondering if she'd die in this abandoned
cabin and be found in humiliating bondage, her bones harnessed,
her arm reaching for a key she couldn't quite grasp. And over her
head this horrible hood, tied tightly in the back in one of his
impossible knots. *Horace,* she thought, remembering his falcon,
the leather cover over Irving's head, how he looked like a sheathed
penis, waiting to be freed to set off after some little mouse of a thing.
"Cock," she whispered, for the sake of saying something, "-a-
doodle-doo."

She thought she heard the sound of someone digging nearby.
"Help," she called, her voice muffled by the heavy cloth about her
head. She knew her cry wouldn't carry and was surprised when the

digging sound stopped. "Help, help." Then the sound resumed. No one came.

She sat on the Bed. Daylight still, late afternoon (the only time the sun was at an angle to penetrate the window slats). Soon it would be getting dark. Ryder would be here then. She hoped and feared he would be. The days were so short, the nights endless.

"Help," she called heartlessly. She sat and listened, hearing only the clomping of her heart. Her ears picked up another rhythm. A hot smell flooded her nostrils. *Calump calump calump.* The beat grew loud, then soft, then merged with another. Then it was gone. It was not the first time she'd heard it, but she feared it was her desire she listened to. The sound of hooves grew louder, the hot smell of horse sharpened.

"Hey!" she cried at the clomping. "Help me!" The sound galloped past, died away, the rider rode on. One time she'd heard several voices, not shouting but talking, laughing. A woman giggled like a bell. Another time someone rushed past, crying, "I can't stop. I can't stop." Someone else yelled, "Pull back on the reins." Hooves like the Lone Ranger. Shouting. Then silence. If she could hear them so well, why couldn't they hear her?

Because they were not listening for the muffled cries of a woman with a sack over her head.

"At least people pass by," she told herself, although what good was it if she couldn't get their attention? She could just reach the window, just touch its shutters with her fingertips if she pulled against the harness with all her stretch. She did so now and tried to grab the bottom plank. She managed to get her fingers around the edge to the first joint. She pulled at it with all her might, using the tension in the rope that held her back. It wouldn't give, but she wouldn't stop trying, knowing how hard it was to grab hold of the wood to begin with. If she got it loose, she thought, she could cry out the opening and have a better chance of being heard. Or maybe she'd remove all the boards, escape before Ryder returned. Ha! In any case, activity was a respite from waiting. And it relieved the hunger she felt, and the cold.

She tore her tips on the edges of wood, leaned back into her heels, grunted like a weightlifter. It didn't budge. It was hopeless. The planks were nailed together and to the window frame in many places. If she got one nail free there would be all the others to contend with. Still, it was something to do. She courted rage, holding Ryder's hair in her hands. Then Dr. Xavier's beard.

"What do you think now?" she asked the old man, furious at him more than anyone. He had thought he was always so right, and he had been so wrong. Just like her father. She remembered the times he had convinced her she was being paranoid when in truth her fears had been prophetic. She gritted her teeth.

"Take that!" she yelled. Her fingers were sore. She was tired. She had to let go. She did and the release sent her flying back into the middle of the room, she lost her footing and swung half off the ground. Sitting, she put the torn tips in her mouth, sucked the skin. Her blood tasted metallic. She wondered how long a person could survive eating herself. She removed the fingers from her mouth. Would that she could as easily remove her thoughts. The smell of her wastes accumulating in a bucket wafted over. Gandhi had done it, she remembered reading, looking that way. If she had to, if Ryder stopped showing up, could she...

She turned away in disgust and walked the length of her rope, stretching her arms and legs again, pulling her body with all her might in the direction of the table, where the key was. He left it there on purpose. She knew he did because he measured its distance each time from the edge of the table before he left. Because he undid the winch and played out the rope, admonishing her with a finger to "be a good girl while I'm gone." Testing her. In hopes of inflicting more punishment, as if he needed a reason.

She took the can of Ensure and threw it at the table. It only pushed the key further away before clattering to the floor. "Dr. Xavier," she said, looking at the window, "you're a blockhead." She remembered a discussion they had had about her difficulty writing after *Bone*. "Remember what I told you about my writer's block?" she asked the plank. She didn't know if he would or not— he forgot so much of what she said, remembering things she hadn't—but this was her fantasy, and so she went on. "I used to be free, knowing no one would ever read what I wrote. Now everyone I know will."

"So?"

"So how do I write with all these people looking over my shoulder?"

"Pen, paper, word processor. However you like."

"Don't you get it? There are characters I want to write about— based on real people, see? But I think how this one will be upset, that one hurt. Whatever I write, no matter how I disguise it, I feel like a criminal in a land of detectives. How can I write about Tanya's incest with her father without betraying her confidences? I can disguise it, sure. I make everyone wear a mask, but it doesn't work. Not only is it all transparent, but the changes necessary to make fiction diminish the impact of reality."

She bit her nails. She thought about how she had disguised Bone's origin in Beau (although why had she bothered, since Beau was dead?). In doing so, she had invented Ryder, only he turned out to be real. It hadn't been her intention to write Ryder into existence. She wasn't even sure it was true. But in any case, Ryder saw himself in the character, and now he was tormenting her like a willful child. She felt like God for a moment, when His creation stood against Him.

Dr. Xavier said she was looking for Beau in the men she had affairs with, so it was possible that whatever qualities drew her to Ryder were ones she had seen in her lost love—and written about: qualities Ryder saw in himself. Of course, Dr. Xavier also said she sought her punishing father in her lovers. "Bah," she told the plank, pulling again at the old man's beard. These discussions with herself were sickening.

Something rustled behind her. She shook her head free of fancy. Had he returned? Was he there, watching her poor attempt at escape? She turned slowly. Ryder was vengeful. If he saw her trying to reach the boards he would mete out some disgusting punishment.

The door was closed. The room was empty. It must have been outside, she thought. Then she heard it again. Across from her was the glint of eyes. Something crouched in the dark and watched. A rat? Too large. A cat? Perhaps. The animal moved. Mabel was afraid, she felt like a bound sacrifice. What would she do, how would she protect herself from a rabid carnivore, a bobcat perhaps?

The creature shambled into the room. Mabel saw the black and white fur, and knew herself to be in the presence of a skunk. Several in fact. A family entered the hut, one by one, through a hole in the floor by the far wall. The mother shuffled her fat body first. Three little ones followed. Then all stood still, watching Mabel.

Intense emotion squeezed out of her, communicating across species, translating into English as, *Don't be afraid, Living Things, I'm happy to see you;* translating into Skunk as an aura of nonthreatening benevolence. In any case the small animals did not run or spray. They walked about, exploring the room.

Mabel moved cautiously to the far side of the room. She watched the mother sniff the chocolate drink on the floor, lap it, turn away. Mother and kittens ambled roly poly, curious as cats, then vanished too soon down the hole.

"Thank you," said Mabel softly, she didn't know to whom.

Cold and boredom once again drew her to explore her limited space. She pulled herself up the length of her ceiling rope, like a fakir doing a trick. If only she disappeared when she reached the top. Instead she slipped back down, giving herself a rope burn across her palms and ascertaining for the umpteenth time that there was no way she could unscrew the pulley system or the eyehooks. Still, it was important to work out every day. She needed to be in good shape if an opportunity to escape arose. She used the metal chain between her hands as a weight and did arm lifts with it, then tried to pull it apart, a variation on an isometric exercise for strengthening triceps. She jogged a bit, then paced back and forth, going to the limits of her rope like a mad dog. Searching, searching for a way out, searching as if she hadn't searched before.

The sound of hooves began to near for the second time. Again she smelled horse and cried for help in the direction of the riders. Voices. Closer this time. In fact, they seemed just outside the door. A man and a woman. "Help!" she called. "I'm in the house!" She pulled herself as close to the cracks in the shuttered window as she could get. Tried to remove, or at least loosen, her hood so her voice had a better chance of carrying through the heavy material. She could so clearly hear the voices outside. "No, Tom," the woman said. "I don't want to. It's locked. It belongs to someone." A male laugh. Murmurs of reassurance. Cooing. Then her again: "Really, I don't. Let's go home. I don't want to anymore. Don't break it." "Break it, break it!" Mabel was yelling, but even in her own ears the sound was *brkin*, hardly audible at that. She tried a high scream. It sounded like a TV playing in someone else's house. She doubted the people outside could even hear it. She banged her hand on the floor, stomped her foot. Banged a can of Ensure. It was unbelievable. She felt like she was screaming in a dream, running on taffy legs. Nothing she did had any effect on the people just outside the door. Were they deaf?

A few moments passed, then the voices died away. She heard the horses ride off. Still she cried through the tiny hole in her hood. "Help help help." It sounded like hiccups. When her throat was raw and her voice had grown raspy she stopped. She put her hands to the sides of her head and pulled at the material. Tight and heavy and strong. She worked her fingers at the knot in back, trying to trace a beginning, a starting place to unravel, before she realized it was hooked in some way to her harness rope in the back. All she was doing by her twisted exertions was strangling herself. She now struggled to undo the damage. She had to get it loose before her air was cut off. She was on the verge of passing out and didn't think she could loosen the hold before she did, but somehow she managed to. She gulped at the air until her heart rate returned to normal and her eyes stopped bugging out. God, Ryder was the devil, clever as the devil. He'd thought of everything.

She sat on the Bed, pulled the blanket around her, looked at the curtained corner he called the Harrow. She shuddered, thinking what lay in store. Oh, what was the sense in trying? she thought. With a sudden decision to give up she threw off her blanket, willing pneumonia as her only escape. Why all this struggle to survive, only to have the madman slice her up like a turkey when he'd had his fill of other pleasures? She sat there, shivering, determined not to give in to the urge to wrap the blanket around herself again.

Cold, however, turned out to be a harder taskmaster than she expected. It wouldn't let her surrender. After some moments she found herself up again, jogging in place, plotting escape.

Even if she died in the attempt she knew she had to try, to keep trying. She walked around her cell, slowly, methodically. Looking with new eyes, willing a sense of freshness, wonder, as self-help books told blocked writers to do. She tried to see as if she'd just regained sight after a lifetime blind.

She paused at the fireplace. She had already investigated it, knew the flue was too small for her to climb through, even if she got herself unchained. Still, she got down on her hands and knees, studied it again, looking up, looking down and sideways. Ryder swept it clean before he left but there were traces of sooty material. Was there anything that could be done with ash? Mabel thought of collecting it, hiding it someplace, storing it up, but for the life of her she couldn't think what to do with it afterward—blow it in Ryder's eyes when he wasn't prepared, yeah sure, that would do a lot of good. And while Ryder was wiping the dirt from his eyes she would bite through the rope with her teeth, steal the key, run outside and away. Uh huh.

She knew the door was locked outside with an iron chain. She had seen it the first night and she always heard Ryder work the padlock before entering. If she had a utensil of some sort, a weapon...but she didn't.

What about the Bed itself? Ryder took measurements of it whenever he came, centering it beneath her hanging body according to some system. She went to it now, made a visual mark with her eye, detecting a particular stain, a scratch on the floor. Putting her straw at one end and a can of Ensure at the side she pushed the mattress back a few feet.

Looking, looking, using her hands to feel what she might not detect with her eyes. And so it was that at first she didn't see anything out of the ordinary. But her fingertips felt a roughness, and then she noticed a crack. It was thin and crooked but looked suspiciously man-made. She traced the line carefully and sure enough—there was another. Could it be, could it open to something beneath the house? She told herself not to get excited, but digging her nails into the cracks she believed she would be able to lift a board. Yes, something did seem to lift up. It was heavy, it was tight, but she thought there was a hole under her, a root cellar perhaps.

Sounds on the walk, someone fumbling with the lock! She just had time to push the mattress back in place, lining it up with the stains and scratches, straw and can, hoping she had marked the exact place. She put the straw in the can and rolled it across the room, sat on the Bed, wrapping the blanket around her. Waiting, a mysterious hooded creature in a darkening room.

Ryder came in with a lit lantern. He took off his knapsack. "Brrrr," he said. "Getting cold out there. You warm enough in your little boneriding hood?" She didn't say anything. She tried not to move at all, maybe he'd be afraid. "Hey, why so glum?" No reply. He came over, pushed her gently. She jumped up, roared, thinking to surprise him into having a heart attack. She knew it unlikely, but she wasn't thinking her best. He grabbed her wrists in one hand and laughed. "You're a tiger." He threw her back on the Bed and went to the winch. "No," she cried, "no no no no no." He smiled in his most charming manner as he lifted her arms above her head, pulled her body off the ground. "Now honey," he said, "just hang on a minute and let me see what you've written today."

He locked the handle in place and went to the notebook, thumbed it, revealing page after blank page. He gave her a long disappointed look. "What you trying to tell me—you want to just hang it up? You can't get the hang of it? You're sick of hanging around, you want to hang out with someone else?" He gave her a mock glare, confronting her. "You got some hang-up?"

Mabel groaned. Whether it was purely the ache in her arm sockets or had more to do with the quality of his puns was hard even for her to tell. Ryder took a small notebook out of his back pocket.

"Maybe you need a little inspiration."

She groaned again, and again it was impossible even for her to tell whether it from physical pain or the foreknowledge that he was going to read some awful stuff. In addition to all that there was the humiliation of her position, the vulnerability—just hanging there, a body sack of nerves and blood to be used, and used against her.

"*I* used to hang out when you gave your readings," he said. "Bet you didn't know that." His manner was almost diffident now. "Yeah, sure thing," he said. "I liked to go to your readings, see you up there. Listen to you speak my words. I liked to look at you, look anyplace on you I wanted. Think about your naked body, your naked mind. And afterward they'd all come running. Hugging and kissing, flattering you, you lapping it like honey till you were sticky with their lies. But me, I didn't reveal myself. Didn't want you to know—just yet. I was plotting something but the time wasn't...you know.

"I knew me a witch doctor once," he went on. "She gave me the power to make myself invisible. It wasn't easy to get that power. It meant burial, hanging, getting strung out. Now I'm giving that to you—free. I'm making you as invisible as a woman gets. No one hears you, right? Scream, yell, cry, it don't matter none. No one sees you— 'ceptin' me a course, and if I close my eyes, *poof*!" He threw out his hands in a cloud of finger smoke.

"My arms," Mabel whimpered. Ryder just smiled. "Speak up," he said. "Got to learn to *pro*ject your words." He paused, she didn't say anything. "Good for a writer," he continued. "That's what I hear. Invisible narration, I mean. Omniscient point of view from an invisible narrator—see, I know a few things. Not much, I sho'nuff ain't edoocated like you all, literary lady, but I read me some of them there books you always giving. To help me with, what you call that again, that big old word, oh yeah, per*spec*tive. Ways to see, right? Spec. Voice, all that."

He twanged her arm strings to make them flutter a bit. Did it absentmindedly, like someone might strum a chord if a guitar was in his hands. "So like I said, I went to your readings, right there at the college that night and the one at the library too. Figure now it sure is nice a you to return the favor at this here *private* reading. Well, don't let me keep you hanging on my every word. Here goes— a little something I wrote last night while you was hanging out."

He took a sip of water, cleared his throat.

"I dreamt of a porcelain hand," he read, "a lady's hand, just the hand, fingers spread in a poignant gesture of beseeching. It was a statue of a gloved hand, and it stood on the mantlepiece in the living room. *Our* living room, though we never had such a mantlepiece, such a hand. I dreamt the memory of it preceding it as it stood there, the fingers intact, though I stood viewing the object with all its fingers broken. Shattered. And I wept, holding the shattered hand, knowing I would never see it again as it once was, in all its perfection. Knowing my mother had died, and my uncle too. And I would never see them again, as they once were, in their prime."

He paused, as if waiting for applause or comment. Cleared his throat, poured more water from the Thermos, drank it. "Well?" he asked finally.

"Please," she begged. With the bag over her head the sound was slurred. Ryder looked annoyed.

"What you saying?" he asked. "Speak up, speak up. What is it?"

"My arms."

He mimicked her. "Mmm amm? Mmmhmm? I don't get you." He made his face look more puzzled than puzzlement. Then put his hand behind his ear like a deaf old man. "All right," he said, laughing. "The jig is up." He boinged her a few times before lowering her slightly so he could more easily remove her hood. He went to do so but before he could she kicked out at his groin. She hadn't been planning it but she saw her opportunity and took it, not thinking how disastrous the consequences could be. Ryder just danced to the side like a bullfighter.

"Okay then," he said. "Have it your way." He left the hood on her, held her legs between his knees and tied them tight with rope. Hoisted her body higher.

"Another one?" he asked shyly. "You want another? Well, I don't know. Oh, all right, maybe a short one. What you think of a little poem then? Listen. I call it 'Spire.'

Respire
Aspire
Perspire
Expire

"Thank you, thank you," he said, holding his hands up to shush the wild stamping of feet. "There's so much I could add," he told her, "to add to the *ire*, but it would ruin the acronym—is that what it's called? There's gyre and fire, mire, liar, crier, but then there wouldn't be no R-A-P-E-, would there?"

He took a joint out of his pocket, lit it, offered her a toke. She shook her head, which shifted her hood slightly so she had to maneuver to get the eye slits back in place. That was when she saw he had drawn smoke into his lungs and was standing next to her. She could do nothing to prevent him from holding her head, blowing into her hole. She tried not to breathe but he was up on her tricks and did it again. It was almost a kiss, but his lips touched the hood, not her lips, and smoke, not a tongue, entered her mouth.

"Do you a world of good," he said as he undid her hood and took it off. He tousled her hair. "Gonna have to wash you soon. Guess it's sweaty in there but want to keep you warm, you know." He smiled. "Don't worry, I'll wash you gentle. Like a baby. Here now, take another hit." She shook her head. He brought the joint to her lips. She couldn't fight him but she tightened her mouth. "Damn!" he said, slapping his leg. "You are one ornery bitch. I could hold your nose, you know that, don't you?"

She closed her eyes, trying to find some way to hold herself up internally so her arms wouldn't pull out the sockets. He looked at her a moment. There was a terrible flash of compassion then. "Wish it didn't have to be this way," he said as he went to the wall, loosened the crank. Let her collapse on the Bed, let her arms fall to her lap.

"Thanks," she said, rubbing her wrists where the shackles had cut into them. "Pot makes me crazy—you know that. I wouldn't mind a cigarette though." He put one in her mouth, lit it for her. She inhaled deep and smiled, smoke streaming dragonlike from her nostrils. It seemed almost normal between them, sultry, as if they were sitting in a bar, not a shack. "Why didn't I think to ask before?" she said. "Jesus, I feel like smoking two at a time, it tastes so good."

"That stuff's poison. I smoke it too but this shit is good for you. Why not try it?" He held out the joint.

She shook her head. "I don't do drugs. Alcohol, yes, cigarettes, yes. Pot and pills, no."

He shrugged. "Suit yourself then," he said, turning to build a fire in the fireplace. He fed it with wood from his backpack, small tinder at first, as if he were giving the tenderest parts to a baby. After he'd gotten it burning well he untied her legs. "What you say we eat? I'm starved."

Mabel was amazed to find she was hungry too. *I am going to have to go on a diet after this,* she thought, then giggled nervously. It seemed a preposterous notion.

He set out paper plates, also from his backpack. "No forks and knives," he said. "Hope you don't mind." She held up her hands to show they were shackled. "Come on," he said. "It ain't so bad. There's a foot and a half of chain between them." He handed her a bloody bag. "Go on, open it," he said. "Little something for you."

For a few moments things had seemed okay, but now the reality of her situation came to her in a rush of horror. Not restricted to plots from her book the madman was capable of any atrocity, she'd learned that too well. Inside the brown bag something dripped blood. A dismembered head? Might be. After all, how did she know she was Bluebeard's first wife. "Go on," he said. "Don't be shy."

She unscrunched the paper. The bag was full of feathers. She pulled out the carcass of a goose.

"Shot it for you myself. Want to see you pluck it." He laughed. "I want to see you stick your hands inside and scoop out its entrails. Clean out its guts, momma. Give it an enema. Hold it between your legs and stuff it." He handed her another bag. "Later though," he said. This bag was even bigger. She opened it and pulled out a turkey, roasted and still warm. "We going to have ourselves," he said, pulling off one drumstick, "a feast."

Ryder ate like someone who had just smoked a joint. Mabel ate more sedately but her hunger kept surprising her. After he'd eaten his fill he opened his notebook again.

"Hear something else?" he asked. "From last spring, from a

time when you and I..." He looked at her and there was a sweetness to his eyes she hadn't seen for a long while, a dreamy quality. Like he was thinking about her and she was the most important woman on earth. Seth's look when he was suckling and the milk ran from her like white love. Holding her finger in his tiny hand, trusting, looking up into her face—couldn't say Momma yet, but with his mouth full of her his lips made a *mmm mmm* sound and the vibration ran through and through.

"Okay," she said softly, unable to deny him. She felt herself that kind of beetle she'd read about, the one who fed her young with her own body when they hatched inside. Ryder smiled back, something warm in his gaze. For a moment she had hope. "Thank you," he said, "kindly." He turned to the page.

"Under fullblown magnolia trees with you," he read. "The fleshy pink flowers with the moist white of cartilage at center. Bones of magnolia branches. The boneness of bone. Trunk atwist, a writhing crazy wood skeleton. Rotting petal carpet, its sweet stink of perfume. Heavy as a corpse's honey, honey, ain't it? Oh, and the large black ants crawling on you and up the trunk and branches, the juicy bi-parts of them. Heavy petaled flowers too drunk to hold up their heads. Lolling brainless. Droop-breasted, pink-nippled centers bleeding onto white skin, brownly bruised. Amputated tits of the magnolia tree. Mastectomy tree of—"

"Ryder!" Mabel said. "Stop, it's terrible."

He looked surprised, then hurt. "What?"

"I mean, it's not terrible writing, the thoughts are terrible. I remember that day. I remember lying with you under those magnolia trees, looking up at the flowers. I remember the light in there, so pink and white, and yes, there was something bonelike in it too, but it was beautiful, sculpted like bone. Didn't you think it was beautiful? I never knew you were thinking such horrible—" She put her head in her hands and began to weep. "Oh God," she cried. "What did she do to you, that mother of yours, what must she have done to you."

Ryder sat beside her on the Bed. "Don't cry, honey," he said softly. "You'll find out."

Mabel looked up. Through tears she saw his face, the bones of his face all angles. "No," she whispered.

"Yes," he whispered back. He stood up, went to the wall, got ready to turn the crank. "Think I'll call this here chapter 'Harrowing the Heroine.'" He pulled her up by the harness, but for the time being didn't tighten the ropes her wrists were attached to, so she dangled free. "Or 'Harrowing the Whore.' What do you like better?"

She made no reply, just tried to keep her heart from fluttering away.

He locked the winch in place and went to the curtain, pulled it back with a "Ta-daaa!" The cylindrical form revealed itself to be a vaulting horse. On its back, a saddle with a rubber-ringed hole in its center.

"This," Ryder said proudly, "is the Harrow."

"Harrow?" She thought she detected pride in his voice and lashed at it. The impulse to destroy was stronger than anything, stronger certainly than reason. "A harrow's got teeth. Don't you know that? How could that be a harrow? There's nothing harrowing about it." She gave a disdainful snort.

"No?" he said.

A chill ran through her, but she continued to fight. "There's no teeth," she insisted. Ryder came around to the table and she twisted her body so she saw him reach under it. *Uh oh*, she thought, and the precariousness of her situation struck her anew. What was she doing, arguing with a lunatic about what he called his torture device? He wanted to think himself a genius, maybe the best thing was to play along.

But all Ryder did was pull out an unabridged dictionary. Webster's Third, she thought she recognized.

"Harrow," he read. "Archaic: to ravish; violate; despoil." He looked at her. "One of its secondary meanings," he explained, pointing his finger. "But teeth is good. Glad you're starting to cooperate." He yucked in his best cracker manner. "Much obliged." Reaching under the table again he pulled out an object about a foot long. It had a sharp head and feathered tail, it was made of wood and painted and looked suspiciously like an arrow. Exactly, in fact, like an arrow.

He worked the pulley, bringing Mabel along until she hung directly over the saddle. He shackled her legs to either side of it and ran a bridle across the horse's belly. She kicked and fought but he was a good deal stronger and not swinging on a rope. When he had her tied in place he inserted the arrow into the rubber-ringed hole, turning a clamp or vise beneath. It was at that point Mabel began to scream.

"Oh, hush up," he scolded. "Just going to do us some boneriding is all. Want to wear your little boneriding hood?"

She forced herself to quiet down, dreading having that heavy material over her head like death itself. She hung about six inches off the arrow, it was aimed into her, her thoughts were running wild. "You better get rid of that," she said, not knowing what she was saying. "Hand it to me now. It's not a toy."

He looked at her sideways, as if flirting. "What," he asked, his grin revealing gapped teeth, "did you say? Don't tell me you women plan to be hunters now instead of prey?" Recognizing rhyme he laughed aloud, shaking his head at his own brilliance. He picked up the notebook and jotted it.

She watched, fascinated, as he began writing more notes, talking to himself. She felt as though she were looking into a mirror, removed from what she saw for all that she recognized the image. After a few moments Ryder looked up. He saw her watching him. "It's for Marrow," he explained. "Need to get to the heart of the matter." He put the book down, took the small notebook from his pants pocket and laid it on top. "Copy some stuff into the big book later," he explained. As if she cared. He went back to the winch, lowered her body till she felt the head tickling her hairs. "'Arrowing the Heroine,'" he said. "What you think, that a better title?"

"Ryder, stop!"

He turned, looking surprised. "Stop? You mean you don't like this idea for a chapter? Okay, I can take criticism. Editorial feedback. You want me to *cut* it. *Insert* it someplace else? It's not *penetrating* enough. *Insideful?* So what should we replace it with? 'Harrowing the Marrow'? Come on, I've shared a lot of my ideas with you. Now I want your response." He stood at the handle, unlocked it. He could let her down hard and she would die a gruesome death.

"Do I make my point?" he said.

"I'll do anything," she said. "I'm not unwilling to help. I just don't know what you want."

"I want a chapter to take the place of this one," he said, no smiles this time. "Something harrowing, that uses the Harrow I've set up—that is, the vaulting horse and saddle. And you, ready to descend to a bonish hello. You can't think of something better we'll just have to go with my idea."

"Okay, wait. Let me think. Give me time."

"Time? I'm sorry," he said, "but we have a deadline. Tell you what though. Think on it a while. I have some chores but I'll be back. Maybe you'll have thought your way out of this one. Let's see what kind of writer you really are. Sorry about this," he said as he took out her hood. "You understand the necessity, I wager." He began singing, "In your Easter Bonnet" as he tied the neck tight, almost to the point of strangulation. He checked her leg shackles, wrist shackles, readjusted the position of the arrow. He built up the fire in the fireplace till it roared, humming happily, as if he were just a merry woodsman in a mountain retreat, as if a manacled woman weren't suspended over an arrow not ten yards away. When he got the fire going so it wouldn't need tending for a while he went out. She heard him monkey with the padlock.

Alone at last.

Hanging heavy in all her bones above the crude arrow, she felt like a sandbag used for target practice. She was trying to think, to see, to plot an escape, to plot a chapter that might get her out of this one. She darted her head around, looking at her circumstances, seeking inspiration. On the Bed the remains of their dinner congealed in its grease. She looked at the tape recorder on the table, saw it was on, although she hadn't noticed when he had done that. Recorded for posterity, research for Ryder's awful work in progress, his Marrow. The dried flower arrangement still sat on the table near the tape recorder. That lovely red cone, she had had ample time to observe, was really a flower. A flower made of many flowers. Autumnal red. Brittle by now, dried out. Maybe stiff. She often saw such conelike flowers on bushes this time of year. Could she get him to replace the arrow with that?

Someone outside was digging. She called for help, as she always did, knowing that no one would hear her, as they always didn't. Digging digging. What was going on just on the other side of the wall? Why all the digging? Why didn't the diggers notice the shack, hear the cries of a woman muffled in a "bonnet"?

Such thoughts were not helpful. She could hardly tell Ryder when he returned that her idea for the chapter consisted of curious diggers breaking open the padlock, finding her, saving her. But such were the fantasies that preoccupied her, and so the time was quickly spent. Before she had thought of an alternative chapter to Ryder's he was back. "Well?" he asked, always the gentleman. "Any ideas?"

"What about what about what about?" she said. Her eye caught on the dried arrangement. "What about what about what about?" He was heading toward the winch, about to uncrank it. "What about," she said, "replacing the arrow with that? That red flower maybe. It might be a comment on, I don't know, on peace, on getting to the marrow of the bone with love, how about?"

He looked at her like she was sick. He turned to see what she was staring at and turned back. "That," he said, "sucks." He went over to the arrangement and plucked the center from it, holding it gingerly by the branch. "Know what this is, don't you?" She shook her head. It was familiar, she saw it everywhere, but she never thought to ask what it was called. She hadn't much interest in nature, she wrote from inside her mind, the great outdoors didn't figure in her writing. "Sumac," he said. "You want that up your cunt?"

He held it up. "It produces a most turrible rash," he said, pausing. "Like poison ivy. Could be interesting to put that there"— he pointed it at her nether-wishbone—"give the bitch an itch to make her twitch." He replaced the branch in order to jot the rhyme. "Yeah, I kind of like that," he said. "It's got possibilities. You're cooking, Annabelle. We could do some interesting experiments, I think. After you get the rash we could try all sorts of ways to scratch it."

He chuckled as he took the arrow out of its hole, using it to rub his scalp. "Yeah. Maybe we'll call the book Cone." Then he stopped. "Wait a minute. Wouldn't the poison infect me too, through you? I mean, if I decide to go that way. I haven't. Spill the seeds of my creativity that way, uh uh. I've been saving it up, for Marrow. Don't want to waste it in you, then you'd suck me dry again and I'd be left with nothing. But with this bush up your bush the decision ain't mine. That it, Mabel, that your plan? Protecting your virginity?"

His eyes were rolling about the room in anger. "Betray me again, did you? I've half a mind to use that arrow, did you really think I would? Let you off that easy, with an arrow in your gut? No, baby girl, I got a few more games to play with you, 'fore we're through. Got to get to that book material, you know. Time's afleeting." His stare caught on their dinner plates. He picked up the drumstick he'd eaten and shook it at her, an evil smile spreading over him.

Still shaggy with meat, a thick ball of cartilage on the end, veins and tendons made an almost wormy head. He inserted it in the saddle, in place of the arrow, adjusted her position, tightening her hands above her head so that even as she kicked and struggled, she couldn't resist. Her center was focused, a wet bullseye above the bone. She looked desperately out the eye slits. The bonehead seemed huge with its shredded meat wig, she could see blood on the bone. That was always the problem with turkey—cook it to keep the white meat moist and the dark meat was underdone, cook it for the dark meat and the white dried out. "No, please," she whispered, struggling as he began to lower her. She strained but there was nothing she could do.

He stopped cranking her down, locked the handle in place, with the ball-in-socket joint just grazing at her. He began playing with the second winch now, making her arms bounce while he sang *Hello Dolly*. "It's so nice to have you back where you belong."

Her voice scarcely audible in the room, Mabel asked, "Why?"

He looked surprised, as if his meanings were clear as a window pane. "I'm writing a scene. I've got the props, the characters." He bowed, then gestured to her, as if she too should take a bow. "It's all here, at the ready, as they say. But I need your perspective, your *point* of view. You convince me not to go any further, I won't. Don't think you can do it. Think I need to drop you down, record your reaction—what do you think? Anything else'd be anti— what's that word, shucks, I sure am a dumb old country boy, ain't I—anticlimax? Yep, that's it! And I want you to have a climax, believe me I do, not no aunty one either. But if you tell me why it's better a different way, I'm open to suggestion. Critical response? Sho'nuff! And remember, speak clearly in the direction of the tape recorder, even if you just groan..."

She shook her head, determined not to make a sound. She knew he was playing with her, that he would do what he would do. And sho'nuff! soon did. Amidst groans of nausea and relief at the lowering of her weight off her arms, he set her to "doing a bit of boneriding for me now." He watched intently, fastening on her the eyes of death. She knew she was in the underworld. "I don't know what you're so upset about," he said, making her jiggle. "I mean, you're living your dreams."

She didn't reply. How could she reason with a madman who was making her an accomplice in his crime against her? Fantasy was not reality, she wanted to tell him. Dreaming something didn't mean wanting it to happen. But she knew the person she really had to convince was herself. What did it mean that a woman spent thirteen years fantasizing scenes of bondage and humiliation? If a man came and entrapped her in her fantasy, was his the sole blame? Or had she in fact willed it to happen?

"Remember," he said. "Mother is the womb of madness." The drumstick penetrated deeper, snaking past the folds of her body. "Now, 'fess up—you love me, don't you?"

She shook her head, unable to respond, trying to protect a core of self.

Ryder bounced her further down. "But Annabelly," he said, "don't everyone love their own shit?"

She snorted at him, still squeezing inner muscles to keep the bone outside her innermost being. It was impossible. Ryder worked her on that bone like it was his own.

"You created me out of yourself, didn't you?" he argued. "I'm your dirt."

She thought about this, she'd have thought about anything now to take her mind off what he was making her body do. "No," she said. "Love is what you have for the Other."

"Haven't I shown how Other I am?"

He had her there. He was confusing her, she was already confused.

"I'm your disease," he said.

She shook her head, unable to respond. "Oh," she moaned. "Oh oh oh."

"Love is sickness, obsession. What have you been if not obsessed...with dirty Bone deeds? If that's not love..."

She thought of Ana and Percy, forced her mind from what was happening. "That's not love," she said, not caring if he heard her or not. "Psychological bondage, to my father's beatings, my mother's silences, that's not love." She heard herself reiterate Dr. Xavier's claptrap. It rang as false in her ears as it had when he'd said it. Was Bone right then? Was there a powerful kind of love in her for him, her creation, her wicked child? Like God who loves humanity even when it sins—didn't she love her Bone, and the evil he made her contemplate?

"No," she said. "Bone is Bone, and maybe what you're saying, I don't know. I'm not sure, but you're not Bone. You're—"

"Know who I am? I'm the man who's not in your novel. Get it? I'm Unbone. You invent me, then I get to invent you too. You're a character in my book now. You're"—he looked around, as if trying to think how to phrase it—"why, you're a living doll. I'm writing *this* book, not you."

This is what happens to a man, Mabel thought, *suffering from an excess of myth. The disease should have a name, hypermythitis or something. Not mythomania, that's a tendency to lie. It—*

"Hey," Ryder said. "Wake up there."

He bounced her hard on the bone till she felt damaged inside. "I like when you groan, Annabelle," he said. "Ain't no one going to know, listening to the tape, that you weren't loving this. You want *more?*" He made it sound as if he were amazed at her appetite. He took his small notebook, opened to the page he wanted. "Here, listen. Hold off the climax to this chapter a bit, okay? I didn't write this, but I think you'll like it well enough."

> *Nothing is forbidden by his murderous laws*
> *And incest, rape, robbery and parricide,*
> *The pleasures of Sodom and delights of Sappho*
> *All that which harms man or entombs him is,*
> *We can be sure, but a means of pleasing him.*

"Recognize your master?" he asked. "The great Marquis."

She didn't answer, just stared dazed through the holes. He went over to her and shoved her. She rocked back and forth on the bone. "Well," he said, growing impatient. "How's it feel? Get to the heart now. How's it feel, riding your juicy bone? How's it feel deep inside?" She still made no reply, she had no words for what she felt. "Maybe I need to taste of *your* bone, that it?" She didn't know what he was planning, but she didn't think she could take anything else.

He hoisted her as high as the bridle around the vaulting horse would allow. He pulled out the drumstick, put it under his nose like someone sniffing a fine cigar. Then, staring at her all the while, he put the head in his mouth, popped it in and out, sucked it, tearing off cartilage, stripping it of meat. He smiled toothily at her as he ripped the final shreds of muscle and membrane, his teeth at their work, pulling, tearing, his eyes all aglow on her belly and breast, making her meat, she was only meat.

"I think this chapter will be central," he said, as he put the bone back in the saddle. She looked down, saw the glistening head of the bald sucked joint. "Don't you?"

But she had turned off and gone someplace else. Someplace green and fragrant, soft, where she could sleep caressed by warm breezes, safe. No harm would come to her while she slept.

And her body was made to ride the bone.

THIRTY-FOUR

Ethel Wutzl was just taking a batch of chocolate cookies out of the oven when the doorbell rang. "That must be her," she told herself. She wiped her hands on her apron and smoothed her hair before opening the door. "Hello, dear."

"Hello, Mrs. Wutzl."

"I was baking cookies. Would you like some with milk?"

Ana nodded. She took off her coat, put her scarf and hat in its sleeve, hung it up.

Nothing like fresh-baked cookies, thought Mrs. Wutzl, *to warm a child's heart*. She bit her lip, wondering why she was so nervous. Somehow this afternoon seemed more important than any she could remember. She so wanted the girl to like her.

Ana followed her into the kitchen and sat at the table. Mrs. Wutzl put the platter in front of her. "Take as many as you like. Don't be shy." She poured a glass of milk. "I have so many fun things for us to do today. After your snack, of course."

"The cookies are delicious, Mrs. Wutzl," said Ana.

Mrs. Wutzl smiled. Such a well-brought-up little girl. Hard to imagine that was Mabel Fleish's influence. "I'll give you the recipe," she said. "I thought we might bake a nut cake for Dr. Wutzl today. Plus marinate a leg of lamb, although that's not as much fun. I'll give you all my favorite recipes. We'll even make things for you to take home. You know what my mother always said..."

Ana nodded. "My daddy's so sad lately. Would cookies help?"

Mrs. Wutzl looked at the girl. "Cookies always help," she said.

After they finished their milk and cookies Ethel gathered ingredients and utensils. Ana wrote down each step of the recipe, then helped measure and stir. The cake was soon in the oven. "If this comes out good," said Mrs. Wutzl, "I've decided you must take it home to your father."

"Oh, I couldn't," Ana protested. "It's Dr. Wutzl's dessert."

"He can eat cookies," Mrs. Wutzl said. "He loves cookies. Now, just watch how I make the marinade and tell me about school."

"It's boring, except for English, when we get to read stories. Mr. Klein teaches Creative Writing once a week too. English is my favorite subject. I love reading."

"Me too," said Mrs. Wutzl, stirring the dark potion. "I read a lot of books, also the newspaper. *The Enquirer* usually has the most interesting stories. What kind of stories do you like?"

"Ghost stories," said Ana.

"Yes," said Mrs. Wutzl. "Especially ones set in different times. That way you learn about history." She poured the mixture over the lamb and put the leg on the counter to soak up the juices. "Newspapers are also full of educational articles about people who come back from the dead or get kidnapped by UFOs."

Ana pulled a lock of her dark red hair. "Do you think, Mrs. Wutzl," she said, "that's what happened to my mother?"

Something lurched inside the old woman. She had never felt as angry at Mabel Fleish as at that moment. What a terrible toll her playing around was taking on the child. "How's that, dear?"

"Do you think my mother got kidnapped by a UFO or something?"

Ethel Wutzl swallowed down what she really thought. "I'm sure she'll come back when she's good and ready," she said.

Ana looked at her. "You think it's up to her, that—"

"Ana, I don't know about such things. I just have a hunch she's fine, someday she'll come back and tell us all a story. She's a writer, isn't she? Don't worry, she's all right, believe me." The girl's hair had fallen forward to cover her face. Mrs. Wutzl wanted to sweep her into her arms, tell her to forget about that worthless mother of hers, she and Dr. Wutzl would adopt her.

"I have an idea," she said. "Why don't we ask the ouija board? It probably knows she's all right."

"Ouija board?"

"Come on. I'll teach you." Mrs. Wutzl wiped her hands on a dish towel and showed Ana into the dining room. "Make yourself comfy," she said. She went upstairs, returning moments later with a home-made board on which she'd pasted cutout gothic letters and words like "yes," "no," and "good buy." The whole thing had been laminated and polished so that it had a smooth surface.

"Wow," said Ana. "Neat."

"I made it," said Mrs. Wutzl. "Madame Tchernofsky showed me how." She placed the board on the table between them and put a plastic object on it. "I didn't make the pointer," she said. "Madame Tchernofsky gave me her spare. Now, the idea is for you and I to put our fingers lightly on the pointer and just go along for the ride. Don't move it, even if it takes a long time. Eventually it will go. Once we get in touch with a spirit guide we can ask questions."

She closed the drapes and kitchen door, which gave the dining room a dark, furry quality. Ethel felt oddly excited, never having done the ouija without her medium. "Maybe my little boy will come."

"I didn't know you had children."

"Only the one. And he didn't live long. My son died when he was a baby, just like your..." She stopped herself. Did the girl know about her brother? It was stupid to bring it up. She quickly put her fingers on the pointer. "Just the tips," she reminded Ana.

The pair sat for some time. Just when Mrs. Wutzl was about to give up, the pointer bolted and took off. The movement was so strong she almost suspected Ana had pushed it, but one look at the girl's surprised face convinced her otherwise. The pointer stopped— "K," said Mrs. Wutzl—then veered off. "O," said Ana. "R," said Mrs. Wutzl. "E," said Ana. Then the pointer was still.

"What's 'K-O-R-E' spell?" asked Ana.

"Kore. Its name maybe," said Mrs. Wutzl. "These spirits sometimes don't always spell good. Maybe it means Cora or Cory."

She cleared her throat. "Are you female?"

The pointer jumped to "yes."

"Must have been Cora then," Mrs. Wutzl told Ana in a stage whisper. "Do you have a question for her, dear?"

Ana paused, then whispered urgently to the board. "Where's my mother?" Mrs. Wutzl swallowed. The pointer took off at once. "H," said Ana. "O," said Mrs. Wutzl. "R," said Ana. *Uh-oh*, thought Mrs. Wutzl. She blushed. Sometimes these spirits were too darn honest, for all that they couldn't spell. She mentally tried to tell the dead guide that the little girl opposite her was not prepared for such information about her mother. The pointer suddenly slid to "S." *Thank you, Cora,* thought Mrs. Wutzl, concentrating hard.

"H-O-R-S. What's that? Hors?"

Mrs. Wutzl shrugged. The pointer didn't move for a while. "Cora," said Mrs. Wutzl. "Don't you have anything more to tell us?"

The plastic piece leaped to life. "Yes," it said, then slid to "no," laboriously spelling out, "D-E-D-A-P-E-R-S-Y." It paused, then spelled, "D-E-D-A-P-E-R-E-R-E-R-S-Y."

"Percy's my daddy's name," said Ana quietly. "Only he spells it with a c."

"I told you, dear. Spelling's the first thing to go. Or second actually."

"I don't understand," said Ana. "Mrs. Wutzl, I'm scared. Is my daddy in trouble?" "No, I'm sure Cora doesn't...shhh. She's taking off again."

The pointer then spelled, "C-E-R-E-O-S-H-O-R-S-H-T-H-O-R-H-O-R-S-H-T."

"Must mean 'serious,'" said Mrs. Wutzl. "I guess it's serious about what it's saying. Or else there's serious trouble."

"Horhorhorhor," continued the spirit, the pointer leaping.

"I don't want to do this anymore," Ana said. "Tell it to stop."

Mrs. Wutzl spoke to the board. "Thank you, Cora. You've been very helpful. Please return to your place now." The pointer began to throb and felt warm to their fingers. "C-E-R-E-O-S-W-I-N-D." It paused, then added, "O-W."

"It's repeating itself," said Mrs. Wutzl, "except for 'wind' and 'ow.' Thank you, Cora," she told the board. "You may go now."

"Cereoshorshor."

"We know you're serious, dear, but you must go now, Cora."

With a sad little hop the pointer slid to the word "good buy" and fell off the edge of the board.

"Well, that was certainly a live wire," said Mrs. Wutzl.

Ana was quiet. "I'm scared," she said. "I just don't know what I'd do if something happens to my daddy." Mrs. Wutzl saw the girl's cheek was wet. "Nothing's going to happen to him, sweetheart," she said. She got up and took the girl around the shoulders. "Don't you worry. Besides, Dr. Wutzl and I are here. We'll always look after you. I promise."

Ana sniffled. "I'm sorry. I'm just being a baby."

"Come now, dear. Don't cry." Mrs. Wutzl patted the girl.

"I wish with all my heart on the wishbone you gave me. Do you think it's only bad wishes that come true? Don't good wishes count?"

"Of course they do. They count twice as much. And you know what? I think our nut cake is done, and it is my wish that you take it home. Why, your father will be pleased as punch, I imagine."

"Oh, Mrs. Wutzl, I wish my mother would come home, don't you?"

THIRTY-FIVE

Ana sat in her room, watching Barbie and Ken coo over their baby. "I'm so happy," Barbie said. "To be honest, Doctor, I used to think about running away, but now I'd just never leave my family."

The door opened downstairs. "Daddy?" Ana went down to see her father. He smelled like cold. "I've a surprise for you," she said, pulling him into the kitchen.

"Oh, Ana, a cake. Did you bake a cake?" Ana smiled, twisting her toe on the ground in front of her. "Here, let me give you a big kiss." Her father squeezed her hard, smunching his cheek into hers. She could feel his bristles.

"Mrs. Wutzl and I baked it," she said.

They went into the living room. "Anyone call?" She shook her head. He nodded, opening a bill.

"Daddy," Ana said. "Have you ever heard of a ouija board?"

He looked up. "I'm familiar with the concept. Why?"

She stared at her foot, concentrating on pointing her toe, turning it from side to side. "Mrs. Wutzl and I used one today, and it didn't make a lot of sense, but I think maybe it was warning me about something." She looked at him quickly, then looked away. "It said its name was Kore, that it was a girl. Then it said your name, only with an *s*. P-E-R-S-Y. Before that it wrote 'D-E-D-A.' So now I'm worried." Ana twisted her foot, watching it intently. "You're not going to die, are you?" She smiled, trying to show the question wasn't as serious as it sounded. The effort of holding her emotions in made tears come to her eyes. She bit her lip and pointed her toes, then twisted her foot again, scrunching her face to show deep concentration on the movements she was making.

Her father put down the mail. He sat in a chair and pulled her on his lap. "Nothing's going to happen to me," he said.

Ana couldn't speak, knowing if she tried her voice would come out too high. A moment later she was crying anyway. "I'm worried."

He held her head to his chest, kissing her scalp. "I don't want you to worry," he said. "There's nothing to worry about. What else did the ouija board say?"

"Oh, Daddy, I'd just die if something happened to you. Mrs. Wutzl thought Cora—that's what she called the spirit guide—was a bad speller. That she meant 'serious' when she wrote 'cereos.'"

Her father took out some paper and a pencil. "Here, Ana. Write down the words just the way the board spelled them."

Ana paused. "I don't remember exactly. I think it was like this." She wrote, "Kore hors dedaPererersy horshthorhorshtcereoscereos horhorhor cereosdedawind ow." She looked up. "There may have been more but it repeated itself a lot."

Her father held the page in his hand. "Ana," he said. "I don't want you fooling with this stuff. It's dangerous. Sometimes you can call up a spirit you can't control."

"Is that what happened to Mommy? Oh, Daddy, you're not going to die, are you?"

Percy's eyes teared. He felt prepared to fight all the demons in hell, that his daughter should never have to mourn him. "I won't die," he promised. "Don't you know? We Furnivals are stronger than death. When they bury us we just get up, kick over our tombstones, and walk away."

Ana smiled through her tears. He wiped her eyes. "Oh, Daddy," she said, hiding her face in his neck. "You're so funny."

THIRTY-SIX

Mabel found herself on the Bed, hooded, shackled, harnessed, covered with several blankets, at her side a thermos. No sign of Ryder. She started to sit up but the terrible pain in her center forced her to lie back. The horror of nightriding came to her.

Groaning, wondering if the damage he had done her was permanent, she touched herself gingerly. The hole was raw but didn't seem to be torn. Of course she couldn't tell the state of her insides, but it hurt, she hurt deeply, a physical and emotional pain.

She forced herself to sit up, thinking to take some soup while it was still warm. She felt it would heal her. She unscrewed the lid, poured some out into the cup, rewarded by the steamy vapor. Chicken soup, just what the doctor ordered. She was about to insert her straw, to sip carefully at the hot liquid, knowing full well she should let it cool off a bit but unable to hold back her eagerness for its solace—when there in the corner she saw it. The Harrow loomed like a figure from a nightmare. Her stomach clenched into a fist, her appetite died. It had stood there all along, watching from behind a screen, awaiting its moment. She had told Ryder it had no teeth but she'd been wrong, for it seemed to grin now most toothily with its shining meatless bone. Leered like a miniature skull, hissing the promise of another ride "soon as I get you in the saddle again, my girl."

She shuddered and turned away, sickened. The effort to sustain an upright position proved too much. She passed out and fell back on the Bed.

When she awoke the second time she found she didn't hurt quite so much. She was either healing or becoming used to pain. Through the tiny cracks in the window shutters she could make out daylight. She didn't know how long she'd been asleep. He'd made her ride for what seemed all night, but then she had gone somewhere else and what happened after that she really couldn't say. He must have taken her down, put her to Bed, covered her, gotten soup and placed it within her reach. Maybe her travels without her body scared him. She could die...before he was ready. After all that had happened to her she knew he couldn't just let her go. Torture was the text of the book he was writing on her body.

He had left the notebook and pen within easy reach of the Bed. Did he really think she would add anything to his infernal work-in-progress? Then he *was* mad. She picked up the book, prepared to throw it as far from herself as she could, but before doing so she saw the pages open. Ryder had written something there. Insanity still made her curious. She stole a peek at his words.

"She rode the dirty bone far into the night," she read, "traveling to another land where pleasure was pain and pain a delight. She made the dirty groans sound all right, and who could say if delight or pain made her cry out her shrieks of O O O?"

"Who's to say?" She yelled at the words scrawled on the page, as if the book itself had ears. She picked up the pen, held it like a knife, and stabbed the paper, tearing her reply into its skin. "I'm to say, you sick bastard. It was pain, hear me? It was pain pain pain!" She threw the book at the Harrow and wept anew that she missed the laughing bone.

Ryder would be back, she knew he would return at dark, like a vampire to suck her dry. "We need to play it safe," he had told her, "in our little mountain hideaway." She figured now was the best time to explore the cracks under the Bed. Quickly, carefully she marked the mattress's location and pushed it aside. She feared memory of lines in the floor might prove a dream, but there they were, thin yet seemingly formed with purpose. Cracks could make a pattern and mean nothing, she realized that, still...a trapdoor of some sort? Oh, that would be splendid. She didn't know what she would do if she found some underworld passage. A tunnel leading into an abandoned mountain mine? A horrible tomb in which the hut's first owner had performed sick sacrifices? Maybe just a root cellar, after all. Whatever. If there was a trapdoor leading down to something, then maybe, just maybe, she could figure out what to do with it.

Her long nails worked under the wood till one broke off. She cursed, trying to bite at the rough edge but the hood material was in her way. She wished for a file to fix the chip. The notion struck her as funny, comical out of all proportion. Prisoners always wish for a file, she thought, but not necessarily for their nails. She began to giggle and roll. It was hysteria, she soon realized, and forced herself to get a grip. She had nine nails left. She focused on them and returned to her task.

It was about that time that she grew aware of digging outside the hut. She wasn't surprised exactly. After all, it wasn't the first time she had heard it. But it struck her as strange, as if someone were working in sync with her, sharing a common goal, like two people digging at opposite ends of a tunnel. Was someone trying to free her? She started to call out, then stopped herself. That way was mere distraction, for no one had heard her call for help before. No, she must be her own salvation, rely on no one but herself. *She* had thought to look under the Bed and discovered a door, so *she* would find a way to get it open, to save her own skin. She dug at the floor.

The pain in her gut was exacerbated by her attempts to lift the boards, but she wouldn't stop. When her strength flagged she had to think only of the midnight ride of Bone Revere for repugnance to refuel her. Finally she succeeded in loosening the edge of one board but it was attached to several others—she was unable to get them all out. Something Ryder had said, bouncing her on the bone, came to her. "Ride that horse!" He whoopee'd. "Yeah, ride it good. When the writing's going it's like riding a horse, ain't it so? You told me that, so now you sit with it pretty, let it take you. Let it trance you away." *Yes,* she thought. Sometimes when you were writing it was like being abducted, carried to a foreign land. You had to let it take you. The rhythm built and you rode it, let it gallop. That was the secret—you had to let it have you. Writer's block interfered with it. Stopped the horse mid-canter, pulled back on the reins with questions: What is the point? Why this, not that? Does it have a higher purpose, is it trash? Get back on that horse, she'd tell herself. Come on, ride! ride! Sometimes she did manage to ride away from the voices, drown them out in the gallop. Other times they pulled her down, ate at her nipples, licked her skin with dry tongues of doubt, leaving paper cuts. What had happened to her the night before—it was revolting, it was painful, but in the end she had ridden, she had ridden away. Escaped him. Escaped everything.

Rode her horse to oblivion, left her carcass behind.

She resumed the task of lifting the board, working steadily. She moved the wood back and forth, back and forth, easing it loose. Concentrating only on the boards and the cracks, working it, working, a kind of Zen. She sat on her haunches. Again she felt something with her, on the other side. A presence. A breath that inhaled when she exhaled, exhaled when she inhaled. Inspiration in time with but not her own. Pushing on the other side of the floor, lifting from underneath. As if something wished to be released, just as she wished to be released.

She looked down at herself and saw the blood then, a thick red ooze on her legs. She stopped working the floor, forced herself to lie back. *I'm hemorrhaging,* she thought as she felt her belly and vagina, to see if she could detect the source of wound. The terrible pain she had felt in her center earlier had been replaced by an ache, a cramping. If she were bleeding from internal wounds wouldn't she feel something more...excruciating? Her belly felt tight, bloated. She mentally calculated the date and laughed. It was her period. Menstruation stoppeth for no man. Good, she thought, hoping she'd have globs all over herself and the hut by the time he came back. He wouldn't know it wasn't from something he'd done. Maybe he'd be more careful. And he'd have to clean it up, and buy her supplies, get rid of bloody napkins. She wouldn't even wrap them up. She'd leave them lying around, open, like accusations from her womb. She thought how she'd been embarrassed at first when he had to clean out her slop bucket, how of late she'd learned to welcome every foul smell from her body, her only revenge, wishing for more beans and less bananas. "Thank you," she now said to the wetness between her legs.

There was a gaiety in her work as she tried to lift the floor. She put all her fingers to it, leaned back into her heels, using her weight. The boards popped out and she fell back. She held the trapdoor in her hand like a shield. "Well," she said proudly, looking down into the hole.

She couldn't tell how deep it went, but dark it most certainly was. It had the smell of wet earth, an almost metallic moistness. She felt around the perimeter till she located what she hoped would be there—a ladder. She knew she would have to descend it and prayed only that the rungs were not rotted through. She stared into the darkness, trying to let her eyes get accustomed before entering it.

Deep below, at the bottom of the rope she thought she saw something. Something roundish and white. Getting larger...no, closer.

"Oh my God," she cried, backing away. A skull was gleaming in the blackness. She saw it now ascending the ladder, she saw it looking at her with a cloudy eye. Mabel screamed as Ryder popped out of the ground.

"What you think we're working on here, darling," he said, "the goddamn Hardy Boys?" He continued to rise up, chortling "Hardy har har," as he climbed.

"What what what—" Mabel stammered.

"There's an opening by the side of the house," he said. "I went to explore it, heard you working away. Decided to surprise you. You like surprises, don't you?" He smiled, then tsked. "But you see, you really got the wrong idea, spending your time looking for trapdoors, crap like that." He took off her hood and forced her to look in his eyes. "What we're trying to do, the point of all this— capturing you, tying you up and all—the point is to make art, not fart." He spoke as if talking to an idiot. "This shit, it don't belong in my book. What you think to do under there anyway? Dig your way out with some dead gal's skull?"

She shook her head, pulling free of his hands. "I wasn't thinking," she said. "I was just going with it. Look," she said, pointing down at herself. "Look what you did to me." He looked and Mabel was not at all pleased with what she saw in his face.

"Yeah," he said. "I'm an artist too, did you know? We could do the book cover this way—what you think? Motherwell. Motherhell."

She didn't know what he was talking about but she soon got the picture when he strung her up, put a sheet on the floor beneath her, and let her drip like she was a human paint tube. She sobbed as he twirled her, swung her, let her dangle, bounced her. The blood ran down her legs, forming drip patterns and smears on the floor.

"Now this is art," he said. "Real art. Jackson Pollock ain't got nothing on me. My mother taught me. She didn't like diapers, washing shitty rags. Sure did toilet train me fast." He laughed, the hollows under his cheekbones fluttered.

She moaned and wept softly, as if she were alone, not trying to beseech or change things, just releasing despair. He fell into a pattern of swinging her back and forth. Her body hissed through the air, globules of blood dripped down her legs, splattering like tears on the sheet. She felt ill from the motion, back and forth, back and forth. Tick tock tick tock. Puke, she knew, would only make for more of his art, but she couldn't help it. She swung wildly out of control and puked up her guts. Pieces of turkey meat floated in a porridge of digested mess, and that made her vomit harder. Retching tore at her viscera, still it felt good to get rid of it. She longed only to vomit up everything that had happened to her since Halloween night, to vomit so hard she turned inside out and was nothing but a writhing red nest of intestinal worms for him.

When she finished she heard a low sound and realized Ryder was chuckling. She writhed in sickness on her hook like a worm. He began pushing her again. With each swing she felt herself descend a bit further. Ryder, now that the momentum had built, had returned to the winch and was playing with it, lowering her slowly till her feet almost grazed the bloody vomit-strewn canvas.

Then he pulled away the sheet, revealing the gaping entrance to the underground that awaited her all along beneath the Bed. His eyes were again the blackblue of newborns. "The Pit," he said, pointing down. He put his hand out, swung her as before. "And the Pendulum." She tried not to scream, thinking he was mad, and madness was a disease, thinking he was not mad as sin, she must not think he was mad as sin, for the devil was implied in that, and she must never give the devil his due.

He set the sheet to dry, draping it over the Harrow. The notebook lay spread where she had thrown it. He picked it up, opened to the page where she had written a response. "All right!" he said. "Starting to break through now, ain't you?" He read what she'd written. "That's it? That's the best you can do? I spend all this time and energy trying to help you and that's how you repay me?"

The cloudy look came over his eyes, and he shook his head. "Guess we're going have to try a few more writing exercises, huh Annabelle? Listen, we been through some stuff together, you and me. What say we reminisce? That stirs the juices. Remember when I strangled you that time, that last time? You liked that, you said it was the best ever. But then you never let me do it again. You wanted me to, you know you did. That's why you wouldn't see me anymore. I know that now. Because you didn't want to reveal your face, your true face. I knew that time, I knew then and there you were stealing it. My soul. My words, my ideas, the memory of those times in the well, other times too. I trusted you, Mabelly, I gave it all to you most willingly. Because we were in it together, exploring the edge, me and you. Then you pulled back, and it was just me then, alone. You had stolen what I gave you most willingly. Planning a book. Without me. Or no, not without me, because Bone was in there, inside me all along. Just, you threw the skin away when you got your bone.

"That time, you know the time with that bit of silk? your face said it all, convulsing and rolling your eyes up, jerking like some fish I'd pull out of water, flopping. I joined you then, you were open as a well and I went in and down and in and in. And it's lucky for you I found my way out 'cause you were gone when I did, traveling far and wide, and I saved your life. I only go into the well when I have to. But when I do I draw up something good, something I can't get no other way. That time I drew up what you were stealing, so don't think you fooled me one bit! And now, my little Annabel Lee, 'twas many and many a year ago in our kingdom by the sea, and I'm going to do it for you. Dangle you like bait to catch the fish this time. You catch it with your wiggling body, gal. I'm going to draw me up a big one. A whale of a novel, a fucking Moby Dickhead."

She shook her head, groaned as he turned the winch handle just for fun. "Ryder," she cried out.

"Ryder—who that?" He grinned boyishly.

"Bone," she said, no longer considering what acquiescence meant.

"I got a few more experiments in mind. Not *too* nasty. I'll make my observations, get my material, make adjustments so it becomes *exquisite*, I know you like it exquisite. I think you just out a practice, that it? Maybe the place to start is in your mind. In *Bone*. Little more boneriding?"

"Please," she begged. "You hurt me, hurt me inside."

"Yeah?" he said. "Funny—you hurt me inside too. But oh, all right. Have it your way. I got other tricks for you." He played out the rope now so that she was descending into the pit, dangling in a hole in the ground.

"And this maiden she lived with no other thought than to love and be loved by me," he recited as she cried, "Stop. Don't do this to me. Please don't do this to me. I'm afraid."

"Yeah," he said, "now you're getting it. That's how I cried

when she lowered me, only it was far deeper than this. But it's a start, it ought to help you get in touch with—as they say in your circles—*yo' inna chile.*" Her head stuck out of the hole. He bent to her, turned the hood around.

"And neither the angels in heaven above," he whispered into her ear, "nor the demons down under the sea, can ever dissever my soul from the soul of the beautiful Annabel Lee."

She was crying, she didn't know if he would hear her or care. Her round covered head, seen from a distance, might seem a ball on the ground, but there was no ground. He lowered her further, testing the rope. "Please," she begged, she knew it was useless but she did it anyway. Before he dropped the trapdoor over her, leaving only a slight opening for the rope, he offered a final poem. "Contemplate this afore we continue your Inquisition," he said. "Bone and Belle went down to hell to fetch a bucket a fire. Belle come back with desire in her crack, but Bone just repose in the mire."

A thud, then black, and it was darker than the vision inside an unholy hood.

THIRTY-SEVEN

Percy dropped Ana off at Pammy's, came home, took out a bunch of yarrow sticks and a book. It was Friday the thirteenth, as good a day as any for consulting the spirit realm. He made bundles of the sticks, threw them and counted the remainder in the accepted manner of *I Ching* divination until he came up with a hexagram. Number twenty-three, Splitting Apart. He read the accompanying text carefully. The lines were said to represent a collapsing house with a broken roof.

"The bed is split up to the skin" was the meaning attached to the fourth line. This yielded a second hexagram, number thirty-five, called Progress. "The powerful prince is honored with horses in large numbers." He tried to understand how he could use these clues to find his wife. His thoughts raced in meaningless circles.

After a while he put away the twigs and oracle, and took out *Bone*. Stichomancy was a form of divination not unlike the *I Ching*. In both, chance or coincidence was used to divine a message. He would use Mabel's novel, he decided, to find Mabel.

He sensed her hiding in its woods of words, peeking out the letters like a scared child. He would examine obfuscations, odd metaphors, discrepancies, look into mystical passages and down dead-end paragraphs as if they were alleyways echoing footfalls. All the places that made Mabel's book strange, the paragraphs that led nowhere, causing editors to sharpen pencils and talk of revision, those were the places most likely to yield clues, he felt. He would force himself to go slowly through such passages, reading between the lines as if with a magnifying glass.

Since he knew that the beginning of her book explored Annabelle's relations with various men, while the end had the orgiastic scenes, he had to figure out a way to fool himself if he didn't wish to will opening to a particular place. He closed his eyes, turning the book over and sideways till he lost track of which end was up. Then, holding *Bone* to his chest, he thought of his wife and opened the pages at random. The book, upside down and back- ward, split to page 169. He began reading where his finger touched.

"...offered what few could refuse—humiliation. A price to be paid. Annabelle, like Rapunzel's mother, must have the radish growing in that witch's yard.

"He sat in the center of the room, surrounded by followers. 'Are you ready?' he asked. A smile stretched across his angular face. Something yearned inside her. Ted was sixteen, dead. 'Damn you,' she told him. The merry band of Boneriders laughed and fluttered their false lashes. Ted had been such a one. He had sat at Bone's feet, worshiping the idol. Temple prostitute. Coke cunt. Runaway who preferred to sell his body for drugs, for the love of Bone, than to live at home with his mother. Annabelle steamed.

"'You're not mad,' said Bo. 'You're jealous.' He twisted and untwisted a silk cord. 'You wish I'd do to you what I did to him. Don't be jealous, little mother.' He smiled. 'I will.'

"'It's your fault he killed himself.'

"'Easy now,' said Bone. 'You know it's your fault.' The Boneriders nodded. 'What did he look for in me that he never got from you?' He paused. 'What is it you want?'

"Her heart opened like a hand, closed like a fist. Bone and his followers nodded in perfect synchronization, pulled by the same string. They wore the grin of brothers. Their shadows, caused by the lamp behind Bone, joined to reach for her in the dark. Annabelle took a step back from guilt, but it danced with her. *Must the mother of a son always play the nun?* she asked.

"'There's a way to bring back the dead,' Bone told her. 'A stolen bone gathers moss. Blood makes the flowers grow. Semen waters the earth.'"

The chapter ended there. Percy went back over the pages, searching for something, anything, to guide his investigation. Should he look for a temple? A Coke distributor? Someone who grew radishes? Boneriders?

"Boneriders" reverberated in that special way he had come to associate with precognition, but that might just be due to Ryder's name. Percy was turning up evidence to confirm Ryder was his man when what he really wanted was a fresh lead.

"A stolen bone gathers moss." The line rolled in his head like a marble. Did it mean Mabel was covered with...? "No," he said aloud. "Something else. It means something else."

He laid the book open on the desk and took out the box of slides, projecting one on the wall to study it. It was not the first time he noticed the strange patty-shaped object in the foreground. And in the distance a long, flat, rectangular building sat on the right, obstructed by woods. Just half a house but long. Poorly constructed, Christ, it didn't look fit for human habitation. Should he comb the countryside looking for architectural blights?

"A rolling stone...a stolen bone." Mabel's line took some of its power from the proverb it echoed, but Percy wondered if there were another source of numina. The saying and its distortion rolled and clicked like ivory dice, spilling repeatedly across his mind. To no purpose. The bones were blank. In any case Percy could not read them.

He focused on the funny shapes instead. He could just make them out, fuzzy, distorted by the closeness of the lens. A shredded, haylike quality to them. Percy squinted. He turned his attention to the photo's left. Mountains. If only he recognized them. They had done a lot of hiking, but it was hard to know mountains you didn't live with. He could tell, however, that the hut itself was on a wooded mountain. The way the dirt road cut through woods and sloped precipitously down indicated as much.

What about the tiny house? The stones that comprised the walls were each shadowed on the right. That meant the sun had been low in the sky. Was it late or early? Probably late, he figured, since Mabel liked to work in the mornings. If that were true, then the left of the picture was west. Something about this didn't sit right.

Dice rattled in his mind till he projected the other slide. Its shadow of a man was cast forward from someone behind the house on the right. How could the stones be shadowed on the right, while the man's shadow reached forward? All shadows stretched together, as did the Boneriders' to unite in darkness against Annabelle. "Rolling stone...stolen bone...moss." He hit his knee and laughed. Of course! How simple. Moss. How stupid of him not to realize it earlier. Any boy scout knows the truth about moss.

He kissed Mabel's novel on its facing pages. Its covers lay open on the desk like arms. *Bone* was deconstructing in its own demise. For the first time in two weeks, Percy felt optimistic.

He put his fingers in his hair, rubbed his scalp hard and fast. Winter made his skin dry. He looked again at the slides, first one, then the other. He concentrated on the strange objects he could see in front. Oddly shaped. Since he had determined the picture's cardinal orientation, he felt sure that the other mysteries would soon crack.

He got up and stood beside the image composed of light. With the back of a pencil he rode his finger along the outline of one lone object, distorted out of proportion by its proximity to the focus. Suddenly, like Helen Keller making sense of language for the first time he recognized with his arm what he couldn't with his eye, but he still couldn't retrieve its name. He traced it again, concentrating on the tactile sense. The word was on the tip of his tongue. He thought of the ouija board, the words it had spelled for Ana. He looked at the long building again. Then he knew. By God, he knew where Mabel was! All he had to do was find her.

He took out maps and telephone books, a pen, paper, and compass. He marked off points and drew circles around them. He was just beginning to consult the phone book when the doorbell rang. He went to answer it.

"Furnival, my lad. Are you all right? I was worried when—"

"Oh, Dr. Wutzl, please come in." Percy led his colleague into the parlor, took his coat and hat. "I'm sorry. I should have called you. I've been busy. There's finally—"

"No, no, not at all, my dear fellow." Dr. Wutzl fluffed his thick hair where his hat had flattened it. "I know you have a lot on your mind. But when you didn't show up in your office...then I saw the Dean and he told me—"

"It's better this way." Percy brushed rain from the old man's hat. "He's right after all. I haven't been able to concentrate on my teaching. It's not fair to the students. A leave of absence is what I need. Time to devote myself to the case. I'm glad you're here. I'm making progress."

"Are you now? That's wonderful. Have you had dinner? Mrs. Wutzl sent this over." He handed Percy a plastic container. "Some lamb stew. She said just put it in a sauce pan and—say, what is all this stuff lying around? Maps, compass. You *have* been busy. And that projection? Is that the house you told me about?"

"Astute of you," said Percy, smiling. "And what can you tell me about the objects in the photograph?"

Dr. Wutzl sat in the chair recently vacated by Percy. "Well, let's see. Not an interesting shot, frankly. Aesthetically, I mean. Taken on a day without much light in a wooded area. A ruined house. Nice touch, how the light glints off that patch of snow, but...basically what I expected from your description."

Percy laughed. "From studying this picture I know where Mabel is." He lowered his voice. "Assuming she is in this house, of course. Which I am positive she is. You don't believe me?"

Dr. Wutzl hemmed, hawed, and erhmmed. "It's just—well, now, so what is all this? Why all these circles on the maps."

"I am listing the counties north of the Catskills."

"Yes, very interesting, and why is that, Furnival?"

"Do you see the beards on the stones of the house?"

"Yes, so?"

"That's moss."

"Splendid," said Dr. Wutzl. "Yes, that's great progress. Perhaps you'd like to warm up the lamb stew and have something to eat? It will do you a world of good."

Percy grew impatient. "I had dinner, Doctor, and I can tell from your remarks that you have never been a boy scout."

"Well, well, indeed. That is astounding. You amaze me." The old man stroked his chin, tried to smooth the furrow between his brows. "And have you been sleeping all right?"

Percy ignored his last question. "But I," he said, "was a boy scout. An Eagle Scout, in fact. And so I know that moss only grows on the north side of rocks."

Dr. Wutzl pulled his right earlobe. "So?"

"So I know that there, on the right, is north. And so this hut is north of those mountains. See them on the left?"

"Mmm hmm. So you're going to look everywhere north of mountains for a hermit's hut? Terrific idea. Oh, I don't know, Furnival. What should I say? I don't like to discourage you but to encourage you in this foolhardy pursuit, I just—"

Percy laughed. "No, of course that's not what I'm going to do. I've narrowed the area of my search considerably. And soon it will be even smaller. First of all, I know this place can't be far from Winegarden. It has to be close enough for Mabel to drive to, hike around, and drive back in an afternoon. She has not gone away for any number of days till...till now."

Dr. Wutzl sat up straight. "Still, my good fellow, it seems a broad area, even if you limit yourself to the counties north of the nearest Catskills. That's what you've been doing with these maps?"

"Excellent," said Percy. "I see you are learning to conclude from your observations. Now, do you see these funny blurred things here, in the foreground?" Percy picked up a ruler and used it to point out the cluster of peculiar shapes at the bottom of the photo. "Do you know what they are?" Dr. Wutzl shook his head. "Neither did I, my good friend, till now. I shall tell you. Horseshit. Spelled H-O-R-S-H-T." Dr. Wutzl looked quizzically at him. Percy laughed. "From riders in the wood."

"Riders in the Wood? You mean like Baal? Clouds?"

Percy smiled. "Not clouds. Here." He traced the shape of the lone figure and again his brain flashed the outline of a man sitting on a horse. "See? In fact, it's a group of riders."

"Hmm," said Dr. Wutzl.

"So clear to me now. Don't you see, it's all a load of horseshit. There must be a bridle path that runs by the house that Mabel is being kept prisoner in."

Dr. Wutzl scratched his scalp, then fluffed his hair again. He took out his pipe and cleaned it. "Please be good enough to explain how it helps you to know some horse riders were on a wooded mountain trail one day near this ruined house?"

"Not a group, Doctor. A class. Turn your attention to the building over here. See the long, flat structure? What is it?"

"An ugly house, no doubt, such as you see coming up more and more in the Pines area and around—"

"No, Dr. Wutzl. I thought so too at first, but when I recognized the manure, then I knew it was a stable. And these shapes way in the distance must be people taking a group ride, possibly a lesson. So that is a riding academy. Or in any case it's a stable that rents horses to people who don't know how to ride well enough to go alone."

Dr. Wutzl nodded. "You are making a persuasive case. So let's suppose this is a riding academy. What then?"

"First I mark off the counties north of the nearest Catskills, as you can see I've done. Then I use these phone books to look up horse stables and riding schools."

"Yes. You may be on to something," said the old professor, catching some of Percy's enthusiasm. "In any case, it's worth a shot. Riders in the wood. Ingenious. Hmmm..."

Dr. Wutzl put fresh tobacco in his pipe, tamped it. "There's something odd here, Furnival," he said. "It just occurs to me. Riders in the wood, do you see?" He paused, brushed the heavy white hair from his brow. "Doesn't that strike you? There's that pun again." He rubbed his scalp. Dead skin snowed on his vest.

"I don't like to disturb you," he went on, "but have you considered how, if that pun exists here, where it cannot have been intended by the artist (in this case, photographer), it casts doubt on its earlier instance where it seemed to answer the question of who would ride her?"

Percy laid down the ruler, aligning its edges with those of the desk. "I'm glad you brought that up." He spoke deliberately, enunciating each word as if he rolled it first on his tongue. "Frankly, it troubled me too. Till I realized that the existence of such an unplanted pun in fact supports my theories." He turned the ruler, aligning it now on the vertical. "You know how hard I have worked on deconstructing literature," he said, "largely through the use of unconscious Jungian archetypes, specializing in genre fiction, which, in its conventionality, is as close to the folk tale as the modern world—"

Seeing Dr. Wutzl's attention wander, Percy changed tack.

"—but that's neither here nor there. The point is, I subscribe to the view that the author has no more authority than any other reader, and is in fact just a reader with a pen or word processor. Well, extend that, and you get a world without higher authority, a world in which we are all authors creating the universe we read around us. Do you see? There are no longer any texts *per se*. That is, nothing is a text, so everything is a text. Texts in ink predicate texts in nature. Observation is an act of literature. Shadows cast by trees spell out meaning in an alphabet of dark and light. Runes in the rocks, Dr. Wutzl, signify as much as any scribbles on paper."

"I don't quite follow. Are you talking about the collective unconscious here?"

"It's even greater than that, I'm afraid. Shakespeare wrote, 'All the world's a stage,' but in fact you and I, Dr. Wutzl, are not characters in, so much as letters of, a novel. Our lives are words. And Anubis over there, asleep by the radiator, his life also has this meaning." The dog looked up when he heard his name.

"Down, boy," said Percy and continued. "The movement of his body along the ground is a script, do you see? Anything that exists, even a passing thought, is part of the text. Existence is largely written in invisible ink. Which, I agree, makes it hard to read." Nubi pattered over, sat at Percy's feet, smiling up.

Dr. Wutzl shook his head. "I don't know. You are either a madman...or a genius. Maybe it is just that I am of a different time. I don't subscribe to newfangled theories. Reader response, deconstruction, feminist criticism. It's—"

"Synchronicity is the key," Percy explained. "Anachronism can't exist in a world in which everything that ever was, is, or will be is squeezed to a seed of potential. The seed bursts, the world flowers into diversity, to accommodate us. Because we are not gods and must live in time. Lost in a dream of chronology, of causality, we forget that this is not a priori reality"—he waved his arm in an arc that crossed the light, making the projection on the wall vanish —"but illusion. *Maya,* the Hindus call it."

A puff of tobacco smoke from the older professor's pipe hung before the beam of the slide projector, the ray of which revealed swirls dancing and disappearing in its light. "Go on," said Dr. Wutzl. "I feel like something is about to clear."

Percy now spoke very fast, as if to an invisible audience. "Puns that exist across time, across language, across intention are as relevant as any others. If a seventeenth-century poet used a word one way that, in the twentieth century, took on another meaning, it doesn't matter that the original poet would not have gotten the pun, let alone made it. The pun is its own relevance."

"So you're saying the photographic pun, shall we call it, confirms your original thesis that Ryder—"

"Exactly!"

Dr. Wutzl began rubbing his scalp furiously, causing static electricity to make an Einstein of his hair. "I say, Furnival. Do you have a drink? Scotch?"

Percy patted him on the shoulder. "You'll be okay. Sit here. I'll bring you a glass." He returned a moment later.

"Nothing for you?"

Percy shook his head.

Dr. Wutzl took a long sip. "I think," he said, "you are a brilliant theorist."

Percy smiled. "Deconstruction is in my blood," he said. "Derrida's glosses are nothing compared to the Talmud—that's the first deconstructive work, centuries of rabbinical dialogue framing a core commentary on a biblical text."

"I didn't know you were religious."

"I'm not," Percy said. "That is, I believe in the spirit, not the hocus-pocus religion has erected around it. My beliefs are eclectic. I'm sort of a monotheistic Hindu soothsayer."

Dr. Wutzl stroked his chin. "Well," he said, "you may be wrong. But then again"—he smiled, his white hair formed a halo about his head—"you may be right."

"Good," said Percy. "Then you'll join me tomorrow for a drive in the country?"

THIRTY-EIGHT

She dangled in darkness queasy. She must have passed out. When she came to she didn't know where she was. All she knew was it was black. It took the greatest of efforts not to throw up again. The hood over her head would make vomit a vile means of suffocation. She concentrated on finding her center of gravity.

Making a magnetic pole of herself, pointing her toes, helped her to swing less wildly around a bottomless pit. Her wrists were shackled and she was completely blind, Ryder having turned the hood before lowering her.

She could smell herself strongly. The tainted odor of her breath filled the sack like a balloon, foul scents reeked from her armpits, and a horsey, salty stink rose in a miasma from between her legs. A veritable perfumeria in hell. Sniffing past the stench of herself she detected the dank heavy air of moist earth too. It left an iron taste in the back of her throat.

How high off the ground she was, what was underneath her, how far she hung from the walls—none of this information would help her; nonetheless she decided to risk nausea again to learn what she could about her environment. She swung out, pumping with her legs, using her feet to reach. At the height of one revolution her toes tapped a surface. The second oscillation brought her even closer so that she detected a wall that was wet and cold, slimy to the touch. Next she tried to reach the opposite wall, but no matter how high she swung she was unable to make contact with it. She learned thus that she was closer to one side than the other, but she still didn't know how big the well was in which she'd been dropped like a bucket.

Ryder would be back and she both dreaded and longed for his

return. She couldn't help wondering what would happen if he were killed or detained by the police. Or what if (and this was the scenario she most feared) he simply decided this was the best ending to the "book" he was writing on her flesh—that she hang and starve, screaming unheard, forgotten, that her last moments be ones in which she felt herself merge with a little boy's terror underground? How could he improve on such a conclusion? At one stroke he would avenge himself on her for "stealing" his material (as he continued to insist she'd done) and on his mother for crimes perpetrated on his childhood, achieving the perfect climax to his fictional situation as well as his actual. *But he said he'd be back.* Mabel tried to remember the rhyme he had made up as he let her down the hole, for it alone held the seeds of her hope; she could recall nothing except Bone and Belle went down to hell, and that much was certainly true.

As the hours passed the novelty of her situation wore off. A person surely can grow used to anything, for after a while she found herself bored, hanging in the cold dark like a soul in purgatory awaiting forgiveness or punishment. She tried screaming, then gave it up, thinking it unlikely she be heard now, when she hung underground, heavy material over eyes and mouth, never having been heard when eye slits and straw hole were nearer her lips and she stood closer to the window. She took it as proof that she had been drugged when she awoke some time later. How else had she managed to fall asleep in this position, she who had a hard enough time sleeping in bed.

Befogged, it took some moments before she discovered a subtle change in her circumstances. Her hood had been turned! She could see! Did this mean that Ryder had been watching all along as she dangled sightless, swinging out with her legs to touch a wall, sniffing deeply to know her space? Was he watching even now? Or was it further proof that she had been drugged—that he knew when sleep would overcome her, calculating from the time she'd drunk tainted water or soup?

It was still dark as death in the pit, but gradually her eyes grew accustomed to the lack of light and she began to make out smudges of gray. The subterranean cell revealed itself as both larger and deeper than she'd expected. Below, the shine of water. Moisture on rocks? but no, the gleam had a depth to it. Having little to lose and being curious beyond sense she swung her body toward the closest wall, kicking out till she managed to dislodge a clump of dirt. It fell with a splosh, confirming that whoever had built the house had erected it over a well! She had never heard of such a thing, she didn't know that it was possible, but now, having proven that somebody had done it she wondered that it hadn't been done many times. Indoor plumbing, she thought, daring a laugh. But the idea of cold black water beneath her wasn't really funny and her laugh died in a descending echo.

Trying to control her rocking she imagined a plumbline dropping from her toes to the bottom of the pit. To her relief the wild rotations steadied. Ryder had conjured a story for her as he let her down into this hell of his devising. Poe had been her first crush, she had read all the stories of the mad necrophiliac writer in an ecstasy of death lust, thinking herself the reincarnated Edgar *and* his fourteen-year-old bride. Thanatos was her god even then. Surely she could remember the ending to "The Pit and the Pendulum." Perhaps it held a clue to what lay ahead, what the mad necrophiliac Ryder had in mind.

She had never liked the conclusion, that she did remember. Because of tragedy? Somehow she thought unintentional comedy was involved. A deux ex machina of some sort. It came to her all at once, like the general himself who appears as the narrator has his toes over the edge of the pit. General LaSalle catches him in his arms, announces the dread Inquisition is in the hands of its enemies. Relief! Swoon! Ah, the nineteenth-century climax!

Ryder would not have had that conclusion in mind, but unsatisfactory as Mabel herself found it, here, at the edge of her pit, she was hardpressed to think of another. Could she make herself fall into the arms of a savior? Try! try! Use your suspension of disbelief. Show the literary detectives your poetic license. But no, she could not. Even for the love of life and liberty she could not make the French army enter the mountain hut in which she hung like a side of beef.

She hung, she hung. Pure boredom caused her at last to swing back and forth on her rope like the hunchback of Notre Dame, to risk nausea just to have something to do, imagining the tintinnabulation of the bell of herself ringing through the land, calling an army of citizens to storm the walls that confined her. She thought she would go mad, she thought she was mad. Mad as a bell no one hears that swings underground, that calls the denizens of hell to sin. She screamed for the sake of screaming now, not because she thought she would be heard, but because she knew she would not be...

How long she dandled herself in the dark she couldn't tell. She fell asleep and awoke several times, but that didn't mean days had passed, just that there was nothing to do. Once she fell asleep hungry and awoke to find a sports bottle hanging nearby. Her arms tied above her head, she had to catch it in her knees, bending and twisting to bring the straw to her lips within the hood's hole. In it, a nourishing milkshake. She sucked suspended like a baby bat. And so the time passed.

Till Ryder returned.

He drew her forth into the light and she couldn't stop blinking. The shack had never struck her as particularly well lit but now the brightness seemed harsh. "Well?" he said, then cracked up.

She shook her head. Physical torture was bad enough without puns. He took off her hood, as if he wished to study her face. Then returned to the winch and lifted her body high, near the ceiling.

"What it was like, hanging like meat in a trap?" he asked, gazing up at her like someone wishing on a star. He turned on the tape recorder, to catch every drip of despair juice.

She thought she would scream from the way he pricked her sores to watch her bleed, that he might have ink. "They're your ideas, they need your words," she said. "I can't write it for you."

"Can't," he said, going to the winch, placing his fingers on the handle, "cunt?" It seemed he would lower her into the well again, dipping her, raising her, dipping her, like a medieval judge testing for a witch by drowning. "Why why why," she was crying. Another descent into hell and she would be beyond reason, he would never catch her in the place she would go. He froze, seemingly mesmerized by her grief. He watched as she hung near the ceiling, crying, "Why?" But as she would not leave off her whys his fascination at the spectacle turned.

"Stop!" he said, but she wouldn't, she couldn't. "Cut it out!" he told her. He took out a gun and showed it to her. She felt like a bird, flapping overhead, cawing *why why*, but the woman in her knew she would never get away by flight. There was no choice but to bring herself back from the edge, ease into a wordless sobbing, make it quiet, hush. She didn't want to taunt the hunter in him into shooting.

"That's better," he said. He laid the gun on the table, within his reach but not hers. "Just quit your whining, we'll do okay." He laughed. "Hey, that's good, that's funny. Coincidence to beat all. I just wrote me a poem but yesterday." He took out his notebook and read to her from it.

> *Stop whining*
> *she whined*
> *drinking the whine of childhood*
> *that drank the wine that drank the wine*
> *distilling a plaint in nasal nagging tones*
> *impossible to obey or refuse*
> *ehhh ehhhh ehhhh*
> *Sto-o-op! Why-y-yning!*

He waited.

"It's great," she said, grimacing from pain.

His face looked insulted, then he drew a curtain across it, making it harder for her to read. "All right now," he said. "Want to play games, let's play games." He shut the trapdoor with his foot. "I'm playful, I think you know. So how 'bout one you like—Cut-the-Cord?" He studied her face. The interest in his eyes would in other circumstances be most flattering, so attentive was he.

She squirmed, tried to look away, tried not to betray her emotions, reminded of that terrible game. She had tried to forget it for a year, but it hung in the back of her mind, a reminder of her sickness. It seemed like centuries ago but it was only last year, the time she and Ryder were together. The last night she had gone with him he had convinced her to play the game. She allowed him to wrap a silk rope around her neck, to strangle her gently while he brought her to orgasm. He swore he would cut the cord in time and he had been good to his word but it had scared her, though it was just as he'd promised, a well of black pleasure that widened and swallowed and gulped her down till she never wanted to come up— or maybe *because* it was as he promised. She hadn't been afraid then, she'd gone beyond fear. It was afterward—when she'd realized how close she'd come to being a corpse on a cord, one of those tragic ridiculous people found with bags over their heads dressed in the beshitted costumes of whores.

Cut-the-Cord.

He hadn't made up the game. He told her that. "I'm no

plagiarist," he said, looking at her with a sick smile, which only now she realized was an accusation. Justine's adventures in the castle of pain. Roland, her captor, making her perform one debasing act after another. He said Sade was the greatest writer who ever lived. Poor Justine. He had laughed at her. Stupid cunt. "Roland, he makes her promise to cut his cord in time, hear?" he said to Mabel. "Bring him back before he comes to death, just like I done for you, my sweet." He stroked her neck where the silk rope had burned. Kissed her there. She closed her eyes, feeling the sweetness of his tongue on her pain, trying not to think of what she'd done, what she'd allowed him to do. "And she did!" he said, hooting in Mabel's ear. She forced her eyes open, forced Ryder's lips away. "Why's that different," she asked, "than what you did for me? You didn't let me die, you wouldn't let me die like that, would you?" He shook his head, looking at her. His eyes seemed to hold the honey of love, and fondness and amazement and something bitter too, like rind, to cut the sweet. "Don't you know you can't hurt me?" he said. "Roland made Justine his slave, and when she freed him what do you think the first thing he did to her was? Suspend her in a pit of rotting corpses!"

It sickened her. The game, the terrible pleasure of the game, the way he mocked the good deeds of Justine. Mabel longed to believe in goodness's reward. Or if not reward, at least not punishment. She knew herself to *be* Justine, just as he said she was. For, even now, when she no longer loved but hated Ryder, hated what he was doing to her, her hate had no teeth—or milkteeth at best. She pitied him! Yes, drawn from the well of his darkness she found herself thinking how horrible it was, how even more horrible it must have been for a child. For a little boy. For a boy who has known no mother but the one who put him down a well for days at a time. Whatever else she had done to him. She began to weep.

"I'll give you a knife," Ryder whispered to her now, as if waiting for this moment. "I'll put the rope around my neck, you pull tight, till I pass out. I leave it to you what you do then. Cut the cord, stab me. All I ask is that you suck me off."

She should say yes, she knew it and forced herself to nod slightly, but there was no conviction in her agreement and he laughed, mocking her hanging there, shackled, harnessed, naked and aloft. "Yeah, that would be fine. Perils of Pauline becomes Justice of Justine. Masochism of Mabel more like it. Listen"—he let the winch unroll so that she fell, screaming, on the Bed—"you don't get it even now, but I *am* going to get a book out of you." He pronounced each word with equal emphasis. "I am going to squeeze a goddamn book out of you. And not any book," he said, "but a good book, a fine book. I want Art, hear me? You keep making pulp. This business with the trapdoor—it's crap. Crap!"

"Ryder, I didn't put the trapdoor here. I was looking for a way out—"

"—and that's what you come up with?"

"You're mixed up. I mean, what did you expect me to do? Sit there, contemplating my—"

"Exactly," he said. "Contemplate your...something. Twat, for all I care. That bloodwell you women got between your legs to drag babies up out of. Your existence. Your sex. Your death. Something, anything, but it's got to be big to pay me back for what you stole, it's got to be of equal worth if—"

"I didn't steal anything, or if I did I didn't know it was yours. You think I set out to steal your life material, but I never meant—"

"Meant! I don't give a fuck about your meaning! You were in error? Now you are in terror." He laughed, gave her that wise smile. "I'm giving you the situation, the rest is up to you. Listen, there's this guy I like to read, almost good as the Marquis, yep yep. Name of Nietzsche, ever *heared* a him?" He seemed to know how she hated when he played the yokel, so he laid it on thick as Grandpappy Amos. "Good old boy, he says...wait now. Let me get it aright for you." When he did his Walter Brennan limp over to the table you could almost hear hoedown fiddles. He thumbed his book till he got to the right page. Cleared his throat. Then enunciated his sentence like a newscaster, deepening his voice. "Almost everything we call higher art is based on the spiritualization of cruelty," he read, shaking his head in admiration. "Oowee!" he squealed, reverting to hickatude. "Think on that a while. You ought to get down on your hands and knees and thank me for what I'm doing for you." He paused, seeming to think of the image that conjured. His eyes rolled back in dreaminess, then he drew them forth. "All I ask," he said, "is that you write it. I'll give you cruelty free of charge. Hey, this is Bone, baby, I know how to be cruel. You give me language, I'll give you pain. None a this thriller-diller shit, I want fucking *literature*."

There it was, out at last. All the hokum gone. The word hung in the air with its smell of sanctity in hell, or maybe it was the other way around—the odor of a fart in church. In any case there was really nothing more they could say. It was in the open now, the stakes were set. I want to be great. I want genius. I am not content with the pleasures of pulp.

"It's for your sake too. Otherwise," he said softly, "your death will be meaningless. Don't you see? You're never going to get out of here...alive. The best you can hope for is life after death. A certain immortality. A book. You know I mean a book. A juicy marrow-bone of a book."

She was scared and wept quietly, not asking anything of him, for he had told her how things were and she accepted his words as the truth she'd always known. Her crying made her ropes tremble and somehow they seemed fragile now, shaking with her sobs.

He gently tightened her harness and hung her again, "to keep you out of trouble a while, honey, don't fret," he explained. She heard him leave, lock the door. She heard digging but she had no hope anymore. She knew that that sound, which she'd once thought meant workmen were near, was caused by Ryder. She still didn't know what he was doing but she had little doubt she'd learn.

He came back, wiping muddy hands on his dungarees. "What do you say? Feel like writing for me some? Remember, it's your only chance...for immortality. Like this you're just a woman who disappeared. The woman who rode away."

"Oh no," she said aloud before she could stop herself. "Don't tell me we're going to do Lawrence now."

"That's it," Ryder said. He went to the wall, then stopped. He turned, his eyes merry with truth. "You secretly like it, don't you?" Smiling, as though it were all clear, the mystery of her resistance solved. "Sure you do. Otherwise you'd give me what I want and that would be that. This way, well, you know you're just playing with yourself, putting off what's coming. You can't admit it but for you, for a fuck-crazy womb-man like you, this is fun."

Mabel felt dazed, her mouth hung open. He was telling her something so shocking she had to take it in deep, to see if it could possibly be true. She turned away, turned back, turned away again. "That's-that's"—she looked around as if for a witness—"that's preposterous. How can you think having all my human dignity stripped away, to be kept filthy, an object of ridicule and hate, is my idea of fun." She shook her head, turning this way and that for confirmation from an invisible audience.

"F-U-C-K," he spelled for her, "F-U-N."

"Fuck is exactly what this isn't about. You can't fuck me," she said, more to herself than him. "You can't, that's why you're doing this. It's you this fantasy's for, not me."

Ryder's usually dead-white countenance reddened. His flesh-colored hair stood in sharp contrast so that he looked like a negative, all the qualities of dark and light reversed. "Shut up." He was seething, she was amazed, never having seen anyone actually seethe before.

He undid his belt and a horrified thrill ran through her. She remembered when her father would take off his belt. "I'm going to give you a licking." The excitement as she ran through the long corridor of the house. His heavy steps after her. Catching her, turning her around. "Laughing, are you? It's all a joke to you? We'll see what's so funny." The giggle screaming in her throat as he pulled her to the bed, pulled up her dress, pulled down her underpants. The sense of her backside, plump and pink, ballooning over his lap. He brought the belt down—not as hard as he could. It was the idea. Splayed, exposed across his legs, the belt coming down. Sammy crying outside the door. "She didn't do it. It was me, I swear it was me. Do it to me, not her."

Ryder's pants were about his legs. He walked toward her, placed himself behind her. She waited for the final indignity, to be stuffed like a turkey. But he stopped. "Almost got me," he said, "that time." She heard the sound of him pulling up his pants, snapping them. She heard his belt buckle jangle. He twisted her on her rope. She felt pieces of herself bulging out of tight places. The harness cut across her belly in a most unflattering way. She hung like an organ grinder's monkey as he spun her to laugh at all the parts displayed for his ridicule. She tried to smile, she tried to believe that what she'd said a moment before had been true. But all she felt now was a sense of her ugliness. The pieces of meat that hung down, flopped about, the sagging, the hair, the protuberances, the bloody raw gashes in her body sack. An unwanted naked woman, a used-up femme fatale on a string, good for sideshows, for freak-fucks, not a real woman, with an allure that was powerful, like a god's. Nothing but a bag to be used and discarded, a pocket pussy.

He undid the rope from the ceiling and held her by her leash, waving his gun in the other hand. "Author," he said, "we gonna finish this Authorian legend." He put the hood over her head and tied it tight. "Outside," he said. She walked outside. "Turn left," he said. "March. Okay, halt." She felt like someone about to be executed before a firing squad and thought of asking for a last cigarette. There was no chance. She found herself at the edge of a hole the size and depth of a grave.

Greedy for sensation, even though, or particularly since, it might be her last, she gulped at the air. The richness of trees and ground, even in the black of night—were stars always so bright? How had she never noticed the moon could smile? And even the cold, which before had seemed unpleasant, now at the brink of death was a delight. To feel, to feel anything...when soon all feeling must cease.

Nearby was a shovel on a mound of dirt. "What are you waiting for?" he asked. "Get in."

She hesitated, unwilling to enter the dirty hole. He put the gun to her. "Ryder," she said in her muffled voice, "I'm tired of this."

"Tired! How do you think I feel, waiting on you day and night, catering to you, having to come back here again and again? Bring you food, empty your slop. Worrying that you're cold!"

"Then let me go. Don't keep me prisoner anymore if—"

"Hey, who's keeping who? You are *my* cross. You nail *me* to this place. I'm being kept to serve you. That's how it is with women and men, us drones serving you queens. So now after all this time I should just let you go?" He whined. "You'd be everywhere, laughing, spying, writing about me, hiding in my closet like an old coat to see what I'm up to when I think I'm alone. And maybe you'd erase me, change me around. There is no such thing as re-vision. There is only vision, the rest is darkness, like before you called me. I remember almost nothing from the time in the well till the time you took me out. Why's that, you suppose? Glimmers here and there when you began thinking of me, of your Bone. Well, now I'm here, there's nothing you can do. You're just where I want you— in your grave."

"But if you kill me what happens to you?"

He shrugged. "Airborne," he said, then pushed. She let herself fall. Landing on her knees she crouched till he clicked the gun off safety. "Lay," he said. She spread full length, belly down, burying her eyes in her arms, waiting to be shattered free of him.

He walked away!

After a minute Mabel peeked out the crook of her arm. She fully expected to see him above her, laughing, having snuck back to do just that. No one was there. Still she lay in her hole, afraid to move. Her thoughts ran laps. Ryder was a lunatic, no doubt about it. Perhaps she'd be lucky. He might forget. He might leave, go off to pursue some other dream. Then, after a while, she'd get out—

He returned a few minutes later, carrying a large crate of books in one arm, dragging another box. At the edge of the hole he paused, then began throwing them at her. He aimed at her head.

"Stop it, Ryder. What are you doing?" She recognized the red cover, her photo on the back. "Ryder, you can't do this."

He leaned over the edge of the grave. "After 'The Pit and the Pendulum,'" he said, "comes 'The Premature Burial.' Think on that a while."

She screamed but it had no effect. "You can't bury me alive. You—"

A book hit her temple. Then all was darkness and the weight of her words.

THIRTY-NINE

Kwestral's dresser was a heavy oak affair. The mirror across the top was framed by matching wood. Slid into the space between glass and oak was a photograph of a policeman holding a young boy, laughing as he bent his head toward the child.

He looked at the picture of his father. Hermie couldn't have been more than five at the time, which would make Officer Kwestral thirty, not much older than Herm was now. He stood before the mirror, trying to summon a father's courage. The computer named Luz hummed behind him. He still hadn't completed the chapter in which his detective self went to Louisiana to find the Barbons, and found something else. He couldn't get his fingers to sit on the keys.

Earlier that evening he'd come home and seen his mother's note. Raced into the kitchen, figuring he had an hour, possibly two, before she got back. He grabbed a beer, a hunk of cheese. He didn't notice the wood handle of the knife was split. It gave when he cut the hard cheddar and the blade sliced his finger. Worse than the pain was the feeling of presentiment: miniature guillotine on mice of the aristocracy. He doctored his finger, took the cheese and beer with him. If it was a sign it was of unreadable significance.

All the while the minutes ticked away like baby bombs. He'd accomplished nothing but a bloody hand. Still hadn't read over the chapter he'd started the day before. He cracked his toe knuckles as if to break every bone, then called up the chapter in Luz. Read it over till a wave of self-hate rode him. Wrong, all wrong, the narrative voice lacked that essential irony. He should go back to the books, Chandler, MacDonald, read till he got the tone right.

Half an hour went by. Half a precious hour and still nothing. Soon the evening would be shot, his mother would be home, and he'd have done nothing but moon about the meaning of a knife. It was time for desperate measures. He washed his hands, took a few breaths, summoned the correct state of mind.

The object he was about to resort to was heavily invested with numina. He feared using it as much as he feared using it up. But sometimes it was the only way. He took the box from the top of his closet. The cardboard was old, by turns brittle and floppy. Detail ran across the top, blue squares, green diamonds, indicating the age of the octagonal container.

Carefully, with the air of someone performing a ritual, he placed his fingertips on the lid. Took a deep breath, let it steam out his nose. Lifted the top. The sight made him gasp—as if he didn't believe it would still be there, that it continued to exist. Yet there it was—faded, cracked, stained with a father's sweat. Powerful, almost too holy to touch.

He rested his fingers lightly on the circle of blue material and closed his eyes, placing the crown on his head. What would he see when he opened them? People said he looked like his father, though John Kwestral had not been albino.

Lifting his eyelids slowly he let his lashes act as a veil before turning his vision to the photograph. He didn't want to see himself in the hat before his father's image imprinted itself on his brain. Slowly, almost meditatively, he moved his eyes left, stopping at his own reflection. Compared it feature by feature to the image in the picture. Surely the resemblance would show Herm to be a man like his father. Herm was twenty-six, his father thirty. Only four years, and yet the shock of disappointment made him want to cry. Why, if it was only four years, did he still look like a child dressed for Halloween?

The police hat was too big, that was one thing. It lay too low on his head. And his white hair, unlined skin, and lack of beard shadow added to the unformed quality of his face.

He didn't look like his father so much as his father's ghost. The features, the shape (not the color) of the eyes. A spirit washed of detail, the incandescent image of a man. There *was* something about the mouth—everyone said so—and the blue eyes, though his father's were royal while his own were baby.

Funny how the eyes stood out in memory. Even now, ten years after he had last seen them see, they seemed to watch from afar. He scarcely recalled the shape of his head or any other feature, but the eyes, the way they laughed when Hermie reached up to grab the hat, and this was more than twenty years ago. Amusement flickering in those deep blue eyes. The moment captured on celluloid was only the skin of the scene. Laughing cop, reaching child. Herm knew his father was bending toward him, to help him steal his crown.

Of course, then he took it back, didn't he?

Kwestral stood at attention before the image of his father, willing some of his bravery to imbue him as well. Officer Kwestral had been a hero, he died a hero's death. Without thought to his own safety he had gone to the aid of a lady in distress. A whore, but still it was in the line of duty. "Son, you have reason to be proud." The cops wore dress blues, they stood erect despite wet faces. It didn't occur to Hermie at the time that they might be crying for themselves, as if they were attendants at their own funerals. He saluted when they did. Would not weep like a woman, sobbing into a hankie, crumpled, leaning on his auntie's arm. No, he cried like a man. Water rolled out of his face unbidden, as from a crag.

The Simple Act of Vanishing, Chapter Two, was written in Kwestral's mind. After all, he was not depending on imagination, having gone to Louisiana in fact to continue the investigation. It was funny, but he hadn't been nearly as afraid in the course of his actions as he was now, alone in his room, trying to find words to record what he'd done. The house on Magazine Street, how to describe it? Faded gentility, was that a cliché? And the various plot twists worked out by fate, how could one make them seem genuinely mysterious, not falsely coincidental?

The first weird knot, he knew, was when Grinn called to tell him Barbon had been released from the psychiatric ward in '81.

"No shit," said Kwestral.

"Into the custody of a Mrs. Lazar."

"No shit."

How was he to convey the chill of precognition that information gave him? The pieces were fitting together, but he still couldn't see the picture, just places where the sky was blue, the ocean green, the man and woman laughing, enjoying their animal selves without a thought to others. He knew Barbon figured somehow in the vanishing act. But what connection did a dead boy's mother have to Mabel's erstwhile lover?

His image of himself in his father's hat blurred as he used memory eyes to see. New Orleans was nothing like he'd expected.

Overgrown lots with sere weeds reminded him of places on Utica Avenue where no one even wanted to sell used cars anymore. Mrs. Lazar, too, was a surprise. Pleasant looking at first, but hard. Still, that was no reason to betray her trust. He faked his way into her confidence, then stole something treasured from her. She was his mother's age, imagine if someone had done that to his mother.

He looked at the postcard taken from Mrs. Lazar's desk. The front showed an aerial view of toothy mountains covered by green velvet. He turned it over, read the print on the bottom. Na Pali Coast, Hawaii, it said, as if it could be mistaken for anyplace else. He reread the message. "Found Eden—BB."

It wasn't dated, the postmark was illegible though the year was current. It could have been mailed months ago. The sender could have left, the sender didn't have to be Beau Barbon.

Of course he knew by then that Mrs. Lazar was Beau's mother. Grinn had told him the news last time he'd gone to Winegarden. "Oh yeah," he'd said, eating a pretzel. "Jake found something else out. About Barbon's mother actually." He sucked salt off the rod, looked along the length of it like someone admiring a cigar.

Kwestral put a stick of gum into his mouth, to stay in the nonchalance game. He had come to greatly admire the detective— his deadpan delivery, sharp vision hiding behind dark lenses.

"Miss Barbon—note I say Miss and not Missus—married Larry Lazar's father in Louisiana. After the kid's death."

Kwestral swallowed his gum. "Jake's sure?"

Grinn bit off the end of his pretzel, chomped noisily. "Jake the Snake make no mistake." He laughed. "She and Lazar lived with old man Barbon till he died, then she inherited the place. Lazar's dead now too."

Kwestral's thoughts returned to Mrs. Lazar. He had duped her, it was repugnant to play tricks on women, especially old women. Of course, that was part of the game, wasn't it? What would Grinn say? *Down these means,* he told himself, *an end must go.* He fixed the brim of the hat so that it made him look the rake and said the line again, in a deeper voice.

Wasn't that what he admired about Grinn? The man didn't waste emotion. Something had to be done, he did it. He didn't feel remorse or pity or guilt. Or even disgust, and in the course of their developing friendship Grinn had told him many a disgusting story about what happens to bodies left in houses for a week or two.

"You wouldn't believe what a bag of crap a human being is," he'd told him. "When the life's gone out of it, then you can see it for what it is." Kwestral nodded to his memory in the mirror. Yeah, that was the thing about Grinn. He was a stoic, even about his wife's cancer death. And if he made an error it was just that—error, not sin. He went on from there. He didn't beat himself on the head. Didn't walk around feeling duplicitous, didn't know the word.

Kwestral felt false all the time, as a reporter, an "investigator," a son. Even in his fiction he worried that he was plagiarizing people's lives. The stories they told, the stories they lived, what right had he to them? A woman murdered, a child lost, and *The Wing* sent him to talk to the family, neighbors. He had to ask questions in a way so that no one could tell what he was thinking. Part of him stood back, watched, noted the color of the stain, its shape (a continent of mud on the ocean of a carpet blue). The other part assumed a holy stance and tsked, getting people to open up.

Oh, come on, he told himself. Mrs. Lazar knew her way around. She wasn't pudgy soft, like his mother. She had long, wiggish hair, Tina Turner style, and the bouncy, girlish manner of a flirt. A determined dimpled way of smiling too. Used to getting her way. She reminded him of someone. It irritated him now, like a word on the tip of the tongue, but he couldn't think of whom.

He looked at the clock on the dresser. An hour wasted, still not a word. Any minute, any minute. Tick tick tick. Her voice, about to go off, exploding, "Honey," up the stairs. He hadn't told her yet that he was leaving for Hawaii the next day. That would be the topic of a long, boring conversation about his responsibilities, about what his father would have expected of him. But Herm had made up his mind. He was going to go, he *had* to go. She would whine, "You just got back from Louisiana. I don't like all this running around you do. You'll get yourself sick."

He cringed in anticipation. He should really try to write at the office, in the library, but he had to be alone, there was no place to be alone. The thought of renting his own apartment just for writing appealed to him, the idea of a secret life, but mundane concerns interfered. What about the computer? Buy a second just for the apartment? And the rent? A lot of money to spend on a place he'd almost never get a chance to use. She'd never let him stay out all night without explanations, and then she'd see through his lies. She saw through him so clearly it was as though he weren't albino but glass.

Think, think. Who was it Mrs. Lazar reminded him of? Rubber goddess, impenetrable despite pinhole earrings. Locks of flaxen plastic. Who? All he could think of was his mother opening his door.

He took off the hat, brushed the top as he had seen his father do, put it in its box, put it back in the closet. His mother would be home soon. If she barged in, caught him staring at himself in the mirror, wearing his father's hat.... Just the thought made him blush. He hurried to the desk where he'd left his Bogie-style fedora. At least it fit him, and if his mother did walk in he could say he'd just gotten home himself.

Row, he told himself, imagining his mind as a soft-bellied fatman he was coaching into shape. When this strategy didn't work he turned to the nighttable. On it was a copy of *Bone.* He looked at the author's photo, trying to see the woman behind the mask. It was a good thing he had this picture, he thought. Without it he couldn't remember what she looked like, only the desire she'd aroused.

Probably laughing at him, at all of them, smiling in the sun with her long-lost love. No, actually, she probably didn't even remember Kwestral. But he remembered her. That's what she hadn't counted on. He'd find her, bring her home. To the victor goes the spoils...if he wanted them. What he really wanted, he told himself, was vindication. He was cleverer than she, and he wanted to prove it by outthinking her plots. She would sink into his arms like a sigh. "You found me," she'd breathe in his ear, "out. Save me, I'm yours." And he'd throw her back. To the sharks.

How could she do it? He looked deep into the photo of her eyes. Abandon her own child? Oh hell, it happened every day, it wasn't news when a woman ran off with the raggle taggle gypsies-o, so why the surprise? But it was the softness that disarmed him. She was a woman of iron in a velvet glove.

There was little doubt in his mind now about where she was. Grinn had come to the same conclusion, putting together the facts, and he was an experienced cop. Of course Beau had showed up in her life—the only bit of truth she had given was when she'd told him about the letter. She must not have thought he'd remember, or come looking for her. Of course not, how could she have figured on that? She'd all but forgotten him, but he knew her well, his Lady

Mystery.

Well, he was writing a book, it would say it all. It would detail his search, his visit to the underworld, how he sought her out. It would be a hero's story, it would tell of courage. He'd picked up the flaming torch and flew off on a quest. And yeah, her lips were the color of cherries, a dark rotten fruit.

So why the hell couldn't he write it?

Because he didn't know how it would end. Oh sure, he knew he'd find her in circumstances seedy, but the glass as to detail was dark. A writer had to have vision. He had to plant clues, lead the reader down the inexorable garden path. How could one write a mystery without knowing how it ended?

Kwestral had read a lot of mysteries in his life, and he'd come to see that the good ones never revealed the truth; they hinted at it. Glimpses behind the door, sounds when they thought him asleep. He hid in the shadows. They were on the bed, Dad with his hat on, Mom with her smile. Royal couple, secret spy. Later, he'd search out the hidden places. Where does she keep her jelly? What is the meaning of hair on the sheets? Cries in the night? What happens if you rip the napkin? How does a girdle taste, feel on the tongue?

For a moment Kwestral relived the horror of childhood, how he'd creep down the long hall between his room and theirs. "I've had a nightmare," the little voice would say. Then he thought he heard the door downstairs.

He listened hard, as he used to those lonely nights. Was his mother about to tear into his fantasy? It was quiet. It was never quiet when she was home. She sang, she whistled, talked to herself.

He would have to wait for reality to write itself, he decided, though part of him wanted to write reality. Writing was a form of magic. He felt he influenced events when he put pen to speculation.

Real-life mysteries more often than not went unresolved. How many times had he seen cop cars going the wrong way down a one-way street, gathering at a corner, lights flashing by the river—any number of things connoting extraordinary events deemed too ordinary for the "Six O'Clock News"? Which was why he'd wanted to be a reporter in the first place. But the novelist in him thought differently. It doesn't matter if the end is real or dreamed, it told him, as long as it makes you *think* that now you understand.

He turned to the front of Fleish's book. The mystery he would write would be something like *Bone*. He'd had the benefit of her mistakes. He saw how to make something resonate with hints of revelation, peeks at truth. Reading that novel he had seen how it was done. Horror stories, with their corpses in the closet, were boring despite the adrenalin rush of surprise. But mystery whispered. The ending should sussurate, sweeping by like a gown.

He pulled the trance over him, fingered Luz, began to dream.

Chapter Two

"Lady of Magazine Street"

The place was one that had seen better days. Rundown gentility, Victorian mansion serving as fleabag boarding house. It needed a paint job. It needed new steps.

I rang the bell. The woman who answered was tall and fair. She had fine features marred by even finer crowsfeet, a girdled Valkyrie torso, hard breasts like Na Pali mountains stripped of velvet, turned sideways. "Looking for a room?" she asked.

"Saw your sign," I said.

She wrinkled her nose, smiling cutely. "Come in. Let me get you a cold drink, show you around."

She fixed me a tall glass of lemonade. I drank thirstily although it was too sweet. "This is a great old house," I said.

"Don't I know it. You should have seen it in the old days. When my dad was alive. He kept the wood, the ornaments, fair to sparkling. I can't keep up with it. We had servants then."

"Hard times," I said.

"Don't I know it."

"You have kids?" I asked casually, looking around.

"A son," she said. "Dead." Her manner slammed shut like a coffin lid. She wasn't smiling now. Her laugh lines vanished, making her face look younger, and less pleasant.

"Sorry to hear that. What happened?"

"Don't like to talk about it, if you wouldn't mind. I'm a private person, despite keeping a boarding house. Let me show you the room."

"I'm sorry," I said. "I hope I didn't—"

She stared, then broke into a smile that seemed genuine. "Come on now," she said. "I'll race you," and the middle-aged woman almost skipped to the stairs, like some sort of weird girl.

We entered the bedroom. I admired the details of the ornate ceiling, the arched windows and carved moldings. "This is my son's room," she said. "He doesn't come home much," then she caught herself. "Larry's been dead twenty years. Can't believe it. Keep thinking he'll come home." She found a tissue in her pocket.

"You know," I said, "when I told my folks I was moving down here they said to look someone up at this address. I mean, it's a great coincidence that you have a room to let and all. But my dad knew a Mr. Barbon used to live here. Do you know him?"

"Why, that must be my dad. Barbon's my maiden name." She gave a maidenly laugh. "What's your dad's name?"

"Kwestral. John Kwestral."

"Well, I don't remember my father mentioning him to me. He passed on a while back."

"Really? I don't think it was your dad he meant. It was someone much younger. More like your son's age, I'd guess. Name of Beau."

"Well, here now," she said. "Let me freshen your drink."

"Oh, that's all right. Do you know Beau Barbon? I mean, that is your last name, or was anyway."

"Actually," she said. "Beau's another son of mine. Lives far away." She smiled with a hard charm, like an aging Barbie.

"My dad would like to know where. He asked me to—"

"What does he want with him?" The smile turned harder, the dimple more determined.

"Oh, I don't know. Nothing much probably."

"What's your interest here?"

"Just my dad has some questions he wants to ask Beau."

"I told you, I don't see him. He doesn't live here. Now, if you're not really interested in this room—"

"Oh, I am. In fact, I want to give you a deposit on it."

"I'm not so sure I want to rent to you. You're kind of snoopy."

"I'd be willing to leave the first month's rent too. To secure a fine room like that."

"Well, maybe, but I don't like snoopers, hear? I—"

"I'd leave the money. Then, if I didn't take the room, I'd forfeit it. You could rent the room but have two months' rent clear. Say, I *am* thirsty now. What do you say to more lemonade after all?"

We went downstairs. Mrs. Lazar walked briskly into the kitchen. Once she was out of the room I hurried to an old secretary that looked promising. Shuffled quickly through papers, a correspondence box full of bills, picked up a book. The place was held by a postcard. I didn't think anything of it and was about to put it back when the signature caught my eye—*BB*. I could hear her heading back in, so I slipped the card into my pocket, never thinking about it.

"Just what do you think you're doing?" Her dimples twinkled hard and fast. I took a frosty glass from her and met a frosty face.

"Good lemonade." I sipped loudly, pretending not to notice her stare. "I was just admiring this desk."

"Seems to me maybe you were admiring it a little too close, is all." Her left dimple twitched on and off till she decided to keep it on. "It was my daddy's," she said.

"Look at that mahogany," I said. "They don't make them like that anymore.

She warmed a bit. "Don't I know it. I'm what they used to call land-rich. Thing-rich, really. Daddy left me things I can't bear to part with. Valuable, fetch a pretty penny. I have all this fine furniture, no cash. But hey, listen here—I don't like people going through my things, no matter how much admiring they do."

"I wasn't, ma'am. I was looking at the hinges. That's how you can tell what a fine piece it is. And the wood. It glows warm and alive, like a woman's hair."

She giggled. "You're a bit of a poet, aren't you?" She brushed a lock of hair out of my eyes. "So fine your hair is," she said. "White, like silk. They could make lovely clothes out of your hair if elves could spin it." She laughed. "You must be what they call albino, aren't you? Like a missing person. Like the blank space left when someone's picture is cut out of a magazine. If only you weren't such a snoop we could have us a good time. Anyway, let me have me your address, so I can get the deposit back to you if I need to."

I fought the urge to shake her hands off me. "Don't," I said, "have one." She looked unbelieving. "I'm staying with friends," I explained. "I'll call." The postcard was crying in my pocket like the blood drops of an ogre's child. "If I don't come back in a week you keep that money, rent out the room."

She walked me to the door, stood in the frame as I went down. "Thanks for dropping by," she called, her face a sudden sunburst of good humor. I smiled back, telling myself a hundred bucks was a fair price for a postcard. *Down these means,* I thought, *an end must go.*

FORTY

Dark, wet, cold. Mabel tried to get up. Something was holding her down. Such a terrible dream—she still smelled worms. Then she remembered. Urine trickled down her legs. She tried to claw at the books pressing down on her, but it was impossible to squirm a hand free. She could scarcely breathe.

Skiing in avalanche country Percy had told her not to struggle if she were buried in snow. Don't panic, don't dig. Just take deep, slow breaths. She lay still now, thinking of breath, of life. Memory fell over her. Long ago, when she was five, she had been captured by boys, held prisoner in their yard. They took turns digging a hole. "Gonna put you in there," they said, pointing to a box. "Bury you alive." They used a plastic shovel, took turns digging.

"You better not dirty my dress" was all she said.

"You stupid?" the brothers yelled. "We're gonna bury you. You'll be dead. No one will care about your stupid dress."

She shook her head. "Just make sure you don't dirty it or my mother'll be mad." She didn't know what else to say. She stood there watching as the hole grew. The boys were bigger than she. They wanted to make her to cry. She talked only of her dress.

"If you're so worried about your stupid dress," said one, "why don't you take it off?"

"Yeah," said the other. "Take it off, why don't you?"

"No," said Mabel slowly. "Just don't you dirty it."

"Take it off," said the boys.

She tried to object. They wouldn't listen. They chanted over her till she had no choice. Slowly she undid the tiny pearl buttons, pulling the dress over her head with great care as they watched. She stood in the yard, shivering in panties and undershirt. Her undies were ripped, she was ashamed.

The boys began to sing, "I see Mabel's titties. I see..."

All they could have seen poking through the material was the brown bud of what would one day be a breast, but she had been warned about boys. Never go anywhere with boys. Never let them touch you. She hadn't listened, so now must pay. They invited her to their yard, and she had gone. Shivering in the sunlight, fighting back tears, she finally understood what her parents had tried to teach her. Boys would come—with plastic shovels, with tarnished spoons. They would make her naked, they would make her dead.

"Time to go home—" their mother started to say when she saw her, the little girl skinny in sunlight. She stopped at the gate. "What do you think you're doing?" she yelled. "Where is your dress?"

"She took it off, Ma, so's it wouldn't get dirty while we were playing," one boy said. Mabel couldn't speak. Her dress was thrown over her, she was pulled from the yard, banished forever.

In the damp dark Mabel now remembered that one of the boys had looked like Ryder. That was the type she craved even then. Cold. With the look of someone watching an experiment. Beau had such eyes, but not Percy. Ryder had once said he wanted to be her Lord Death, and something inside her stirred. She willingly gave him her breasts to devour, submitting to something not unlike evil. Had she summoned a demon in her writing of *Bone?*

She tried to lift her arm to her face; the books wouldn't let her. *Demons,* she thought. *I'm losing my mind.* Evil seemed so...medieval. In contemporary terms the practices of totalitarian regimes—nazis, khmer rouge—were certainly evil, but what she was contemplating was different. Something incarnate, capitalized. An opposition to Good as pure as Life to Death. Was Ryder *Evil?* Did demons have clouds pass through their eyes when they took their pleasure? A demon fucking she imagined would have fire orbs. She wouldn't expect him to cry in her arms, talking of the boy he'd been, how he hardly remembered anything since the time in the well.

"I don't believe in demons," she said aloud. Dirt fell into her mouth but couldn't silence her. "They're the gods of a conquered people," she insisted. "Beelzebub means Baal Prince of Earth."

The grave seemed to accept this. At least it voiced no dissent.

"Ryder's a madman," she said. "Madness may be evil, but not Evil." Centuries had passed since the world believed otherwise. Now there were different names for devils—schizophrenia, paranoia, sociopathology—treatments other than burning at the stake, too.

What about the law, would it consider Ryder insane? Criminal? The legal definition of sanity had something to do with premeditation. Malice aforethought. Surely Ryder had premeditated this crime, his forethought malicious in the extreme, but just as surely he was mad. A conundrum. Maybe it *was* all the work of demons then, voices that said, Don't listen to those bloody angels of empathy. What you want to do is okay *because you want to do it.*

Her nose itched. She lay pinned beneath books, unable to scratch. This was getting preposterous. Why was she wasting time, thinking about such things as devils now, when she should be plotting her escape? She rubbed her face against a cover. She thought of "The Premature Burial." Poe making fun of himself, hokey journalism. But wasn't there a graveyard somewhere with a mausoleum that had a bell rigged up to the caretaker's cottage? She felt herself start to panic. She didn't want to die this way, buried alive. Maybe she'd been right as a girl, maybe she was Poe reincarnated, and the price for that was this. Devils, evil, premature burials, life after death—such thoughts! All at once she laughed, using up valuable air perhaps but she couldn't stop. It had come to her so clearly, almost as if a voice outside her spoke: What was better to think of in a grave than the meaning of life and death? Demons *did* exist. She knew that now. Maybe they didn't have the same objective reality as French toast. Maybe they were only voices in one's mind. Maybe they functioned as metaphors for fallen aspirations. Still, they existed, creating havoc with their unattainable desires.

The weight on her chest compressed her into dirt. She tried to push it away with the power of breath. She tried not to think of worms. Lucifer fell, she told herself, because he thought God loved humanity more than him. Demons were the angels of unrequited love, the spawn of jealousy. Rape, steal, murder. Do it *because you want to,* because even if you don't, you will not be loved as much as the others.

That she should have been kidnapped and punished in this way, just when she'd decided to be good, struck her as a final irony. For, if she hadn't turned Horace down that night she'd have been with him, not alone and vulnerable while Ryder waited behind a curtain in her living room.

Waves of thought, of realizations come too late, crashed over her. She felt as if she were drowning in notions vast and gray, uncaring. Lifted up by ideas, only to be dropped down, buried beneath others. Realization upon realization. Maybe it was the scarcity of air that produced that sense of drowning. It was horrible and wonderful all at once, to lose the sense of herself alone, to gain acceptance by a great swallowing ocean.

Another idea rolled in her mind. An image presented itself. She tried to turn to a different part of the sea, but it remained before her eyes, wherever she looked. For there was once a girl who gave a baby a bath, and nothing after was the same. She shook her head, as if her mind were a paperweight with a sudsy scene, but the idea would not disperse. It settled on her again, demanding to be thought. Gallons of water would not wash it away. Had there been evil intent in the child's deed? Immediately she said no. She always countered her scrutiny of Ana with easy denial. The grave demanded greater honesty. These might be her last thoughts. She conjured a three-year-old face. "I gave Sethy his bath." The girl held the foot of her brother like a rag doll's.

The scene was suspended as if in a magic glass. Mabel examined Ana's eyes, the way her mouth moved when she spoke. She looked for Evil acting through her child, but all she could see, on the verge of her own death, was a child playing. One could as easily say Seth was the demon as Ana, tempting her to murder with his helplessness. In that sense, Mabel *was* an accomplice to Ryder's crime, having been alone that night. She shook her head and saw the scene with Ana and little Sethy again.

Something came to rest beside her, and she sighed deeply. Had Seth wandered ghostlike in her doubts all these years? There was a time, she realized—it had existed till now—when she'd been afraid to look at what had happened. And so the thought of Evil floated ever between mother and child, an invisible curtain. "There are no demons," she now said aloud to her books. "There are only humans, and the terrible things they do." Those acts were human acts, born of hurt, misunderstanding, fear. Jealousy too. Easy to put it off on demons, to invent demons to blame it on. Ana did not kill Seth anymore than Mabel had, and Mabel, lying underground like a great hidden root, could forgive herself and her daughter and her husband for the ridiculous pain they had caused one another. Ana had played with a doll—maybe to help, maybe to hurt—she had been jealous, but she was still a child playing.

But what of Ryder's mother, what of all she did, all she created with her childrearing practices? In other circumstances, in other cultures, hers might be the methods for creating the tribal holy man, a shaman gifted in healing, accustomed to negotiating with devils and gods. But in this place, now...

She didn't know what to think anymore. She was tired, too tired to think.

The books on top of her stank of mold. There was no wisdom in their words, she knew that only too well. She had researched *Bone* for many years, contemplating the symbolism of myths, the acts of gods. All in a detached manner. The pursuit of story. A treasure hunter seeking something useful for fiction (like all else she valued in life). Now the weight of her own lies held her in place. A person was responsible for her words. What had she accomplished with hers but the creation of another myth of demon love? And if a demon chose to use her own words against her...

Mabel gnashed her teeth, as if her writing of *Bone* were to blame for what had now become of her. She wore guilt in her mouth like a bit, it pulled her this way and that. She kept trying to bite through but it rubbed hard against her gums. She felt that she was being made to pay for all her infidelities—to her husband, to her children, to her writing—and the moment when she had said no, I love Percy and Ana, and I will not act out this craving of dirt for dirt, was too little, too late.

A jacket spine had been crushing her face, and she had been unable to free her hands to move it or twist her nose out of the way. But suddenly she felt its weight lifted from her. Her jaw just as suddenly relaxed. She knew herself to be in the presence of a witness. Somehow that made the difference. Something had come, not to intercede, but to listen. She no longer felt betrayed, and so she could see she'd felt betrayed all her life. Prayer flooded her. It had nothing to do with hope. It was not a bargain one struck with God, this welling of love she suddenly felt. It was the mere, perfect, exquisite knowledge that someone knew her story. There was significance to the narrative she'd been telling with her life.

Her ears filled with the sound of wind. Leaves were blowing, it seemed to her. Then she recognized the rustling of pages. The weight of words was being eased from her chest. She was being brought into light. "I can't talk now," she used to tell people when she didn't want to be disturbed. "I'm buried in a book." This suddenly struck her as quite funny, and she began to laugh, crazy with relief.

If this were a story of mine, she thought, giggling, *I'd make it Percy who lifts the books.* The notion at first was playful but the thought took hold. *Imagine it, imagine it,* she told herself. *Make it happen.* She was a writer, she was a god. It could be Percy, it had to be. If only she could think of a way for him to find her. There wasn't much time, but she couldn't cheat. It had to be an event she could believe in. Only if she believed it could she bring it into being. The books were being lifted off and thrown. Soon a face would reveal itself. It had to be Percy's. How, how? Find a way to make it Percy's face. He might be hiking in the woods, she told herself, and see the pile of her novels. He might have seen Ryder one day, remembered him, followed him. He might, he could...

But no, it was no good. She could think of none but a great coincidence that would bring Percy here. Mabel was too good a writer for that. She would not discover that the grave she was buried in was really the berth of a ship at sea. A general would not appear to catch her in his arms as she fell into the abyss. Book after book was discarded. Long before Ryder's gap-toothed grin appeared she knew it for the only possibility.

He crouched above her chest, spoke into the hole of her face. "What's the matter, darling?" he asked. "Catalepsy got your tongue?"

His balding death's head, his perverse word worship. Mabel almost smiled. He'd thought to overcome her with his premature burial, as if a woman were an onion that could be made to yield stinking shoots. Instead he had made her stronger. She would fight him, she would never succumb to a bugaboo tale such as this. One day, no matter what else happened, one day she would die. Then she would exist everywhere. He would never escape.

FORTY-ONE

"Nubi!" The dog bounded over snow like a leaping ghost. "Sit." He sat. Percy patted him. "Good boy. Here, smell." He held out a pair of Mabel's sweatpants. Nubi sniffed it, offered his paw.

"No, you stupid mutt. Just remember that scent. That's who we're looking for, okay?" He let the dog into the car, put the sweatpants back into Mabel's gym bag, and drove to the Wutzls.

Dr. Wutzl was waiting at the window. "Furnival," he said as he got into the car. "Why the hound of the Baskervilles?"

Percy kept one hand on the steering wheel. With the other he pointed to the county they were going to, pushing the road map toward Dr. Wutzl. "It occurred to me last night," he said. "Nubi might come in handy. Could scent her out. As in Lyon yesterday— didn't you think that kid seemed suspicious?"

"You mean just because he didn't want to look at the photograph? I don't think so. He was grooming a horse. Maybe he thought you were a lunatic. When he saw me he calmed down."

Percy sighed. "Maybe. I just thought, I don't know, we feed him half a ton of dog chow each week, I thought maybe he can do something to earn his keep—besides shake hands with invisible men."

Dr. Wutzl looked out the window. He had been going with Percy on these escapades all weekend, from early till late. Nothing had turned up. His original enthusiasm, a spark at best, had dampened considerably. "Furnival," he said. "Has it occurred to you that maybe, if we find that house, she might not, you know—"

"None of that, Dr. Wutzl. I've had it to here with rational pessimism. Just got off the phone with Sammy—Mabel's brother." He took his eyes off the road to glance at his colleague. The old man looked tired. "Want to close your eyes a while?"

"No, no." Dr. Wutzl protested like a child being sent to bed. "I'm not in the least bit tired. What did Sam say?"

Percy took a deep breath, held it, let it out through his nose. "It seems he told their dad about Mabel. I guess sooner or later he had to. Her mother's beyond knowing or caring, but her father's been in a panic ever since. So now Pop Fleish's got it in his head that we have to have a memorial service. Can you believe this? Mabel's been missing just over two weeks. I mean, it feels like two centuries, but I'm not ready to throw in the towel. Her father says it's time for the family to sit *shiva*."

He looked at Dr. Wutzl's blank face. "That's what you do when someone dies," he explained. "After the funeral you sit on these box crates and mourn. People come over with food, they try to keep your spirits up. I'm thrilled to hear this from Sammy first thing Saturday morning." Percy rubbed his nose. "What exit is it?"

The old man started. He had been dozing while listening, as if Percy were a radio. Now he abruptly turned his attention to the map, trying to disguise his lapse. He led his finger up the blue line of highway, held the map to his nose. He moved it far away, then close again, turning it slightly left, slightly right. "I'm sorry," he said. "My eyesight's not what it used to be."

"That's okay. I think this is it. I'll ask at the toll."

Percy slowed on to the exit ramp, a long gliding circle that felt like flying.

Dr. Wutzl sat up. "How did this happen?" he asked with unnatural alertness. "Sam and his father, I mean."

"What? Oh, a few days ago he and Debbie wanted me to bring Ana to their house. 'Let's take Pop and Momma out of the home. Debbie will make a nice dinner. It will be fun, relieve some of this gloom. Ana's a child too, after all. It's a pity on her.' I should have gone along, but I said no." He shrugged and pulled behind several cars waiting for the toll.

"This *has* been hard on Ana, you know," he continued, glancing at Dr. Wutzl. "She's worried about me dying. Ever since she and your wife contacted a ouija-board spirit—"

Dr. Wutzl turned to him. "What? My wife did what?"

"Didn't you know?"

"Oh, it's too embarrassing." The old man held his head in his hands. "This spiritualism claptrap she's involved in is bad enough, but when she starts bringing in others, publicly humiliating me...I tell you, that old woman is going too far." He rubbed his scalp, making his hair stand on end.

"Belief," said Percy firmly, "not disbelief, is the basis of my objection to this. I don't discount communications from spirits. I'll take all the help I can get." He laughed. "It was eerie, how the board spelled out stuff about a window, for instance. That is, it spelled 'wind' and then 'ow.' You know how Matt gets stuck in the window at the end of Mabel's novel, and Bone chops him up? It also kept saying, 'dedapersy,' which Ana interpreted as referring to my death. Strange, don't you think? Did your wife happen to read *Bone?*"

"Ethel? Ha!"

"It also kept writing 'hor.' First I thought of Horace and wondered if I *was* on the wrong track. You know, that the obvious was the inevitable, like Poe's 'Purloined Letter'? The poem we found seems to implicate Horace Byrrd, but that doesn't mean he is innocent, right? But then I realized it wasn't 'hor' but 'horsht,' or *horseshit*, that Mabel was being held near a stable."

"Preposterous." Dr. Wutzl hmphed. "Coincidence."

"There are no such things as coincidences."

"In a literary sense perhaps, but surely..."

"Why shouldn't our lives have as much meaning as those of characters in a novel? Oh, I grant you some of it is narrative sense, a function of reminiscence, but when I look back I find great meaning in events, the import of which was hidden at the time. 'The Purloined Letter' again. The clues are all around us, if we but had eyes to see. No better hiding place than out in the open. We live among clues to a crime not yet committed. If we are not dreamed by a creator we are dreamed by ourselves. In any case, anything can have a meaning greater than itself. The pattern of sticks falling. The movements of a pointer over a board."

"I don't know." Dr. Wutzl's voice had an air of concession.

"Just this morning," Percy continued, "I opened Mabel's book to a quotation from a Canaanite poem. 'Puissant Baal rejoiced. He summoned *weeds* into his house.' That seemed prophetic."

Dr. Wutzl nodded reluctantly. "Yeats was caught up in mysticism too," he acknowledged. "I don't know. I don't know anything any more. I suppose I can view a spiritual quest as a form of literary research, if nothing else."

"All right then," said Percy. "Anyway, it made me wonder about life imitating art, poetry being prophecy. If you consider— hi, uh, how much? No, that's okay, Dr. Wutzl, I have it. Here. Can you tell me how to get to Bald Eagle Dude Ranch? Hmm? Okay, thanks, you too." Percy rolled his window up.

Dr. Wutzl shivered. "It's certainly cold today," he said.

Percy looked at him. The old man's color didn't seem right. White, pasty. Eyes bleary. "You know, Dr. Wutzl," he said. "I really appreciate your coming with me on these trips. I like your company, being able to talk things out. But you don't always have to. Especially now. I mean, it's cold, the roads can get icy. I understand if you want to sleep late."

Dr. Wutzl smiled. "Thank you. I appreciate your concern. I'd hate to miss these rides, though the old rheumatism—"

"You just tell me then, okay? I'll understand."

They drove on in silence, the slippery roads taking all of Percy's concentration, till they came to the turnoff to Bald Eagle. "This isn't it," he said. "Not on a mountain. Not on a dirt road. Damn. Well, since we're here we might as well talk to somebody, have some coffee. Okay with you?"

They entered the main house, went to the check-in counter. Percy showed the photographs he'd made from slides to the clerk. The young man picked one up, held it under the light, shook his head. "I'm not from around here," he said. "I just work part-time. Why don't you ask that pretty girl in the apron? See her? Mona!"

The waitress turned around. Percy showed her the picture.

"Well, I don't know," she said. "Seems like maybe I've seen it, but maybe I haven't. I mean, I don't think I saw it, but maybe."

They accompanied her to the dining room, where they ordered rolls and coffee. She brought over a basket of freshly baked breads. Percy sipped the dark liquid, trying not to hope. "The food is excellent," Dr. Wutzl said, his mouth full of muffin. "I must remember to come back here with Mrs. Wutzl."

The girl returned. "No, I'm sorry," she said, giving Percy back his photograph. "I can't think of where I might've seen it. Or even if I really did, know how that is? I showed it in the kitchen. Nobody there knows it. But if you're looking for a riding school in the mountains, did you try Horse 'N' Things, up on top of Baldy?"

Percy thanked her. The girl left. "Ready to go, Dr. Wutzl?"

"In a minute, Furnival my lad. Just, before we do, there's

something I want to say." Percy sat back. The old professor seemed uncomfortable. "I think," he said, "though I'm much older and it's a sign of respect, that is, well, anyway—" He er*hmm*ed and fidgeted and finally blurted, "I think it's time you called me Rufus."

Percy smiled. "Thank you, Dr. Wutzl—Rufus," he said. "And you must call me Percy, okay?" His face felt hot, he knew he was blushing. It was silly to be so touched by the old man's gesture, yet he was. He felt as if he'd made peace with the dead.

He paid the bill. "Wait here, er uh, Rufus," he said, "while I call Horse 'N' Things for directions."

Rufus smiled shyly. "I'm raring to go, Percy my lad."

Horse 'N' Things turned out to be yet another dead end. No one had seen the hut or had any suggestions. Percy was soon back in his car. He consulted his list of stables and riding schools. He crossed out Horse 'N' Things. Next to Bald Eagle Dude Ranch he put a question mark and wrote Mona's name. He drove on.

"Here we are," he said as they arrived at the next stable. "What do you think?" Dr. Wutzl did not reply. Percy glanced over. The old man's mouth hung open, he emitted a gentle snore like the shushing of waves. Percy smiled. He closed the door quietly on the sleeping professor and left Anubis standing guard.

Here too his questions led nowhere. He returned, consulted his list again, drove away. Rufus snored on.

Two more stables. Nothing. People pocketed the slip of paper with Percy's name and phone number, promising to call if they thought of anything, anything at all, but they were so absentminded about it he was sure they wouldn't. Other people's anguish was easy to dismiss. Thinking this, Percy tsked. As if in reply Rufus closed his mouth and made a noise like a baby sucking. Percy hoped he would soon stop.

On the ride down from Fryer's, where a kid took the photo and said he'd show it to his great-granddad who knew the area really well, Anubis began to whine. "What? Oh, uh," said Rufus, waking up as Percy pulled over.

"It's Nubi. I have to let him out." Percy opened the door. The dog ran across the road and through the woods.

"I must have fallen asleep for a second," Rufus said.

Percy nodded. He waited five minutes. The dog did not return. "I better go after him," he said. "Sorry, Dr. uh, Rufus. I'll be back soon." He slammed the door and crossed the road.

He was annoyed. More than annoyed. He was angry as he hiked up the side of the brushy mountain. There was no trail. He had to pick his way through deer runs, along slippery wet patches of rock, testing for holes buried under rotted leaves, avoiding fallen branches. He was soon sweating. When he rested, his perspiration turned icy. *That dumb beast,* he thought. *That jackal-headed traitor.* He could hear the dog running through bushes somewhere ahead of him. He called him, but Anubis did not respond.

Then the idea crossed his mind that the dog was leading him. Percy's anger turned to expectation. Everything assumed a rightness that had been missing since Halloween. It made sense. This was how it would happen. First the paths that led nowhere. Then the following of random chance. Coincidence. It had to be.

"Good boy," he said. "You've found her, haven't you?" He followed the sound of dog in wood.

It was not easy to bushwack up the slippery mountain. He thought of the time he and friends had stalked the deer. Then too his face had gotten scratched, and he had been both hot and cold. He wondered now if he would have to pay for the murder of that doe. He shook the thought from his mind like a hound his wet coat.

For each step up it felt as though he slipped back two, but when he looked around he saw he was making progress. He had to rest, despite the sweat running cold down his back. He looked up to see how much further to the top. There was Anubis, standing on an rocky outcrop, looking down. The dog barked once, wagged his tail. "Good boy," Percy called. "Stay there. I'll meet you."

But Nubi didn't wait. He disappeared into the brush. Percy hurried after him. At each partial clearing in the woods he expected to see the stone hut; at each clearing he was disappointed. Wood, cloud, rock. As far as the eye could see. He got to the pinnacle where Anubis had stood. He pulled himself up, went to the edge to look around. He didn't notice the patch of wet rock. He slipped and would have fallen thirty feet if he hadn't caught hold of a fir sapling. He dragged himself back on to the dirt where the traction, though soggy, was good. "Shit," he said. He had torn his glove, gotten mud in both boots. All at once he knew he'd been had. He called Anubis, whistled, but the animal, if he heard him, did not make his whereabouts known.

Percy stood there, wondering what to do. It was cold, late. Soon it would be dark. Anubis had led him on a wild goose chase. "I'm leaving," he said aloud. "You can stay if you want."

The dog suddenly bolted from between rocks. He was chasing what appeared to be a fat black squirrel. "Oh no, Nubi," Percy called in a frenzied voice when he recognized the small animal. "Anubis, come here!" The skunk had its tail up. "Come here, you stupid mutt!" he shouted. Too late. Anubis barked, the skunk sprayed, the dog yelped. The skunk sprayed again and again, its body rigidly jerking, as if it were having orgasms. Anubis ran, tail between legs, crying. He approached Percy for help.

"Get away from me, dummy," Percy said, raising his hand. The only thing that kept him from hitting the dog was not wanting to touch the stenchy hair. He started down the mountain, a chagrined Anubis in tow. "God fucking damn." He sniffed himself, confirming what he knew. His down jacket stank of skunk.

When they got to the car, he looked at it. And looked at Anubis. And at the car again. "I've half a mind to make you run alongside," he said. But he had no choice. He opened the door.

"Whew," said Rufus. "Smells like Nubi's been skunked."

"I am not in a good mood," said Percy. They drove home in silence, the windows wide open, the heater turned on full blast.

FORTY-TWO

Mabel ran in place, trying to keep warm. She was exhausted. She put her hands in the pockets of the jacket Ryder had left for her. Started dancing around again, trying to build up heat. Since her premature burial she had felt the cold of the grave on her continually. There was a moldy smell in her nose. She thought at first it was the hood itself, mildewed from the damp of her breath. But it wasn't any better when he took it off. She just smelled death all the time, felt its cold, clammy embrace. *I don't want to die.* She wept in amazement of that fact. What meaning had survival—it all would end in the pit anyway. Still, she hoped by taking each event singly something might yet save her—at least from the end Ryder had planned, a corpse rotting lonesome in an unmarked hole.

She hopped to the corner where she kept her calendar. Hopped while noting the dot, then counting the slashes since the dot before. Dots represented days on which she'd heard riders. She had noticed a pattern. There had been two days in a row when she heard people on the trail that must run through the woods near the hut. These were followed by five when she heard only an occasional rider; a single, not a group, at that. It didn't take a detective to figure out that the days she heard several voices were the weekend. The days and nights had begun to run into each other, what with Ryder's "experiments" and his drugging her food. But this system of dots and slashes helped her keep track of time.

She stood still now, listening for the sound of hooves. All she heard was a dog barking. Someone's stupid dog was chasing animals in the woods. She tried to hear beyond it, but the bark was familiar. It drew her. She shook her head. "Damn dog," she said. "How can anyone hear? Be quiet"—as if barking could bury the sound she hoped to hear.

Someone whistled and that was like...but couldn't be. "I'm losing my mind," she told herself. "Hallucinating." Somewhere in the forest the dog yelped. It whined, it cried, then stopped. She listened intently but heard no more till the other sound began. *Calump calump calump.*

Yes, that proved it. Today must be Sunday. Cold but bright. She'd heard a few riders yesterday but not many. Today's riders confirmed it was the weekend. She'd lost track of time when he'd buried her. It felt like days that she'd been held underground, but according to this calendar it couldn't have been more than a few hours.

Occasionally he came in the day but never on a weekend. He wouldn't want to risk being seen going into the abandoned hut. He wouldn't want to build a fire for her either, not if he thought someone might be around to see the smoke of it. Mabel was glad of the time alone, time in which to think, to plot. She sat on the Bed. His anger had been building till murder was all that was left. What could she do to stave off his fury? He saw her as holding back, unwilling to help him in his project. She had to show him that she was trying. She took the notebook, picked up the pen. *Write, write.* Something, anything, just show him that it wasn't for lack of effort on her part. He was getting meaner with each visit. Who knew what he'd do next—the bastard had raped her with a turkey bone, hung her like a marionette, dropped her down a well, buried her alive. She shuddered to think of the constructs in his mind, a dungeon of creaky tortures. Writing something for him was her only chance, and it was slim enough at that.

Yes, if she could pull a Scheherezade, get a plot going and leave him hanging each time...yeah, ha. She started to shake with laughter—not the joyous kind, it rode too close to terror, thinking how he kept her hanging and how perfect if she could do the same to him. Oh, but if she could, if she could find a story and get it going, not ending it but each time leaving a hook.... Again she started to spasm mirthlessly, giggles quickly dissolving into tears. A hook, a hook. She had only to gaze up to see the hook on which he kept her hanging. She just hadn't it in her to compete with him. He was the master of suspense (*suspension*, chortled the tragic comic). She fought the urge to throw the book away from her. *Just get something down, something that will appease him; don't be clever, just let him see the attempt, then maybe he won't bury me alive.*

She sat there, trying to think of an idea. She remembered that when she first uncovered the trapdoor beneath the Bed she'd had a momentary fantasy, quick but full, that it led into a tomblike space under the house. She'd imagined an altarlike niche in which she would find the skeleton of a young girl—a child sacrificed by the hut's original builder. She didn't know why she thought of that now. It had been only a flitting fantasy, she was surprised she even recalled it while sitting, trying to write. But the story idea was starting to take over. She imagined uncovering bones, seeing the faded pink of a dress, a corn-kernel necklace; she saw herself weeping over the sacrificed girl. She even saw herself reading a note. In it the child wrote how the old man was holding her prisoner until she agreed to marry him. Could she do it, could she get a plot going along those lines?

She tried to force the words. They dropped dead on the page. She made their tiny black bones appear. "The sleeve of the dress writhed," she wrote, "and I almost screamed in horror till a snake poked itself out the neck, then wriggled away down a hole." She worked all day on her tale, not letting herself stop. It wasn't any good, but it was the best she could do. She hoped it would be good enough.

When a rush of wind blew over her that evening she knew without looking up that Ryder was standing there. She acted the possessed writer for him. Put the pen in her mouth, inserting it in the strawhole, in case he had missed the point—she was writing, okay? She was writing. She looked up, pretending to be surprised to see him there. Let him think she'd been galloping that horse of trance, riding to the land of make-believe.

But one glance at his face told her he didn't buy it. He didn't look pleased. As if he had a different scenario in mind, and this was just putting it off. There was a bottle of red wine in his hand. *Uh-oh*, she thought. *"A Cask of Amontillado."* Get her drunk and wall her up forever. "Got something good for me?" he asked.

"Trying," she answered, a little shyly. "I don't know, I had an idea that I—"

Ryder had picked up the notebook and started reading. He hadn't finished the first page before he threw it down. "This is crap," he told her, "and you know it. Hardy Boys find the Golden Bough."

"It's a first draft," she said, disappointed and hurt—it was ridiculous but she was hurt by his rejection. "Can't you see that? Maybe I'm just not that good a writer, maybe I don't have it in me."

His eyes glittered, he gave her one of his devilish smiles. "We'll see," he said, "what you got in you." He went to the Harrow, pulled out the drumstick that had stood erect, rotting in her liquids, since the night of her ride. He replaced it with the poison sumac. "I think maybe *this* is your best idea. I didn't know how *dry* you were. You're all dried up. See if we can't get your juices flowing again."

She tried to reason with him, but her words became groans as he pulled her up by the arm ropes, placing her over the Harrow, tying her legs around the vaulting-horse belly with the bridle. "You look pretty as a picture," he said, "with that hood o'er your head."

Mabel didn't feel pretty. She felt ugly and scared and oozing with death, bloody and caked in her hole, the very maw of death. "You'll fill me with poison, remember? You said you don't want to do that in case, in case you, I mean maybe you'll be inspired to do something and you won't be able to, I mean you don't want..." She went on and on, her words streaming out, making little sense even to her. She was rambling, her arguments wouldn't work on him even if he could hear them clearly, which he couldn't because of the hood. And because he didn't care what she said.

"I know you're a better writer than this." He kicked the notebook with the toe of his boot. "*Bone* ain't as good a book as I'd a wrote but it is better than the shit you do for me. Let me read you some. Maybe you'll get the idea of the sort of thing I want. " He looked at her, then down at his small notebook.

"Yes," she said. "Read to me. I love your writing. You're a great writer. Read your stuff to me."

"Shut up," he said, but not in an unfriendly way. He turned to the page. "Irises fullbloom, spread like an exploded cock," he read. She said nothing, she tried not to moan. "Purple scrotum flower aglisten with raindrop tears." He licked his fingers as he turned the page. Sipped water from a jar. "Big old cock of a tree," he went on. "Fat beech, couple hundred years old, judging by the girth of its dick. Grandfather Cock." She looked at him. His face had the poet's madness. He was on fire with his own words.

"Mabel," he said to her, "remember that time, that spring with me? That was real, wasn't it? You and me. That was a time. All nature rutting, everywhere we looked we saw randy animals, swollen flowers. I remember how you drank the lilacs with your nose, holding the face of the delicate flower in two hands, bending down to thrust your nose in among the shy blooms, stealing their essence in great gulps. Deflowering the flowers with your nosy nose." She nodded. "Now it's autumn," he went on, "and a different bloom awaits you, my love. A fragrant flower, alas no, but coned like a lilac bouquet. Not so sweet perhaps. Like you."

"Ryder," she said, thinking she caught in him a speck of tenderness, something she could appeal to. "I'm sorry I hurt you. I took material from you, plagiarized your pain. I didn't mean...I didn't know." Her words were mumbled, but she knew he heard them, for he was listening intently. Perhaps this was it, all he needed to hear: *I am sorry.* Someone in the world was sorry for the wrongs he had suffered. She went on. "Once you loved me. You wept to think of the carcass I must become." *No, this was wrong, the wrong note to sound, don't bring that up now, that time they found that decaying animal in the woods and he insisted on examining the maggots, the way it seemed to breathe and heave with their movements, no.* "I can't," she began to weep, "I can't take any...." She trembled in the air on her rope.

He stroked her leg and looked up at her. "'And we nourish our lovely moments of remorse,'" he said, quoting another poet of evil, "'as beggars give sustenance to their own vermin.'"

Shocked at these words she stopped crying to look at him. About his lips a playful smile. The gaze of his eyes intense. He looked like the angel stabbing Saint Teresa with ecstasy, except that he was below her, staring up. The evil of innocence, the evil that plays with animals till they bleed to death.

He went to the winch handle and started to lower her, then stopped. "I have to do this," he said, "unless..." He held out the bottle of wine. "Drink it," he said, "and we won't have to ride that tired horse." He looked bored suddenly, as if saying his lines by rote, but she detected the excitement behind his lying tone. He shook the bottle, held it out, like he was trading firewater with an Indian.

"I don't drink," she said softly, although it wasn't true. She was compelled by the script, her own script.

He laughed, knowing she was. "Sure. Like Annabelle. At first. Of course, I know better. I know you like a fox." He put his hand in his pocket, pulled out some oval pills. "You can take these," he said, "and get into what's going to happen. Don't and you won't. Up to you." He shrugged, as if he didn't care, but his eyes glinted like death's-head lapis lazuli. "See, I think if we go back to *Bone* a while, well then I think you might be able to find your inspiration again. What you think, or would you rather ride into the sunset with this idea you been working on?"

Mabel's heart pounded. She had recognized that he was using her own words against her, quoting from her book in the context of their conversation, compelling her to respond in kind. She had to force herself to steer clear of *Bone*.

"What is it?" she asked, because Annabelle had not.

"You know damn well it's powder from the cantharis beetle. Stick to your lines."

"Spanish fly's illegal." Fighting for time. *Save me,* she cried to an invisible general she couldn't believe in.

"These are 'ludes. Just as good, maybe better. Here, take them."

"No," Mabel said. "Ryder, I—"

"We're doing it by the book, goddammit—your book!" he screamed. "You are going to take these damn pills. You are going to get into this, hear me? You know how it goes. You have no choice. And stop calling for that rider. I'm your rider. Your Bonerider."

He took a step toward her, then back toward the winch. He lowered her down. She struggled to avoid having the poison enter her but couldn't. It tunneled into her, its dry flowers of evil brittling, cracking, exposing a sticky sap. She screamed as death entered her, she felt the terrible burning. He came to where she sat, grabbed her head, pulled the hood off. He forced the wine bottle into her mouth, pinched her nose shut, smiling like a mother force-feeding a child. Reciting as he did so, as if it were a nursery rhyme to calm the brat.

> *Her shriek is in my voice itself,*
> *Black poison is my blood through her,*
> *I am the mirror sinister*
> *Wherein the shrew regards herself!*
>
> *I am the wound, and I the knife,*
> *I am the cheek, the vicious smack,*
> *I am the limbs and I the rack,*
> *The life and taker of the life!*

When he took the bottle neck away she sputtered a bloody liquid, screaming, "No! Baudelaire had genius, you have no genius," but before she could finish her words he had put two pills down her throat, pushed the wine bottle back in her mouth. She was gasping, choking, but he would not relent till the bottle was drained. Then he let go of her nose. "You made me do that," he said. "I'd rather you did what you were supposed to, you know. I hate violence."

"You hate violence," she snarled, her face purple from rage and wine. She sat woozy in her saddle, lolling. Drunk despite herself. Dizzy and reeling. She spit, hoping she looked as ugly as she felt. Wild, bloody with hate. She sucked on the sumac flower, drawing up its poison kiss, the nectar of evil entering her. She drank death like wine.

Ryder walked to the corner where she marked her calendar. He erased the strokes with his boot. "No more time," he said. "In this hole day night wet dark hairy slimy..."

He talked on and on. She saw his mouth move. He was talking. She couldn't catch the meaning of his words. "Ahwah ahwah ahwah," he seemed to say over and over. Space telescoped itself backward so that he seemed a tiny doll. She could pick him up, toss him on the fire like a twig. *Who cares about you?* she thought, or did she say it aloud? Then something turned upside down, and he was larger than life. So big, in fact, her eyes couldn't take him all in at once. He stood over her. How did he get there? She didn't see him move. She strained her neck to look up. His angular snake head. How could she not have known? Arms on his waist. Glaring down. Something bigger than a man. Her mouth hung open. He held her on her horse. "I can bring your son back to life," he whispered. She turned to stare. Seth? The slit of his mouth was closed. Seamless.

Had he said that, or did she just hear it? "Yes," she said, she didn't know to what. The words reverberated in her womb as if she had said them herself, long ago. Read them in a book. Seen them inscribed somewhere, on a tablet maybe. Written in stone. Somewhere far away. Long ago. Her eyes closed, opened, closed. The world rolled itself up like a scroll and disappeared. He pushed her deeper into the saddle. Commanded her to sit, to pussy sip. And she sat.

Something in his hand, she didn't know what. She tried to focus on it. So familiar, staring back, but her eyes bleared out, her mind couldn't figure. Then she recognized her face. How could that be? And so tiny. A mirror? How come her reflection was there, on the back of that thing he was looking into? How come he was looking but it showed her face?

"I thought, I thought." She laughed. Tried to explain why she was laughing, but she was laughing too hard. She couldn't catch her words before another convulsion shook her. It didn't matter anyway. He wasn't listening. He was reading. He had a copy of *Bone* with her photo on the back. Her picture winked. "Don't be afraid," it told her in the secret language of images. She wasn't afraid. She tried to explain. "Shhh," said her tiny face. "Listen to him." She listened. The words rang, so clear, each vowel orotund, like church bells on a winter Sunday. The sounds bubbled in her chest and burst, a million fragments piercing her with splinters of glass and soap. So familiar, as if he were reading something inside her, as if she were the book in his hands. "Concentrate," the headshot sang. "Myth is the story of ritual."

"I'm trying," she said. "I'm only trying to please."

"...and gave her pills." He was reading aloud. The slivers of words entered her like needles. "They gave her booze. She was not aware of what she was doing half the time, the other half she didn't want to be. Taken out of herself, transformed into a vessel to be filled and emptied and tasted and probed and discarded. Over and over. No matter what she felt then it was better than what she felt otherwise—that she had lost her child through her own depravity."

Something tickled Mabel's cheek. A bug? She was not afraid of the thing crawling down her face, merely curious. She scratched the spot, with no evil intent. The moisture on her finger was transparent. She tasted it. It was salt. "Kill me," she whispered, she didn't know to whom. "Kill me kill me kill me." The narrator didn't turn his attention from the page. He continued reciting her own words, throwing them back in her face.

"'I can bring your son back to life,' Bone promised her, away from the others. 'Not for long but briefly.' He revealed kindness in secrecy like a flaw. The others would find such kindness weak. When the king weakened, they chopped him up, buried him in the yard, in the cellar—let a new king grow. Bone had affection for her but not enough to risk a *coup d'état*. As long as he was inventive in his rituals they would follow him. The moment he let kindness rule he would join, not lead, the dance.

"It was his job to supervise. 'Okay, boys and girl,' he said, clapping. 'Time to build us an angel. Make the beating wings of the pulsation machine.'

"That night, after the Boneriders had drunk their fill—making sure Annabelle did too—and the music and dark had turned them immortal, Bone gave the signal. His devotees turned to their god. He motioned one of them to bring her to the center.

"'Kneel,' he commanded. She kneeled in her place. He snapped his fingers, pointed, directing one to go behind. He snapped, pointed, another stood in front. He looked at two, they inserted themselves beneath. He clapped his hands. 'Begin,' he said, and they began. It took a little while for the movements to throb together, it always did, but soon enough they pulsed in power.

"She believed in him, his secret promise like a fragrance. She had not been a follower of her own free will, but now she would do anything. She willingly became meat, and went down. It was then, when she had forgotten womanhood and motherhood, descending in darkness, and the plain hoods pumped around, that her son appeared. She opened her eyes to let out a tear and saw him sitting beside Bone like a prince. She tried to call, but the words couldn't get past her mouth. She tried to stand but couldn't unbend. Tried to greet him but was held back. She wanted to run, to hold her longlost child. She was fixed as firmly as a pinned butterfly, stuck in the center of the void of pulsation that brought him to being. Through the sacrifice of flesh she had given him life. Not once but twice.

"Ted was laughing. Sitting beside Bone, pointing and laughing, fluttering his lids. She watched him, filling her eyes with the sight. He whispered into Bone's ear. 'Send that one there. Those two here.' He made good suggestions. Bone nodded, proud as any father.

"'Why don't you join them?' Ted told Bone at last. 'I'll sit here and watch. Direct it a while. Go on, have some fun.'

"But Bone was still king. He gestured in a courtly manner. He said, 'After you.'"

Mabel put her head in her hands.

"Dream the others now," said Ryder. "Make them come." He

threw the book, it hit her head. Sparks flew into the air. She pointed at the fireworks.

"You're a lousy writer," he said. "I want you to know what shit this is. Listen how a master writes." He took a small black book from his pocket, opened it to a marked page, began to read.

"He felt that a violent disturbance imposed on any adversary relayed to the cluster of our nerves a vibration whose effect, stimulating the animal instincts which flow into the reservoir of these nerves, compels them to alert the erectional nerves and then produce this quivering known as a lubricious sensation."

He looked up from the page. His eyes glowed red with reflected fire. He licked his thin lips. They had no more color than the rest of his skin.

"I don't understand," she said.

"You don't understand what?"

She shook her head. "I don't feel well. I think I'm sick."

He stared as if observing an animal. She retched a few times, but nothing came up. He watched as she convulsed, bent over, trying to vomit. He undid her bonds, took her down from her high horse, holding her with his arm about her waist. "Your legs tremble like a newborn colt's," he said gently, as if she was someone he had saved from a natural disaster. Then she somersaulted over and lay in the dirt.

"The great marquis deflowers your eye," he said, continuing his lesson though his student was passing out. "Makes you see what he describes. You can't help it if you're weak. You're nothing but a woman. Woman is weakness. Here, look at me now, don't turn your face. I want to rape you through your eye."

Mabel wondered how he made the room spin. Or was it she who danced? She wiped her forehead and found purple sweat on her hand. Blood? Was she sixteen again, in an old rundown house, naked in the moonlight? Beau had a fat kitten in his hand. A switchblade in the other. He brought the two together. "No!" she cried. The animal's legs were tied. Kitten, knife. Kitten, knife. She looked from one to the other. Close, closer. Then—she covered her face. The horrible screaming of a cat. She held hands to her ears. "No!" she wept. "Please don't, Beau, please don't."

He laid the sacrifice down, blood tiptoed cross the floor. With his still-bloody hands he wiped her eyes. "Don't cry, honey," he said, his voice soft as fur. She felt sticky. When he pulled her hands from her ears he left bloodstains on her skin. Her hands, her breasts, everywhere she looked she saw blood. It was in her hair.

"You have to watch," he said, his voice falling like rain, so quiet she struggled to hear. "For your own good, don't you see? You're weak. Women are weak. You got to make yourself strong. Strong enough to bear anything. That's where the power comes from. Obeah-lady said so, you know I wouldn't lie. Not to you. She used to cook and clean for us, took care of me. She said, 'You grew from your father's stick, came out your mother's hole, but you are my child. You hear? My own.' She taught me magic. Now I'll teach you."

Then he cut the animal up. She refused to look away. She watched for his sake, grew sickly excited at the strange rituals he performed. But where was he, that mighty magician, when it came time for the most important sacrifice, of the tiny animal that mattered most? By then he was dead. She didn't want an abortion—the only child of a dead boy—but she was sixteen. Her father found a doctor to rip up Beau's seed.

"—is now. You ready?" asked Bone.

She stared at the giant with his red eyes. How did he fit in the room when he was so big? Why was it so hot?

He held out his hands. One was empty. The other held a pill.

She took the pill. The text dictated as much. If—or rather, when—it killed her she'd have paid, but only then. All the boys she had devoured. Beau. The abortion. Seth. She *was* the very maw of death, she must be made to bear it.

She looked around. Boneriders were entering through cracks. Between the wood planks over the windows Boneriders squeezed through. Boneriders jumped down the chimney, they seeped under the door. She stared in the corners at the Boneriders who giggled in groups. Everywhere they gathered, waiting for King Bone to lead the dirty dance.

FORTY-THREE

It was crazy to undertake such a hike. Not that Kwestral was in bad shape. Despite his loose-jointed appearance, daily workouts at the gym had given him stamina. Nonetheless, he kept thinking of the salamander he'd left on top of the stove when he was a kid, how after dinner he'd come back to find him a rusty puddle.

Ten miles up and down the needle cliffs of the Na Pali coast carrying a full pack, alone, an albino beneath the Hawaiian sun— only a crazy man would do it. One possessed. He was wearing loose cotton pants, long sleeves, a hat, sunglasses, sunscreen, and could feel himself burning through the fibers of the material. He figured that at best he'd end up covered with crimson freckles.

The cliffs looked soft and green in aerial photos, but the rocks closest to the ocean, the ones he was on, were crispy brown, life torn out by its roots at the very edge. Further in was jungle, but especially around each finger cliff the wind let nothing live. It tried to blow him away at every turn. At one point it stole his hat. He kept coating his head with sunscreen, thinking he was going to die of exposure. The sun hammered him with gold blows.

Well, he'd die moving. Maybe he'd get lucky and hit a patch of shade. He tried to remember why he was sure Fleish and Barbon would be here. It was the postcard from Na Pali. And this hike was known as a hellish walk to paradise. Just the kind of place they'd want—hard to get to, no roads except a footpath of eroded dust. Cinder and volcanic ash washed down in the rains fell like hour-glass sand in the sun as he hiked. Kalalau was the Eden of dopes coming to bliss their lives away. If they were on Kauai they were on Na Pali, and if they were on Na Pali they would be in the vicinity of the waterfall at the end of the accessible coastline.

There were flaws in his thinking—after all, the postcard had been mailed months ago. He'd arranged the trip as soon as he'd gotten back from Louisiana, where he'd stolen it from Mrs. Lazar. It was easy to do once he decided to do it. He had lots of money, that was the good part of living with his mom. Still, first he asked Grinn for the cash. "You expect *me* to pay for your vacation in Hawaii," he said. But Kwestral had a hunch, and it was that hunch he was following, even if it cost him his freelance job (which he didn't think it would. No one wrote an obituary like Herm Kwestral, that's what they said around *The Wing*'s water cooler.)

The surf twirled below, from a distance the sort of blue of his father's eyes, taking it all in. Kwestral was working hard, going down for a spot of shade, a moment of relief, only to begin climbing the pointy lava gravel on the other side. *The waves danced their Salome, asking for head*, he thought, but for once he was too tired to take his notebook out, too tired to care. Surrounded by astonishing blues, greens, reds, white, he had to look away in order to see it. Part of him didn't want to see it anymore.

Spring, he remembered. Especially after his father died. Flowers poking up their green noses, opening leafy arms, blue eyes. It got to a point where he didn't want to look. Too painful, remembering how shortlived everything was. Each day it would demand something—feel, feel—only to vanish below, bulbs blowing their heads off in petal explosions. When he was young he'd been stupid in his joy. Go running into spring like a dog, looking, jumping—c'mon Dad, let's play. Then something happened, and the flowers looked cannibalistic, beauty growing from a father's dead eye.

He was hot, sweaty. His feet ached, he was tired. He contemplated a broad-leafed plant several feet below the path, growing in the shade of a rocky overhang. Could he pull the green hand free, plaster it on his head with sunscreen, or would he crash in the attempt like a red and white wave on the rocks below?

His mother hadn't wanted him to go. He should have stuck to his original story, that he was going on a sudden vacation, but then she had said she wanted to go too, what fun! So he told her he'd be working, looking for this missing woman, all about his hunch where she and her lover were hiding. "I'm doing a little police work," he said, laughing, "on the side. The kind of thing Dad would have done."

She brushed his hair back from his brow, about to plant one of her wet kisses when he backed away. "Your father wasn't a hero," she said. "You don't have to be one either." He looked at her as if she'd said something dirty. "Listen," she said. "The other cops, they concocted that story for our sake, for the pension. For their sakes too. They were all involved in something, and that battered woman was part of it. I don't know the whole thing, but you have to hear this. He was my husband. I knew him. Something was going on. And the way you see him, like you're still fifteen and—"

"Ma, that's nice and all, but hey, I've got obits to write."

"Herman, I want you to hear this! Your father was on the take and he got took, that's all. Now you want to be a hero. Like him. Only, he was no hero. And what you're planning sounds dangerous."

"Don't worry. I'm not—"

"You don't have the right," she said sharply, "to play with your life." He started at the anger, so she softened her voice. "Honey," she explained, "you're my baby. My only child."

He took her hand, stroked it, saw the swollen, weary fingers. "Yeah, Ma," he said, "but I can't be only your child."

So now he was dragging his feet on the narrow path, forcing himself to concentrate on the dangerous trail so as not to break his mother's heart. One slip and he'd be plummeting, hardly a bush to stop his fall. Some brown vegetation with short, gnarled roots clung between him and wet death, that was all. He paused, looking at the sea, willing vertigo like a man on a bridge. The thought came to him that he could jump, and he was terrified.

"Excuse me!" someone shouted, startling him from his reverie. He turned to see a scantily clad woman leap around him on the path. She wore only visor, running shoes, and a purple net bikini. The last was sure to produce an odd tan. "How far you going?" he called. "All the way," she shouted back.

That was it. She was gone and he was dead. He leaned his pack into the side of the cliff, slipped it off, sat on it. Guzzled water from his canteen, knowing it wouldn't last the trip. He imagined the trouble the authorities would have, getting his bones out of here. Maybe they'd leave him to rot.

Suddenly an old man appeared, short, dark, stocky. "You hot, man?" he asked. "Sure's hot."

Kwestral nodded, not willing to expend any energy on this conversation. He figured he should probably offer the fellow a sip of water, but he didn't. Anyway, he looked to be a native and was probably better adapted than an albino of Scottish descent.

"Nasty hike in the sun. Just wait till you get to Red Mountain. It's a bitch." He laughed. "Only time worse is in the rain. Dirt turns slick, people slide like flies on wet manure. Trail washes out, you have to dig into the cliff with your hands and feet, pray till the ledge starts again."

Great, Kwestral thought. *Maybe that's what I'll get on the way back. If I get back.*

"Hey, you are the reddest white man I ever saw. You got to get out of the sun." He took out his canteen, swallowed hard, relieving Kwestral of any residue of guilt he'd felt about his lack of hospitality.

"Don't you think I know? There's no damn shade."

"Sure there is." The old man laughed, the creases of his face deepened. "Around the bend. Here, man, follow me. There's a nice log to sit on too."

Kwestral picked up his pack. As soon as they turned the corner the wind stopped and the trail descended to blessed blackness. He hurried toward it like a man who sees a mirage. The shade was cool, and there was indeed a log to sit on.

"Feels good, huh," said the little man. "You should've worn a hat. Pretty though, ain't it? I mean, the way those cliffs in the back rise up all covered green, like antler velvet—ever seen deer velvet? It's just the mountains near the water that are bare—from sticking out into the ocean I guess. Like, what you call that thing on old sailing vessels—the maidenhead?"

"Something like that," he answered, too tired to correct him.

"It's lava, you know. Mountains. Beach. This island is the oldest, that's why it's green. You been to the Big Island? All rock, something to see, like the moon, you know? Hey, what you doing here, anyway? You don't seem to be enjoying yourself."

Kwestral squinted. He felt burn lines around his eyes. Maybe he'd have some wrinkles after this. "Looking for someone."

"No one's supposed to be living here. That doesn't mean no one lives here, just no one's supposed to. How you expect to find him?"

Kwestral took out his sunscreen, began applying it to the backs of his legs. The little man watched intently, as if he were observing a strange rite. Kwestral didn't care. It was good to sit in the cool, amazing really how cool the shade was. "Ask around."

"You a cop?"

He considered some moments, looking into the old man's eyes. "No," he said. Yellow orbs. That was odd. And the pupils were slits, not round. Didn't look quite human, Kwestral thought, then felt ashamed, as if he'd betrayed feelings of racism—but Hawaiians had dark eyes, didn't they? He wasn't sure. There were Hawaiians around, but he hadn't had a chance to stare into anyone's eyes.

"I am, was, sort of," the old man was saying. "Before I retired. I was a ranger actually. These cliffs here, especially when you get to the beach and back behind it, people used to live here. Families. Marijuana farmers—big plantations. Hippies. My job was to get them all out. Felt bad about the families. I mean, it was their land. There was once a whole civilization living here. Can still see temples, groves. But the government bought their land, the ones who were descended from the original Hawaiians here, I mean. It was done fair, as fair as these things are done. They made the park. No one's supposed to be here without a permit, no permit for more than two weeks." He sighed. Took out a granola bar.

"Got the families out easy," he continued. "They didn't want trouble. Pot farmers were harder. You find a marijuana field, next thing you know someone's shooting your head. We got them out too.

"The worst were the naked people. Hippies full of love, and they were good at hiding. No houses, no signs 'less you knew where to look. I knew. 'Cause I knew where all the fruit trees are. This place, Na Pali, is like a woman. If you imagine it like that you always have a map. Where the waterfall is, that's her hair. And the two pools back of there, those are her eyes. The mountains that come up, first one, then the other, are her breasts. And in these cliffs you can see her legs, see, bent at the knees. That part in there, you can't tell but it gets rounded and sweet. Her belly is there, and her belly is full of fruit trees. Guava, passion fruit, avocado, papaya, banana too. You have to know where to look though. It's all hidden by other stuff. And especially mango, there are groves. Big, ancient mango trees. The thing about mangos is you can't keep humans away. That's how I got the hippies out. Some came back since then, but I'm retired now, I did my turn. I don't care."

Kwestral's feet were hot. His boots felt like iron maidens. "Maybe you can help me find this guy?"

"What's in it for me?"

"You want money?"

"I don't want bananas."

He took out a military photograph of Beau Barbon. The old man squinted. "Yeah, I know him. Red-haired girl with him. What you want him for?"

Kwestral hid his excitement. "Just talk. Some questions."

"Give me an extra twenty and I'll convince him to talk."

"Ten up front, twenty more after I talk to him."

The old man said okay. "You better get going if you want to get around Red Mountain before three. That's when it's hottest."

He groaned. "How will I find you?"

"Tomorrow morning, man—I'll find you. Take you where the locals and hippies used to talk story. Nice there. Good mangos." He extended his hand.

"Hey, what's your name?"

"You couldn't pronounce it. Call me Goat."

Kwestral smiled. "How far to the beach, Goat?"

"Not bad. You see it when you get around the next point. Two hours. You got water to last?"

He shook his head. "I thought three canteens would be plenty, but I'm on the last."

"Take my advice," Goat said. "When you get to the beach, fill up at the fall but treat the water. Here." He handed him three small tablets. "One in each quart. Let it sit ten minutes before drinking. You don't want to drink the water, no matter how sweet people tell you it is. It's full of shit."

"Thanks," he said. "Appreciate it."

The old man vanished with a wave of his hand, and Kwestral was alone once more. He sat a while, trying to convince himself to get up. It was three on the dot when he saw big Red. The mountain was composed entirely of loose gravel that refracted sunlight like a mirror. The stuff afforded him poor footing. He kept slipping back.

When he finally reached the top he stopped to check out the view. He could see Kalalau ahead of him. It was indeed a pretty sight, one mile of white sand bordered by growling blue on one side, humming green on the other. Two hours later it looked distinctly less beautiful. No, that wasn't true. The blue arms of the Pacific beckoned like a goddess floating naked on her back. She waved, promising cool, wet pleasures. Foam and a tumble. She promised, she promised, but slipping down Red Mountain was worse than slipping up. He braked his knees so hard he smelled smoke. And every time he looked from the path (he had to concentrate so as not to lose his footing on the sharp incline) he caught sight of Beauty taunting. He was probably getting sunstroke, he thought, because he thought he saw a red-haired woman floating in the belly of each wave. He liked the image but he was too exhausted to write it down.

He descended into deep vegetation. At first the shade brought relief, but it also brought tiny flies that ate at his skin like it was rotten fruit. When he thought he'd never make it to camp he saw a site, then another. He could hear the ocean but not see it. Then there was a break in the ferns and he stood amazed to watch huge breakers roll in.

He felt like collapsing, but the flies drove him on. He threw down his tent. Unable to set it up yet he walked over to the hundred-foot fall people used as a shower. He'd read about it in the guidebook, knew it the antidote to exhaustion. Just the sight of it was. Naked men and women took turns standing under the hard, cold spray, then stood around talking as the sun dried them. What the hell, he figured, pulling off his sticky shorts, although he was by nature somewhat shy. But it was too hot to be modest.

A tribe of little children sat on the rocks, watching the adults frolic. He was ashamed of his whiteness, his redness. He heard a woman say, "Don't worry about the kids. They're used to nudity. It's nothing to them," but he didn't believe it. Not the way those kids were staring. Feeling like a prude he turned his back, put his filthy shorts back on. He walked past them, the little girls giggling. At his site he put on clean clothes and, feeling rejuvenated, decided to explore the beach. He was one of the few people dressed.

There were two huge caves just past the fall. The first had people camping in it—at least four tents set up inside, more further in. The second cave was wet. A pool formed in its mouth that led back to a black river. He stood in the warm brine, watching tiny fish dart. Hypnotized by the sound of water dripping, he headed into the cave. Echos like rings drew him. The cave was cool, strange as silver and lovely. He stood in warm water up to his thighs, afraid to go further, unwilling to leave.

This is *Eden,* he thought, then ridiculed himself. He trudged out as if marching from a swamp. His legs were sticky. He figured he'd wash them at the waterfall. Going past the dry cave he saw a woman with hip-length blond hair. She was waving. He turned. There was no one behind him. She beckoned, shaking her head impatiently.

"Hi," she said when he came up. "Want a mango?" She was modestly dressed, wearing both the top and bottom of a bikini.

"I don't dance," Kwestral said.

She giggled politely. "You didn't really think I said tango?"

He shook his head. "I have a nervous sense of humor. Anyway, why do you want to give me a mango?"

"You're cute," she said, "and burned all to hell. I'm leaving tomorrow morning. Here, look. I got a whole bag of them."

She did indeed, and another bag of hard green fruits that looked like limes, another of yellow ones. "Passion fruit," she said. "And guavas. I was greedy. I picked more than I can eat."

He held a mango in his hand. It weighed heavy and soft, like a breast. He put it down. "I don't know how to eat one."

She smiled. "Eat it like a woman." Before Kwestral could figure out if she meant what he thought, she showed him she did. She cut the fruit in half, dug her face into it, slurping loudly, licking up juice with her tongue. When she lifted her mouth from the orange-yellow fruit she had a matching mustache. He laughed.

"Here, you try it. Don't be shy. Just stick your face right in it, that's right. Now just nibble and suck. Mmm, good." She poured water from her canteen into her hand and washed her face.

Despite the messiness he found it delicious. He had never tasted anything like it before. He thought it would be too sweet, but his whole body cried out at the first swallow, as if he'd waited all his life for the tangy fibers. When he was done scraping the skin with his teeth, searching out extra bits of tender flesh, he took water from her to wash his face.

"You just get here today?" she asked.

"Yeah. Hell of a hike."

"I know it. That's why I'm taking Captain Horoscope back." Seeing his confusion, she explained it was a boat that went from trail head to campground. He almost wept from joy at the thought of not hiking back. Then it occurred to him. "How much he charge?"

"Fifty-five," she said.

"Damn," said Kwestral, calculating what he'd have left after paying Goat. "I don't have enough."

"He takes plastic," she said. "He's got one of those card things in a waterproof pouch." She laughed. "Plastic in Paradise."

"I could kiss you," he said. She smiled. Her thick blond hair was coarse and wavy. It had a Polynesian quality except for the color. Her skin was dark, her eyes were dark, her features thick and sexy. Miscegenated beauty.

"There was a full moon last night," she said. "I slept on the beach. It came up over the cliffs. Look at the rock faces. Don't they look like Easter Island statues, like incredible green gods? Hey, see over there, that's a temple. It looks like a rock pile but it's not. The missionaries took it down, just left the bottom. It's incredibly old."

She leaned back on her arms, her breasts fell open beneath her top. "It's so beautiful here it makes me horny."

They shared a dinner of Ramen noodles and passion fruit as the sun went down. He got his mat. They placed their bedrolls side by side, feeling as alone in the dark as the last survivors of the apocalypse. She tasted in his arms of the ocean, she moved like a fish. He wondered how he could use her in his book.

In the middle of the night he dreamed that a mouse gnawed his hand. Then he realized something was indeed gnawing his hand. He screamed awake. A crab darted into a hole. "Go back to sleep," the girl said. "There are no monsters in Eden."

The next time he opened his eyes Goat was staring into them.

"Sweet dreams?" he said, glancing at the girl.

"What time is it?"

"Time."

He got up, put on his shorts. He poked the girl. "Got to go."

"Bye." She rolled back over into sleep.

He wanted to wash but the man said no. The moon was still up. On the other side of the beach the sun was poking its rays past the cliffs. The sky was dusty pink, as lovely as anything he had ever seen. "Come on," said Goat. "You want to meet this guy, you got to do it now."

Sleepily he tied on his boots. He took a mango from the girl's bag. "Want one?" he asked. The old man caught his throw.

They hiked two miles on a tiny trail that seemed to be used only by goats. Kwestral felt good. Aside from blisters on his feet he found he'd weathered yesterday's hike surprisingly well. There was a place on his neck he must have missed with the sunscreen, but he had to hand it to modern science. Yesterday's redness must have been from exertion. The stuff had worked fine.

Goat stopped. "Give me money now," he said. Kwestral gave him some bills. "All of it."

"That's not our deal."

"It is now."

"Are we near?"

"You're so near he can smell you, but till you give me the money you won't find him." Kwestral sighed, flipped more bills. "Okay," said the man. "Go up this path, take a left at the top. You will see a meadow with a big flat rock. Sit there. He'll be along."

"What kind of a fool do you take me for? You're coming with me. You said you'd take me to him."

Goat laughed. "So I did, man. So I did." He turned and scurried down the path, disappearing in the scrub before Kwestral could grab him. Vanishing like a Hawaiian leprechaun, only he kept the gold.

With a distinct lack of optimism Kwestral headed up the path. To his surprise he found the vegetation giving way to an opening, in the center of which sat a large, flat rock. There was no one in sight. He sat down, realizing he'd been had, figuring what his next move should be.

All at once he felt someone behind him. He turned. No one there. Still, he could feel eyes watching. He kept looking around, peering into the jungle surrounding him. It took a while before he saw the skinny, lanky-haired man standing in weedy trees like one of them. The fellow was sinewed and dark, like something left out in the sun and wind too long. His arms, back, and chest were tattooed with strange symbols. Even at this distance Kwestral could see that none of the skinwork had been done with craftsmanship. The marks looked old, cragged, as if cut with a kitchen knife and stained with a pen.

The man stood in the trees like a shadow, watching Kwestral watching. He was tiny, that surprised Kwestral, and skinny as a sickness. All at once he smiled, a surfer's smile, and walked into the clearing. Behind him a woman swayed to an inner samba. She wore a blue sarong tied around her waist. Her breasts were tan. She did not look at the men. Stopping on the other side of the meadow she untied her skirt, refolded the sash. Kwestral could not take his eyes off her. The girl had red hair. The girl was not Mabel Fleish.

He shook his head and turned to Beau. Now that he saw him up close he noticed Barbon's skin was not only tattooed but marked by unhealthy pustules. Sun poisoning? Leprosy? Wasn't there a lepers' colony around here?

"Old man said you wanted something."

"You Beau Barbon?"

He had dope eyes, crazy blue run with red. Maybe he'd been a boy who made the young girls cry, but it was absurd to imagine a woman like Mabel with him now.

Barbon didn't answer. He snapped his fingers. The girl stood up and turned toward them. Now Kwestral could see one of her breasts was cut up in a peculiar, Mayan-looking design. He couldn't make out if he saw figures or just geometric patterns. Her breast looked raw, though it swelled to perfection, matching the other one like it was crosshatched by a mad cartoonist. She sat down in the lotus, facing them, and began to hum.

Kwestral turned his attention entirely to Barbon. At least, that was the plan, but when he looked to his right he saw the man was gone. He jumped up, about to run in the direction he'd last seen him, when he saw Barbon sitting on his left. Again the guy gave him his surfer's smile. *These people,* thought Kwestral, *have some quiet feet.*

"Do you know a woman named Mabel Fleish?"

For a moment Barbon looked genuinely surprised. And surprise softened him, so that he seemed ten years younger. Now Kwestral could see the boy Mabel had loved. His face melted in memory and Kwestral felt ashamed, looking at him, as if he stared at the naked face of a dreamer. Then Barbon pulled the screen back across his eyes.

"Sure," he said. "Chick I knew in school."

"Seen her lately?"

"Kidding? I wouldn't know her if I fell over her."

"You sure?"

"What's going on?" Barbon said. "You a cop? Something happen?"

"She disappeared. Couple of weeks ago."

"Yeah?" Barbon took this in, processed it behind his ringed eyes. "What do I have to do with it?"

"Thought you might know something."

"I haven't seen her in...must be twenty years. Haven't thought about her in as long. Jesus, how'd you even know about me?"

Kwestral shrugged. "A hunch." Barbon wasn't lying. He could tell. Call it another hunch, though he wasn't doing so good with hunches maybe, still another one popped into his mind and he had nothing to lose. "And Larry Lazar?"

Barbon paused. "Stepbrother," he then said, "after death."

"You kill him?"

The tattooed man rolled a cigarette. Lit it. Took a toke. Handed it over. Kwestral closed his eyes, inhaled, knowing full well that when he opened them he and the girl would be gone. Sure enough, he blinked. And was alone. Gone, the two of them. In a wisp of smoke. As fleet of foot as forest animals. It didn't matter. Nothing did. His disappearance was a confession, and there was nothing Kwestral could do about it. Or wanted to, for that matter. He was preoccupied with something more important, namely how he could incorporate this material—gorgeous locale, great love scene, exciting adventure—in a book in which he'd been dead wrong about his central character.

Love, he told himself, *is the story of how we become each other's gods.* He didn't know what it meant, but he jotted it into his notebook, then checked to see if the flashlight on his pen was working.

The next morning he sailed out of paradise on Captain Horoscope's boat. As they floated past the spot where he'd set up camp he saw an ancient temple on the cliff above. On a jut of rock ten feet below he saw a goat. The animal stared yellow-eyed at him, as if he could see that far, to see a particular man in a boat bouncing over waves. It seemed peculiar, the way the animal stared. How would he get down from the tiny ledge on which he balanced on two feet, the other two extended above to an even smaller shelf?

The boat rocked past, the goat turned his head. Perhaps the light caught oddly on his horns. For a moment Kwestral could have sworn he saw a man with a crown. Then he heard a gay tune piped. He looked around to see who played. Nobody on the boat was even whistling. He looked back at the goat. Gone. The fluting stopped.

The Pacific was anything but. It threw itself against me like a woman. He repeated it to himself like a mantra. He didn't want to risk getting his notepad wet and he didn't want to forget the line.

FORTY-FOUR

Dr. Xavier stroked his short grizzled beard. "So you're going to follow this ridiculous lead," he said, "and the next, and the next. Where will it stop? Why won't you let the detectives handle the case? Don't you think it's possible someone else can be right?"

"No," Percy snapped. "I don't think so. And I also don't know why you're so negative about it. Unless you're also an idiot."

"Good," said Dr. Xavier. "Now we're getting somewhere. Let's explore the root of this anger. Whom do I remind you—"

"You remind me of an idiot. I mean that etymologically, from *idios*, meaning one's own. You're too self-involved. Listen, I thought you'd be excited. When that kid up at Fryer's called I almost jumped out of my skin. I mean, I didn't expect anything when he asked me to leave the photo. What the hell, I figured, I have duplicates. He said he'd heard of a hut or lean-to or something off the trail that you couldn't see unless you knew where to look. I didn't get excited. It wasn't the first time I'd heard that sort of thing. I didn't think twice, never expected him or anyone else to call. If I had, then you could call me crazy, but this—"

"Did I call you crazy? Have I ever called you crazy? Have you ever heard me call anyone crazy? Do you think a man..."

The small gray psychiatrist was like a terrier worrying a toy mouse. Every time Percy started to say something, Dr. Xavier swatted him with a question. "Okay," Percy said. "You didn't call me crazy. I surrender." He waited for Dr. Xavier to say something else. When he didn't—unless you counted sniffling, a persistent, annoying habit of the analyst's—he continued.

"All right. Let me finish. I just want to prove I didn't jump to any conclusions, okay? So the kid asked to show the photo to his great-grandfather 'cause the old man grew up in the area. I didn't think anything of it. I hope you can see how blasé I was about the whole thing. Until the old man called. Can't you see? I didn't expect to hear from the kid. I certainly didn't expect Mr. Fryer to call. When he did I almost canceled our session to drive—"

"You wouldn't have liked anything better than to run away from the truth, right, Percy? Be honest."

"I'm here, aren't I? I'm not meeting Fryer till tomorrow. Oh hell, I don't want to talk to you anymore. You've really brought me down. I'm pissed. I came here full of good news and now.... If I knew you'd be like this I wouldn't have bothered. I thought you'd be happy. Instead, you only want to talk about how I'm pursuing a fantasy, dreaming instead of living."

"Exactly. And who does that sound like?"

"You! It sounds like you. Look, I know you want me to say my mother, but I'm not going to. That's a digression. That's the fantasy, see? This, what I've been telling you, is reality. Fryer called, he really called. And he really said, 'Looks like what you got here's a picture of Old Man Weavel's place.' Just like that. Old Man Weavel's place. 'Can't be sure,' he says. 'Been years since I was there. Don't ride much myself anymore. But I recollect it like that.' That's how he talks. 'I recollect. I warrant.' Look at you, staring like a fish. Why do you want to bring me down?"

"Turn around. You're not supposed to face me. Now, what makes you say I want to bring you down?"

"Your attitude. I mean, what has really happened is that my driving around, going to stables with my photographs of that old house, reading Mabel's novel, looking for clues, has paid off. But you're not excited. Why? Because you advised me to give up. You always have to be the one who's right."

"Is that how it seems to you? That I always have to be right? That's very interesting. So I remind you of yourself, not your father or mother. I'm a mirror for your own aggres—"

"Oh for chrissake, will you stop?"

Dr. Xavier was quiet, except for his sniffle. Percy refused to say anything. Each tested the other's will with silence till Dr. Xavier sniffed, snorted, and coughed so wildly Percy feared he would erupt like a volcano of phlegm.

"Can we get back to your wife for a moment?" Dr. Xavier said.

Percy threw his hands up. "By all means."

Dr. Xavier *er*hmmed. "Maybe you don't want to hear this. Maybe you're not ready to hear this. Do you want me to tell you want I think? If you can't handle it, I won't but—"

"I said we could get back to Mabel. If you have something to say, just say it. Stop ramming my ego, trying to stuff your shit down my throat. Okay?" Dr. Xavier coughed. "Okay?"

"A telling metaphor, but never mind. It seems"—sniff sniff—"to me you have concocted a fantasy about your wife being abducted and held against her will in order to protect yourself from the truth." Sniff cough sniff. "It is clear to the police, it is clear to your colleagues and your neighbors, it is even clear to—"

"Will you just get on with it, Perry Mason? What is it so clear to everybody but poor misguided me?"

"That your wife has run off with a lover." Dr. Xavier waited for his words to sink in. Percy said nothing. The clock ticked loudly. "Isn't that true?"

Percy sat up, turned around, faced his psychiatrist. "No, it's not true. And if you think so, you're a bigger idiot—"

"What are you doing?"

"What do you mean?"

"Get back on that couch. Don't turn around. Lie down."

"No. I will not. Didn't you hear what you just told me? Why should I lie down for you?"

"Down, down," said Dr. Xavier, as if taming a lion.

"No."

"Please. For your own good. Down, Percy, down. If you don't lie down you're committing suicide"—sniff sniff—"that's what it means. You have to lie down"—cough hack snort—"I'm telling you, for your own good." The desperation in Dr. Xavier's voice finally moved Percy to lie back before the old man choked to death.

"Okay?" he said. "I'm down. You can relax. You okay?"

"That's better," Dr. Xavier said. "Now, I don't know if you're ready to hear the things I know about your wife. I can't repeat them to you verbatim, but you must admit I know things about her that you don't. Before she quit analysis she told me—"

Percy sat up again. "How dare you!" he said, confronting the old man. Dr. Xavier held both hands over his face, crossing his arms as if protecting himself from a vampire. "Down, down!" he screamed, but Percy wasn't having any.

"Don't you believe in the Hippocratic Oath? Isn't Mabel

entitled to her privacy, even if she left you?"

"This is a special case," Dr. Xavier said. "If a murderer tells me about a crime he is going to commit I must let the police know. And if you insist on pursuing this folly to your own detriment I must tell you the truth about your wife. She was—"

Percy stood up. "Not another word. I won't have anyone, not even you—especially not you!—say anything against her. You think you know her so well. You don't know sh—"

"Percy, if you won't lie down, at least sit. We have ten minutes left to our session. You must stay seated. There, that's better. Listen to me," he said, sniffling madly. "I just want to say, I was thinking about you last night. About your father-in-law, in fact, his idea."

"What exactly are you talking about?"

"The memorial service, of course. What did you think I meant? It's not so outrageous to lay her to rest and get on—"

"But she's not dead. You only want to kill her off, you and her father. What did she ever do to you, except leave?"

Dr. Xavier waited till Percy calmed down. "I'm not saying she's dead. But don't Orthodox Jews sit *shiva* for people who convert? Wouldn't it be a good idea for you, in this sense, to mourn her passing and accept it? She has passed on. You must—"

Percy put his hands to his ears. "I won't listen to this. You're the one who should sit *shiva*, she left you, not me. She wouldn't—I know. I can't explain how I know, I just know. This is the last straw. I'm never coming back here."

He walked to the door, opened it, let it slam behind him. He grabbed his coat, walked across the empty waiting room. He did not turn around when Dr. Xavier screamed, "You can never run from the truth." He did not stop pulling the doorknob when Dr. Xavier yelled, "You'll be back." He walked down the hall. "You owe me for three sessions!" called Dr. Xavier. His voice was high, annoying as a small dog's yip.

When he got home Percy phoned Rufus. "I have good news," he said. "Fryer thinks he recognizes the house."

"Wonderful," said Rufus. His enthusiasm rang false.

"Yes, indeed. I'm heading up there tomorrow. Meet with him, try to find the place. Want to join me?"

"Well uh uh I'd love to uh Percy. But I don't, that is, I have some place I'm expected. Someone my wife wants me to meet. And my rheumatism. I don't feel so well, nothing serious, just tired—"

"You don't have to make excuses."

"I'm not making excuses, I just don't feel—"

"Fine," said Percy. "I'll call when I get back. Oh listen, Ana just walked in. Got to go." He hung up. He looked around the empty hall. Ana had band practice and wouldn't be home till five.

He hadn't wanted to let on that he was disappointed in the old man. Did it show in his voice? His one friend, a person who had helped him, who had listened to his theories and showed concern, offering his own crackpot ideas, Rufus Wutzl now seemed to have joined the other side. Did he think, like the rest of them, that Percy was out of his mind?

He sat in the dark, resisting despair, wondering how the day had turned gloomy. "I've had good news," he said. "Fryer's call was good news. So why did everything get turned around?"

More than two weeks had gone by. The police had found no clues of their own but discarded all of Percy's. The city tabloids had never had more than a passing interest in the story. Mabel was only a first-time novelist whose book had gotten some unexpectedly good reviews, but she wasn't a star—except in Winegarden. And even there, only in the eyes of those who knew her...well. The local paper still wrote small bits about the case, but people had lost interest. It was being played as runaway wife, publicity-hound author. Grinn was evasive about the outcome of his investigations. Kwestral didn't return his calls. A woman once answered his phone and gave some bogus excuse—he was vacationing in Hawaii or something like that.

"She's alive," Percy told the dark.

There was something between them—a marriage bond, a love tie, whatever it was, the tension existing between husband and wife was as palpable as a rope around both of them. If she weren't alive he'd have known it. The bond would have snapped and sent him reeling. If she didn't love him anymore the severed tie would drop him like a stone. He had always known when she was with another man. He had known of her attractions before she did. It was in just such a way that he knew she was alive. Suffering. He also knew he didn't have much longer. He had to find her before she was convinced of a terrible mistake.

It had come to him last night. They had misread *Bone*, they had all misread *Bone*. And if Ryder were the sort of madman Percy knew he was he would try to make Mabel play out a false conclusion.

As Percy sat contemplating interpretations of his wife's ending he lost consciousness of time. When Ana came in and turned on the light he was surprised. "Oh, hello," she said. "I didn't know you were here. Why are you sitting in the dark?"

He pulled himself up, kissed her. "Sorry, sweetie. Fell asleep, I guess." He went into the kitchen. She followed. He turned on the gas. He lit the oven. "Go up and start your homework," he said. "I'll call you when dinner's ready." Ana, banished from her father's presence, clumped away like a sad elephant.

That night Ana was afraid to sleep. She asked her father to read her a story. She was too old to be read to, but these were special circumstances. Sometimes just the sound of his voice, just his presence, was enough to help Ana fall.

The story was called "Maria Marevna," and it was about a prince who marries the beautiful Maria Marevna. She tells him not to open the closet while she's gone, so as soon as she is, he does. In it a naked old man is tied in chains. He cries he's thirsty, so Prince Ivan gives him water. The chains melt away. The old man becomes a hunter and says, "I am Dirty Bone the Deathless, and now I shall steal your bride." He kidnaps Maria Marevna. Prince Ivan searches, weeping and sleepless, till he finds her again. She tells him to hide. "If Dirty Bone finds you he will cut you into little pieces." Prince Ivan doesn't listen, and Dirty Bone chops him up, putting the pieces in a pickle barrel, throwing it far to sea (at which point Ana began to cry).

"It's okay," Percy said. "Honey, it's okay in the end. The magic animals he's been kind to put the pieces back together and splash Prince Ivan with the water of life. He finds a magic horse and catches Dirty Bone the Deathless, destroys him. He saves his wife, they live happily ever after."

"Fairy tales are like that, Daddy," Ana said, "but life is not a fairy tale."

"Little Ana," said Percy. "How did you get to be so wise?"

The next morning, after the schoolbus picked Ana up, Percy sat sipping coffee. It had snowed in the mountains the night before and he could see the dusting on the ground outside. He rinsed his coffee cup, went out to the car. Nubi, tied to his doghouse, whimpered. Percy looked at him. "You want to come?" The dog barked. "If I bring you, do you promise not to be a pain?" He jumped, strangled himself on his collar, fell back. "No chasing skunks, no whining, no getting lost?" Nubi barked three times, sat down, offered his paw. Percy smiled. "Okay then." He untied him and let him in the car. Went back to the house and got his leash.

After an hour's drive Percy found himself at Fryer's stable. He asked for Mr. Fryer's house. "What you do is go down the road a bit. You'll see it up past the pillars," said a girl. "Can't miss it. Looks like a castle, sort of. But real tiny."

Percy found the house easily. He drove through the gate, up the drive. "Be good," he told the dog. He got out of the car and climbed the rickety stairs. He let the eagle-winged knocker fall.

Mrs. Fryer opened the door. She wore a pink gingham apron over a plain gray dress. Mr. Fryer wore overalls and a flannel workshirt. He looked to be ninety. She returned to the stove, motioning Percy to sit at the table. The cloth was checked, the walls were yellow, the windows had curtains, frilly and hand-sewn. Coffee was brewing.

"Pull up a chair," Mrs. Fryer told Percy. "Coffee?" she asked. "Pie?" Mr. Fryer watched him, not smiling, not frowning. Percy stirred sugar in his cup. Mr. Fryer began studying the photograph.

"Yep," he said. Percy waited for him to say something more. "Remember Old Man Weavel?" he asked his wife.

"Heard a him, Orph, never saw him myself. You're older than me, you know, by a bit."

Mr. Fryer laughed. "And she won't never let me forget it," he stage-whispered to Percy. "Anyways, I remember him. Was a hermit once lived up on this mountain in those days when there weren't no one else around. This place was just trees. We used to farm below. You know that good pasture land where they built them houses in the valley? That was our farm. Pop had to sell it. Shame, but...well. We had this here piece. Good thing too. We came up here. Old Man Weavel lived up here alone. Didn't take to having neighbors. Ornery! I's just a boy. Went over to his place, we being neighbors, and dang if he didn't take a gun to me. Shoot o'er my head, but just the same I'm glad to be ninety-one, I tell you. The things I seen. The things I could tell you. I was in World War One, you know. Over in that there France. Saw fighting, let me tell you, then I come home. Five my uncles had what they called the Spanish influenza. Everybody got it. Going around. Lot a death, I tell you. You should see them all in the graveyard. One after another—all the stones, 1917, 1918. My brothers and I, we was strong, we built this house ourselves, stone by stone. They call it the Castle, you know that? Yep, Fryer's Castle. Ain't that right, Emily?"

The young Mrs. Fryer, not a day over seventy, nodded. "That's right, they sure do. But listen here, Orpheus, this young fellow don't want to sit here yapping. He's got business at the hermit's."

"Orpheus?" Percy asked.

Mr. Fryer turned around. "Yep?"

"Your name's Orpheus?"

"What's a matter with that?" The old man became belligerent. "You don't like that name?"

"No, no," said Percy. "I mean, I like it a lot, I'm just surprised. You don't look like an Orpheus."

"Yeah, well, that's okay, I know. Took a lot of flak about it in my day, believe me. My mother, bless her, fancied poetry. Wrote some nice rhymes herself. 'Orpheus sang his wife free, but then couldn't stand her liberty.' Remember, Emily? She named us all like that. Me, I'm Orpheus. My older brother, he's gone now, his name was Virgil, only that's not so strange as Orpheus. My second brother, he's gone too, she was going to name him Zeus but Pop talked her out of that, and a good thing too. Orpheus was bad, but Zeus! Can you imagine? They'd a tarred and feathered him. Pop told her that, so she named him Icarus, that was okay, we called him Icky, didn't let on to strangers right off what his real name was. Then there was my sister, my only sister. Let me tell you, they say time heals all wounds, but don't you believe it, son. I still miss her till I feel I'm busting, and it's nigh on seventy years since Persy disappeared. I tell you, my mother didn't stop grieving a day in her life. Oh and how we—"

"Persy?"

"Yeah, Persy. What's a matter, you got a hearing problem?"

"No, I'm sorry. Just, my name is Percy."

"Yeah, you don't say? I always kind of figured Persephone was a girl's name. How do you like that?"

After a while Mr. Fryer drew an invisible map on the table with his finger. "This here's the back road we took to bring the old man down, after he passed on. They say he froze to death up there, but

I think he died a meanness. I mean, folks offered him help. Cut wood. I'd a done it but—"

"Orph, now stop chewing the fellow's ear off."

"Oh hush," said Mr. Fryer. "Now, where was I? Oh yeah, I recollect. This here's the trail the horses take. Lessen I go with you, you won't see the place. Like to ride? Stable won't charge you for the horse, if I says so. I've a mind to ride some myself."

"Now, Orpheus," said Mrs. Fryer. "Doc says—"

Mr. Fryer waved his hand at her. "Quiet now."

"I don't ride," said Percy. "I sit on a horse and let it go where it wants. I don't think—"

"Well, you need teaching is all. You and your missus, you come back here, my grandson'll have you jumping in no time. Anyway, what I showed you before is the road. Not traveled much, mind. Not plowed. Don't know if you can get a car up it. You have chains? Well, anyway, you know how to go."

"You've been very kind. Both of you. The pie was delicious, Mrs. Fryer. I've enjoyed talking to you. Thanks so much."

"Weren't nothing," said Orpheus. "You come back here any time, you and your missus. We be happy to have company."

Percy swallowed hard. "I swear we will," he said.

"Serious young fellow," he heard Mr. Fryer tell his wife as he walked down the steps. "Shame about his hearing."

In the car Nubi was running from the back seat to the front like a caged lion. "Quiet," said Percy. "I'll let you out in a minute." He drove far enough away from the stable that the dog wouldn't be able to do something stupid to the horses. He put the leash on Anubis's neck. The dog pulled and bit it.

"I'll let you off," said Percy, "but if you run into the woods like last time I'm leaving. Understand?" Anubis whined. Percy took off the leash. The dog bolted across the road. "Damn you, I'll wait two minutes, hear me?" He got in the car, revved the engine. Nubi reappeared from behind trees, leaped in front of an old Chevy and just made it across the road. The driver yelled something out of the window, which the Doppler effect kept from being rude.

Percy drove to the turnoff the old man described. "You know," he said, "I think this is the other side of the mountain where you got skunked. Remember that? Boy, was I mad."

He began driving up. The road was steep, but other cars seemed to have made it—in any case, there were ruts in the muddy snow, and enough gravel had been churned for traction. It felt as if each wheel reached out to take a step, as if Percy were driving a cartoon car. "Come on, Ping," he said, using the name Mabel had given the old Plymouth. "You can do it." Step by step the car inched up the side of the mountain. Percy encouraged it till they were about halfway up. Then it wouldn't go anymore. The road leveled out just before a sharp rise where there was a patch of ice. The wheels spun but couldn't grip. After several tries Percy got out. He put rocks behind the wheels, which enabled the car to move slightly before spinning. When it slipped back it almost went off the road.

Percy gave up. There was barely enough room to turn the car around. He made several careful maneuvers to get it facing down. He turned the wheels in toward the mountain and put on the brake.

"Nubi," he said. "Watch the car. I'll be back soon."

Anubis sniffed the air and cocked his head. He whimpered and cried, scratching at the window. "No way," said Percy. He started up the road to the hermit's hut.

FORTY-FIVE

"The bus is here, Dad," Ana had called, knowing full well that her father wasn't paying attention. She had looked down the road, seen the yellow van turning the corner, and hid by the side of the house. The driver, not seeing anyone, had slowed, then gone on.

With a sigh Ana had placed her bookbag behind the naked azalea bush and peeked in the window. Her father was still mooning over his coffee, looking at the river that ran behind the house. She went to the car and got in. Good, the blanket they kept in the back was there.

The night before she had heard her father on the phone with Dr. Wutzl. He'd said, "I'm heading up there tomorrow." She figured he meant to see her mother. If he knew where she was then Ana was going to go with him. She had questions she needed answered. Like, why won't you come home, why don't you love us anymore, why do you want to stay wherever you are instead of with me?

Then she was lying on the back seat, using her plastic periscope to look out so her father wouldn't see her. She watched him free a copy of *Sam's Corner Gazette* from the azalea bush and throw it on the porch. *So this is what it's like when I'm not home,* she had thought, feeling exhilarated by her invisibility and impatient with her father's procrastination. *Come on, Daddy,* she had mentally ordered. But when she saw him head down the path with Nubi's leash she had gone uh-oh and folded herself into a bag of girl on the floor behind the driver's seat, using the blanket for cover. She hoped it looked casually fallen.

Don't give me away, she had thought loudly as the door opened and Nubi jumped in. He stood on her, barking, nosing, trying to pull the blanket off. For once she was glad her father was preoccupied. He merely warned the dog not to give him any trouble. He got into his seat, drove off. Ana lifted an edge of the blanket, revealing herself to Nubi. She put her finger to her lips, whispered, "Shhh." The dog eyed her, his mouth open and drooling. He seemed to smile, but she knew that was merely the shape of the shepherd's snout. Then suddenly he closed one eye. It was quick and strange, and for the life of her Ana couldn't help but see the action as a wink.

When they stopped at the stone house Ana used her periscope to stake it out. This must be where her mother was, but all she could see was an old couple drinking coffee with her dad. It grew cold in the car and she was glad of the blanket.

Finally her father came down the steps, got into the car, and drove off. Nubi was whining and crying, as if he'd decided to give Ana away after all. Percy let him out, then let him back in. He drove down a small twisty road, then turned the car up a bumpy dirt one.

After a short hard climb he stopped the car. With a sharp warning to Nubi he got out. There was no house in sight. Ana watched him through her periscope, trying to think what to do as her father shrank into the distance.

When she could no longer see him she got out. With a similar warning to the dog she set forth on the path her father had followed.

FORTY-SIX

When Mrs. Wutzl came into her husband's study to tell him luncheon was ready he was rubbing his neck. "What is it, dear?" she asked. "Your back bothering you again?"

Before he had a chance to reply the phone rang. "Yes, hello?" he said. Mrs. Wutzl took the opportunity to neaten the papers on his desk. He signaled her away with his hand, but she was so taken with her task that she did not see.

"Of course I remember you, young man," he was saying. "Hmm, yes. I believe so. That is, he asked me to go too. I was feeling rather poorly so I declined, but let's see...Fryer, I believe the name was. The town, now that's a tough one. It's up around Sam's Corner, do you know where that is? Hold on one minute." He covered the receiver with his hand. "Dear," he said to his wife. "Do you mind? I can't concentrate with you fluttering about."

"I'm so sorry," Mrs. Wutzl replied, busying herself with adjusting her husband's window shades instead. When he gave her an angry look she left the room, clomping heavily down the hall to check her roast. She was careful to make less noise on her return so as not to disturb him. She stood outside the door. Dr. Wutzl had returned to his conversation. He laughed. "'That is no country for old men,'" he said. How elegantly he spoke his mind, she thought. "But," he went on, "I should very much like to accompany you." Mrs. Wutzl marched into the room, flailing her arms desperately. "Yes, yes, hold on," he said. "What is it, dear?"

"Madame Tchernofsky," she whispered.

"I know, but this is important. One minute. Yes, Mr. Kwestral, are you still there? Good. Because, although I have a previous engagement I should very much like to accompany you. Could you, that is, I hope it's not too much trouble for you to pick me up on your way? Oh good, good. Then I shall see you this afternoon."

He hung up the phone and closed his eyes.

"Madame Tchernofsky will be terribly disappointed," Mrs. Wutzl said. "She so looks forward to your literary discussions. She has told me that she has never seen a young spirit such as yours make headway so fast, and now you're about—"

"Dear," Dr. Wutzl said, "I must go. 'An aged man is but a paltry thing, a tattered coat upon a stick, unless soul clap its hands and sing.' That is to say, Percy, his wife. Oh, I know Madame Tchernofsky has my soul in mind too, but it isn't just study that's important. There are our deeds. Percy needs me. Mabel—"

"What are you so worried about her for? She's nothing to us."

"She's like"—he looked at his wife's tight mouth—"she's like a daughter. I'm worried, just as if she were my own daughter."

Ethel sighed. "Oh, I didn't know, dear. That you felt—"

"Yes," he said, "and Percy is more and more the son I never had. Or rather, I don't mean to forget Felix, but when we learned that Percy and Felix had the same birthday, well, we both felt it, the bond, the revelation of one of heaven's mysteries. It was an epiphany. A veil pulled away. I saw why he and I have been drawn together. So now I must be with him. There are actions one must take at the end of one's life."

"My *dear* dear!" She ran to him. "Please don't talk that way."

He took her hand. "Of course. I'm sorry."

"Come, have something to eat. It will make you feel better."

"I'll be along shortly," he said, picking up a well-thumbed book of Yeats. "I wish to meditate a moment: 'You think it horrible that lust and rage should dance attention upon my old age.'"

"Not at all, dear," she said. "I used to, but Madame Tchernofsky explained it was part of your young spirit. My communicators have said as much. They've told me..."

Dr. Wutzl didn't appear to be listening. He browsed through the poetry volume, smiling sadly. "'One man...'" he mused to himself, "'loved the sorrows of your changing face.'"

Ethel knelt at her husband's feet. "Darling," she said, "you express yourself so beautifully, so sadly. I wish, I wish"—she looked about the room as if for hidden words—"I wish I could have been more of the wife for you, the sort of woman you deserved."

He patted her head. "Butler Yeats," he said.

She nodded. "The fellow at the Big House? I didn't know his last name. What about him?"

He bent his torso, kissed the air above her skull. "You are the woman who was made for me. I deserve no more...or less."

She looked up, eyes glittering. "Do you forgive me, the sins I've made in the name of love? I never meant for them to—"

"Pooh," he said. "What sins? You've been nothing but a most excellent wife. Why, the meals alone that you've served should—"

"Oh yes, dear," she said uncomfortably. "That reminds me. The meat will burn. Come along." She led him into the dining room, left him there while she went to bring in the pot roast with creamed onions. "The way to a man's heart..." she told an imaginary daughter as she spooned gravy into a bowl. When she returned, pot roast and gravy in hand, she was alarmed to see how white her husband's face had become.

"It was never my intention," she said, "despite the doctor's warnings, to—are you sure you're okay?"

Dr. Wutzl nodded and began to reach for the roast. He stopped midway, looking up as if he heard something. He grabbed his belly, lurched forward, clutched his heart. Before she could put down the platter he was lying on the floor.

"Rufus!" she called. "Oh Woofy, what is it?" She fell to the floor beside him, put his great head in her lap.

"'Horseman,'" he mumbled, "'pass on.'"

"Rufus, don't go, oh Rufus, please, please, dear." The tears splattered his papery cheeks so that it looked as if he were the one crying. She stroked his brow, pushing the white hair back from his face. "Oh Rufus, don't leave me. Please Woofy, please don't go." She wept like a child, as if begging the dead could convince them to stay. "Rufus! Woofy!" she yelled, trying to startle him back to life. It did no good. The shell of the old man had already fallen away and was growing cold, leaving the bone of a new death glistening.

FORTY-SEVEN

Percy glanced at his watch. Two thirty. It was a gray afternoon, the weather turning cold, smelling of snow. He walked quickly. Not much daylight left. The mountains grew dark early this time of year. He figured he had two hours.

He almost passed the clearing with the hermit's hut, it was so overgrown, the house fallen down tiny. Could anyone really live in that? It was like a dilapidated mausoleum in a rundown cemetery. The whole building hardly seemed bigger than a grave. He bit his tongue, hurrying to the woods' edge, pausing to look for signs of life.

It seemed smaller than the hut in the photo, but it was clearly the same place. No one could live in there, he decided. A stone cage. Iron bars ran vertically across two tiny boarded windows. The openings themselves were hardly as wide as a man's shoulders.

The door was partially collapsed too. Then Percy saw the padlock. Whoever had boarded up the windows and locked the broken door had gone to some trouble to keep folks from looking in. Percy decided to do just that.

He stayed hidden in the woods, going around the back of the house. Car tracks continued up the road, ending just beyond the house. He could make out a rusted Volkswagen. Like the hut it had an abandoned look. Then he noticed the footprints. Someone's heavy boots had beaten a path in the light snow, going up the mountain from behind the house.

Stealthily he approached, prepared to duck back into the woods at any sound. When he got to the door he put his ear to it, listening. He couldn't hear a thing.

"Mabel?" he whispered. No response. Around the back was a

pit filled with branches, as if to disguise it. He couldn't figure out its purpose—collapsed root cellar entrance? He went to a window, listened. Nothing stirred inside. "Mabel?" No answer.

She couldn't be there, otherwise why wouldn't she respond? *Unless she can't,* Percy suddenly thought. He began pulling at the bars, as if they were the steel arms of soldiers keeping him from his wife. He took a thick branch on the pit and used it to pry the bars. They were held in place by screws embedded in stone. The stone was rotten, crumbling in the holes, and the bars pulled out easily once he had leverage.

He pushed at the boards, but they were harder to loosen, nailed in as they were on the other side. If only he could kick at them, but the window was too high. He beat with his fist. A board started to crack. He kept pounding. The sun came out—just for a moment, long enough to glint on an ax and catch his eye. Percy walked to the tree stump that was used as a chopping block. He saw fresh chips. The house was not as abandoned as it looked. He pulled the ax free. A bolt of power surged through him. The handle in his hand felt like an extension of his arm. He swung at the window. The wood broke open. He pushed away the splintered boards, stuck his head through, looked in.

A lifesize doll had been placed on a mattress, its head covered by a bag. "Mabel!" he called. She was unresponsive. "Mabel! Turn around." She didn't move. Her arm dangled at her side, pale as death.

It was her corpse tied in place, suddenly he knew that. The form was hers, the way her back curved to her buttocks, the shoulders that seemed like wings. Tears burned his eyes as he continued to break up the planks, determined to get inside and hold her, even if she was dead. "Mabel," he cried. "Mabel!"

Then, slow as syrup, she turned, seeming bored, barely willing to acknowledge him through the eye slits. "What are you doing here?" she asked, as if they were acquaintances running into each other in a mall.

"It's me," he said. "Aren't you glad—"

"Shhh." She put her finger to her lips. The rattling of the chain between her hands was louder than her voice, muffled by the heavy material. He struggled to hear her. "Better go now. He was here. He'll be back. Chop you up. You mean well, Matt, but why don't you go? It's too late."

She wore a filthy blanket poncho, like a homeless person, and held a tattered red rag—her Halloween dress, Percy realized with a start—in her lap. The edges of the torn dress were burned, and her whole getup was stained, as if she'd sat in blood. A rope attached to her back hung down from the ceiling. More than that he couldn't see, didn't want to see, but there were the shadows of things lurking in corners, darknesses whispering among themselves of what had been, of what would be.

"You're alive," he said. "That's all that matters." She didn't respond. "Let's get out of here. There isn't much time."

She stared as if he spoke a foreign tongue. She pointed at something coming in the other window. There was nothing. He watched her. He wanted to shake her, pull her along. Time was running out. Ryder was close. But there was no way to free her unless she agreed to help. "Mabel," he said. "Let's go."

She faced him. "Go?" she asked. "Leave here? But it's not over. I can't go. How can I leave Bone?" She laughed at the notion. "I have to take whatever he dishes out. There was a knife in the saddle and he promised to lower me gently. The itch, oh my, you can't imagine. The relief, I thought. He swung me up and started to drop me. On the knife, don't you see? But stopped just short of death. Took my pulse, my temperature, looked in my eyes. Made notes. It's all there." She stared under the table, where Percy could see books and what appeared to be a tape recorder. "I can't fight him anymore," she said. "He told me he wouldn't resort to surgeon skills first. He'd try other means to extract the story. You don't know. You can't imagine. But Matt gets chopped in the end. Oh, don't come in here, Percy, Matt is all chopped up. Bone will chop you with his ax, he'll—"

Percy pulled his torso back out of the small window. "I've got the ax. Look," he said, showing her the tool in his hand. She went on mumbling about Matt coming through the window to save Annabelle, Bone chopping him up, planting him in the floor, and "oh, it was terrible, the blood everywhere I looked, but I didn't turn away, I'm a woman but I'm magic, obeah says..."

Percy wasn't listening. He was trying to squeeze through the small window. He managed to get his head and shoulders through by twisting, but his hips wouldn't pass. He wiggled like a fat woman squeezing into a girdle, feeling vulnerable as he dangled half in, half out of the window, with Mabel chanting, "Chop chop." She stared at something along the wall. Percy couldn't see what. Or whom? Terror surged in him. He popped through the window and fell on to the floor, jumped up, ready to fight Bone ax to ax. There was no one there. Just Mabel, oblivious on a bed, staring at space, as if she were reading some script other than the one he was in. "...blood to pay for blood, and the woman made to bear down..."

"Shhh," he said. "Listen to me. You listening?" He tugged at her hood, trying to get it off her head. She gagged and he saw he was strangling her. He used the ax edge to cut the rope and remove the sack. Her eyes stared at him, alternating between daze and craze. Black rings circled them, accentuating the expression (or lack of) in them. Her hair, those long dark-red curls that were her one vanity, was matted wild. The clumps stood out from her head like shaman hair. She looked damned and damning.

With the ax blade he cut the harness rope, released her body, her arms. Her wrists were still shackled, but the chain was lax. Her shoes were under a table. He told her to put them on. She dawdled, like a kid not wanting to go to school. There was a key on the tabletop. He tried it on her manacles and was surprised when they opened. She just sat, watching him. She still hadn't slipped her feet into the shoes.

"Okay, listen," he said. "Matt doesn't get chopped up. Not really. You made that up. That's just fiction. In myth, Mot, the god of death, enters Baal's house through the window and chops up Baal, not the other way. Baal's pieces are planted, not Mot's. You twisted it." He pulled her arm. "Come on."

She fought him. "You don't know," she said. "Matt came in through the window. He stuck his head in. Bone was waiting with his ax. Pow! Slish! It rained blood, and a field of poppies bloomed. No, wait." Her eyes focused for a moment. "I remember—Matt entered through the window. Bone had an ax. But you have an ax, you entered through the window." Her eyes clouded over again. "Mot was death." She looked at him, wild with confusion. "I don't understand."

"I'll explain later," he said, pulling her.

"I can't!" she wailed. "Don't you see? I'm trying to save you. Percy, I love you. Please go. I have to stay. End bondage by choosing bondage. That's how it's written."

"Jesus fucking damn, Mabel. Who are you—God? That's how it's written *by you*, that's all. This isn't fiction. It's life. We aren't characters in a story you or anyone else wrote. We have to get out of here before Ryder gets back."

She wasn't paying attention. She was laughing. Percy stopped talking and waited. Perhaps it was a good sign. Something funny had broken her spell. Soon she would share the joke. "It was my idea," she was saying, "the sumac. I thought it would be better than the arrow, but the itch made me wish for a knife—do you see? Then he came with medicine. I don't know how he found an ice mold in the shape of a dick, but he froze apple-cider vinegar, put it in the saddle. "Tell me you want it," he said. But I wouldn't. I thought I was standing up to him, but I was only playing into his hands. He said, 'I never would have guessed. Virtue is so important, even to a slut, that she refuses medical treatment unless it's her own idea.' He made me beg, do you see? He made me beg to be raped with a frozen dick. The burning inside, oh you can't..." She began to laugh, great sobs of laughter convulsed out of her. She pointed at something only she could see. He walked to where she pointed, stood between her and it, forcing her eyes to see him.

"There isn't time for this," he said. But he had no choice. He looked out the window. The view it offered was tiny but empty. "I'll try to prove it, okay, based on *Bone*? You have to listen. Okay, you listening? Look at me, Mabel, don't do that."

She had turned her face to the other wall. He put his hands on her cheeks, pulled her toward him, holding her face before his. She closed her eyes.

"Damn you, listen to me," he shouted. "Ryder will be back soon. I saw his car. There isn't time. Listen, you think Annabelle chose slavery and death, but she didn't. She chose life. Listen to me. I can prove it if you'd just listen."

She didn't say anything. Her eyes remained closed. But her head relaxed in his hands, and she didn't pull away. He went on.

"Remember when Annabelle apologizes to Bone? Nobody could figure it out, I mean why it was powerful. Even you didn't know. But I do. Want to know why?" He thought he felt her head nod. Percy quickly looked out the window again. The view was still vacant, but Ryder might be back any moment. It was absurd to be having this discussion now, here, as if they were making literary chitchat.

"She chose the empty hand," Percy said. "Not the one with the pill that everyone assumed she chose. That was suicide. She'd never choose suicide, don't you see? She apologized because she was killing *him*, not herself. Her choice of freedom meant his death. Bone has to kill himself if she doesn't, right? He only exists to darklord it over her. I'll prove it. Pay attention." He shook her. She was like a ragdoll. She offered no resistance.

Something creaked outside. Percy went to the window. No one was in sight. That didn't mean Ryder wasn't hiding. He saw a tree sway nearby. He went back to the mattress.

"Please," he said. "We have to get out of here."

She wouldn't move.

"Okay," Percy said. "Then listen. Bone has the pill in one hand. The other's empty, right? Remember when she says the empty hand has been dealt her?"

She opened her eyes. He saw her there, behind her eyes. She was taking it in. He didn't know if she agreed, but she was drinking his thought. He nursed her slowly, though time was running out. He couldn't force her to swallow if she refused. He spoke softly, listening for any sound of approach he might hear.

"Bone tells her to choose, right?" She nodded. *Good,* Percy thought. *That's progress.* "Everyone assumed she chose the hand with the pill. It was an ambiguous ending, lady or tiger. We all assumed it was the tiger, but she chose the right hand, didn't she? Well, the right hand was empty."

Her eyes cleared, her mouth opened. No words came out.

"Want to know how I know?" She nodded. Percy laughed, carried away for a moment by his own cleverness. "Remember how they shook hands?" he said. "People use their right hands to shake with, so how could it have had the pill? Okay, now stand up."

She wouldn't budge. Except for the almost imperceptible nodding of her head she hardly responded.

"Oh Mabel, there really isn't time to keep singing this song."

Nonetheless there had to be. She still wasn't won.

"Look at it in mythic terms then," he whispered, in case someone was near. He went to the window, looked out. If only he could see around the other side of the house. Ryder, approaching one way, would see the open window, but at least Percy might see him too. If he came the other way, neither he nor Percy would know of each other till they were face to face. The thought of that horrible surprise made him shudder.

"Annabelle is Anathe at first, right?" Percy said. "Goddess of war. But the Anathic figure becomes Inannic—a fertility goddess whose sacrifice causes crops to grow. Life again after time under ground. At first Annabelle is described in terms of blood. Toward the end she is described in vegetal terms, as corn—tall and thin, flaxen-haired, pale green complexion. Listen to me, the goddess is sacrificed only so she can be saved."

Mabel in no way indicated that Percy's words were more than sounds. He pulled her arm, she resisted. Yet she seemed to be listening. He felt he was in a hell designed for professors of archetypal literature. Only God or Dante could invent such a perfect punishment for a pedant, forcing him to lecture to a bored student while the walls of his classroom closed in.

He rubbed his head. "Persephone," he said, desperate to prove his thesis, "is taken to the underworld, right?" At that, Mabel's eyes widened. He continued the point that seemed to shock her into recognition. "And Inanna descends to save her son. Agriculture/ fertility deities are brought to the realm of death—whether they are kidnapped or choose to descend to bring someone else back, or even if they are chopped up the way Baal is. The important thing is that they are always brought back. You can't leave them there. Don't you see? Baal is planted and grows. Persephone spends part of the year with her mother. Inanna comes out of the meat state in the underworld and returns to heaven. For the fertility god to be kept forever underground is absurd. Every escatology has a judgment and a new creation. So on the mythic level too *Bone* can't work unless the ending, ambiguous as it is, implies a choice of light."

Mabel rolled her eyes up and intoned:

> *"To the Land of No Return,...*
> *Ishtar...[set] her mind...*
> *To the dark house,...*
> *To the house, which none leaves who has en-*
> * tered it,*
> *To the road from which there is no way back,*
> *Where dust is their fare and clay their food,*
> *(Where) they see no light, residing in darkness,*
> *(Where) they are clothed like birds, with wings*
> * for garments,*
> *(And where) over door and bolt is spread dust."*

Percy had not studied Mabel's book all that time for nothing. He recognized the Mesopotamian poem housed in *Bone*, and he knew the retort and continued the fragment.

> "'O Gatekeeper, open thy gate...
> If thou openest not the gate so that I cannot enter
> I will smash the door, I will shatter the bolt...
> I will raise up the dead, eating the living,
> So that the dead will outnumber the living.'"

"We create each other in love," she mumbled. "Bone says this all the time. He says I created him, and now he's creating me. He's only following my text, after all, he's my child, and I'm his, and if that's not love, a woman plotting for years and years how to make a devil come, then what is, it's not you or Ana, I created him from nothing and now he wants to bring me to nothing so I can..."

"Stop it!" Percy yelled, then lowered his voice. "You're babbling. Listen, you're a person, not a character in some book. And he's Ryder, not Bone. All the rest is madness."

"Madness." She laughed mirthlessly. "If he's mad then I created his madness. So I am responsible and must bear..."

"Okay," he interrupted her, shook her. "He says he's following the text. What about what I told you? Annabelle's hand was empty. I proved it. That means Bone commits suicide, not Anna."

Her eyes rolled for a moment. She shook her head. Percy felt as if he had turned on a computer and was watching it boot into memory.

"She chose the right hand," she muttered to herself. "Right/left, right/wrong. But if...but if..." All Percy had said to her, plus her own knowledge of the book's genesis, zipped past the screen of her face. She seemed to overload. In any case, the fog drifted back and her eyes grew blank. "No," she said. "Your interpretations are wrong. I never intended it that way. I—"

"Damn it, I don't care what you intended. It doesn't mean a thing, do you hear me?" Percy shouted, not caring for the moment who heard him, exasperated at having been so close, only to lose her again. "I've told you, the author is no longer an authority even in his or her own work. You have to accept it. 'The birth of the reader must be at the cost of the death of the author.' That's Barthes.

That's the twentieth century talking."

Her eyes opened, then closed halfway. When Percy understood what he had just said, he shook his head. "No," he cried, as if he'd been tricked to betray himself. "I didn't mean it that way. I didn't mean death literally."

"How come," she asked in a voice so quiet he could barely hear it, "your intentions count when mine don't?"

He was powerless to answer. He lowered his head. When he raised it he saw she was smiling. "Mabel," he said. "You're there, aren't you? Help me."

She looked around, stretched as if waking up. "We can't leave, Percy, not that way," she said. "At least, I can't climb out the window. He'll be back soon. He's got a gun."

"It's Ryder, isn't it?"

She nodded. "How did you find me?"

"In your work," he said. "I knew you were there. I just kept reading and reading, and..."

"But that's no different from what Ryder says."

"It's completely different. I looked for you in your book. Places where you went of your own free will. He wanted to capture you, imprison you in a book of his making, force his interpretation on you. Make you succumb to his will."

Mabel paused, as if tasting his words for truth. All at once she took his arm and pulled herself up. "Percy," she said. "Ryder has a gun. You know Chekhov." He looked at her, nodded.

"I don't know if it holds anymore that a gun appearing in the first act must go off in the end. That's rather passé, don't you—"

"Someone's coming," she whispered.

He heard the sound of footsteps on the path. The padlock began to rattle. He could hear heavy breathing: his own. An overwhelming urge to urinate took him. He thought he might vomit.

"I'm scared," Mabel said. He swallowed hard, grabbed his ax, hid by the door. He motioned her into the opposite corner. Had Ryder seen his car? The open window, footprints in the snow? Did he know someone was here? If he'd gone down the mountain...but he might not have. His yellow Bug was here, his own footprints led up.

They heard him fumble with the chain. Percy signaled to Mabel. He pointed to the ax. She nodded. She seemed to understand. Could he trust her? She might again decide to follow fiction, but that was a chance he'd have to take.

Outside, Ryder jiggled with the lock. He threw open the door and stood grinning like a skull. Gun in hand he stepped toward her. She cowered in a corner, then assumed her death face. "Bone," she said, beckoning with pale hands. Ryder seemed surprised to see her hoodless and free, but he stupidly continued walking forward. "What—" he started to say when Percy swung the ax. He brought it down on what would have been his head if Ryder hadn't stepped to the side.

He got him in the shoulder. The blunt ax didn't penetrate deeply, but it hurt considerably. Ryder dropped the gun, shouting in pain. It clattered to the floor and lay waiting like an animal. He looked at Mabel, then Percy. "You can't do this," he said, singling her out. "You know you can't. It's not—"

"Yes, I can," she said.

He reached into his pocket. Put both hands behind him, then brought them around. He held them out before her, closed. "Choose," he said.

"No!" she shouted, putting a fist into his stomach. He doubled up and pills rolled from both hands when he clutched himself. "You cheat," she said. "You had both hands full. You weren't playing by the book either." She came after him with her fingers out as if to scratch him to death. Ryder looked horrified, although it wasn't clear at what. All at once Mabel kicked the gun back and ran to pick it up. Before she could aim he was out the door. She shot once, dropped the gun, put her fingers in her mouth. Percy picked it up and ran out the door. He saw Ryder escaping into the woods.

He started after him, following the trail of bright blood in the snow. Mabel tried to follow but was too weak. "I can't," she said. "Please, don't leave me." He stared at the spot where Ryder was vanishing. He let the gun fall into his pocket, like a stone picked up as a souvenir. He'd almost shot a man, he thought. He hadn't even been able to shoot a deer, but a man.... He shuddered, put his arm under her. "Wait," she said. She pointed at the tape recorder, the notebook. He picked them up and carried her down the mountain. She was all that mattered, she was as light as paper.

Even before they saw the car they heard barking. "Anubis." Mabel laughed. "Look at him." The dog clawed at the back window, whining and barking and whimpering, trying to get out.

Percy opened the door. The dog ran to Mabel, sniffed her. She petted him. He sat in the snow and offered his paw. When she went to pat his head again he snapped and darted into the woods. "Oh Christ," said Percy. "Not again. I'm not going after him. Let him freeze. I'm sick of that damn dog. He's been nothing but trouble. You'd almost think he was intentionally sabotaging my efforts to find you."

Mabel got in the car. She touched the dials, the glove compartment, the seat. Percy got in the other side. He started the engine, turned on the heat. Mabel looked at him. "You can't leave him," she said. "I know he's a pain but he's just a dog. Go after him, Percy. I'll wait here. I'm all right."

He sighed and kissed her for the first time. "Lock the doors," he said. "Don't let anyone in."

She smiled. "You sound like the seven dwarfs to Snow White."

With foreboding he left her in the car. He noticed small footprints by the front wheel. They soon vanished, and he didn't think anything more of them. He followed dog tracks up the mountain. Not far from where they started the prints met up with a man's. Percy saw blood. There was no sign of a struggle. It was as if the dog had found his wounded master and gone off with him. Percy couldn't shake the notion that Anubis was with Ryder. He touched the gun in his pocket. He followed the red snow.

He stalked man and dog till both prints vanished. The rocky terrain was thinly covered with snow. The brush told no tales. One way or another, he decided, Anubis had found Death.

Mabel grew sleepy, waiting for Percy to return. She closed her eyes. It was dusk. Grayness crept over her like an unwelcome doze, hiding specters in its indistinguishable light. Then she was startled awake. The car was cold. The engine had died. She sat up.

Dusk had turned to night while she napped. She moved into the driver's seat, started the car. It stalled twice, then turned over. She felt something watching her. In the rearview mirror she saw a flash of white. When she turned to look behind her it vanished. She caught it again from the corner of her eye. It was on the right side. Then she realized the right side was reflecting something on the left. Wherever she looked it seemed at that moment to disappear.

She was uneasy, she felt exposed. Turning her head every which way, she tried to catch sight of the elusive watcher. When a face suddenly appeared and looked in she screamed. He opened the door. Percy held her. "It's okay, Minky," he said. "It's okay now."

He released the brake, let the car ease itself down the mountain. "Where's Anubis?" Mabel asked.

"Anubis is dead."

FORTY-EIGHT

*T*his was a case riddled with corpses, Kwestral thought as he drove
along. *This was a riddle cased with corpses this was a corpse ridden
by cases.* He put on the radio to turn off the brain brat. His mind
circled back to upsetting images. As an obit writer he was used to
dealing with death second hand. He didn't have to see things like
poor Mrs. Wutzl sitting on the floor beside her dead husband, his
head in her lap. "Please," she'd beseeched him with animal eyes. "I
don't think Dr. Wutzl's feeling well enough today to go with you."
The old man's pupils were glazed, sticky, as if made of resin.

*Dr. Rufus Wutzl, English professor emeritus at Jones College,
died today of...*

"Let me help you." Kwestral pulled her to her feet. "Can I call
a neighbor?" She gave him her phone book, saying, "Harriet Hook
might be persuaded to come for tea," wiped her hands on the front
of her dress and hurried into the kitchen.

*He was blank years old and had taught at the college since
nineteen blank blank...*

The two elderly women were sitting on the couch when he left,
sipping hot liquid from delicate china cups, nibbling on nut bread.
Dr. Wutzl still lay on the dining-room floor. He looked like a large
game animal shot by aging huntresses.

"I'm sorry to have to rush off," Kwestral said.

"Not at all." Mrs. Wutzl looked up. She'd been staring into her
teacup, seemingly absorbed in watching her tears salt the liquid.
She gave him a grandmotherly wave. He'd left quickly, feeling as if
he were abandoning his own mother in her need. Nothing could
have been further from the truth. Though he'd only been a boy he
had sat beside her, her rock, from the time his father's partner came

with the news till long after the wake.

The esteemed professor of Romantic poetry...

Kwestral could see the form his obituary would take. He only had to fill in the facts. He knew that blocking it out this way was a way to block out his feelings too. He forced himself to remember the old man as he was, lying there, not as he would look on the page. He'd known at once, of course. That death could be mistaken for sleep was a device credible only in novels and fairy tales. The color, the ghastly pallor of death was unmistakable, even if you'd never seen it before. And he had, and could never forget the color his father had turned, that hideous white, whiter than his son.

Though he'd started out early it was now late afternoon. He was trying not to be annoyed at the delay the death had caused him. He focused instead on the strange sequence of events that had led him to Dr. Wutzl's stiffening side.

He'd returned from Hawaii just the day before, and was still jetlagged, but had called Grinn that morning, eager to tell him he'd found Barbon. That was when he learned about the letter *Sam's Corner Gazette* had received in the morning mail, an oddly spelled note, the envelope of which was signed *BB*. Grinn, the desk sergeant told him, had gone to Sam's Corner to investigate. Kwestral called Percy, to find out what he knew about the note, but he wasn't home. Dr. Wutzl was next on Kwestral's list. The old man not only said his friend had gone to talk to a Mr. Fryer in Sam's Corner but had insisted upon accompanying Kwestral there. Little did he know he'd be unable to cancel a previous engagement.

Well, okay, so the old man's death had cost him some time, but if he hadn't called him he'd have no lead at all about where to go next. So now he was on his way, and it was a lucky thing that Wutzl, before deciding to join him, had given directions to Sam's Corner.

Kwestral turned off the highway at the appropriate exit and followed county roads till he got to the four-corner stop with the flagpole in its center. "Excuse me," he said to a tired-looking woman. "Do you know where I can find a man named Fryer? I think—"

"Orph Fryer?" she said. "Sure do. Everyone knows Old Orph. He's our living history. If it weren't for Orph Fryer we wouldn't know how the village got its name or that the railroad wanted—"

"Yes, yes," Kwestral said, "but I'm in a rush, so if you could just..." And so, ruffling her feathers a bit, she did.

"This is something," Fryer said upon seeing him. "First that other fellow, then you. Never seen a albina before. Sure are pale."

Kwestral didn't know how to reply. "Please, can you tell me how to get to the house in the photograph?"

"Sure I can." Kwestral waited. "But I won't."

Mrs. Fryer looked up. "Now, Orph."

"Oh, hush. I tell you, two men running up to that hermit's house, something's going on and I aim to be part of it."

"Now, you know what Doc—"

"Doc, my foot! A man can go crazy, sitting in a kitchen with no one but you to talk to all day."

"Well, that's how you feel, is it?" She turned her back.

Kwestral sensed he'd interrupted a long-running argument. "I don't think it's such a good idea—" he started to say.

"I don't give a hoot what you think, neither," Fryer replied. "I'm going. I'm intent on going, and if I don't go you don't go, so there!" He stuck out his chin like a petulant boy, and Kwestral sighed. Time was running away, and they were still jabbering. What harm could the old man do—he'd direct Kwestral, then sit in the car and wait for him by the hermit's house. There probably wouldn't be any trouble. At most, maybe a body and a grief-stricken husband, nothing that Fryer could really screw up.

"Okay," Kwestral said. "Let's go then."

"Really?" Fryer looked young in his surprise.

"Orph," said Mrs. Fryer, wiping her hands. "I won't have it."

Kwestral turned. "I'll watch him," he said. "I'm sorry, but I can't waste any more time. If things are as I fear, then there's a professor in these mountains with a broken heart. Who knows what—"

From the corner of his eye he saw the old man slip a rifle under his coat. "Uh-uh," said Kwestral. "No way, Jose. You are not taking that thing with you."

"I always tote it along. Never know what you might see. Get us a turkey, right, Emily?"

"Don't you talk to me. I don't want you going, and that's—"

"Come on, boy. Let's get out of here 'fore she turns on the water. Can't stand when she does that." He hobbled down the steps, almost ran into the car, where he waited like a dog for a ride.

"I'm sorry," Kwestral told Mrs. Fryer's back, feeling as always the traitor. She dabbed at her eyes.

"Come on! What you waiting on? Git!" called the old man. Kwestral saw the gun by his side. *What am I supposed to do?* he thought. *Have him arrested?* He hoped he knew enough to keep the safety on. They started down the drive.

Fryer's memory of the roads wasn't as good as he'd let on. "It's changed a mite," he said. "Wasn't all this hardtop last time I went to the hermit's. Rode mostly. That was back in, let's see, it was after the Spanish influenza, so that's... Hey, you want to see the grave-yard where they's buried from back then? It was sad—"

"Do I go left or right here?"

"Huh?"

"Left or right?"

"Well, that depends on where you's going."

He gritted his teeth. "We're going to the hermit's, remember?"

"Sure I do. Nothing wrong with my memory. I tell you I remember way back to the Great War, and that's a lot..." Meanwhile the cars behind them were beginning to give hesitant country honks.

"Left or right?"

"Hmmm. Well, left, of course. I done told you that."

So Kwestral made a left and Fryer yelled, "Left, I say! Left, you bloodless pale excuse for an imbecile."

"This is left!" Kwestral yelled back. He pulled on to the shoulder. Fryer was pointing behind them. "Left. Don't you know your left from your right?" Kwestral made a difficult U-turn on the two-lane but heavily trafficked road. And so it went till somehow they made it into the mountains.

"Yeah, this is it. Turn here." Fryer pointed to what looked like a carriage road.

"You sure?"

"Sure I'm sure. Hey now, who's lived here all his life and who comes from downstate where folks don't even give you the time of day, let alone go for the ride to show you directly where to turn."

Kwestral sighed and made the turn.

The jeep got stuck on the rough road, just as he knew it would. It couldn't make the icy incline and didn't seem to be the first car to have gotten stuck in that spot. "This can't be right. We must have turned off at the fork."

"I told you make a right," Fryer said. "What happen to your brains? They bleached out too?"

Kwestral snorted with disgust and shook back his spider-web hair. "I think there's some sort of clearing ahead. Maybe I can get directions. Stay here," he said. "Don't move from this car. The heat's on. You should be comfortable. Only, don't you touch anything either. I'll be right back."

"We missed the turn to the hermit's place 'cause of you," Fryer said. "No one else lives up this mountain. Just the hermit, and he's dead. Dead, you hear me!"

Kwestral slammed the door harder than he intended and walked briskly up the path. When he got to where the woods thinned he was just able to make out the hut in the dusk. *Old fool didn't even know he'd told me right after all.* He hurried to the open door.

There was an abandoned feeling to the place. At first he thought it despair and ruin, but there was a smell of habitation about it. Stale fire, food, waste...struggle. He stood in the doorway, taking it in, his eyes growing accustomed to the dark. Something hung in the center, like a giant spider's web. He approached it. Despite the lack of light he made out the ropes threaded through eye hooks in the ceiling, the winch. His stomach turned over. The hoist, the winch, the vaulting horse. Everywhere he looked he saw horror upon horror, as if he'd fallen into a nightmare department store and was checking out the displays. There was a hole in the floor—an oubliette?

He knelt beside it, peered in. A great wet space breathed sick exhalations at him. He could have been looking down a well—he thought of Nietzche's abyss. If you looked too long into it, it looked into you. He wanted to turn away but couldn't. Instead he stuck his hand into darkness, groping till he found something. A ladder rung! That was when he felt pressure on his backside. In his vulnerable position he was unable to keep himself from toppling. He fell for what seemed an inordinate amount of time. In any case there were ample seconds as he tumbled for him to figure out he'd been pushed, realize there was nothing he could do about it, decide it was a good idea to hold tight to the slimy ladder rung and hang quietly while his body thudded into a wall.

There was a square of dim light above him, then the square filled with shadow. He recognized he was staring at a head. Darkness poured into the hollow bones of the face, producing a skull-like effect. He or it didn't seem to see him. Then the head disappeared, the square closed in on him, banging shut with a sound he imagined a coffin lid might make. From inside. It was dark. He could see nothing at all. He held the ladder with two hands and worked his feet onto a rung.

Herm Kwestral was a writer who took his craft seriously and knew his muse was inclined to whisper in darkened movie theaters, concert halls, restaurants. So now he took out his penlight and used its tiny blade to look around.

He couldn't see much with its ray of weak light, but it did show him he was surrounded by rocky walls, that the ladder hung down from a lip above and he was behind it, in a recess. Below, water waited for him to make a wish. A ledge of harder stone stuck out from the body of rockwall. At one point on the far side was a darker darkness. It might be a tunnel, it might be an animal burrow. It could be nothing at all. He had a choice. He could hug the wall and inch along the ledge, sucking with his fingertips the way rock climbers did, till he got to the other side. Or he could swing the ladder over. There was a third choice of course. Do nothing and rot in the "safe" place he had lucked into...till that madman, whoever he was, came back.

He heard footsteps above him, low voices. Putting the penlight away he prepared to try the impossible. With his weight he got momentum going on the ladder and forced himself to think of nothing but landing safely in the niche on the opposite wall. For a second he felt like a sightless white slug in the moist dark, a creature that lived underground, without light, that lived by feel, by taste. Then he made the leap and found himself clinging to the ground, amazed that he had done the impossible so easily. He would have been more impressed with himself if he hadn't let the ladder fall away, thereby cutting off one of his escape routes to the other side.

He took out his penlight again and directed the thin beam across the dug-out floor of a passageway. The cool air on his face told him that it led out. He climbed on his knees through intestines of earth, having to wiggle like a worm in places, so small was the space. Then the tunnel opened out and he saw something dug from the wall. He shone his light and revealed a blanketed form. It had the shape of a body.

He lifted his hand stealthily, as if he feared to awaken the sleeping Mabel Fleish. He pointed the light at what seemed the roundness of a head. "No!" a child seemed to cry from far away, from long ago, as a blank eye stared. Death grinned, and he was falling once more into a hole. "Father," he heard himself say. "I didn't mean, I never meant," then he was out, as was the penlight, which rolled from his hand.

FORTY-NINE

Ana followed the path her father had taken till it branched into three twisted limbs. Then she had to eeney-meeney-miney-moe it and subsequently found herself on a trail that brambled out. When she turned around she realized she had walked off the path some time before and didn't know which animal trail led back.

The woods were already darkening, overwhelming her with shadow. She walked in one direction, only to decide she needed the path to her left, then the right, and so on, till she'd gone in circles. It was almost dusk.

That was when the ghost of a dog darted by. "Nubi!" she shouted, so delighted to see the shepherd that she didn't stop to wonder how he'd gotten out of the locked car.

Anubis stopped on a rocky overhang, barked once, wagged his tail. *He wants me to follow him,* she thought. She hurried in the direction he led her. He paused regularly so she could catch up but didn't let her come near enough to touch. All at once he vanished in the gray day. She was as lost as before, only the woods were darker. "Nubi?" she called in a scared voice. Then she saw the man.

He was someone she thought she knew, although it took a moment to place him—a friend of her mother's! She even remembered he had a funny accent, and a funny name. Writer, that was it. She recalled coming home early from school one day and there they were, in the kitchen. "Ana," her mother said. "This is a friend of mine...Writer." He smiled, he had the most *gorgeous* smile, sexy like a rock star. "Hey there, sweet lips," he said. "Spitting image of your mom, ain't you?"

"Hi," she now said, running up to him. "I'm Ana, you know, Mabel's daughter? Remember me?"

She saw the grin spread over his face. The surprised delight seemed intense but not that uncommon when she met her parents' friends. *So this is little Ana. I haven't seen her since she was a twinkle.*

Now he had that twinkle. "Well, well," he said. "Looky what we've got here."

She smiled down at her feet, hoping this grownup banter would be over soon and they could get to the point. When it didn't seem impolite to disrupt his glee she asked if he knew how to get to the main road. "Sure do, sweet lips," he said. "Main road, right this way." He began to lead her up the little path. That's when she noticed the blood. "Your shoulder," she said. "You're hurt."

He turned to her, his smile gone. "Yes, I am," he said. "Badly hurt, but seeing you"—she blushed from his flattery—"is healing me fine."

Happily she followed behind, glad to have found an adult to trust. A friend of her mother's too. Maybe he knew.... She remembered why she had hidden herself in her father's car. And this man, her mother's *friend*, a man named Writer.... "What are you doing here?" she asked as he held a branch out of her way.

"A little boneriding expedition," he said, laughing to himself.

"*Bone* writing?"

He looked surprised. "You read that?"

"Sure," she said, proud of herself, although she knew there was a lot in there she didn't quite get. "So you must have been here with my mom, huh?" He didn't answer. That clinched it. He must know where her mother was. "Are you two through now?" she asked. "Can you take me to her?"

His delighted face mimicked her own prideful one. "Sure thing, sweet lips," he said. "Just follow me. I could teach you to ride, you'd like that?" She heard *ride* but thought it was his funny way of saying *write*. At first. She felt clever, having found her mom, having found her writing place, soon to learn her writing method—and it wasn't anything like fat old Mrs. Blum said. It was like her mother did when she tried to explain why she couldn't work with Ana in the house. You have to be alone, someplace where you can't be interrupted. Still it was wrong of her to go off like that, worrying them all. She could have told them before she left. And when she'd be back.

Ana was thinking such thoughts, following the bloody man, till they got to the clearing. The little house sent a chill of warning through her. Something seemed wrong. This was a place of evil. You could feel it even at this distance. It was cold and ugly, a shuttered, barred, rundown hole. "She's in there," he said, pulling her. "Come on. I'll show you how she likes to hang out when she's writing."

She followed reluctantly, dragging her feet, till she spotted the faint outline of Nubi in the woods behind Writer. He didn't seem to know the dog was there. She let herself be led a bit further, thinking she didn't care for the way the man was looking at her with his weirdly bright eyes. But she'd been brought up never to be rude to grownups, and she didn't quite know how to object to going along with him.

"Um," she said. "Uh, I don't think...I don't want to, um, I'd better not," she said. "Thank you anyway. I have to get home now." She turned. He stood in front of her.

"What's your hurry?" he asked.

"I'm late. I have to—"

"Nonsense. You're going the wrong way. Here, come with me, Little Red. Your mother and I were working on *Bone*, you can work on a *Bone* too."

A flash of intuition detonated like a bomb. There was no longer any doubt. Something was very wrong. "No," she cried as he took her hand. "Nubi," she called. The dog watched, cocking his head, then trailing after the man as he tugged Ana through the woods.

"The first thing you must learn is not to struggle," he said. "It enrages a man"—he grabbed her hair so that her head was forced up and she had to meet his crazy eyes—"like me, Little Red."

She tried to nod but he held her against his chest all of a sudden, looking through the woods at the cabin. "Shit," he said, then smiled at the frightened child. "Excuse my French." He took her to a tree. "Don't fight and this won't hurt." He leaned her against the tree and undid his belt. A thrill of fear shivered through her. And righteousness. *Now I'm going to get it,* she thought as he pulled the belt through the loops. *Now I'm really going to get it.* But he didn't hit her. He tied her with the leather and walked away.

She stood like that, tied to the tree, as if playing Wendy with invisible pirates. She wondered if she should call for help or if that would make Writer come back. It didn't matter because then he was back. He undid the belt and forced her to go with him to the hut.

"Oh, what a terrible place," she said even before he lit a lantern. She could see the bloody, ugly thing on the floor like a popped balloon, all the ropes dangling above. She smelled the rank odor of evil, as if an animal had been sacrificed and butchered there. Over and over. The sight of the bloody sheet and mattress, the pulleys, the sling only confirmed what she knew. This was a meathouse, just the way the vegetarians in her lunchroom described it. A place of cruelty and filth, where living beings were made into hamburger, to be served to you on a bun by ladies with hairnets and angry faces.

She tried to get out. He grabbed her, slapped her. He went to hit her again. She cried, "No!" and cowered on the floor. He pointed a scolding finger and smiled. "I got your riding hood, Little Red," he said. "You want me to put it on you?" He showed her a velvet-looking bag with holes and a drawstring. "No!" she cried. "Please. I'll be good." He patted her head and went to start a fire. He said it was cold. She didn't feel cold. He had his back turned. His neck was caked with old blood. Nubi had followed them in. *A dog knows his true master*, she thought. He was the only one watching her. The man didn't seem to know Nubi was *her* dog. He seemed to think he was his.

She put her finger to her lips, winked. She would have to get up fast, then run like anything. In the dark he'd never catch her. Besides, she was going to sic Nubi on him. Nubi could be pretty smart when he wanted. He knew she was in trouble.

Her clothes rustled when she got up. The man turned around. "Nubi," Ana called, "sic him!" She started to run. Writer grabbed her jacket, held her back by its material. She tried to pull herself free, shouting, "Sic him, sic him!"

Anubis gave a puzzled cock to his head. He looked at her, looked at the man, looked at her. He smiled, panting, then licked his lips and bared his teeth at her. Ana screamed. Terror renewed her. She twisted free, began running, shrieking as man and dog pursued.

Anubis leaped ahead and stood growling in her path. She began running to the left. Suddenly there was an explosion and a giant bumblebee buzzed by, stinging him. Blood bloomed from his side like the speeded-up film of a rose she once saw. The dog ran limping, yelping, into the woods. Writer ran after him.

She still didn't know what had happened or that she was screaming or that she had turned around. She had no idea who the old man with the rifle was or how he had gotten there or why he was calling "Persy!" or why she was crying "Daddy!" But somehow she found herself hugging a skeleton of an old man, and he was stroking her head, crying, "All these years, Persy, all these years," and she was crying, "Daddy, that's my daddy's name." And that was when the ghost-faced man dug himself out of the side of the house and ran at them shaking branches.

FIFTY

Kwestral came to when he heard the shot. The grave he was in was pitch, but he groped along, seeking the source of cool air on his face. He heard water rumbling behind him, gurgling like a hungry stomach. *In Xanadu,* he thought, surprised at the Coleridge poem that came as he crawled, *did Kubla Khan a stately pleasure dome decree; where Alph, the sacred river, ran through caverns measureless to man down to a sunless sea.* And then he was at a hole dug under the side of the building. He saw up through a puzzle of tree limbs, but when he pushed they easily lifted off and he was free.

He pulled himself out, expecting to find another dead child, like the one whose skeleton he had just found, only this one would still have her meat. The shout of *No!* still reverberated in his bones. Instead he saw Fryer embracing a little girl. "Persy," he heard him crying. "All these years...I told Mother I'd bring you home."

"Daddy," the girl was crying in counterpoint. "My daddy is Percy Furnival. My mother's Mabel Fleish. I am Ana Fleish Furnival. I live at 9 Wood Street, Winegarden, New York. My number is 221-3091"—reciting the mantra of lost children.

Kwestral came up to them. "I know where you live. I know your dad. Are you okay?" She nodded. He turned to Fryer. "You?"

The old man was quiet. "I thought," he said, "my sister...my baby sister. Losing my brains, I reckon." But he didn't stop stroking the child's head.

"This the hermit's place?" Kwestral asked, swallowing hard.

Fryer nodded, but Kwestral wasn't sure he'd heard. "My sister," he was saying. "I promised Mother. Swore I'd never rest. I ain't been up here since...I'm ready, you know, dead tired. Wasn't till now, but I feel old. That little face starting to look a woman's..."

He held Ana's skull in the cup of his hand. "I best go in there," he said, still stroking her hair.

"Don't," Kwestral said. He took the old man's arm and could feel bone through the skin. "There's a body," he said. "A child's body."

The old man nodded. "I know," he said. "I'm ready." Fryer started to stumble off to the hut, dragging his rifle, then just dropping it.

"The promises we make the dead," Kwestral called after him, "you think they mean more than what we owe the living?" He didn't expect an answer and he didn't get one. He was just talking in his own head.

FIFTY-ONE

Rufus Wutzl Is Dead;
Romantic Authority, 79

Dr. Rufus Wutzl, English professor emeritus at Jones College, died of gastrocardiovascular trauma yesterday afternoon, his family said. He was 79 years old and lived in Winegarden, New York.

The esteemed scholar of Romantic poetry was well known for his critical analyses of Byron, Shelley, and Keats. In 1953, his seminal work, *The Romantic Revolution*, was published to international acclaim; the textbook has been widely used in college English literature courses ever since. It was followed by *The Byronic Hero* in 1958, *English Romantics* in 1964, *Wedding Conclusions in Romantic Comedies* in 1967, among other critical books and essays.

At the time of his death he was writing what many assumed would be his magnum opus, Professor Percival Furnival, a colleague at Jones College, told reporters. Professor Furnival, in an oral agreement, was named literary executor by Dr. Wutzl, with whom he spent much time in the last weeks of his life.

"I haven't had a chance to do more than glance at Dr. Wutzl's notes," Professor Furnival said, "but it seems he was tracing the influence of the Romantics on Yeats as well as on my wife." Mabel Fleish, Professor Furnival's wife, is the author of *Bone*, a recently published first novel that affected Dr. Wutzl deeply, as did the disappearance of Ms. Fleish herself for the past two and a half weeks, according to Professor Furnival.

"Dr. Wutzl felt almost as worried as I did by what happened," Professor Furnival said, referring to the alleged abduction of Ms.

Fleish by a transient as yet to be found by police. "He accompanied me on many of my searches. It was during one of these that he named me his literary executor. I only wish he hadn't died before we found her, that he could have known, before his own death, that she was okay. He often told me that he thought of her as the daughter he never had."

Professor Furnival expects to edit a posthumous edition of Dr. Wutzl's last work.

Elena Tchernofsky, head of a mystical study group Dr. Wutzl joined shortly before his death, the Order of Hermetic Hermits, eulogized him in a service held at their temple. "Rufus Wutzl was exploring spiritual avenues that would have profoundly influenced his work," she told a gathering of colleagues, students, and co-religionists. "Let us not grieve," she continued, "but wish him bon voyage." She broke a bottle of 1967 Perrier Jouet, supplied from Dr. Wutzl's own wine cellar, over the coffin.

Dr. Wutzl is survived by his wife of 51 years, Ethel Wutzl. They have no children.

FIFTY-TWO

The English department turned out en masse for Dr. Wutzl's funeral. In addition to Elena Tchernofsky he was eulogized by Dean Hook, who told how the respected scholar was never too busy to talk to students and faculty, how he was always eager to offer advice. Mrs. Wutzl sobbed noisily. Women from the community offered tissues.

Mabel and Percy entered the chapel quietly and stood in the back. When people started to leave they saw her. The air of mourning took on a sparkle of joy. In subdued voices well-wishers gathered to welcome her home. No one could take their eyes off her. She was a woman returned from death, a miracle in their midst.

People walked out into the crisp November air, smiling despite the solemn occasion. "Have you heard?" "Have you seen?" "Over there, look." "She looks great." "She looks tired." "He looks wonderful." "It's the most wonderful thing that ever..." They congregated outside the chapel to smile at the happy couple. Mabel and Percy, hurrying past with bowed heads, would not have been surprised if someone threw rice.

At the cemetery those who had not yet had the opportunity to congratulate them did so. The only one oblivious to the excitement was Mrs. Wutzl. She was wrapped in her grief and had not noticed the buzz of excitement that had started with Mabel's appearance.

The last honorary shovel of dirt was thrown on the coffin. The rest of the work was left for the gravediggers. Mrs. Wutzl turned to walk away. For the first time she saw her. Giving a sniff of distaste she noticed the scent of *joie de vivre* in the air.

Disgraceful, she thought. Festivity at such an important funeral. The leavetaking of a great man. Dr. Rufus Wutzl, professor emeritus, scholar, distinguished lecturer on the English Romantics—the world would not see his like again for many days. And his passing was to be upstaged by a woman hardly better than a whore!

She was angry, furious in fact. Walking from the grave she shook off comforting arms as people tried to steady her on the lumpy dirt. She made it clear she expected everyone to come back to the house. Even in her mourning she had been busy—preparing food for the funeral guests. She wanted people to see that some women still knew how to send their men on royally. Rufus was like a Viking in a burning barque. She would set his memory ablaze, float it down rivers of gastric juices. His funeral would be talked about for a long time to come. People would groan to think of the hams and petit fours they'd consumed. There would be heartburn in Winegarden tonight.

But at the house it was the same. Conviviality reigned. The atmosphere was partylike as people drank and ate. With cheery miens they toasted Mabel on her return, then assumed lugubrious masks to console Mrs. Wutzl.

Before leaving, Mabel and Percy went up to the new widow. "I'm so sorry," Mabel said. "Dr. Wutzl was always kind to me."

Percy took Mrs. Wutzl's hand. It felt cold and wet. "You know how much your husband meant to me," he said. "He was a good friend. Like a father. This was so sudden."

"The doctor said he died of gastrocardiovascular trauma," Mrs. Wutzl told him, then turned her eye on Mabel. "But I say he died of a broken heart."

"Oh," said Mabel. "I thought it was from overeating. I mean, I mean—" She began to stammer, as if her insult had been unintended.

Mrs. Wutzl glared. Before she could stomp off, Ana came up. All she did was squeeze the old woman's hand, but it seemed to say more than easy condolences. Mabel lifted one of Ana's braids, swung it like a jump rope for a moment, then dropped it. "I just want to say thank you," she said, stuttering slightly. "For, you know, looking after Ana. She's told me how kind—"

Mrs. Wutzl frowned happily. "Pooh," she said, hugging Ana, starting to pull her along. "Come, dear," she said. "I want you to taste the honey loaf I made. One of Dr. Wutzl's favorites. He had so many favorites. Such an easy man to please, and—"

Mabel took the old woman's arm. "Please, Mrs. Wutzl," she

said. "It would mean a great deal to me, to all of us if.... Oh, I don't quite know how to put it, I hope you won't be insulted or find it presumptuous. Just, if you'd think of yourself as Ana thinks of you. Sort of a grandmother, if you don't mind. It would mean so much to her. And I hope you'll visit us. Often."

"Yes," said Ana. "I always wanted a grandma like you."

"Pooh," said Mrs. Wutzl, her eyes glittering brightly.

EPILOGUE

Percy and Mabel sat on the couch, leaning back on its arms to face one another. Each had a foot in the other's crotch, the other leg bent at the knee. The peculiar symmetry of their pose made them seem like bookends.

He smiled at her, she smiled back. "What's this?" he said, slapping a rhythm on her thigh.

"'Way Down Upon the Sewanee River'?"

He laughed, lifted her foot, put it to his lips, kissed it.

"What's this?" she asked, opening her mouth wide, distorting her face sideways.

"Edvard Munch's 'The Scream'?"

"Good." She laughed. "Poyfect. We're almost ready for 'Ed Sullivan,' except he's dead."

Percy kissed her foot again. "Everytime I see you I can't believe it. Or else I can't believe the other. I don't want to believe the other. That was a nightmare. This is real. But it's as if I have to look away to see the miracle of you here beside me."

She stroked his foot. "You know," she said, "you can read sometimes. Watch TV, take a walk. You don't have to look at me all the time. I'm not going anywhere."

He nodded but didn't do any of those things.

"Ana, too," Mabel said. "She doesn't want to let me out of her sight. I've been home a week, and we haven't fought once. I'm not complaining, but it's not normal. She has to—"

"Don't worry. She will."

"I suppose."

"How does she seem, I mean about the whole thing?"

"Pretty good, on the whole. I was up there just a little while ago.

I wanted to talk about wishes, tell her that wishes don't make things happen. She'd shown me this wishbone Mrs. Wutzl gave her, how she'd shellacked it and had been wearing it on a chain around her neck. She had made some sort of pact—about how she'd wear the bone till I returned."

"Really? I had no idea."

"And she was kind of afraid that if she threw it away I'd disappear again. I tried to straighten her out, but it was hard, me being neurotically superstitious too."

"So what did you say?"

"Well, it was good, really. Convincing her helped convince me. I told her not only that wishes don't make things happen, but that we're not responsible for our wishes, only for our deeds. If something bad happens, even if you did wish for it, you don't bear guilt for it."

"Did she accept that?"

"I think so. I hope so. It's one of the hardest things I have to work on, you know—that Ryder was not acting out my wishes, that he is not the evil that's in me."

"What makes you think Ana believes it if you can't?"

"For one thing she did throw out the wishbone." Mabel laughed. "And I'm still here, aren't I? For another, she gave me an old photo. Seth was in it. God knows where she found it. She asked about him. 'That was your brother,' I said. 'He died when he was a few months old. An accident.' I didn't say anything more."

Percy nodded. "I think that's good. It was time she knew."

"Yeah, I thought so. You know what else? She gave me her Barbie and Ken dolls. Case, clothing, the works. Says she's too old to play with dolls. I said, 'You sure?' and she stood up straight. 'Mother,' she said. "I am going to be twelve in a month.'"

Percy laughed. "Amazing. She's growing up so fast. What's she want for her birthday?"

Mabel smiled. "She said she didn't want anything, that she already had her greatest wish—me coming home. Isn't that sweet? But I pressed her. Finally she said pierced ears and pearl earrings."

"Gads, no! Pearl earrings?" He moved his foot. "Want a drink?"

She shook her head. He walked away, she watched him. She stared at his back, thinking he would turn around. Couldn't he feel the intensity of her gaze? She kept expecting him to look back and smile, wink, say, Gotcha! Do anything to acknowledge that he could feel her mind. He didn't. He had entered another space. For a brief moment he was part of a different world. He was there, outside her, removed and away. She closed her eyes and felt dizzy, as if something had snapped. When she opened them he was on his way back. He smiled, took his place on the couch, put her foot in his crotch. "Did you see the doctor today?"

She nodded. "He says the rash is almost gone. At least that terrible itch went away. He wants me to keep using the medicine for another week."

"Oh, uh, this guy called," he said. "Kwestral. You know, the reporter?" He looked closely at her. "He's got a new address and phone number, he just moved. Wanted you to have them. Said you should look him up when you're in the city."

Mabel wiggled down into the cushions. "I don't expect to be going that way again." She fell quiet for a few minutes.

"Um, well—he also wanted you to know he's written up a first-person account of the rescue. Asked if that's okay. I said you'd call him back if you had a problem."

"I don't."

"I figured."

"He say anything else?"

"No. Or wait, yeah, he did. He said he was working on a book based loosely on your experience. A kind of non-fiction novel or bloody hybrid. I think he was hoping you'd volunteer to look at it when it was done."

She shrugged. "Sure," she said. "I'll do what I can. He's a good kid. Introduce him to Max, maybe. If the book's got something to it Max'll find him a publisher." She was quiet for some moments, watching Percy sip his drink. She cleared her throat, looking dreamy. "I think I've got a book in me too," she said softly, as if she were telling Percy she was pregnant.

"That's great! I th—"

She quieted him, holding up her hand. "Let me finish," she said. "You see, I don't know, this experience—I felt so dried up before. Dead. But now life is precious. Every second sparkles. It's all miraculous, water spilling out the faucet, the ability to go into a car, to open a door and step outside. To—" She lost the ability to talk, and her eyes filled. Percy stroked her leg.

"I know," he said. "If only there was a way to keep it alive."

"Just being with you," she said at last. "And Ana. Oh, I'm so full of ideas, Percy, I can't tell you—it's almost too much. I'm bursting with it. Despair seems such a waste of time." She paused, still holding her hand up.

"I've been looking through his notes," Mabel went on. "You know, from the...experience. I mean, he had ideas. Just, he was...undisciplined." She looked up at her husband. "The book I'm thinking of writing, well, this is the thing. I'm thinking about writing *his* book, the one he wanted us to...you know—Marrow? Like, how he kept accusing me of stealing his material, using it in *Bone?* Well, this feels like it's *my* material. His ideas but my sweat and blood, my pain, my terror and tears and rage."

Percy studied his wife. "Honey," he said softly, "have you thought this through? Have you considered the ramifications?" He watched her nod grimly. She seemed so small, so sad. It broke his heart to see her that way.

"There's no other peace," she said. "If he's alive...and he hears I'm writing his book.... Don't you think it'll flush him out? And if he's dead...this is what he'd want me to do, what I want to do for him. Can you understand that? Is that too weird?" She searched his face for repugnance; finding none she went on. "Not the lunatic who held me prisoner. The other Ryder...who could have been. If his mother hadn't...if *I* had, you know. I was just so caught up with my own stuff I didn't really pay much attention to his. But he had it in him—he was rough, but he had depth. What he did to me I can't forgive, but what was done to him I can't forget."

Percy took her hand. He knew it was hard for her to voice such things, especially to him.

"Don't get me wrong," she said, the urgency in her tone sounding like that of a condemned convict in his last moments. "I hope with all my soul he *is* dead. He's too damaged to ever do the good he might have if...." She shrugged her shoulders up, then let them drop, as if in resignation. "It came to me yesterday, when I was reading over his notes, thinking about the letter." A shiver of fear ran through her as she looked at the copy of *Sam's Corner Gazette* on the floor, folded open to the Letters column. "I want to write this book, I *need* to write this book. Shit! It's my book, material he squeezed and pulled and jerked out of me, as though I were some frog he was dissecting, for chrissake!" She looked angry for a moment, but Percy knew she was yelling at ghosts. She swallowed hard, not speaking till she regained her composure.

"This will either catch him by his ambition and they'll put him where he can't hurt me again. Or"—she lowered her voice till Percy struggled to hear—"it will stand as a tribute to a murdered soul. Because, you know, Percy, he had it in him to be something... magnificent."

Her eyes shone fully and they both looked away.

He cleared his throat after some moments. "What time does Mrs. Wutzl want us? Did she say who else is coming to Thanksgiving dinner?"

"Four-thirty, I think. It's just you, me, Ana." She smiled at her husband. "Rufus's family, she called us. Isn't that sweet?"

He nodded. "She makes delicious turkey," he said. "I had a drumstick that was out of this world."

"Yes," Mabel said. "Me too."

Her face seemed to fall. Percy glanced at the paper. "You're thinking about that damn letter again, aren't you?" She didn't respond. "It's a coincidence," he insisted. "Listen, he had to have mailed that letter before I showed up at the hut. It arrived at the paper the same day."

"I just have this feeling," she said, patting her chest repeatedly.

"Maybe you shouldn't write this book then," he said. "I mean, I *know* he's dead. And writing is the best thing you can do...for you. I don't give a fuck about him and his magnificent murdered soul. It's you, Mabel, it's you I care about. If I lost you again, I—"

His voice cracked. He had to stop speaking, for he was on the brink of crying and was ashamed to break down before his wife. "I don't know what I'd do," he said finally. "That's why I say this: If he *is* alive, which I don't believe, but if he is, and if he hears about the book you're writing, and if he decides to come back, tries to do it all over again, take you, and....oh, Mabel, I can't go through it again. And neither can Ana, and neither can you. Honey, can't you write a different book?"

She took a deep breath and sighed. "I can't live my whole life in fear," she said. "Afraid to write. Afraid to be alone. This will expose the truth. And there's something else." He sat up, she adjusted her position to his.

"I'm not a naturally good person, Percy," she said. "I'm not the person you think I am. Ryder needed a break. I could have helped him. I can pretend I didn't see the spark in him, but that would be a lie. Instead of helping him get that spark to burn brighter I used it to ignite something in my own work. This new book, this Marrow, well, it's a tribute *and* a trap. Payback, in both senses."

Percy looked amazed, as if the depth of his wife's compassion was astounding. "Don't," she told him, reading that adoration. "I don't belong on a pedestal. This is what I should have done all along. What one writer owes another. Believe me, if he's alive then he's one dead fucker—I will see him put away forever. But if he's dead then I want to give the dead their due." She looked away. "No big deal."

He sat quietly, sucking ice cubes from his drink, considering his wife. "I wonder," he said conversationally, "if we'll ever find Nubi. I mean, he was a pest but he was our dog. I'm surprised no one's called us to say they've found his body. You know, combing the woods for Ryder they have to have found him, don't you think?"

She made a face, as if tasting something rancid. "Ana told me how he turned on her," she said. "I've kind of felt it all along. I didn't say anything to you, but I always thought there was something wrong. Do dogs get mentally ill? Dr. Xavier convinced me my feelings were just a projection of my wishes."

They were both silent. The newspaper rustled as if whispering. They both knew they were thinking about the letter. "Okay," she said finally. "Let me see the paper." He reached over to pick up *The Gazette* and handed it to her.

> *I abslutly forbd tht my bdy be viewd fr any reasn whtsoevr. Once my grve is flled in, it wll be seeded with acrns, so tht the dirt of the sd grve wll evntlly hold vgtation, and once the thcket is grwn bck to its orignl state, the trces of my grve wll disappear frm the fce of the erth.*
> *—Mrquis de Sod*

"I tell you, Percy, he's out there," she cried, throwing down the paper. "Waiting, watching. Not dead, not alive. It's as though he can't, I don't know...settle. He's my own bad dream."

"Seems we were all living bad dreams," he said. "Wishes coming true in a monkey-paw way."

She twirled a lock of her hair around a finger. "Yes," she said.

"Wishes we dream about but don't want to come true."

"Next time I start wishing for something maybe I'll ask, 'Are you a good wish or a bad wish?'" He mimicked Glinda's voice in *The Wizard of Oz*.

She laughed, then frowned, and it was such a characteristic gesture he squeezed her foot again. "Must we always live in fear of our own minds?" she asked. "Jesus, even prisoners are allowed to dream."

"The thing in the paper," he said, shifting all at once. "It's Sade's Last Will and Testament. Did you know? Things didn't turn out as he wished. He ended his life in a madhouse—albeit as a privileged inmate allowed to direct others in a theater of cruelty we can only imagine. In the end he was buried, then his body exhumed. His skull was explored by a respected phrenologist who decided he was a man of 'benevolent and religious faith.'"

"Leave it to head doctors," said Mabel. "Speaking of whom—"

Their conversation was interrupted by an animal howling outside. The bookends fell silent, pulled apart. They looked out the window, horrified as children who hear a ghost. The wolf howled again. They were filled with the presentiment of death, as if a denizen of the underworld were crying his desire for them. When the animal howled a third, and final, time they looked at each other and laughed. Why, it was just a dog somewhere baying at the early moon.

Percy tapped a riff on her thigh. "What's this?" he asked.

"Do it again." Such a familiar little rhythm. So cheerfully mundane. All at once she giggled. "Life is but a dream."

He smiled. "That Kwestral kid was always humming it. It drove me *crrr*azy." He rolled his *r* like a madman, pointed an imaginary gun at his head, and fired.